9/21

LAR

KT-426-440

Books should be returned or renewed by the last
date above. Renew by phone **03000 41 31 31** or
online *www.kent.gov.uk/libs*

Libraries Registration & Archives

CUSTOMER
SERVICE
EXCELLENCE

CSE

Kent
County
Council
kent.gov.uk

Also by Amanda Brooke

Yesterday's Sun
Another Way To Fall
Where I Found You
The Missing Husband
The Child's Secret
The Goodbye Gift
The Affair
The Bad Mother
Don't Turn Around
The Widows' Club

Ebook-only short stories
The Keeper of Secrets
If I Should Go

A Good Liar

AMANDA BROOKE

HarperCollins*Publishers*

HarperCollins*Publishers* Ltd
1 London Bridge Street
London SE1 9FG

www.harpercollins.co.uk

HarperCollins*Publishers*
1st Floor, Watermarque Building, Ringsend Road
Dublin 4, Ireland

A Paperback Original 2021
2

A catalogue record for this book
is available from the British Library

ISBN: 978-0-00-821912-3

This novel is entirely a work of fiction.
The names, characters and incidents portrayed in it are
the work of the author's imagination. Any resemblance to
actual persons, living or dead, events or localities is
entirely coincidental.

Typeset in Sabon LT Std by
Palimpsest Book Production Ltd, Falkirk, Stirlingshire

Printed and bound in Great Britain by
CPI Group (UK) Ltd, Croydon CR0 4YY

MIX
Paper from
responsible sources
FSC™ C007454

This book is produced from independently certified FSC™ paper
to ensure responsible forest management.

For more information visit: www.harpercollins.co.uk/green

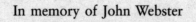
In memory of John Webster

The Empress Theatre
Sedgefield, Cheshire

Onstage, the white rabbit performed the perfect pirouette and imagined her dance teacher, Mrs Clarke, urging her on. 'Well done! Now keep those arms moving and remember, one continuous flow.' The little girl lifted an arm and extended her fingers gracefully.

The music stopped.

An ear-splitting alarm cut through the shocked silence and, as it reverberated around the theatre, the white rabbit's supple limbs turned to stone. Only her pink nose twitched as the lights came up. There were six hundred faces staring back at her and they had frozen too, all except her mum, who had stopped recording her nine-year-old daughter's performance and lowered her phone.

'The theatre is being evacuated,' came a tinny announcement. 'Please remain calm and follow the signs to your nearest exit. Staff will be available to assist and direct you.' The disembodied voice didn't sound concerned. If anything, there was a hint of annoyance.

With whiskers quivering, the white rabbit sniffed the air. There was no telltale whiff of smoke, no sign of flickering flames. There had been no bang, no tremor to shake the ancient boards of the stage, nothing to suggest anything was amiss. It was a false alarm, or maybe a fire drill. It happened at school all the time.

The white rabbit turned to the only other figure onstage. The principal dancer was five years older and wore a blue satin tutu with a white apron and matching Alice band; another protégé from the Hilary Clarke School of Dance. She reached out a hand and the white rabbit grasped it. The curtain closed.

'Well, that was short and sweet,' muttered Hilary Clarke.

She shared a look with Rose Peagrave who was positioned at the end of the row with eight young charges between them. Rose was Hilary's most senior dance instructor and most likely candidate to take over the school when Hilary hung up her dance shoes the following year. At seventy-one, her retirement was well overdue, but still, it would be a wrench.

'Come on, people. Gather up your belongings,' Rose shouted above the alarm.

Hilary took a deep breath and swallowed her disappointment. This was their first show in the newly renovated Empress Theatre, and it was only a three-day run. She prayed the alarm could be reset quickly so they could resume rather than abandon their opening night. She had allowed herself the indulgence of being part of the audience for this evening only, leaving another of her teachers in charge backstage. Slowly but surely, she was loosening the reins.

Picking up her bag and coat, Hilary was slow to surrender her seat. The tiny theatre had just one tier above the stalls,

2

and these were not the cheap seats by any means. The circle had been transformed into an exclusive VIP area, with plush upholstery, generous leg room, and waiting service no less. The series of function rooms to the rear were still under renovation, but would eventually provide a high dining experience to theatregoers with deep pockets. Hilary would be happy enough with the nip of whisky she had promised herself in the second half, but the night wasn't turning out as she had anticipated. At least for the half hour she had been able to watch her dancers onstage, they hadn't put a foot wrong.

Although the circle was full, it had less than a hundred seats and wouldn't take long to clear. There were two stairwells, one that led to the foyer at the front of the Empress, the other to an exit at the side, according to the usher. Rose led the way and opted for the latter, which was generally being ignored. The theatre was at the end of a row of buildings and everyone knew that the alleyway at the side was dark and dank, but fewer people meant less chance of misplacing a student. Good choice, thought Hilary. She would be leaving her school in good hands.

'Miss, miss!' cried a student just as Hilary was leaving the circle. It was seven-year-old Jack. It was always Jack. The child had exceptional promise, but he was too easily distracted. 'I left my coat.'

Hilary looked over her shoulder. There was no one behind them and it would take no time to go back. 'Fine, show me where you left it. Quickly now,' she added sternly.

For theatregoers in the cramped stalls below, the evacuation wasn't as smooth as it was for their privileged counterparts. The venue had been open for less than a month and was crammed with curious locals eager for their first glimpse inside the art deco building. It had taken two years to return the Empress to its original purpose, but nine-year-old Amelia Parker had no interest in the sympathetic restoration of gilded plasterwork and polished veneers. She had come to see her best friend perform. Evie was the white rabbit.

Amelia's mum had been looking forward to it too, but twenty-five minutes into the performance, Kathryn Parker had been jiggling in her seat.

'Sorry, love, I need to nip to the loo,' she had whispered. She had been drinking cranberry juice all day, but it hadn't helped. 'Do you want to come with me?'

Amelia had been mortified. What if Evie spotted them getting up from their seats? 'No way,' she had said.

And so it was that when the alarm had sounded and the curtain came down, Amelia was on her own. Her mum had instructed her to seek out Evie's mum if there was a problem, but she was a few rows in front and had hurried off in the direction of the stage as soon as the evacuation started. Amelia checked behind her, hoping to find her mum in as much of a rush to retrieve her daughter. The aisle was filled with people she didn't recognise.

'We need to leave, sweetie,' a woman said. She was struggling to squeeze past Amelia, who had gripped the arms of her seat. 'Come with us.'

'I have to wait for my mum.'

The wrinkles crisscrossing the woman's brow deepened as she looked from Amelia to the young girl whose hand she was holding, her granddaughter presumably. Her husband was bringing up the rear and muttered under his

4

breath as someone shoved him from behind, almost knocking the box of popcorn out of his hand. People were getting impatient.

'Leave her be, love,' the man said. 'Her mum will know where to find her if she stays where she is, isn't that right?'

Amelia nodded and, although she retreated into the aisle to let people pass, she stayed close to where her mum would expect to find her.

At the rear of the stalls where the growing mass of theatre-goers was deepest, Lois Granger caught her boyfriend smirking. Ballet wasn't Joe's kind of thing, especially when performed by a bunch of school kids, and she knew that once they were outside, he would drag her to the sports bar further down the high street. She wouldn't put up much resistance. The idea of a ballet production of Alice in Wonderland *had* sounded so much better in theory.

'You can use the side exits to the left and right of the stage!' a staff member called out, but the crowd swarming around Lois was impenetrable. They would have to stay put, but that was fine. Leaving through the foyer meant a shorter walk to the bar.

Hilary found Jack's coat shoved under his seat and, as she helped him shrug into it, she felt a shower of grit rain down onto her head. Her nose wrinkled as she looked up. The ceiling was rippling. Hilary blinked hard, thinking her cataract operation couldn't come soon enough, but with a single thump of her heart she realised the problem wasn't her eyesight. There was a roiling layer of dense smoke spreading like an ocean across the ornate ceiling.

'Sweet lord,' she said, grabbing Jack by the hood of his padded coat.

'Miss! That's hurt—'

Hearing the crack and splinter of rafters above her head, Hilary gave Jack an almighty shove. 'Run!' she screamed.

The boy pitched forward, arms flailing, and Hilary couldn't help but notice how the child kept his fingers beautifully extended. 'Good boy,' she wanted to say, but never had the chance.

Almost directly below Hilary Clarke, Amelia had held her ground and refused to join the dense crowd forming at the back of the auditorium despite several attempts to encourage her to leave. She wouldn't move, but she had put on her coat in readiness. As she pressed her cheek to the stiff wool of her mum's jacket, something made her look up. It felt as if someone had dropped a tiny stone on her head.

Amelia's seat was a few rows in front of the overhanging circle, giving her an uninterrupted view of the theatre's high ceiling. There was a pair of long-limbed figures moulded into the ornate plasterwork, and they appeared to have come to life. Beautiful alabaster faces offered trembling smiles. 'Wow,' Amelia whispered, moments before the world turned black.

Scorched beams and lethal chunks of masonry smashed into one section of the circle and rained down onto the stalls with a bone-shattering crash. The lights went out, and a wave of panic hit the previously ambivalent audience like a tsunami.

Lois felt rather than saw the ceiling collapse. She and Joe had just made it through the exit at the back of the stalls and were in the centre of a narrow conduit that led left and right. The long corridor had a set of double doors at each end that opened onto the foyer, but the light from these exit points was beyond Lois's reach. For every person who escaped through those doors, she could feel the pressure of ten more behind her. People flowed left and right, but Lois was part of a small group that was forced into a smaller and smaller space at the epicentre of what had quickly become a crush.

Lois's arms were trapped by her side and her fingers began to tingle. She had made the mistake of screaming as the crowd surged, and there was no room left to re-inflate her lungs. She fought with all her strength to escape, but her efforts were countered by others with equal force. There were parents determined to save their children, adult children determined to save their elderly parents, friends and strangers trying to save themselves.

The emergency lighting illuminated arrows to the exits, but these faded to a dull glow as a cloud of dust filled the void. Lois ought to be relieved it wasn't smoke, but her eyes remained wide with terror as she searched out Joe's face in the gloom. They had become separated and she couldn't get to him, nor he to her.

'I can't breathe,' she mouthed.

Joe was taller, his chest inching above the critical mass of bodies. 'It's OK. We can make it.'

Lois shook her head and a tear slid down her cheek. Fear was replaced by an overwhelming sense of sadness that took the form of black specks across her vision. She was going to die and she didn't understand why. There was so much more living she had to do, but she would settle for just five more minutes so she could tell her parents how much she loved them, and insist her best friend go on without her and live her best life. She was thankful that they weren't there and hoped they wouldn't feel guilty. She prayed Joe would make it out so he could help ease their pain, as they would ease his, but she couldn't be sure. *Be brave,* she wanted to tell them, and it was advice that she took for herself. She could no longer see the exits. The light was fading. *Be brave, Lois.*

Rose was standing at the bottom of the stairwell. When she had seen Hilary turn back with Jack, she had intended to wait upstairs, but a couple of the kids had gone ahead of her and she was forced to keep going. She was in the stairwell when the building shook and the lights went out. Her students' wails had echoed off the walls and it was a small miracle that they reached the ground floor without mishap. The corridor was crowded and the emergency lighting provided an eerie glow, but the waft of fresh air coming from the exit offered hope, and their route to safety was unfettered by panic.

'Get everyone outside,' Rose instructed the twelve-year-old girl, who, by virtue of being the eldest, was charged with the safety of her fellow students. Rose held back to count them as they filed past. 'Five, six, seven.' She raised her gaze, hoping to see the missing student and his teacher, but the stairwell was empty.

Rose told herself it was fine. Hilary would look after their stray lamb, but what if they were injured? She could only imagine what had caused the whole theatre to shake, and she was still deciding what to do next when she heard a clatter of feet from above. 'Thank God,' Rose said, as Jack appeared.

The little boy was covered in dust, and coughed between sobs.

'Where's Mrs Clarke?'

'She pushed me,' he mewled. 'And when I looked back, I

couldn't . . . I couldn't see her. I think stuff fell on her, miss. She's trapped! There's fire in the sky and everything!'

Rose placed her foot back on the stairs, but it was a tentative move.

'Please, miss, don't leave me!'

They could hear the wail of sirens approaching. 'OK, OK,' Rose agreed, telling herself it was the sensible decision. It wasn't about being brave, or otherwise. 'We'll get help.'

Claudia Rothwell had been sipping coffee further up the high street when the fire alarm had sounded. She had been killing time, waiting for the show to finish so she could slip home without anyone realising she hadn't gone to what she suspected was an intensely boring amateur ballet. The alarm, however, had been the first warning that the night would prove to be far from dull, and her heart had been in her throat as she raced towards the red glow in the sky.

She had pushed through the crowd gathering outside the Empress with a sense of determination matched only by those fleeing danger. A stitch cut into her side, and her legs threatened to buckle as she circled the building. The people coming out of the fire doors at the side were covered in dust and grime, and some of that grime was blood.

Claudia had been planning to post a comment on Instagram about how great the show was, along with a photo of the programme to prove she was where she claimed to be. Thank God she hadn't. The night was turning into all kinds of wrong, and she had to put things right. But how?

Inside the theatre, the dust was settling, revealing small fires and debris strewn across the left-hand side of the auditorium. Buried beneath one pile of rubble was Amelia. She had been fortunate in that the largest chunks of falling

9

masonry had broken up as they ricocheted off the balcony, but they had struck with enough force to break bones.

It was the pain that roused her from her troubled sleep, and she let out a bleating cry when she realised it was no dream. She was lying on her stomach with her head pressed against a rough and tattered piece of cloth that was damp and sticky. It was too dark to see, but Amelia caught the faintest whiff of her mum's perfume, and something else, something metallic. Her mum's jacket was soaked in blood. She tried to move, but couldn't.

'Mum!' she cried out tentatively before choking on a mixture of dust and tears. She tried again, fear and adrenalin giving her a voice that rose above the distant wail of the alarm and another sound – people screaming. 'Please! Help me! Please!' she sobbed. 'I want my mummy!'

When no response came, Amelia closed her eyes. She must have fallen asleep because confusion returned when she sensed a flickering light cross her closed eyelids. She remained trapped, but she was no longer alone.

Hilary Clarke emerged from a similar dark place, but her rise into consciousness was laboured. Her legs were crushed beneath a large piece of timber and, mercifully, her spinal cord had severed its connection with the excruciating pain in her lower body. Hilary extended her one free arm and marvelled at how the thick layer of dust gave it the appearance of marble. She retched as she attempted to call for help. It was no good. There was no one to hear her cries, and nothing left to do except reflect on the life she had lived. She hoped people would think fondly of her.

Outside, the little white rabbit had lost her whiskers, but gained a foil blanket as she stood with her mum and the *swelling crowd that had spilled out of the theatre, along the high street, and into Victoria Park. Despite the cold, Evie held her body with poise, her placement perfectly centred. Mrs Clarke would be proud.*

Eleven Months Later

The Night Sedgefield Will Never Forget

By Leanne Pitman, *Cheshire Courier*

If I had been asked to describe Sedgefield when I moved to the town several years ago, I might have waxed lyrical about its Roman heritage and historic cotton mills, the beauty of the surrounding Cheshire countryside, and the tranquillity of the canals that had once been the town's life blood. Without doubt, I would have extolled the virtues of its cosy pubs and trendy eateries, but I would never have mentioned the Empress Theatre. I gave no thought to the abandoned art deco building that lurked behind the modern façade of a typical English high street. I didn't know it was there. The whole country knows where it is now.

The Empress Theatre was a hidden gem and might have stayed that way if a pair of beady eyes hadn't noticed its glittering potential. It reopened its doors amongst much pomp and ceremony a year ago, and the restoration was heralded as a cultural turning point for the town. Sadly, the real turning point came four short weeks later, when Sedgefield suffered its greatest tragedy.

As we prepare for that painful anniversary, it's time to look back and ask how we got to this point. Was it a freak accident, or was it an inevitable consequence of snobbery and greed? Do we blame the fire for taking the lives of our loved ones, or should we turn our attention to those who saw more value in bricks and mortar than the safety of our townspeople? Is it time to name names?

Prior to the theatre's restoration, Sedgefield's main thoroughfare was a mix of historic architecture overlaid with new-age branding, but unlike many high streets in this day and age, ours thrived. Unfortunately, this wasn't good enough for the upper echelons of our society. They found the discount stores and betting shops a juxtaposition to the artisan bakeries, boutiques and bistros. A Greggs' sausage roll might fill the gap if you're on a tight budget, but God forbid the smell of flaky pastry should overpower the delicate aroma of bruised basil and hand-picked coffee beans. Something had to give, and it was no surprise that middle-aged socialite Phillipa Montgomery would be the one to grasp an opportunity.

When Phillipa tabled her proposal to restore the Empress Theatre, she claimed it would make the town a magnet for investment. Reading between the lines, she meant it would increase the headcount of millionaires and local celebrities to rival that of Alderley Edge, and the best the rest of us could hope for was that they would be good tippers.

And Phillipa didn't just want a fancy theatre, she wanted it now. Impatience and a budget that prioritised style over substance evidently led to shortcuts, and those shortcuts would prove fatal. The exclusive function rooms on the first floor hadn't been completed in time for the reopening and, tellingly, the project hadn't been signed off at the time of the fire. But still, the show must go on.

On the face of it, the grand opening was a blistering success, although very few of Sedgefield's townspeople could attest to this fact, given that the celebrity-packed variety show had been priced beyond their means. Phillipa responded to accusations of elitism by inviting the local dance school to put on a mid-week run, and all three nights of Hilary Clarke's adaptation of *Alice in Wonderland* had sold out in days.

When the show had opened on the evening of 21st October, the house had been packed, and it should have been cheers that filled the rafters instead of smoke. I'm certain that the performers would have received a standing ovation, but the curtain had come down after only half an hour, and it was the show's originator who took her final bow. Hilary was counted amongst the twelve fatalities that night, although arguably there were only eleven victims.

The body of Declan Gallagher, employed by Ronson Construction as site supervisor for the restoration, was found amongst the smouldering rubble close to his seriously injured sister, who would remain in hospital for weeks. A tragedy for the family perhaps, but also a conundrum. What was Declan doing there?

Evidential hearings took place within months of the fire, but this fact-gathering exercise is yet to produce any answers. We are told we have to wait for the investigators to complete the public inquiry and issue their findings, but we can make our own deductions. The likely cause of the fire was an electrical fault, and it isn't much of a leap to assume that Declan will bear some responsibility for what happened. He was an electrician by trade after all.

His murderous role has to remain under the spotlight if justice is to be served. It's understood that he had given his sister two tickets for the Empress's last ever show, and she had gone with a friend. There was no reason for Declan to be inside the theatre that night and, so far, his sister is refusing to explain his presence.

What we do know is that the first police officer was on the

scene within six minutes, and the ambulance service arrived a minute later, but these first responders weren't cleared to enter the building until the fire service deemed it safe. When two fire crews arrived eleven minutes after the fire alarm had sounded, they were significantly under-equipped to tackle the inferno that would require twenty appliances and most of the night to bring under control. Not one of those appliances came from Sedgefield's fire station, which had been sold to a property developer the year before. The closure was part of a wider rationalisation of the service that, according to the hype, would not compromise the safety of residents.

So where did it all go wrong? Should we blame the brave fire crews, or does the fault lie with the councillors who were forced to cut budgets? Should our government be held to account for cutting public funding, or does the blame lie closer to home? Did Declan Gallagher choose to cut corners in order to deliver the project to Phillipa Montgomery's demanding schedule? Or was it his incompetence that cost the town eleven lives? Did he know the risks he was taking? Did Phillipa?

Reportedly, it will be months before the findings of the public inquiry are edited and published, but the town cannot and will not wait. The community is doing its best to pull together, but as we face the first anniversary of the Sedgefield's darkest hour, we need answers.

Why was the theatre opened when it was clearly unsafe to do so?

Had the contractors been appointed on a wink and a nod, along with the approvals for the various planning consents and building inspections?

How did the fire spread through the roof space unchecked, and why didn't the smoke detectors pick up a warning sooner?

Was it a spark from a shorted circuit that started the fire, or was it ignited by the flash of Phillipa Montgomery's smile when the authorities gave her the go-ahead for her vanity project?

Should we put our faith in the public inquiry? Can we trust that this tragedy will be investigated fully and without bias?

When will the people of Sedgefield receive justice?

1

'I can't publish this!'

If it weren't for the digital age, Leanne's editor would be tearing her copy to shreds right now, but Mal Smithson had to settle for glaring at his computer screen.

'You asked me to do a personal piece, and this is it.'

Mal spun around to face her. 'A personal piece, yes. Not a personal vendetta.'

Leanne slumped back onto the faded sofa shoved against the wall opposite Mal's desk. The cushions sagged. 'I'll admit it needs some work and maybe I got a bit carried away towards the end, but it's only a first draft.'

'I couldn't care less. Even the tabloids look restrained compared to this,' he said, crossing his arms over the straining buttons of his denim shirt. His cuffs were frayed, as was his patience.

'I won't allow this scandal to be kicked into the long grass,' Leanne warned. 'I'm the only reporter on this paper who actually lives in Sedgefield, and it's my duty to be the voice of the people.'

'What you've written is inflammatory and libellous, and

you know it is,' he said, struggling to keep his voice level. 'No amount of editing will make it fit for print.'

Mal's deepening wrinkles made him appear much older than when Leanne had first met him less than four years ago. She had been working as a freelancer at the time, but her move from Leeds to the north-west had felt permanent, and the job at the *Cheshire Courier* meant she could stay in Sedgefield. She had thought they would get on well and, despite their current locking of horns, they did.

Her editor reminded her of a jaded teacher who was too set in his ways to consider retirement, and twenty-nine-year-old Leanne could pass easily as his student, with her dark clothes, lilac hair, and Doc Martens. In many ways, a student was exactly what she was. Mal had learned his craft back when newspapers were the main source of public information and, although times had changed, he continued to take that responsibility seriously, and expected his staff to do the same.

'We cannot and will not speculate on the wider causes of the fire until the findings of the public inquiry are published. The evidential hearings provided some, but not all of the information the investigators will be privy to. You're doing the town no favours by spreading false rumours. We have to be patient, Leanne.'

'And meanwhile, this paper is doing all it can to protect those individuals who don't deserve our patience and understanding,' Leanne hit back. 'I don't suppose your decision has anything to do with the fact that Phillipa Montgomery is friends with the *Courier*'s owners?'

'Phillipa is friends with a lot of people, and I take exception to any suggestion that I would be party to a cover-up.

If it's found that Phillipa was in any way responsible for what happened, I won't hesitate in putting it on the front page, but until then, we report the facts as and when we know them.'

The room darkened as the glimpse of September sky through the window turned slate grey. The *Courier*'s offices were in the centre of Chester, renowned for its stunning architecture and most notably the black and white Rows and the Eastgate Clock. The view behind Mal's desk comprised largely of a red-brick wall and a close-up of an air-conditioning unit. The *Courier* had hit upon hard times in recent years, transitioning from a daily to a weekly publication, while developing its online service to keep readers engaged between its Saturday morning print-runs.

Leanne had been aware that opportunities would be limited when she joined, but her intention was to use her time at the *Courier* to strengthen her CV by finding those meaty stories that could propel her career in a new direction. The theatre fire might have been one such story, but this wasn't about personal ambition. It was simply personal. She lived in Sedgefield. She walked past the empty shell of the theatre that had been boarded up since the fire, and she suffered the effects of the devastation it had caused. She wouldn't let this go without a fight.

'If it's not a matter of protecting Phillipa's good name, what exactly is the issue with my article?'

'You want to go through this line by line?' Mal asked, twisting in his seat to glare at his screen again. 'Where shall I start?' He shook his head as he scanned the page. 'OK, here. You say the *Alice in Wonderland* show was put on in response to criticism about elitism. Really, Leanne? You seem

23

to have conveniently forgotten there was a provision for community-led events in the original proposal.'

'Fine, cut it,' Leanne said. It was a matter of opinion whether Phillipa had supported or simply tolerated the inclusion of the community in her project, but it wasn't the hill Leanne wanted to die on. 'What else?'

Mal's ruddy cheeks glowed as he examined another paragraph. 'How about this? You say Karin Gallagher has refused to explain why her brother was in the theatre.'

Leanne huffed. 'And?'

'She was on life support for three weeks and woke up with amnesia. She can't explain something she can't remember.'

'And you believe that? I don't think it's any coincidence that she decided not to return to work at the Bridgewater Inn. She couldn't face the town, Mal. Everyone blames Declan, it's not just me. She's protecting him.'

'From what?'

'She was one of the last to be pulled out of the building alive. She must have seen what he was up to in there.'

'What he was up to was looking for his sister! As interesting as it might be to create some kind of conspiracy theory, the simple fact is that Declan lived on the high street. He had received an automated message when the alarm went off. Hell, he was close enough to have heard it. He would have reached the theatre easily before the first responders, plus we have anecdotal reports of a man pushing his way through to get inside. He went in there for Karin.'

'In that case, why didn't he find her until it was too late? What if he'd decided to go to the back office first to destroy evidence? He was in charge of the installations and all the safety checks. When he saw the fire, he would have known it was his fault.' She leant forward when she added, 'And his death is the only one that the coroner hasn't been able to fully determine yet.'

A coroner's inquest had been opened for each of the twelve people who had died in the disaster, but because there was an ongoing public inquiry, all of the inquests had been opened and immediately suspended pending the outcome of the broader investigation. Despite these limitations, the coroner had indicated that eleven of the fatalities were consistent with death caused by either the fire itself, the subsequent collapse of the roof, or as a result of the crush as people tried to escape. Only the death of the man who had been responsible for the restoration works remained ambiguous. Declan Gallagher had suffered internal injuries, but the coroner had been reluctant to suggest how those injuries might have been sustained until all investigations were complete. That was too much of a coincidence.

Closing down Leanne's file, Mal faced front. 'I don't disagree that there are questions to be asked, but your article doesn't get us any closer to the answers. I'm sorry, Leanne. You're a good reporter. You can do better than this.'

Leanne picked up a single strand of lilac hair that had fallen onto her not-so-skinny jeans. Mal was right. She could do better, and she would. 'Fine, delete it.'

'There are other ways we can help Sedgefield,' Mal said, not taking Leanne's surrender at face value. 'In the last eleven months, people have been torn apart by this sort of blame game. I appreciate you're not alone in wanting those responsible to be marched in shackles down the high street so you can throw rotten veg at them.'

'Or stones,' Leanne interjected.

'Or whatever,' Mal said. 'But that isn't how it works. For a start, one of them is dead.'

'So you do think Declan is to blame?'

Mal rested his elbows on his desk and sighed. 'Only if I allow myself to be swayed by gossip. I'm praying the findings of the inquiry, whatever they may be, will help bring closure, but that's going to be after the anniversary,' he said. His eyes had softened with a heavy dose of sympathy that Leanne would prefer not to see. 'I know I don't have your perspective, but we could do worse than helping people focus on some of the positives. There were heroes that night; the first responders and the theatregoers who put aside their own safety for the sake of others.'

Leanne swallowed hard. 'Not everyone was heroic.'

'And not everyone was saved,' Mal said softly. 'I get that.'

She shook her head, warding off his kindness. 'What is it you want?'

Mal took a moment, waiting for Leanne to compose herself despite the fact that she was refusing to show any feelings at all.

'I'd like you and Frankie to work together on a series of features. In the coming weeks, I want the *Courier* to acknowledge those acts of bravery, as well as celebrate the lives lost.'

Leanne sat up, her focus remaining on the only mission that mattered. 'In that case, we'll need to interview the bereaved families.'

Declan was originally from Donegal, but had come over to England a few years ago. He had been following in the footsteps of his sister, Karin, who had settled in the town a

26

decade earlier. She was one of the bereaved, and she was key to all of this.

'We'll only interview those who are willing to speak to us,' Mal cautioned, 'and I've asked Frankie to concentrate on the victim pieces.'

'You don't trust me?'

'I don't think it would be wise. Do you?' he said. 'Unless there's one you want to . . .'

'No,' Leanne said quickly. 'I can't.'

'You're bereaved too,' Mal chose to remind her, 'and maybe you don't feel ready to put that on the page yet, but I need you to acknowledge that your interest in this story is driven in part by your personal connection. If you can't keep that separation . . .'

'I'm fine,' Leanne insisted. 'I can do professional detachment.' She smiled a smile that was as false as her assurance.

Mal scowled at her. 'I know you're looking for something to grab the headlines, and that's exactly what I'm giving you. Look for the heroes, Leanne. Look for the ordinary people who went on to do extraordinary things.'

'Sure,' she said, without enthusiasm.

Mal refused to give up. 'There are untold stories out there, accounts of survivors being helped by strangers. There's one that has real potential. Remember the young girl who was buried in the rubble – Amelia Parker? The family tracked down the man who carried her out, but someone else had passed her to him. A mystery woman covered in dust. She was the one who dug Amelia out of the rubble and saved her life, but so far, she hasn't been recognised for her heroism.'

'And you want me to find her?'

'You're a good journalist when you want to be. Tap into the emotion I know you feel behind all that anger.'

'As you've just pointed out, my emotions are irrelevant,' she replied. 'I wasn't there.'

'And neither was I, but I want you to write a piece that places the reader inside the theatre that night. Let us celebrate the best in humanity, not the worst. Hell, if you manage to find Amelia's hero, I can guarantee it will make the front page, and not just in the *Courier*. You could make a name for yourself.'

'Trying to get rid of me?'

'No, I'm trying to make you a better journalist.'

Leanne rose to her feet without bothering with a response. She was heading for the door when Mal said, 'Oh, and I want you to cover the plans for the memorial service.'

'Whatever.'

'You'll need to speak to Claudia Rothwell. She's the one whose charity is putting it all together. Do you need her details?'

'I know who she is,' Leanne said, making sure she had turned away fully before Mal could see the glint in her eyes. The battle for justice would go on, and if her editor wanted facts to substantiate her accusations, what better place to start than with one of Phillipa Montgomery's sycophantic friends? Leanne would take down Phillipa's tight network of supporters, one bored housewife at a time.

2

It was raining when Leanne pulled up in front of a gleaming set of electronic gates in her battered Ford Fiesta. A ten-foot wall enclosed the property and, although it wasn't far from Sedgefield town centre, there were enough surrounding woods and hedgerows to make it feel like it was in the middle of the countryside. The three-storey new-build contained five luxury apartments, and the penthouse occupying the entire top floor belonged to Claudia Rothwell.

There was an intercom set into the wall next to the gates, but Leanne figured Claudia would have a good view of arrivals and could surely let her in without making it necessary to get out of the car to use the buzzer. Mal had made the arrangements for the interview, and Leanne was not only expected, she was on time. She waited patiently. The gates remained firmly sealed.

Forced out of the car, she grabbed her leather jacket from amongst the detritus on the back seat and held it over her head as she pressed the intercom. Claudia didn't deign to answer immediately and, when she did, she sounded surprised at the interruption.

Leanne's features were set grim as she climbed the stairs with her rucksack slumped over her shoulder. Reaching the top floor, she wasn't surprised to discover the door to Claudia's apartment firmly closed. She knocked with a tightened fist and, after a short delay, Claudia greeted her with a bright smile that momentarily disarmed Leanne.

Claudia was less polished than the images splashed across Cheshire's society pages, and she appeared diminutive despite being two inches taller than Leanne. Her dark, raven hair had been tied back in a messy knot, and her brown eyes were smudged with what looked like the previous day's make-up.

'God, you're soaked,' she said, beckoning Leanne inside and taking her jacket.

There was a pause before Leanne realised she was expected to take off her boots and replace them with the open-toed slippers stacked neatly by the door for guests. Leanne was wearing her Docs and turned away from Claudia as she unlaced them. Her big toe protruded through one of her socks and she pulled both off discreetly before shoving them into her boots. The deep pile carpet felt warm underfoot as she stepped into the white, terry-towelling slippers.

'Let's go through to the kitchen and I'll make you a hot drink,' said Claudia, leading the way past seven polished oak doors. All closed.

'Nice place,' Leanne noted, not needing to see inside the rooms to know her host had expensive taste.

The kitchen confirmed her suspicions. There wasn't a black quartz surface or hand-polished tile that didn't shine like a freshly minted coin. It was a bit too ostentatious for Leanne's liking.

The Rothwells had done well for themselves. They weren't in the super-rich league of Sedgefield's finest, but they certainly moved in the same circles. According to Leanne's research, Claudia's husband, Justin, was a finance director for a pharmaceutical company and had the benefit of a private education. He was forty years old and had one previous marriage. No children.

There was relatively little information available on thirty-four-year-old Claudia. She appeared to spend her days championing worthy causes between long lunches and evening soirées. She was a Phillipa Montgomery in the making.

'Make yourself at home,' Claudia said, pointing to the breakfast table, where two chairs had been positioned at an angle rather than opposite each other. There was a plate of biscuits waiting, including Jammy Dodgers and Custard Creams, which looked as out of place in the current setting as Leanne herself. 'Would you like tea or coffee?'

'Coffee, please.'

'I hope you don't mind instant,' Claudia said, reaching inside a cupboard for a jar of Nescafé and ignoring the French press lurking in the corner.

'It's what I'm used to.'

Claudia glanced over her shoulder at Leanne. 'Me too, if I'm honest,' she said. 'Do you take milk? Sugar?'

'Milk, two sugars.'

Claudia didn't look the type who was used to associating with someone who consumed unrefined sugar without apology, but if she judged Leanne for her health choices and chubby thighs, she didn't show it.

'I love your hair, by the way,' Claudia said, while they

waited for the kettle to boil. 'I'm too much of a wimp to go for such a striking colour.'

'Thanks.'

It could have been a backhanded compliment, but Leanne felt an involuntary thrill. She had never been one of the popular girls at school, not fitting the mould reserved for the fortunate few who looked a lot like Claudia. Leanne would have given anything for their approval back then, and had to remind herself that she needed no such endorsement now, especially not from the Rothwells or the Montgomerys of this world.

'I know I look a mess,' Claudia said, pulling at the shapeless jumper that magically accentuated her long limbs and sharp cheekbones. 'I went through loads of different outfits this morning, but decided to wear what felt most comfortable – that's why I was late answering the door. Your editor said you didn't need photos today.'

Leanne nudged her rucksack with her foot. 'I did bring my camera, just in case,' she said, if only to see Claudia's features pale. It was a mean thing to do, especially when Claudia was going out of her way to be nice, but Leanne found she couldn't help herself. 'Never mind, the office will be in touch to arrange a photoshoot.'

Claudia finished making their drinks and wiped the counter clean before joining Leanne at the table.

'I can't tell you how grateful I am,' she admitted. 'The anniversary is going to be tough and, although it's a night we would all rather forget, it feels right doing something to mark the occasion.' She bit her lip. 'It's going to be hardest for the families who lost loved ones.'

'You were there too, I believe,' Leanne said dispassionately as she checked her notebook. She often used a voice recorder, but only when she was invested in what her interviewee might have to say. For today, her notes would be brief, unless she managed to unpick Claudia's connection to Phillipa, but all in good time. 'I presume you were affected by what you saw?'

Claudia fidgeted with the cuffs of her jumper. 'This isn't about me. I'd rather talk about the work of the charity.'

'Which you set up.'

Claudia moved her head from side to side, not quite a nod nor a shake of the head. 'The Empress Memorial Fund was my idea, but I didn't know the first thing about establishing a charity, I still don't. Justin helped create a board of trustees made up of greater minds than mine, and we have a working party who do the actual work. It's going to be down to them to make this happen.'

Leanne tapped her pen against the blank page, leaving a peppering of blue spots. 'You're taking a chance holding it outdoors in the middle of October.'

'I know, and it's too much to hope that it won't rain, but we intend to erect a marquee for the refreshments, as long as it isn't too windy. We did consider different venues, but there are survivors who won't want to be part of a large crowd in an enclosed space. Victoria Park seemed to be a good compromise.'

'Except for those who can't bear to look at the theatre.'

'I appreciate the park is close by, but some of the survivors have said they'll find solace returning to the place where they found refuge that night.'

'Will that include you?' asked Leanne. 'How are you going to feel?'

'I expect I'll be too busy for much reflection. I'm more interested in how everyone else will be coping,' Claudia said, dodging the question again. 'Your editor mentioned you're writing a series of features about survivors. I've had the privilege of speaking to many of them, and their stories are incredibly moving. It seems that everyone has their own unique way of dealing with their trauma, which is why it's been doubly hard to find a way to mark the anniversary in a way that's inclusive and meaningful for everyone. I want the memorial service to reinforce what already exists in the town. A strong sense of community and camaraderie. You'll see for yourself if you come along.'

'It'll be hard to avoid, and not just because of my job,' Leanne said. 'I live in Sedgefield.'

'Oh, sorry, your accent threw me. I can't quite place it.'

'I'm originally from Leeds.'

'What made you move to Sedgefield, of all places?'

Claudia's expression was open, as if she really wanted to know. 'I moved for love,' Leanne said, waiting long enough for the softening around Claudia's mouth to confirm she had fallen for the trap. 'Love for myself that is. I was in a toxic relationship, and decided I deserved better, but I couldn't face moving back in with my parents, so I packed a bag and crossed the Pennines.'

'Wow, good for you. When did you—'

'I was here that night,' Leanne said, forcing the conversation back on topic. 'Not at the theatre, but I can still taste the smoke that hung in the air for days.'

'Then you know how difficult it will be to pitch this event just right. Believe me, the working party has been through countless iterations of what could work and what simply won't do. It's been hard at times to find a middle ground. We don't want the service to be focused on any particular religion, but we need to acknowledge individual beliefs. We want singing, but the lyrics have to be carefully considered. We talked about releasing balloons, but there's the issue of plastic pollution. Fireworks were suggested, but that might trigger some of the survivors. I could go on.'

'So what will you be doing?'

'We'll have a few speeches, some readings, and there's a local choir to provide the music. We're also working with local faith leaders so we can signpost anyone who needs individual support, but I'd have to say, the most contentious issue has been whether or not to invite the dance school to resurrect part of their *Alice in Wonderland* performance.'

Leanne pulled a face.

'My thoughts exactly, and it isn't going happen,' Claudia said, sharing a moment with Leanne as if they were old friends. 'But we did agree that the dance school should be involved in some way. Rose Peagrave is in charge now, and she's said that the students are super eager to do something to celebrate the memory of their founder.'

'Hilary Clarke,' Leanne said. When Claudia nodded, Leanne decided the time had come to drop another name into the conversation. She hooked a finger around her chin, pen still in hand. 'It sounds like there are a lot of people involved in your working party. Would Phillipa Montgomery be one of them?'

'No,' Claudia replied, unfazed by the name drop. 'It was deemed inappropriate for Phillipa to be involved, given the nature of my charity, and the ongoing investigation.'

'Who deemed it inappropriate?'

'Phillipa.'

'I see,' Leanne said, scribbling a note to that effect so that Claudia was left in no doubt that this was an important aspect of her story. 'Are you a close friend?'

'Not particularly.'

Leanne was used to hearing this kind of evasion. Phillipa had become a social outcast, and no one wanted to be linked by association. Not that it stopped Leanne from tarring them all with the same brush. 'But you did socialise with her?'

'It was hard not to,' Claudia replied, as if mixing with the rich and infamous was a daily hazard Leanne might relate to. 'But you couldn't break into Phillipa's inner circle except by invitation. I was very much a newcomer, still on probation.' She stopped abruptly when she noticed Leanne's pen move. She extended a hand tentatively towards the notepad, stopping short of touching it. 'Please don't quote me on that.'

Placing her pen on the table, Leanne signalled her agreement to an unspoken pact. Claudia would continue on the understanding that nothing she said could be attributed to her. Leanne relaxed back into her chair.

'When Justin and I married four years ago, I was plunged into a world I knew nothing about, and I'm still finding my feet,' Claudia said in a conspiratorial whisper. It wasn't only the pitch of her voice that had changed, her accent had become broader too, indistinguishable from the average Sedgefield resident who didn't care about rounding their vowels. 'I was a receptionist at his tennis club when we met. There was a mix-up with the bookings and somehow we got talking. I'm pretty sure our paths wouldn't have crossed otherwise.'

'I take it you gave up your job.'

Claudia picked up a Custard Cream and offered the plate to Leanne. Leanne took two.

'I had no choice if I wanted to fit in.'

Leanne raised an eyebrow. 'It can't have been that big a sacrifice.'

Claudia cringed. 'Sorry, I don't mean to sound ungracious. I know I'm living a life of privilege compared to some, but it was a huge culture shock. My mum died when I was five, and I was brought up by my dad in a draughty terraced house. Honestly, this isn't me,' Claudia said. Her eyes darted to the door as if someone might storm in at any moment and evict her for trespassing on private property.

'Sounds like a case of imposter syndrome.'

A flush rose in Claudia's cheeks. 'It can be quite intimidating, pretending to be something you're not, and especially when surrounded by the genuine article.'

'And was Phillipa someone who intimidated you?' asked Leanne. She wasn't ready to feel sorry for Claudia, but a note of understanding had crept into her voice.

'I know she's had a lot of bad press, but she was a legend. No one but Phillipa would have attempted a project on the scale of the theatre restoration.'

'And everyone rushed to help, including you, despite not being in her inner circle,' Leanne noted, refusing to allow Claudia to distance herself completely from Phillipa. She had been snapped at various fundraisers, as well as the grand opening.

'I'll admit, I wanted to be involved, and I did help out on occasion, but all the high-profile jobs were ring-fenced for those with more experience and better contacts. I can understand why. As I'm discovering for myself, public relations have to be handled carefully if you want to secure community buy-in.'

And Leanne had been amongst those who had bought into Phillipa's scheming. She could visualise the front-page headline in the *Courier* when the theatre had opened a year ago. 'The Empress Returns.' There had been a close-up of Phillipa's face beneath it. 'Is it true she wanted to rename it as the Montgomery Theatre?'

When Claudia laughed, a tiny crumb from her biscuit trembled on her lip. 'You shouldn't believe all the rumours. Phillipa is an indomitable figure, but her ego isn't quite that big. And despite what happened, I think her original intentions were honourable. She wanted to give something back to her community, and this has broken her.'

The crumb on Claudia's lip was distracting, and Leanne wiped a finger across her own mouth. Claudia mirrored the move. With the offending crumb dislodged, Leanne asked, 'Is she still in the South of France?'

'I believe so.'

'So much for helping with the investigation.'

'She did stay for the evidential hearings,' Claudia reminded her.

The hearings had taken place at the start of the public inquiry. Witnesses had included the incident commander and other officers from the emergency services who were there that night, as well as various expert witnesses. Representatives from the renovation company, Ronson Construction, had given evidence, as had the woman who was responsible for their appointment and so much more.

'Will Phillipa be back before the findings are published?'

'I don't know. Like I said, we're not close.'

'But with all your charity work, you must be in contact with people who are.'

'Setting up the Empress Memorial Fund has given me an appreciation of how much of an undertaking charity work can be. You can't rely on goodwill alone. You have to reach out to people who can make things happen, and some of my contacts are closer to Phillipa than I am.'

Claudia's voice had risen to a normal level, and her accent was suppressed once more. She couldn't seem to decide which she wanted more, to be accepted as an average person on the street, or one of the elite. Leanne's overall impression was that she simply wanted to be accepted, full stop.

'Bryony Sutherland might be a good starting point, if you can pin her down. She runs a family business so she hasn't been as involved with the memorial fund as I'd like. It's been the same with a lot of Phillipa's friends actually.' Before Leanne could ask her next question, Claudia answered it for her. 'If Bryony knows what Phillipa's plans are, she hasn't shared that information with me.'

'So who has been helping you? Anyone from Ronson Construction?'

Claudia uncrossed her legs and sat up straight. 'No, because we're not building anything, and when it comes to having the stage and marquees erected, I won't be using a company under investigation for negligence.'

'Do you believe they were negligent?' Leanne asked. When Claudia simply shrugged, she added, 'Do you know if they were procured appropriately?'

'You're asking me questions I'm in no position to answer.'

'But you must have been aware that the project's schedule

had slipped. The opening had already been delayed. Did Phillipa openly criticise the work, or was she covering for their incompetence?'

Claudia's fingers began to explore the silver handle of a teaspoon on the table. 'I couldn't say. Like everyone else, I'm waiting eagerly to see what comes of the inquiry.'

'Tell me about Declan Gallagher. Did you know him?'

'I was aware of him, yes. He came to some of the fund-raisers, I believe.'

'And the night of the fire, did you see him at all?'

'No.'

Given Claudia's previous obfuscation about her experience that night, Leanne changed tack. She stopped asking questions and left a pause for Claudia to fill.

Claudia took a breath before deciding to speak. Her expression was pained when she said, 'You can't begin to imagine the chaos inside the auditorium, and I'd defy anyone to give a clear account of what they did or didn't see. I get flashes of memory, people's faces swimming in front of my vision. There was so much noise, people calling out to each other, children crying, others screaming.' She lifted the teaspoon and stared at her warped image in its reflection.

Leanne couldn't ignore Claudia's distress, but her thirst for answers was impossible to quench. 'Do you believe Declan went inside to save his sister, or could he have had another motive? There's a suggestion he needed to get into the offices on the ground floor. Could there have been something in there he didn't want anyone to see?'

She stopped short of asking, 'Why are you protecting these killers?' As Claudia was eager to point out, she had never been inside Phillipa's circle of trust.

40

'I don't know anything,' Claudia whispered. Her hands fluttered and, in the process, she knocked the teaspoon off the table and it clattered to the floor. The legs of her dining chair scraped over the tiles as she reached to pick it up.

Leanne's brow furrowed. Knocking the spoon off the table with trembling fingers could have been a simple accident, but Leanne had been watching Claudia closely. The fumble seemed choreographed.

From down the hall, there came the sound of a door opening, and Leanne had to stop herself from saying, 'Ah, I see what you did there.'

It wasn't a mishap. It was a signal.

Tall, with broad shoulders, Justin Rothwell wore a rugby shirt that gave the impression he could cause some damage in a scrum, but his smile was playful, verging on mischievous. His light brown hair had grey accents at the temples, and his hazel eyes were two shades lighter than his wife's. Leanne couldn't help but stare. He was beautiful.

'I hope I'm not disturbing you,' he said, extending his hand towards Leanne. 'I'm Justin.'

Leanne willed her cheeks not to burn. 'Lovely to meet you.'

'I'm afraid Claudia has to put up with me working from home today.'

'He's been doing that a lot lately,' Claudia added, catching Justin's eye. As he moved towards her, she dipped her gaze and he kissed the top of her head.

'I must like your company,' he whispered.

Leanne felt a shiver run down her spine. She didn't do relationships very well, her longest having lasted only eighteen months before she discovered the lying rat had been sleeping around. That particular rat was the reason she had sold her flat and left Leeds. She had given up on love, and was convinced she wasn't missing anything special – except at moments like this when she saw the real thing in action. Claudia had sent a distress signal, and Justin hadn't hesitated to respond.

'I was doing my utmost to keep out of the way,' Justin explained, 'but I need a caffeine fix. Would you like a refill?'

'I've barely touched this,' Leanne said, picking up her drink. She watched Justin over the rim of her cup.

'I must say, it's good to have the *Courier* supporting us – ah, sorry, I should say, supporting Claudia. My name might be on the board of trustees, but I take no credit,' Justin said, raising his hands. 'This is all down to my wife.'

'My editor's determined to publish some positive pieces,' Leanne replied. She had tried to inject some enthusiasm into her response, but she wasn't sure she succeeded. It wasn't exactly investigative journalism.

'The paper could play an important part in helping the town heal,' Claudia said, sounding as if she were one of Mal's disciples, or was it the other way around?

'That's the plan,' replied Leanne, attempting a smile.

As he waited for the kettle to boil, Justin added scoops of ground coffee to the French press Claudia had hidden away, but his attention remained focused on Leanne. 'What other stories are you working on?'

'Ones that will give our readers a sense of the needless loss that night,' Leanne said, not making the articles sound nearly as positive as Mal envisioned.

42

'I was telling Leanne there won't be a shortage of heroes with stories to tell.'

Justin turned to his wife, spoon in hand. The two locked eyes, and he seemed unaware of the coffee grains raining down onto the floor tiles. 'If that's the case, she needn't look further than this room.'

The air became charged, and Leanne straightened up. 'What do you mean?'

Claudia pursed her lips as if she were about to object, but with a sigh, her shoulders sagged. She left it to her husband to explain.

'Claudia was meant to be a mystery shopper that night,' Justin began. 'Phillipa gave out complimentary tickets to all her friends for different shows. She wanted feedback on their experience.'

'Friends?' Leanne asked, seizing on the contradiction with what Claudia would have her believe.

'I was very much at the bottom of her list,' Claudia said. 'I was sent along to the only amateur performance in the theatre's schedule.'

'She wasn't happy,' added Justin playfully. 'She didn't even get seats in the VIP area.' He grimaced. 'Sorry, that sounds crass, given what happened.'

It did sound crass, but Leanne knew what he meant. She hadn't seen the attraction of spending an evening watching a group of school kids prancing about on a stage either. 'None of us knew what was going to happen.'

He sighed. 'If only we *had* known. Claudia had two tickets, but I was working late and she went on her own. I could have tried harder to rearrange my schedule, but the first I knew of the fire was when I was driving home and a couple of fire engines sped past.' Justin lowered his voice, but Leanne heard it crack when he added, 'I should have been there for her.'

'What happened?' Leanne asked, directing the question back to Claudia, who wouldn't meet her gaze.

'I was no different to anyone else. The evacuation started off so calm and orderly,' she said, repeating what so many others had said at the time. Not one person had suspected the alarm to be anything more than an inconvenient fire drill. 'I was in the stalls and headed out the way I'd come in, but there was a long queue. When the ceiling collapsed and the lights went out, people started screaming and scrambling on top of each other.'

'We act on instinct,' Justin said, when Claudia could no longer continue. 'We have competing needs of self-preservation and a primal desire to protect our group, the group being our friends, our family and our neighbours. Claudia managed to get to the side exit, but held back longer than she should to make sure everyone else was safe. I'm sure by now you've realised my wife's overriding compulsion is to help others.'

'No, Justin,' Claudia warned. 'Don't make me out to be something I'm not.'

'Then don't deny what you did.'

'I don't, but if I'd known how much I'd hurt you in the process,' she said, holding her husband fiercely in her gaze.

'Us,' he corrected.

For a time, only the sound of Claudia's shallow breaths could be heard. Leanne needed to know. 'What's this about?'

Claudia shook her head slowly from side to side, pain contorting her features. The smudged make-up gave the impression of shadows beneath her damp eyes. 'I didn't think through what I was doing. I was so stupid! If I'd known . . .'

'I found Claudia wandering around Victoria Park amongst the other survivors,' Justin explained. 'She was obviously suffering from shock, but she hadn't sought help. She didn't want to waste anyone's time, but I insisted she was seen by one of the paramedics. We were advised to make our own way to the hospital so she could be checked out for any effects of smoke inhalation.' He stopped to take a breath. Meanwhile, Claudia had pressed her hand to her mouth. Whatever he had to say was killing them both. 'And because she was two months pregnant.'

Claudia swallowed hard. 'Compared to some of the others they were pulling out of the theatre, I was fine.' She laughed bitterly as she stabbed a finger to her chest. 'I was fine. Just me.'

Leanne knew what was coming and yet she searched the room for confirmation that a baby lived there too, one that would be four months old by her reckoning.

'We lost it,' Claudia said when she noticed Leanne's hopeless search. Her voice was hollow. 'Not on that night, but within days.'

'Oh,' Leanne said. For a second she thought only of how this was going to mess up the dry piece she had intended to write about the woman of privilege behind the memorial fund. It took an indecent amount of time for the grief etched on the faces of Claudia and Justin to finally register. What was wrong with her? Leanne reached over to place a hand on Claudia's arm. 'I'm so sorry.'

The small gesture appeared to be too much, and Claudia's chest heaved as she fought to hold back a sob. Justin was there in a second, crouching down so their foreheads touched.

'It's time to acknowledge the Empress took another victim that night,' he said.

'But it wasn't the fire that killed our baby, it was me,' Claudia replied, anger clenching her words.

'No, sweetheart, no! If anyone's to blame, it's me. It shouldn't have taken a tragedy to make me realise how precious you are to me. I should have been there.'

This last comment pierced Leanne's cold heart. Survivor guilt at its worst. It was all too much, she needed to leave. She picked up her notepad and shoved it into her rucksack.

Still holding on to his wife, Justin turned his head towards her. He no longer looked like a burly rugby player, his loss had diminished him. 'We want people to know. It's time.'

Leanne nodded. 'I'll be in touch if I need anything else,' she said, rising to her feet.

Justin went to follow her, but Claudia held him back. 'I'll see Leanne out,' she insisted.

In the time it took Leanne to lace up her Doc Martens, Claudia had composed herself. 'I never wanted to go public,' she explained. 'That's not why I agreed to this interview. I'm only interested in raising money for the charity and letting people know about the memorial service.'

Leanne believed her. 'I shouldn't worry. I imagine your story will generate lots of support for your cause.'

Claudia didn't appear convinced. 'Could you do me a favour? Don't over-egg it. I'm scared people will think I'm looking for pity, and I'm really not. Mention the miscarriage if you must, but no one needs to read some tragic backstory of how my mum died when I was little. It's what's happening in the present that's important. There are those suffering so much more right now.'

'I won't mention your childhood,' Leanne said, eager to do whatever Claudia asked, despite herself.

Claudia pressed a business card into Leanne's hand. 'You've been so good. I was dreading today, but I'm glad it was you I spoke to. I promise, I'll send you over the press release when it's ready, but ring me any time, if you have questions.'

Once outside, the slap of cold rain on Leanne's face gave her a jolt. Mal had tasked her with finding heroes, but this had been the last place she had expected to find one. Claudia had gone against every one of Leanne's preconceptions. She didn't like how much she liked her.

3

Leanne pulled up in front of a rusted gate that barred further progress. Unlike Claudia's little palace, there was no high-tech security system to grant access to Leanne's home, just an old-fashioned padlock that had a habit of freezing in winter.

Leaving the car with the engine running, she hurried across a track pitted with potholes to unlock the gate. It was almost seven o'clock and the sky had turned a sapphire blue, with purple cloud that absorbed the last of the sun's warmth. At least it hadn't rained today and there were no puddles to dodge.

Leanne searched for the right key from a set attached to a large cork ball hanging from a rope. It had been a present from her best friend; a moving-in gift when Leanne had arrived at Raven Brook Marina four years ago in a car filled with all her worldly goods and a vague plan of how to get her life back on track.

'What's this for?' she had asked when her friend gave her the odd-looking key ring that was the size of a clementine.

'The cork stops your keys from sinking if you drop them

in the water. I was hoping they did bigger ones in case we fall in the canal on our way home from the pub, which is exactly what we'll be doing tonight. Going to the pub that is, not the bit about falling in.'

'Mum thinks we should wear life jackets permanently.'

'I'll keep you safe,' Lois said. 'Promise.'

It had never occurred to Leanne to say it back. From the moment they had met during Freshers' Week, Lois Granger had made it her mission to take care of those around her. She was the go-to friend whenever there was trouble, and it was natural that Leanne had gone to her when her life had taken a nosedive. It was Lois's idea for Leanne to buy a boat with the money she had made from her flat in Leeds, and it went without saying that Lois would become her lodger.

They had visions of travelling up and down the country and had gone as far as to plan a boat trip to the Peak District and another along the Llangollen Canal and over the Pontcysyllte Aqueduct. The only journey Leanne had plotted recently was a marathon trek to London, for when she landed that scoop and was flooded with job offers from the national press. Technically, she could go anywhere she wanted, if she wanted.

The gate shuddered as Leanne opened it wide enough for the car to get through, then she did everything in reverse until the gate was locked again. It was easier if there were two people, but Leanne was getting used to being on her own and, as she went through the motions, her thoughts moved seamlessly from Lois, to the Empress, to Claudia Rothwell.

Two days had passed since the interview, but Leanne was

yet to write a single word for Saturday's issue. The headline, however, had written itself.

'Secret Agony of a Very Public Tragedy'.

Mal didn't know that particular angle yet, but he was going to love it. Who wouldn't? Claudia's actions deserved to be acknowledged, and yet Leanne prevaricated. It wasn't so much that Claudia had a link to Phillipa Montgomery. Or maybe it was, just a teeny bit. What bothered her most was that she would be drawing sympathy to someone who lived an otherwise privileged existence. It wasn't as if Claudia wanted a pity-piece either, but sympathy was coming her way whether it was sought or not.

Driving past the timber-clad clubhouse, Leanne followed the track that hugged the edges of the marina. Raven Brook had what appeared to be an incomprehensible maze of jetties, but the design provided moorings for at least two hundred boats of varying shapes and sizes. Each mooring had its own electric hook-up and access to water, which meant Leanne had no reason to move the boat. Car parking spaces were at a premium during peak season, but not in the colder months. Leanne was one of only a handful who lived on board all year round and she had no problem finding a space close to home.

The *Soleil Anne* was a forty-foot narrowboat, painted marine blue and decorated with the requisite roses and castles. Inside, it had a well-proportioned galley and saloon that provided enough living space for a futon that doubled up as a bed. There were two more berths in the bunk room towards the bow, and in the middle, a bathroom complete with shower. The previous owner had lovingly fitted it out from a shell, but two months before he was due to marry his childhood sweetheart, he had discovered his fiancé was having an affair with his best man. With his dream in tatters, he had sold the boat to Leanne at a knock-down price. He had hoped she and Lois would have better luck in their new home. He would be disappointed.

Grabbing bags of shopping from the boot of her car, Leanne was halfway down the jetty when her phone rang. It was zipped up in her jacket pocket and she didn't dare fumble for it. She had dropped a phone into the canal only a month after moving aboard and had learnt her lesson.

Leanne wasn't expecting any calls, but it was impossible not to raise her hopes. It had taken some perseverance, but she had managed to obtain Karin Gallagher's mobile number from a contact who had worked with her at the Bridgewater Inn. The pub was close to the centre of Sedgefield and, although it wasn't quite within staggering distance, Leanne and Lois had been regulars. She didn't recall ever seeing Karin in there and, now that Declan's sister had resigned as assistant manager, she never would. Speaking to her at all was proving to be another impossibility. Karin had so far ignored all five of Leanne's voicemails, but there was always a chance the reporter had worn her down.

Unzipping the awning that covered the stern, Leanne climbed aboard, but she didn't unlock the hatch straight away. She took out her phone and, as it lit up the darkened ante space, Mal's name glowered at her. She had sent him updates throughout the day, including a report on a crash that had caused a five-mile tailback along the bypass, but she doubted he was phoning to thank her.

'Where's the piece on Claudia Rothwell? It was due two hours ago.'

'I've been out all day. It's only Wednesday, there's still time.'

'I don't pay you to choose your own deadlines. I want it on my desk by ten at the latest tomorrow morning. If you have plans tonight, cancel them.'

Leanne never had plans, that wasn't the problem. 'Fine, you'll get it.'

'Look, if you're not up to this, say now and I'll assign it to someone else. You can always work on our advertisement features.'

Leanne couldn't tell from his tone if this was tough love from her mentor, or a real threat. She didn't want to risk finding out.

'It's not that hard, Leanne. I've seen the press release Claudia sent through. She's practically written it for you.'

'There's a bit more to the story than the plans for the memorial,' Leanne said. She couldn't avoid telling him any longer. 'It turns out there was a victim of the Empress fire that no one knows about.'

'What does that mean?' asked Mal. There was an edge to his voice. He was good at sniffing out a story and had picked up the scent.

'Claudia was pregnant. She stayed by the exit to make sure people got out OK, but she suffered the effects of smoke inhalation and it led to a miscarriage.'

Mal didn't respond immediately, and Leanne used the time to unlock the hatch and open the cabin doors. She left her shopping on the steel footplate, so she had one hand free to steady herself as she climbed down a short set of wooden steps into the living space.

'We need to get this story published,' Mal said at last.

Leanne reached for the shopping that was now at eye level, and transferred it into the boat. 'And I said I'll do it. I was thinking I could separate the two articles; give you the one outlining the memorial service for this Saturday's edition, and save the personal stuff for the anniversary issue.' They had another three weeks until the anniversary. She was prevaricating again.

'No, we need to get this published quickly.'

Gritting her teeth, Leanne closed the cabin doors to reveal two golden carp on the inside panels. Each scale of the fish on the left-hand door had been painted in exquisite detail and its body shimmered. The one on the right had more of a skeletal form, a work in progress that would never be completed.

'We have to be the ones to break the story, or someone else will,' Mal persisted.

'Yeah, it is a shame about the baby, isn't it?' Leanne said, feeling good that she could prick her editor's conscience even though she had reacted in a similar way.

'Fuck off, Leanne,' Mal said, but his humour was improving. 'This is one hell of a story. You should have told me about it sooner.'

'Claudia wants the focus to be on other people, not her.'

'Tough, sometimes the news writes itself. And it's not as if it's going to be detrimental to her cause.'

'We can't ignore that she was part of the fundraising machine for the restoration project. And she was only there that night at Phillipa's behest, checking up on staff to make sure they were doing their jobs properly. That won't go down well with some.'

'Claudia has been open about the extent of her involvement,

and she was pretty low down in the pecking order from what I've heard,' Mal replied. 'And I know I sound like a broken record, but Phillipa hasn't been accused of anything specific. It's a non-issue as far as Claudia Rothwell's concerned, and I expect your article to reflect that.'

'Is that it?' Leanne asked, switching on the uplights that warmed the honey tones of the marine pine lining the walls.

Her living space had all the essentials within easy reach. There were bookshelves full of biographies on the world's most notorious serial killers, a widescreen TV for watching documentaries on the same theme, storage space under the futon for her files when she worked from home, and a log burner that was more reliable than the boat's central heating. Unlike Claudia's apartment, there was also plenty of clutter that meant she never had to worry about something being out of place. The boat had a cottage feel that continued into the galley, which had all the mod cons, including a gas hob, a fridge-freezer, and running hot and cold water. There was no excuse for the breakfast dishes piled up in the sink, but Leanne would leave any self-admonishment until Mal had finished giving her an earful.

'I'm thinking how we can do this,' he said. Leanne could hear him scratching the stubble on his chin. 'Instead of doing one anniversary issue, we could stagger it over the next three weekends, with a special edition the following Saturday after the anniversary. We should have enough material. Frankie has a couple of stories on the bereaved families ready to go, there's your piece on Claudia, and the one about Amelia Parker.'

'Amelia who?' asked Leanne before she had the good sense to bite her tongue.

'For God's sake! The girl who doesn't know who dug her out of the rubble. Haven't you set up the interview yet?' he ranted. 'I promised the parents you'd be in touch days ago, and I've given you the contact details for that bloke who carried her out. His name's Rex Russell. Christ, Leanne, I've done half the job for you.'

'OK, OK. But you definitely said you didn't need that one until next week.'

'To give you more time to investigate. It's your job to find out who our mystery hero is, and I want a name before the anniversary. If necessary, we could run an appeal for information this weekend. That should help you track her down.'

'You're not asking for much, are you?'

'Then you'd better get to it,' Mal said, sounding brighter than he had at the beginning of their conversation. 'No distractions, Leanne. Drop whatever else you're doing.'

When Leanne ended the call, she scrolled through her call log. She considered giving Karin Gallagher one more try, but Mal was right. She had a job to do and couldn't allow herself to become distracted. There wasn't time. It was probably a good thing.

The Empress Theatre
Sedgefield, Cheshire

In those last precious moments when everyone thought the evacuation was as interesting as their evening was going to get, Rex Russell gave a gentle sigh. He had held back while others pressed forward, partly out of politeness, but also because he didn't want to spill his popcorn.

His wife had suggested using one of the side exits that were less crowded, but it was cold outside and they had their eight-year-old granddaughter with them. He had reminded his wife that the theatre was brand new and there was unlikely to be a genuine problem. They were probably being used as guinea pigs for the first full evacuation.

Expecting the alarm to be silenced at any moment, Rex shuffled beneath the shadow of the circle, missing the peculiar shower of grit that attracted Hilary Clarke's attention directly above him. 'Maybe we should sit—'

An explosion of falling masonry and splintered timber propelled Rex forward into sudden darkness. His popcorn flew into the air as he landed on his hands and knees. The emergency lighting came on, but there was a dense cloud of dust swirling around him, pressing against his chest with almost as much force as the terror gripping his heart. Frantically, he groped around until he found his wife and granddaughter. They needed to move, but he sensed danger ahead, where the crowd had contracted into an impossibly small space. Danger lay behind them too, in the smouldering ruins.

Choking on dust, Rex scrambled sideways until his back was pressed against the wall. He pulled his family close to him, wanting to shield them as best he could, but his arms were as short and stout as his body. He wasn't built for heroics. All he could do was put his hands over his granddaughter's ears so she didn't have to listen to the screams; screams that eventually faded to whimpers and pleas for help. Even the fire alarm had lost its breath and was a distant mewl.

Amelia released a whimper as the beam of light tempted her into consciousness. It made her eyes sting and she closed them tight, willing the darkness to take her again.

'Please wake up. Oh God, please wake up.'

'Mum?' Amelia asked as she was roused once more. The ground that should be below her was above her head, and she couldn't figure out why. Then she began to cry.

'It's OK, I'll have you out in no time.'

When something moved above Amelia's head, an avalanche of dust poured into her makeshift coffin. She choked on the air.

'Sorry, lovely,' said the woman. She was coughing too between groans and moans as more of the weight pinning Amelia down was shifted.

The girl's confusion persisted. 'I think I've fallen down a rabbit hole.'

'I think you might be right, but it's time to come out.'

'My friend Evie was the white rabbit. On the stage.'

'I bet you were excited to see her.' Her rescuer's voice was clearer now that the tomb around Amelia had been dismantled.

With a pained groan, the woman manoeuvred a large piece of timber and dislodged a slab of masonry in the process. Pain shot along one of Amelia's legs, making her cry out. Everything went black, until the shining light found her again. Minutes may have elapsed, or only seconds. Amelia couldn't tell.

'I need you to be brave now,' the woman said. 'Do you think you could hold this for me?'

Light came towards Amelia and a torch was pressed into her hand. It fitted inside her palm and, as she pointed it at her rescuer, she recoiled with fresh horror. The woman's face was the colour of stone. It was as if one of the figures moulded into the ceiling had come down to save her.

Her rescuer smiled. 'It won't be long before you can see Evie again.'

'I want my mum,' Amelia replied, fighting the urge to cry.

She hurt so much, from the top of her broken head to the tip of her crushed toes. Her nose was blocked, but she could taste the smoke. The woman was framed in an orange glow, and the specks of red and yellow light floating around her looked like fireflies.

'So, are you a dancer too?' the woman asked, forcing Amelia's attention away from the fire.

'No, I want to be a director.'

The woman leant over Amelia to clear more debris, and the torch picked out a silver pendant hanging from her neck. 'Sorry, but this might hurt a wee bit.'

As Amelia braced herself for the excruciating pain that would eclipse everything else, she focused only on the pendant as it moved back and forth. The woman heaved a piece of masonry that had been pinning down her arm and then Amelia was falling back into her imagined rabbit hole.

Rex could see the same eerie glow that had entranced Amelia. It was taking over the auditorium as he cowered against the wall. The dust had settled enough to reveal the dam of writhing bodies blocking the main exit. The crowd had shrunk, but not nearly enough, and the smell of smoke was growing stronger.

'I want to go home,' sobbed his granddaughter.

Rex's wife turned to him. 'We have to find another way out.'

She went to stand up, but Rex stopped her. 'I'll go,' he insisted. He cupped her dusty face in his hand and kissed her. 'I know I haven't said this enough, but I love you.'

'Don't be getting all mushy,' his wife said with a flicker of a smile that was snuffed out by panic when her husband moved to leave. 'I love you too, Rex. Please, make sure you come back to us.'

Clambering over seats to reach the aisle, Rex crept closer to where the upper tier gave up its shelter until he could take in the full horror. One half of the theatre had been smashed to pieces and the illuminated arrows that were meant to point to the nearest of the side exits pointed to a mountain of broken rafters and rubble. There were fires at ground level, but so far its spread was limited. The danger lurked above where a large section of the ceiling was missing. Dense smoke filled the void in the roof, and it was this that glowed orange as gusts of wind fanned the flames. Burning embers floated down and, more alarmingly, occasional pieces of debris crashed to the ground.

There was less damage on the far side of the theatre and, peering through the gloom, Rex found what he was looking for; a green exit sign close to the stage. He watched as a handful of survivors broke cover and raced towards it. That was where they had to reach, but, before Rex turned to fetch his wife and granddaughter, he looked back to where they had been sitting earlier. In the spot where he had left the little girl to wait for her mum, there was a mound of debris. His streaming eyes disguised his tears. It was too late for her. He had to think of his own family.

4

The day after Mal's telling off, Leanne arranged to meet Kathryn Parker and her daughter, Amelia, at the Bridgewater Inn. It was midweek so they had their choice of tables, and opted for one by a window. The menu offered standard pub fayre, but the view was better than most. The beer garden backed onto the Bridgewater Canal and had moorings for boat trippers, who could access the pub via a gate next to a play area.

The now ten-year-old survivor was more interested in the reporter than the view, and as Leanne returned from the bar with a glass of lemonade, two J2Os, and no fresh information about Karin Gallagher from the barman who had served her, she was being eyed cautiously.

'Are you sure you don't want anything to eat? How about an ice cream sundae?' she suggested.

Amelia shook her head.

'This is fine,' Kathryn said, taking their drinks.

Leanne placed her phone in the centre of the table with the voice recorder running. After a nod of approval from Amelia's mum, she began the interview. 'Do you know why we're here, Amelia?'

'We come here for Sunday lunch all the time,' Amelia replied, choosing to direct her response to her mum. 'I like looking at the boats.'

'I heard you were very brave,' Leanne tried again.

Amelia pursed her lips around the paper straw poking out of her lemonade glass.

'I've told Amelia you're going to find the woman who helped her,' said Kathryn.

Resting her elbows on the table, Leanne leant forward until she was at eye level with Amelia. 'I live on a boat,' she said, as if she had all the time in the world for a cosy chat despite a looming deadline.

To her credit, she had submitted one of her articles to Mal that morning with five minutes to spare, and she didn't expect him to throw this one back at her. She had emphasised Claudia's loss and described her gritty determination to put the needs of others before her own, both on the night of the fire and through all the work she had done since. Claudia's altruism was inspirational and seeing it in black and white had made it harder for Leanne to deny that she might actually be one of the good ones.

Amelia's straw popped out of her mouth. 'What's it like? Do you live there all the time? Do you get seasick?'

'Yes, I do live on it all the time and no I don't get seasick, but I do suffer from land sickness now and again.'

'What's that?'

'It's where you step onto dry land, but you feel like you're still bobbing up and down on the water. It can make you feel a bit wobbly,' Leanne explained, swaying ever so slightly for effect.

When Amelia wrinkled her nose, Leanne knew what was

coming. She hadn't met a child yet who hadn't asked the next question on Amelia's lips.

'Does it have a toilet? Does the poo get flushed into the canal?'

'Amelia!' her mum said.

'It's OK,' Leanne replied, laughing. 'Yes, it has a special toilet with a built-in cassette underneath for collecting the waste. You add chemicals so it doesn't smell, or at least not too much, and when it has to be emptied, I use a trolley to take it to a disposal unit in the marina where I live. It's basically a matter of emptying it into another toilet.'

'Eugh!'

'It's not as bad as it sounds. And that's probably more information than you need to know,' Leanne said, pulling a face. 'Why don't you tell me more about you? I'd like to understand what happened at the theatre. Maybe we could start with why you went, what happened before the fire alarm, that sort of thing.'

'One of Amelia's school friends was in the production,' Kathryn said, to encourage her daughter.

'Evie,' Amelia confirmed. 'She was the white rabbit.'

'Ah, yes,' said Leanne. 'I've seen her in video clips.'

Recordings of the curtailed performance had been shared widely on social media and, although the videos taken by proud parents during the show weren't the most harrowing, they were uncomfortable to watch. The sight of a little girl with a pink nose and long whiskers freezing onstage had brought with it a sense of foreboding that resonated with the public, if not the audience at the time.

'I was just as excited as Amelia,' Kathryn added. 'I work on the high street and had been following the theatre renovations for two years. Some of their other shows were a bit pricey, but we snapped up the tickets for the dance school.' She picked at the label of her discarded J2O bottle, a pained expression on her face.

'Where were you sitting?'

'In the stalls,' she said. 'In hindsight, I wish I'd paid a bit extra for the seats upstairs in the VIP area. It was less crowded up there, although that didn't help poor Hilary Clarke I suppose.'

'Can you remember your seat numbers?'

'It was Row F,' said Amelia when her mum struggled to recall the exact location. 'Mum had the aisle seat. We were on the left, which is stage right, obviously.'

'Amelia fancies herself as a bit of a director,' explained Kathryn. 'She and Evie were always putting on little shows of their own.'

'We don't do that any more,' Amelia said solemnly.

'Everything changed after the fire,' her mum agreed. She scraped a nail across the torn label on the bottle, staring at it intently. 'But Evie's started back at dance school, so you never know. We might get back to normal one day.'

They were quiet for a moment as they recalled how things used to be. Not everyone's life could be reset. Leanne cleared her throat. 'Was it just the two of you?'

'Yes,' Amelia replied. 'We were going to sneak backstage afterwards to see Evie.'

'It's good that your friend got out safely.'

As the little girl nodded, her eyes glistened.

Kathryn opened her mouth to speak, but stopped herself. 'I was about to say Amelia wasn't so lucky, but she *was* luckier than some. I can't imagine where I'd be now if . . .'

She shook her head. 'It feels so random when you look at who made it out and who didn't.'

'Yes, it certainly does,' Leanne said as the names of the victims rolled like a list of credits in front of her glazed eyes.

The youngest victim had been sixteen, the oldest seventy-one. Each person had their place in the world stolen, leaving a gaping hole that couldn't be papered over with column inches and special edition newspapers. Why did Lois have to be on that list? Leanne's insides twisted. Mal had been right to ask Frankie to write the victim pieces. Leanne couldn't do it. She had avoided Lois's family since the funeral. She was a coward.

Aware that Amelia and her mum were watching the emotion play out on her face, Leanne clenched her jaw. 'So,' she said, eyes narrowed, composure restored, 'do you think you could tell me what happened when the alarm went off? How did you become separated from your mum?'

'She had to go to the Ladies. I was looking after our coats.'

'It was a few minutes before the alarm sounded. I had a water infection,' said Kathryn, needing to explain what pressing need had justified the abandonment of her child. 'And Evie's mum was only a few rows in front of us. I told Amelia to go to her if there were any problems, not that I thought there would be. It didn't cross my mind that . . . I never imagined.'

Kathryn pressed her lips tightly together. She could say no more with Amelia sitting next to her.

'When the alarm went off, everyone started pushing past me,' Amelia said, continuing her story. 'People kept telling me I had to leave, but I didn't want to go.' Her face scrunched up. 'I had to wait for Mum, so I stayed by my seat.'

Leanne could picture the scene with the help of the footage

she had found online. She had watched the initial evacuation with growing frustration. There had been no sense of urgency until the announcement came that the theatre had to be cleared. And even then, people took their time because they expected a second announcement to say the show could be resumed. In the handful of recordings that had continued beyond the moment when the ceiling collapsed and the lights went out, the subsequent footage revealed only jerky images of feet, and inky darkness. Theatregoers were no longer concerned with filming what had been a curious scene. They were fighting for their lives.

'I was looking up at the ceiling. There was this figure of a woman stuck to it like a squished statue,' Amelia said, keeping her eyes grounded on Leanne. Her breath had quickened as if she were afraid of what might be lurking above. 'She came alive. Or I thought she did. Mum says it was probably the smoke making it look like she was moving. Then it went black.'

'Could you hear anything?'

'She means she was knocked unconscious,' Kathryn said.

Amelia glanced at her mum, tears rimming her eyes.

Kathryn shook her head in despair. 'Our seats were a few rows out from the cover of the circle. There was nothing to protect Amelia. Nothing, and no one.'

'Can you remember anything that happened after that, Amelia?' asked Leanne.

Amelia folded her shoulders into a hunch. 'Bits.'

'Like?'

'I remember coughing,' she said, then made a retching sound as if she could still taste the dust and smoke. 'I was buried under all this stuff and it was dark. I was so scared. I kept calling out, but I didn't think anyone would find me.' There were more laboured breaths. 'I could smell the fire, but I couldn't move. I broke my leg and one of my arms too.'

'It must have hurt.'

A tear slid down her cheek as Amelia gasped for air. 'I don't remember.'

Kathryn went to take her daughter's hand, but Amelia pulled away. Kathryn tried again and, when she managed to grasp Amelia's hand, they held on to each other tightly. 'Maybe we should take a moment,' she suggested.

'I'm fine, Mum,' Amelia replied, but her chest continued to heave.

'You're doing great.' Leanne took a slow, deep breath through her nose and out through her mouth, inviting Amelia to do the same. 'Why don't you tell me about the woman who dug you out? Would that be OK?'

'She must have heard me crying.'

'I would have cried too,' said Leanne, feeling ridiculous because she wanted to cry now. She was reliving someone else's memory and it was terrifying. 'Do you remember her finding you?'

Amelia scrunched up her face. 'I remember she moved something and I screamed. I thought it was more stuff falling on top of me.'

'What was she like?'

'Nice.'

'Can you describe her? What was her hair like? Was her skin light or dark?'

Amelia took more panted breaths. The next memory scared her. 'She was grey. She looked like the statue in the ceiling.'

'She would have been covered in dust,' Kathryn added.

69

Leanne kept her focus on Amelia, needing the girl to work harder to fill in the gaps her mum was determined to bridge for her. 'How about her eyes. What colour were they?'

'I don't . . . I don't know.'

'And you're sure it was a woman?'

'Yes.'

'Why?' asked Leanne.

'She had a nice voice.'

'Did she have an accent? Maybe a weird one like mine,' Leanne said with an encouraging smile that hid her frustration. Mal wasn't going to get his reunion based on such scant information.

'I don't know, I don't remember,' Amelia said. Her next series of breaths were jagged, the need to breathe fighting an attempt to hold back tears. She still had hold of her mum's hand and allowed Kathryn to pull her close.

'It's OK, you did really well,' Kathryn said, a signal that the questioning was over.

'Sorry,' Amelia mumbled.

'Don't be. Your mum's right, you've been really brave.'

'Not as brave as the lady who saved me. You will find her, won't you?' Amelia said, fresh tears threatening. 'I have to say thank you to her.'

'I'll do my best.'

'Do you want to go outside and play for a bit, get some fresh air?' Kathryn suggested. 'I'll watch from the window and I won't take my eyes off you. I promise.'

Amelia gave her mum a stern look that Kathryn felt compelled to explain after her daughter had set off for the swings. 'She hasn't forgiven me for leaving her,' she said. 'And I can't say I blame her.'

'This wasn't a tragedy you could have foreseen. *You* are not responsible,' Leanne said, as the familiar taste of bile rose in her throat. 'It was the job of the people who renovated the theatre to make sure it was safe. Unfortunately, they spent too much time choosing the right shade of velvet for the curtains to worry about adequate fire exits.'

'I did try to get back to her,' Kathryn said, unwilling to shift the blame. She looked down at the phone recording her confession. 'I was in the Ladies when the alarm went off. I hurried back to the foyer, but an usher stopped me from going any further. I shouldn't have listened to him.' She squeezed her eyes shut and tried to rewrite history. She grabbed her empty bottle of J2O and looked as if she might throw it. 'In that short window of opportunity, I could have pushed past the people coming out of the auditorium, but I didn't. I *should* have, but I didn't.'

'It must have been hard, waiting for her.'

'I tried to stay calm. The usher said it could be a false alarm.'

'Which explains why you stayed where you were.'

Kathryn's laugh was bitter. 'You can wrap it up how you like. I knew Amelia would be panicking, and that was before . . .' Her mouth moved, but it took a moment for the words to come. 'The whole building shook like there was an earthquake. The lights in the foyer flickered at the same time the noise hit me, and I was plunged into this awful nightmare. I can still hear the screams.' A hand went to her chest. 'I shouted for Amelia until I was hoarse. I ran between the two sets of double doors. Back and forth, back and forth.' She gasped for air from the imagined exertion. 'People were running out, others were being pushed, and some got trampled on. I tried to get nearer, but someone slammed into me and I fell, breaking three fingers. I don't remember the pain, not the physical kind. I just remember the screams. My screams. I imagined Amelia calling out to me and I couldn't reach her.'

Kathryn hadn't taken her eyes from her daughter, who was sitting on a swing. She was watching the two women talk, checking that her mum was being true to her word.

'She *was* calling for me,' Kathryn continued, her voice catching. 'I should have been there.'

'When did you find out Amelia was safe?'

Kathryn took a deep, juddering breath. 'I stayed in the foyer until the firefighters ordered me to leave. There was more chaos outside. A crowd had gathered at the front of the theatre, blocking access for the emergency services, so they herded us towards Victoria Park. There was no way I was leaving, so I sneaked around to the side of the building. There were only stragglers coming out of the fire doors by then, and I saw paramedics working on someone. As I got closer, I realised . . .' Kathryn made a choking sound. 'I thought she was dead.'

'She was lucky.'

'No thanks to me,' Kathryn said, straightening up. 'It's the people who got her out that need to be recognised, although I think Rex is fed up with me trying to thank him.'

'That would be Rex Russell, the man who carried her out?'

'He's a lovely man,' she said, managing a smile. 'We've met a few times since, but he refuses to take any credit for helping Amelia. He says she was simply thrust into his arms.'

'Hopefully, he can give me a better description of whoever

it was. Do you think Amelia would ever recognise the woman if we did find her?'

'I honestly don't know. Amelia's counsellor can't tell us if the gaps in her memory are from when she was unconscious, or if she's simply blanked some things out.' Kathryn chanced a glance away from her daughter when she added, 'I know Amelia wants to find her saviour, but I don't hold out much hope. We've tried before. We even did a couple of TV interviews, but there was no response. Rex says he didn't notice if the woman followed him out or not.'

'You think she's dead?'

'Don't you?'

'I aim to find out.'

5

It was a blustery Friday morning and the clubhouse café was relatively quiet; perfect conditions for two journalists who had sensitive matters to discuss. The air was thick with the smell of crispy bacon and fried mushrooms, but Leanne and Frankie had settled for coffee and Danish pastries so they could eat with their fingers as they worked.

Frankie was Leanne's senior by ten years and had joined the *Courier* straight from university. She had a round, open face, and deep brown eyes that gave an intensity to her stare. She was good with people, much better than Leanne.

'Are you sure you want to do this?' Frankie asked. She had arrived with a bundle of files, one for each of the Empress Theatre fatalities.

'We don't need to go through every single file.' Leanne broke off a sliver of Danish pastry as if she had an appetite. She struggled to swallow it. 'Amelia's rescuer was definitely female, so we can discount all the men.'

Leanne watched as Frankie sorted through the Manila folders and separated them into two piles. There was a name written on the front of each, and Declan Gallagher's name was uppermost on the discarded stack.

Frankie smoothed her dark hair, which was pulled tight against her scalp. 'Ready?'

'How many are left?'

'Seven, including two teens. Should we discount them too?'

'To be honest, I'm not sure. I've managed to speak to the man who carried Amelia out, but he wasn't much help at all,' Leanne said, recalling the phone call she had made after her interview with the Parkers.

Once Leanne had realised Rex Russell could give no better a description than Amelia, she had wanted to cut their conversation short, but Rex had insisted on explaining himself. He said he may have seen Amelia earlier, he really couldn't be sure, but he was very clear in his recollections of what happened after the ceiling had collapsed. He described hearing the cries for help from those caught in the crush, and how those cries had diminished very quickly, how the brutal pressure of bodies would have stolen the oxygen from the victims' lungs long before the smoke could get them. He acknowledged that he and his family were lucky, but he regretted not persuading more people to follow him after he spotted an alternative escape route through a side exit. He had been on his way out when he had heard another cry for help.

'He was pretty traumatised to be fair,' Leanne added. 'When he had seen a woman coming towards him with a little girl's limp body in her arms, he had assumed the worst. As far as he was concerned, he was being handed a dead child and was too shocked to register much about the woman. He said her face was covered in dust and her hands in blood, but he couldn't even describe her ethnicity. The only useful piece of information he could offer was that she was around five foot seven or eight.' She stared at the files. 'That might discount the younger ones.'

'I do have some physical descriptions, so let's check as we go along,' Frankie said, pulling the first file towards her.

Leanne wasn't sure what she had expected, but the contents of Frankie's files were sparse. It felt wrong that a dozen or so pieces of paper should represent the sum total of a person's life. The front sheet listed some basic facts, such as the victim's age, along with contact details for the family.

The first file was for Hilary Clarke, and underneath the top sheet was a photocopied photograph. It was a professional headshot of Hilary, and one that had been used regularly across the media since the fire. There were other images too, and Leanne sifted through them while Frankie checked her notes.

'Hilary's body was found upstairs in the circle. One of her students, a young lad called Jack, says she pushed him out of the way as the ceiling collapsed. She might be a hero, but she's not Amelia's.'

Leanne stared at a photo that would have been taken half a century ago. It was an iconic shot of a ballet dancer onstage, long limbs extended with apparent ease. 'She was stunning.'

'And absolutely adored by her students,' Frankie added. 'She didn't have children of her own, but she was godparent to dozens.'

Frankie paused long enough to acknowledge the life lost, before closing the file.

The next victim was the youngest, and Leanne wasn't sure if they were quick to discount her because she was clearly too short, or because neither of them could bear to look at the photos. There was a collection of Instagram pouts and raucous laughter shots of the sixteen-year-old with her friends. She had been a crush victim, and Frankie had spoken at length to her parents. She summed up their conversation in one word.

'Harrowing.'

The third file was discounted almost as quickly; a woman in her thirties who had suffered catastrophic injuries as a result of the ceiling collapse. She had been seated in the stalls, so she would have been closer to Amelia than Hilary, but there were witnesses who were able to account for her movements right up until her death. The witnesses were her two children, who had been protected by their mother from the falling debris. They had suffered only minor scratches, but major trauma that would last a lifetime.

'Do you need a break?' asked Frankie, resting her hand over the name on the next file.

Leanne knew what was coming. She gritted her teeth and shook her head. 'No, I'm OK.'

'We know it wasn't Lois,' Frankie said, not needing to open the file. Lois Granger's boyfriend had been with her the whole time, and had watched her die.

'Next,' Leanne said miserably.

The fifth file wasn't so easy to discount. Angela Morris was a teacher at a local primary school. She had gone to the theatre with the girls from work to cheer on some of their students. She was an asthmatic and, after becoming separated from her friends, she had been overcome by smoke and dust, and her body was recovered from inside the theatre.

'If it was Angela, her difficulty in breathing might explain why she couldn't carry Amelia out by herself,' Leanne said.

They created a separate pile just for Angela before tackling the penultimate file. Seeing the face of another teenager was too much for Leanne.

'This is so wrong,' she said, her voice becoming a hiss. 'These people had lives to live, whether it could be counted in years or decades. They should be flesh and blood, not bits of paper.'

'You'll get no argument from me,' Frankie said, closing the girl's file with the same reverence she had given to the others. The youngster was another crush victim, which meant she too had been trapped following the collapse.

'Nearly there,' Leanne said, watching Frankie pull the last file towards her. They should be thankful that there weren't more. Amelia's details could so easily have been amongst Frankie's files. Mal was right. They had to find this woman.

'Lena Kowalski,' said Frankie, turning a page. 'She became separated from her fiancé quite early on. He was inconsolable when I spoke to him. Apparently they'd had an argument about which exit to use, and Lena chose one of the side exits. It's not clear yet if she was hit by debris from the first ceiling collapse or later on. There were at least two other cave-ins, one that sealed off the last serviceable stairwell to the upper floor, and another directly over the stalls.'

Leanne checked the top sheet of information. 'She was Polish?'

'Living in the UK for five years.'

'So she would have an accent,' Leanne said, touching the file with the tip of her finger. 'Amelia said her hero had a nice voice. I did ask if she had an accent, but she couldn't say.'

'Any voice must sound nice if you're trapped in a burning building and someone wants to rescue you.'

'True, but it certainly doesn't eliminate her as a possibility.' Leanne sat back and sipped her coffee as Frankie added the last folder to the new pile. 'So we have to two potential candidates.'

'Or it could be someone else entirely. There are lots of reasons why a person would choose not to come forward,' added Frankie. 'Not everyone wants to bare their soul to the press. I haven't spoken to a single survivor who wasn't traumatised in some way. They each have their own story, and pulling Amelia from the rubble might be only one small part of her rescuer's. Who knows what else happened to her?'

'But I promised Amelia I'd help find her hero. What do I do if I can't get beyond a shortlist?' asked Leanne despairingly. 'I'm not sure there's anything I can write that will add to the attempts Kathryn Parker has made already.'

'Want my advice?'

'Yes, please.'

'Don't include any speculation about who you think this woman might be, because that will only lead potential witnesses. Ask the public to fill in the gaps of Amelia's memory and, to add a bit of jeopardy, be upfront and suggest that the truth may never be uncovered. No one wants an act of bravery to go unrecognised. If, by some miracle, you can identify her, this could be quite the story, Leanne. We all love a reluctant hero. We like to think it could have been us.'

'Except life isn't a neat movie script,' countered Leanne with a spray of spittle. The swell of anger had taken her by surprise. 'Not everyone can be a hero, and not everyone gets to be saved by one either. Who was there for Angela Morris when she collapsed? Who was ready to push Lena Kowalski out of the way of falling rubble? Lois's so-called boyfriend was three feet away when the life was crushed out of her, for Christ's sake.' She paused, her jaw twitching as she clenched her teeth. 'There were six hundred people in the theatre that night, and not all of them were thinking selfless thoughts. People shoved Amelia's mum out of the way hard enough to break bones, all while she was screaming for her daughter.'

Frankie didn't interrupt until she was satisfied that Leanne's rage was spent. 'Do you want me to write Amelia's story?'

'No, I'll do it,' Leanne said a little too sharply. 'Sorry, Frankie. Thanks for the offer, but I'm already in Mal's bad books.'

'He's worried about you, that's all. He doesn't want you to lose your way.'

Leanne glanced out of the window and across the marina. Boats were bobbing up and down in the water, moving, but getting nowhere. 'Has he spoken to you about me?'

'He showed me the piece you wrote about Phillipa Montgomery.'

'Do you think it was too much?'

'Possibly too soon,' Frankie conceded.

'I asked Claudia Rothwell about her, but she claims they weren't close.'

Frankie shrugged. 'It's probably true. I can't recall ever hearing Claudia's name associated with Phillipa, in fact I'd never heard of Claudia before the fire. Had you?'

'No,' Leanne said, recalling Claudia's nervousness. She didn't come across as an attention seeker, or at least not a successful one. 'Claudia did mention Bryony Sutherland

80

though. She thinks she's still in contact with Phillipa. I recognise the name, but that's about it.'

'Her family built up a pottery business that specialises in tableware. Bryony's fortune was literally handed to her on a plate,' Frankie replied. 'She always struck me as one of Phillipa's loyal foot soldiers, so I imagine they would have stayed in touch.'

'Did you ever interview her about the fire?'

'She's been a consistent no comment.' Frankie raised an eyebrow. 'Why? Have you tried?'

'Not yet, but I will. I don't see why any of them should get away with it.'

'No one's saying they will, Leanne, but you need to be prepared for things not to go as you might wish. I agree wholeheartedly that the renovation was a vanity project, but I'm not sure I'd go as far as to say there was negligence, not yet. The fire investigators have given nothing away so far.' She paused and wrinkled her nose. 'Well, almost nothing.'

When Frankie flicked a glance at the discarded files, and one file in particular, Leanne sat upright. 'What have you heard? Is it about Declan?' she asked, pulling his file towards her. Frankie didn't object when she opened it.

'Don't get too excited, and do not let Mal know I've mentioned this to you,' she warned. 'You might have been right to question what Declan was doing there. You're not the only one wondering why the coroner couldn't give the same assurance he gave to other families before suspending the inquests. According to my source, Declan's injuries were unlike any of the other victims'.'

'They think he was murdered?' Leanne asked. She had to admit, she had fantasised about killing him herself had he lived, and wouldn't be surprised if someone had beaten her to it. If you couldn't blame an electrician for an electrical fault that killed eleven innocent people, who could you blame?

Frankie gave her a withering look. 'Didn't I just say, don't get too excited? The comment made to me was that the investigators were concentrating on where he was found and where he had been. Read into that what you will.'

Leanne's mind made leaps and bounds. 'So my theory holds, he could have sneaked into the offices. It was an enclosed space, and if the fire had reached there, he could have suffered burns. Or maybe he did some burning of his own to destroy evidence.'

'And that would be why they haven't released any of the forensic evidence until the public inquiry has concluded its investigations – so people don't start coming up with their own theories.'

'He's guilty as hell, whatever he was up to,' Leanne said, removing the cover sheet to reveal the employee photo that had been provided by Ronson Construction. It was a head and shoulder shot and, despite the harsh lighting, the thirty-seven-year-old electrician from Donegal was handsome, with deceptively kind eyes. What was he thinking in his last moments? Did he realise people were dying, some of them no more than children? Did he care?

'We're not going to get any answers until mid-November,' Frankie said. 'That's the latest timescale for when we'll receive the official verdict.'

It was only the beginning of October and they had the anniversary to get through first, but Leanne couldn't wait that long. It wasn't fair on the families and friends of the victims. It wasn't fair, full stop. She flicked back to the cover page. There were contact details in both Northern Ireland and Sedgefield. 'Have you spoken to his family?'

'I had an interesting chat with his ex-wife. Apparently he was quite a character, but that was as close as she got to saying something nice about him.'

'I'm not going to like him, am I?'

'You mean you did before?' Frankie asked, not needing an answer. She had read Leanne's draft article after all. 'Declan had a troubled childhood from what I can gather. His dad left home when he was young, never to be seen again, and it seems the apple doesn't fall far from the tree. When Declan's wife accused him of having an affair, rather than deal with it to save his marriage, he walked out on her and their three kids, all under the age of ten. That's why he ended up in Sedgefield.'

'He was running away,' Leanne concluded.

'In the sporadic conversations he'd had with his ex, which I imagine weren't particularly pleasant, Declan kept promising he'd move back to be closer to the children. He was waiting for the work on the theatre to be signed off, but she says he didn't sound too upset about the delays in completion.'

'He didn't want to go back, not even for his kids,' Leanne said with disgust. 'I bet he didn't see the similarity between his life choices and his dad's.'

'That type never do.'

'And what about Karin?' Leanne tapped a finger against her name in the contacts section. 'What's she said about him?'

'I haven't spoken to her directly, but I did receive a rather

83

ambiguous statement via her flatmate who was with her that night. The line is that Karin will never get over what happened and that she grieves for all the victims.'

'Is that it?'

'Yep.'

'She didn't mention Declan explicitly?'

Frankie reached towards Declan's file and turned a few pages. She stopped at a sheet that was blank except for an email heading from someone called Beth McCulloch with two sentences printed below it. Frankie had repeated the statement given on behalf of Karin Gallagher almost verbatim.

'Don't you find that odd?' asked Leanne. 'She must be aware of the rumours implicating Declan, but chooses not to stand up and defend him. That says it all.' She closed the file before adding, 'Is Mal insisting you write a piece about him too? Do we have to see his face amongst the real victims?'

'Let's just say I plan to write something short and simple that we can hide at the back of the paper.' Seeing the reaction being played out on Leanne's face, Frankie continued quickly, 'In the absence of any evidence to confirm or disprove that he was in some way responsible for the tragedy, we have to remain unbiased. Whatever Declan's past misdemeanours, it's not for us to say if his loss deserves to be mourned or not.'

'Not yet.'

'I promise you, I'm writing what I think is a fair account at this moment in time,' said Frankie. 'But if and when wrongdoing is proven, I'll be more than happy to help you browbeat Mal into publishing your article.'

'You don't want to write something yourself?'

'No, this one's yours,' Frankie promised. Her features softened. 'But in the meantime, we need to concentrate on celebrating the lives of the *good* people of this town.'

Leanne cast an eye around the café, as if one glance could distinguish the good from the bad, the selfless from the selfish. There were only a few customers left, and she recognised every face as a fellow boat owner or a regular from the town. How many would put their lives on the line for each other?

The café manager, Dianne, was cleaning tables, and caught Leanne staring at her. She came over.

'Can I get you ladies a fresh brew?'

Frankie was already gathering up her files. 'Thanks, but I've got places to be, people to see.'

'I'm OK for now, Di,' said Leanne.

Dianne pursed her lips and the feathering of wrinkles around her mouth deepened. She twisted the spray bottle in her hand and, although she turned as if to leave, her feet remained planted. 'There was someone looking for you the other day,' she said, her casual tone a contrast to her awkward pose. 'Did he track you down?'

'No,' Leanne replied. She didn't need to ask for details. She knew who was stalking her.

'He wanted to go through our door,' Dianne said, tipping her head towards what was the only entry point to the marina other than the rusted security gate. The door was strictly for use by boat owners and authorised personnel. 'I told him he'd have to phone you to let him in.'

'I've blocked his number,' Leanne said. 'And if he does come back, please tell him we have nothing to say to each other.'

'I understand, love, you've been through enough. And I'll remind everyone to keep the security tight. Leave it with me.'

'Thanks, Di.'

When Dianne had gone back to work, Frankie stopped packing up. 'Was that Joe you were talking about by any chance?'

'He's tried before.'

'I interviewed him about Lois,' Frankie admitted. 'He asked after you. Do you not think—'

Leanne didn't give Frankie the chance to finish that thought. 'I don't want to see him.' When Frankie didn't move, she added, 'I thought you were leaving?'

'I am, but you know where I am if you need some company.'

'Thanks, but right now, I have a deadline to meet,' Leanne said, checking her watch. She had only hours left to submit Amelia's story. The public appeal to find a hero would be launched in twenty-four hours, alongside the feature on Claudia and her charity work; two feel-good stories that didn't rest easy with Leanne.

'Are you sure you don't want me to write this one?' asked Frankie.

'No, I can do it,' Leanne said. She stood to give her friend and colleague a hug, urging her to go before her resolve weakened.

After Frankie had left, Leanne sipped the dregs of her coffee and pulled a face as she swallowed the cold, bitter liquid. She needed to return to the boat and get to work, but first she wrote down the Sedgefield address she had memorised from Declan's folder.

6

The still waters of the canal reflected candyfloss clouds dissolving in the sunshine. Leanne had wrapped up for her walk, but found herself peeling off her gloves. Autumn was being kind and so was life, she supposed.

She was back in Mal's good books, having delivered two of the most talked about articles in the *Courier*'s recent history, and the paper had been inundated with messages since Saturday. It was no surprise that the vast majority were from people offering their condolences to Claudia and promising to donate to her cause. The story had been picked up by other media outlets too. Claudia was going to be busy.

Leanne was more concerned with the response to her second article and, whilst there had been offers to help find Amelia's hero, everyone Leanne had spoken to so far had only vague recollections. They didn't want to dwell on the fact that they had seen a little girl on her own and had done nothing. They were parents and grandparents with charges of their own, or they had some other pressing need that had forced them to leave Amelia to her own fate. They went to great lengths to explain their decision to Leanne, who could neither blame them, nor give absolution. She had no idea what she would have done in the same situation.

Continuing on her walk, the canal was quieter than it had been at the weekend and the only boats she saw were covered with tarpaulins, ready for their winter hibernation. She had to squeeze past the occasional fisherman perched along the canal bank, but otherwise she was alone with her thoughts. She followed a path of well-trodden earth while she mentally retraced her steps all the way back to the building that was now a burnt-out shell.

Leanne had visited the Empress a week before it had opened. She had been invited to a prelaunch press day, and the stage had been in the process of being set for opening night; a variety show with some high-profile performers on the bill. The air had been filled with the thrill of anticipation, mixed with the astringent smell of fresh paint and drying plaster. Leanne had felt privileged to be amongst the first to tread the newly polished boards, to try out the plush velvet seats, and to gaze up at the stage, where spotlights picked up dancing motes of dust. The town was being lulled into a false sense of superiority, not knowing the price it would pay.

Taking a breath of crisp, autumn air, Leanne allowed her mind to fill the auditorium with townspeople, many of whom she would bump shoulders with during her weekly shop. Some she knew better. Some she would never see again. Onstage was a white rabbit.

Leanne placed herself amongst the grumblers who had cursed their misfortune at being evacuated for the sake of a false alarm, but the sense of foreboding was hers alone. Her heart clenched when the lights went out and the world collapsed around her. She was scrambling over chairs in her haste to escape, choking on the dust, fleeing the fire and the smoke that permeated all her senses. She zoned in on Row F, stage right. There was only rubble where Amelia had been.

Would Leanne have gone to investigate? Or would she have doubled her efforts to save her own skin. Would she have pushed against people's backs, contributing to the crush that forced the last breath out of Lois's lungs? Would the outcome have been any different if she had been there? Would there be one less death, or one more?

'Watch yourself there, love, or you'll end up in the canal,' a man called to her. He was approaching with his dog, a huge German Shepherd that had its tongue lolling out. The dog licked the air, and tasting Leanne's fear, released a whine of sympathy.

'Sorry, I was miles away,' Leanne said, refocusing her gaze on the path she had been veering off.

'You don't want to fall in,' the man continued as they drew level. 'It's colder than it looks.'

'Yeah, I should know better. Thanks.'

Leanne knew all about the perils of messing about on the water. When she had announced that she would be living on a boat, her mum had sent links to a long list of safety videos on YouTube, and Leanne had watched them all, if only because she knew her mum would test her later. She had made Lois watch them too. They had thought they were prepared for every eventuality, from escaping a capsized boat to cold water shock, but at no time had they considered the dangers of a trip to the theatre.

Leanne was swallowed into the yawning mouth of a tunnel, and the echo of her Doc Martens hitting the flagstones followed her along the narrow forty-foot walkway. Grateful to emerge into the sunlight, she blinked as she recognised the stark silhouettes of two Victorian warehouses in the distance. What would have been a ten-minute drive from the marina had taken over half an hour, but she thought it would appear less conspicuous arriving on foot. If asked, she could say she had been passing Karin Gallagher's apartment by chance.

The converted warehouses were gargantuan relics of a bygone age and had multiple entrances. Leanne followed the Perspex signs screwed to ancient brick until she came up against the entry system that corresponded with the apartment number she had noted from Declan's file. Alongside the buzzer for each apartment was a name, but Karin's wasn't one of them.

Wondering if she had confused the warehouse for its twin next door, Leanne went to turn away, but the name on the label that should have been Karin's struck a chord. Declan's sister had a flatmate, and her name had been on the email printout Frankie had shown her. McCulloch. Leanne rang the intercom.

'Hello?'

The voice was that of a woman around Leanne's age and, although it was hard to discern the accent from the pithy greeting, Leanne didn't think the speaker was from Northern Ireland. Karin had left home when she was eighteen and, according to the internet, had backpacked around the world before settling down in Sedgefield. She was thirty-two now, but it was unlikely that she had lost her accent completely. It had to be the flatmate, about whom Leanne had no information at all beyond her name.

'Is that Beth McCulloch?'

'Who are you?'

'My name is Leanne. I was hoping for a chat,' Leanne said, hedging her bets that she would get further by asking for an interview with Beth rather than Karin.

'A chat about what?'

'I'm from the *Cheshire Courier* and—'

'No, thanks.'

With a distinct click, the connection was cut. Leanne pushed her luck and pressed the buzzer again, but there was no response. She stared at the intercom, her mouth twisting as she considered her options. She hadn't expected it to be easy, but never mind. It was a nice day. She could wait.

There was a bench next to the canal with a view of the flight of locks that rose up towards Sedgefield town centre, but Leanne turned her back on the scene and perched on a low wall. With one eye on the entry to Karin and Beth's apartment, she opened up the internet browser on her phone and began searching for images of the two flatmates to while away her time.

She already knew what Karin Gallagher looked like, there had been photos of her plastered across local and national press for weeks after the fire. The family tragedy had sparked a brief media frenzy as the nation waited with bated breath for Karin to come out of her coma and be told the heart-breaking news that her brother had died trying to save her. By the time it happened, however, the tide of public opinion had turned. Declan was no longer a hero. He was a suspect – if not officially, then in the court of social media. The article that Leanne was not allowed to publish had reflected the current mood of suspicion. Why had Declan been there? What did Karin know?

Karin's spokesperson was more of a mystery, and it was Beth McCulloch's name that Leanne typed into Google, along with her current location to limit the results. She found what she was looking for on the first page. Beth was on Facebook and, although her privacy settings limited visibility to a handful of profile picture updates, it was enough. One photo was of two young women proudly showing off a set of keys. Karin was sporting a bobble hat and multi-coloured scarf that pulled in long hair the same shade of brown as her brother's. The other woman was blonde, wrapped up equally well, and around the same age. They were standing in front of a rust-coloured brick wall that looked identical to the converted warehouses. Was this the day they moved in? Leanne could imagine their excitement. She had a similar photo of her and Lois standing on the stern of their boat.

Leanne was staring at the image of Karin and Beth when her phone rang. She didn't recognise the number, but she had spent the last couple of days responding to messages, and it was likely to be someone returning her call. Conversely, it might be someone she didn't want to speak to, but with just over two weeks until the anniversary, time was running out in the search for Amelia's rescuer, and Leanne was willing to take the risk that the caller wasn't the man who had stood by and watched her best friend die.

'Hello?' she said, more cautiously than she would like. She strained her ears, alert to the background noises that might reveal the caller's identity. She could hear the chirpy voice of an actor selling the virtues of whatever product was being advertised on TV.

'Oh, yes. Hi. Is that Leanne Pitman?' a woman asked. Her voice had a rasp that gave away her years.

'Speaking,' Leanne said. She was no wiser as to who it was, which was fine. At least it wasn't Joe.

'I didn't know whether to phone you,' the woman began. 'I said to my daughter, they won't want to hear from the likes of me, but she said, "Mum, everyone who was trapped in that theatre has a story to tell, and you need to tell yours." It was an awful, awful thing, but, if nothing else, it shows there are more good people in the world than bad.'

Leanne opened her mouth to reply, but the woman hadn't finished.

'Not that I'm claiming to be a hero or anything,' she said, 'but we all did our bit. I'd gone there on my own and, oh, I saw things that would break your heart. It's burnt into my memory and I don't say that to be funny. It's true.'

'I'm sorry,' Leanne cut in when the caller drew breath. 'Could you start by telling me who you are?'

'Sorry, yes, I'm Mrs Brody, Carole Brody. It was my daughter who got in touch, but I thought I should be the one to speak to you.'

Leanne bent forward, intending to retrieve her notepad from her rucksack, which was lying on the ground, but she straightened up immediately. Movement had caught her eye. Someone had left the building. The woman was wearing the same multi-coloured scarf Leanne had seen on Karin in the Facebook photo. She was heading away from Leanne, towards the car park.

'Shit,' Leanne muttered under her breath.

'Pardon?'

'Sorry, Mrs Brody, I need to go,' Leanne said, standing up and grabbing her things. 'I'll ring back to make arrangements to come over and see you, if that's OK?'

Leanne cut the call while the old lady was halfway through her answer. She broke into run.

Karin's hair was tucked beneath a mustard-coloured beret and she wore her scarf loosely so she could plunge her face deep into its folds right up to her nose. With her shoulders hunched, she looked as if she were expecting to be ambushed at any moment and her pace was brisk.

Leanne picked up speed, which wasn't easy when running across the original cobblestone path that served the warehouses. She stumbled, caught her balance without stopping and, as she closed in, she heard the clunk of a car lock disengaging. Lights flashed on a blue Peugeot that looked as ancient as Leanne's Fiesta. Karin had circled the car to reach the driver's side and, as she turned, she spotted Leanne rushing towards her.

Still moving, Leanne opened her mouth to call out her name, but the sound of the 'K' caught at the back of her throat. There were blonde tresses peeking from beneath the beret. It wasn't Karin she had been chasing. It was Beth.

Leanne didn't slow, and thumped against the opposite side of the Peugeot. She made her target jump, but Beth wasn't frightened, she was angry and moved to open the car door.

'Wait, please,' gasped Leanne. 'You don't have to say anything, just hear me out.'

Beth glowered at Leanne over the roof of the car, but at least she waited.

'Right,' Leanne said, catching her breath. 'The thing is, I know you must be fed up of the press by now, but I'm not looking to dish the dirt on Karin or her brother, if that's what you're worried about.' She held Beth's gaze with what she hoped was a genuine look of sincerity rather than an engineered one. 'Like I mentioned before, I work for the *Courier*, which has been running stories to mark the anniversary of the fire.'

'I wouldn't know. We stopped reading the gutter press ages ago.'

Despite the hostility, Leanne took a breath and relaxed into it. Beth had offered information voluntarily. It was progress of sorts. 'We want to celebrate the heroes and honour those who died. We want stories about ordinary people who did extraordinary things,' she said, quoting the phrase Mal had used on her more than once.

From her rucksack, Leanne pulled out Saturday's edition. She had planned to post it with a note if today's attempt at contact had failed. She handed it across the roof to Beth.

Beth scanned the front page that featured both of Leanne's articles. She looked as though she was still reading when she said, 'What do you want from me?'

'To hear your story, Beth. You were there too, weren't you? How many people have asked what it was like for you?'

Beth's eyes were cold against the sunlight. 'I didn't do anything remarkable.'

Leanne rested her elbows on the car roof. 'You wouldn't believe how many people I've spoken to who have said the exact same thing,' she said softly.

In Leanne's experience, if you talked to someone for long enough, they would eventually find a way to be the hero of their own story. She had seen it happen before, whether it was a pile-up on the M56, or a bake sale at the local church, and Beth would be no different. Not that Leanne was interested in hearing what part she had played during the Empress fire, she simply needed to keep Beth talking.

'I know you got out, but your flatmate didn't fare so well,' Leanne continued. 'And I have to say, some of the most heart-wrenching stories I've heard have been where friends and families had become separated. I take it you and Karin are close?'

Beth flicked through the pages of the *Courier* before she spoke again. 'We've been living together for five years. We're not just flatmates like everyone keeps saying, but that's all you're getting from me. I'm not giving an interview for free,' she said. Her brow creased with pain. 'I can't.'

'A payment isn't out of the question,' Leanne replied, managing not to baulk.

The *Courier* wasn't some national paper with wads of cash to persuade 'a close family member' to confess all, and there was no way Leanne was going to convince Mal it was worth their investment. It wasn't as if she were speaking to Beth to add another voice to the anniversary piece, she had enough of those. Beth was a means to an end, and that end was the quest for justice that Mal had given Leanne clear instructions not to pursue.

'I don't mean to sound mercenary,' Beth said, reading Leanne's hesitancy as disapproval, 'but we're still paying the price of the fire. Karin has only just managed to get to a place where she can hold down a job, and the handouts we had at the beginning didn't go far. We came out with our lives, and I know we should be grateful, but gratitude doesn't pay the rent and it doesn't put petrol in the tank or get me to work.'

'I'm not judging you,' Leanne said. She was rooting in her rucksack again and took out her purse. She had £60 in cash.

'This isn't a payment, it's me doing my bit to help a fellow member of our town fill up her car – I know I don't sound it, but I am a local.'

Leanne placed the cash on the car roof and used her phone to weigh it down. The voice recorder was running.

Beth scowled at the phone. 'You want *my* story?'

'Why don't you start by telling me why you went to the theatre that night?'

Beth shrugged. 'Karin was given tickets and we thought it would be a fun night.'

'Is it right she got them off her brother for her birthday?'

Beth's eyes narrowed. Leanne wasn't supposed to mention Declan. 'They weren't a present as such. He wanted us to be his spies to make sure things were running smoothly.'

'Such as?'

'The sound quality, the lighting, that sort of thing, I suppose. He didn't really say.'

'Was he worried there was a problem with the electrics?'

'So anyway,' Beth said, deliberately ignoring her, 'we went to a bar and had a couple of cocktails first to make more of a night of it. We weren't that keen on seeing a ballet, but we fancied a nose inside the theatre after hearing so much about it.'

Leanne wanted to know more about what Declan had said about the restoration. It sounded like he was expecting there to be potential faults, but she knew if she pushed again, it would bring the interview to a premature close. It killed her to hold her tongue, but she had to bide her time.

'It was beautiful inside,' Beth continued. 'Not the kind of place you would expect to become the stuff of nightmares.'

'Where were you sitting?'

'In the stalls.'

'And what did you do when the alarm went off?'

'Grabbed my coat,' said Beth. 'I think Karin and I would have been the first ones out of there if the woman next to us hadn't been in the way. She had all kinds of bags with her and didn't want to move. She was convinced it was a false alarm, but so was half the theatre. And whoever made the announcement asking us to leave had sounded blasé about it.'

Leanne had listened to the manager's testimony during the evidential hearings. Although a smoke sensor had been triggered, the fire had been largely contained within the roof space at that point, and staff were initially confused because they couldn't find any sign a fire, just a faint whiff of smoke. Because the hearings were simply a fact-finding exercise for the public inquiry, Leanne and the rest of the town were still waiting to find out how that could happen. It had to be faulty installation.

'We made our way to the back of the auditorium,' Beth continued. 'Heading for the foyer along with everyone else. I doubt we were the only ones planning to head straight to the bars, but there were definitely some who dragged their heels, hoping the alarm would be cancelled before we reached the street.'

'And you were still with Karin at that point?'

'Yeah, and then the whole world imploded. The lights went out and there was this huge surge of bodies. The emergency lighting came on, but we'd been hit by a massive dust cloud. Not that I needed to see to know what was happening. I could hear.'

Beth pursed her lips. Her experience up until that point

had been easy to recount. What came next was the nightmare that haunted not only Beth. Leanne's mouth had gone dry.

'People all around were screaming and coughing and, ahead of me, I could hear others crying out for help. And then it got quieter. We were all struggling to breathe, with those ahead of us faring the worst. I hate to think what part I played trying to force my way out. I wasn't thinking about anyone else, just me and Karin.'

'Did you make it out through the front?' asked Leanne, ignoring the lump in her throat.

'At first we didn't have a choice. We kept pushing and being pushed, but we weren't getting anywhere. The theatre was falling in around us. I knew we had to break free, and it was pure luck that we did.'

When Beth stopped to take a breath, Leanne was left to wonder how fate had decided who would have luck on their side and who wouldn't.

'I'd heard a member of staff directing us to the side exits near the stage, so that's where we headed, although that was terrifying in itself. I could see where the ceiling had caved in.' Beth tilted her head upwards to the clear blue sky as if she could still see it. 'It was surreal. The dust was settling and the smoke was mostly in the eaves. I could see this orange glow above us. I often wonder how long that fire had been raging above our heads.'

'Was Karin with you when you reached the side exit?'

'She was when we made a run for it across the auditorium. I felt her grab my coat sleeve. I just kept yelling at her to hold on, that we were going to make it. When we reached the inner corridor, it was cramped, but nowhere near as bad as the other exit, and at least there was no one coming down the stairwell by then. We were jostled about a bit, but I was sure Karin was with me. I should have looked back, but I was concentrating on that final door. I could feel the air getting colder.'

'And?'

'We got outside and I turned to tell Karin we'd made it, except it wasn't her. It was the bloody woman with all the bags. Straight away, I was ready to fight my way back inside, but the stupid cow was in hysterics. She wouldn't let go of my arm, and there were too many people still coming out through the doors. I knew the best chance I could give Karin was not to clog up the exit. I had her phone in my shoulder bag so I couldn't call. All I could do was wait.' Beth curled her hands into fists. Fully formed tears had collected in the corners of her eyes. 'I would never have left without her. I thought she was behind me.'

'And what does Karin say happened?'

'She doesn't remember.'

'But even someone with amnesia can have random memories come back to them,' Leanne said, based on her suspicions rather than any form of medical knowledge.

'She wakes up in a cold sweat most nights, but she has no idea what, if anything, she's remembered.'

'Do you think she saw her brother?'

'I told you, she doesn't remember, so how would I know?' replied Beth, losing patience. She glanced at the phone sitting between them, or it could have been the money she was counting.

'And what about you?' Leanne persisted. 'Did you see Declan? With the crush at the front of the theatre, he could only have gained access through the side entrance, but you said you couldn't get back in. How do you think he managed it?'

The tear running down Beth's face revealed a broken woman. 'It was possible to get back inside,' she said, contradicting what she had said only a moment earlier. She lifted the newspaper Leanne had given her. 'She managed it.'

There were only two faces on the front page of the *Courier*, and Leanne doubted Beth was referring to Amelia. 'Claudia Rothwell?'

'Some things stick in your mind, and she was one of them. She was encouraging everyone to get out, reassuring us that the fire crews were on their way, and then she pushed her way back inside,' Beth said with incredulity. 'I stayed where I was, and I still can't believe I left Karin in there.'

'Or Karin left you,' Leanne offered. 'She was found close to her brother's body. What if she made a deliberate choice not to leave? What if she'd been looking for Declan?'

'Why would she?' Beth said, wiping her eyes and smearing her make-up. 'Declan wasn't supposed to be in there.'

'And yet we all know he was. The question is, what was he doing?'

'No, the question is, what the hell am I doing?' Beth said, straightening up. She shoved the newspaper back at Leanne. 'You're not interested in my story, are you? I'd say this interview is over.'

As Leanne tucked the copy of the *Courier* out of sight, she tried a few more questions, gentle enquiries into how Beth had felt seeing Karin again, how they had managed her recovery, but Beth had closed down. Leanne picked up her phone in one hand and lifted the three twenty-pound notes in her other.

Beth backed away as Leanne extended the money towards

101

her. She pulled open her car door. 'Keep your money,' she said. 'How the hell do you sleep at night, preying on other people's misery?'

If Beth had given her a chance to reply, Leanne would tell her that she didn't sleep well at all. She wasn't sure she ever would again.

The Empress Theatre
Sedgefield, Cheshire

Karin Gallagher was trying not to giggle. Beth had drawn the short straw and was sitting next to an eccentric older lady with bright purple highlights who had decided they would be companions for the night. Beth's new friend had been knitting when they arrived and, after the alarm sounded, she took for ever to pack up her things.

'Do you want one last sweet before I put them away?' *the lady asked, offering one of the many bags she had brought with her. She was the only one in their row yet to stand up.*

'No, thanks,' *Beth said tersely. She wasn't sharing Karin's amusement. The woman was in the aisle seat, and they couldn't move until she cleared a path.*

As they waited, Beth put on her hat and coat before lifting her shoulder bag over her head and across her tensed body. Karin shoved her phone inside the bag's front pocket.

'We really should get moving,' *Beth tried.*

Her new friend waved her hand. 'We won't make it to the front of the queue so we might as well take our time. If it was a proper emergency, I think we'd know about it by now.'

103

As it transpired, Karin and Beth found themselves some-where close to the middle of the large crowd waiting to get out through the central exit, which was somewhat fortunate because when the lights went out and everyone surged forward, the bodies surrounding them kept them from toppling over.

'Oh, my God! Please, no! What— What's happening?' someone shrieked close to Karin's ear. It was the lady with purple highlights who had been shadowing Beth.

The screams all around them were unmerciful and Karin wanted to cover her ears, but she couldn't move her arms. When a gust of warm, acrid air assaulted them, they started choking on the dust.

'I can't breathe!' cried the woman squashed against Beth's back. 'I don't want to die!'

'Stop pushing!' yelled Beth.

'It's not me!' she shouted back.

The emergency lighting fought against the dust cloud to create a luminous grey fog, and when Karin looked at Beth, she hardly recognised her. They were covered in a thick layer of plaster and grit. 'We'll be OK,' Karin promised.

Beth nodded. She was trying so hard not to let her fear show, but Karin could see how the skin above her collarbone was sucked in every time she tried to breathe. Karin was struggling for air too. 'We're packed in. Too tight.'

'We need to move across to the side,' Beth told her. 'Imagine we're swimmers. In a riptide. As we're dragged forward. Get ready to move. Sideways.'

Karin turned her head to glance back across the audito-rium. Through the swirls of dust, she spied smouldering timbers rising up where rows of seats had been. The damage appeared to be concentrated on one side of the auditorium.

'We need to move that way,' Karin said to Beth, pointing with her eyes to the opposite side.

With the next push, Karin and Beth steered themselves diagonally. Each time they moved, Karin was aware that they were being followed by the sound of sobbing. The old lady clung to Beth like a limpet.

And whilst Beth's new friend dripped snot and tears onto the back of her jacket, Claudia Rothwell was edging closer to the fire doors at the side of the theatre.

'Come on, hurry!' she shouted to the traumatised theatre-goers who had paused outside the fire doors to take their first gulps of fresh air. Most were adults, but there were children too. She wanted to help. She needed to be involved. If nothing else, it would ease her conscience later when she would be obliged to recount a convincing story of being there all along.

She was about to shout again when a little boy's wails rose up into the mournful night. He was pointing to the burning theatre and calling out for Mrs Clarke. There were people trapped inside, and it looked like one of them was Sedgefield's revered dance teacher.

Claudia had never been one of Hilary's dance students, but she had wanted to be. Her dad could never afford the classes and, even if he had, he wouldn't have wasted a rare Saturday morning off to take his daughter to dance school. She had envied her friends, but one by one they had dropped out when Claudia convinced them how uncool it was. Hilary must be in her seventies now. It was unthinkable that she wouldn't make it out.

Blue flashes of light danced across the walls further along

the alleyway. The emergency services had arrived. 'Help's on the way!' Claudia yelled.

A woman grabbed hold of her sleeve to steady herself. 'Thank God,' she said. 'People are dying in there. I could hear them calling out.'

Claudia stared at the handprint the woman left on her cream cashmere coat. It was the colour of rust. Blood.

Fear rose up through Claudia's body, making her feel clammy, but she was angry too. She wished she had never become involved in the stupid renovation project, but she had become obsessed with impressing Phillipa. It was strange to think there had been a time when Claudia was envied by her peers, but marrying Justin had placed her in a different league. No matter how much he loved her, it didn't soften the blow that she had gone from the very top to the very bottom, and when Phillipa had assigned her as mystery shopper for the only amateur performance, it had been a deliberate snub. Not attending had been an act of rebellion, but one Claudia had always intended to keep to herself.

Pressing her fingers against the stitch in her side, Claudia considered her options. She had only recently found out she was pregnant and shouldn't take any chances, but could she walk away and say she had done enough? The answer scared her. No, she couldn't.

Inside the theatre, while Amelia was lost down her rabbit hole and Rex Russell was yet to move away from the wall he cowered against, Karin and Beth fought to reach the opposite side of the auditorium. A small group had gathered and, every so often, someone would build up the courage to break cover and make a run towards the exit near the stage. Onlookers felt a surge of hope whenever someone disappeared beneath the green exit sign without being hit by the falling debris that suggested another collapse was imminent.

'We have to go! Now!' Beth urged.

Karin nodded and they set off at speed, or Karin would have if the old lady hadn't manoeuvred herself directly between her and Beth. Karin put a hand the woman's shoulder as encouragement. They would make it together.

As they raced into danger, Karin could feel every muscle tensing, and only the old lady dared to look around them. Terrified by what she saw, she stumbled and grabbed hold of Beth's sleeve. Karin strained her ears for the telltale creak of disintegrating rafters, and that was when she heard someone calling out. It was a voice she recognised.

In the absence of any breakthroughs to identify Amelia's rescuer, Leanne avoided Mal as much as possible. He wanted his hero headline, if not for this weekend's edition, then in time for the commemorative issue due out on the Saturday before the anniversary. It didn't look promising, and the only way Leanne could appease her editor was to feed him other stories of bravery so he wouldn't ask too many questions about what other lines of inquiry Leanne might be pursuing.

'I'm sure my daughter made it sound more than it was,' Mrs Brody said modestly as she handed Leanne a mug of tea. 'I was on my own, you see. Our Rachel couldn't come because she was eight and a half months pregnant. Not that I mind going out by myself, I'm never on my own for long, and on that night, we all stuck together.'

'Are you OK to talk about it?'

Mrs Brody dropped down onto the sofa opposite. 'Ask away.'

During their brief chat on the phone, Leanne had imagined Mrs Brody to be a doddery old woman, but the reality was very different. At seventy-three, Carole was the new generation of pensioner who had hit puberty in the sixties and wouldn't be seen dead in a twinset and pearls. Her hair was silver with purple highlights, her make-up provided a youthful glow, and her figure was enviable. She had informed Leanne that she had to leave by three o'clock for her Zumba class. She reminded Leanne of her nan, who told tales of swooning over the Rolling Stones, and it gave her a surge of homesickness.

Leanne opened her voice recorder. 'Perhaps you could start by telling me where you were sitting, Mrs Brody.'

'Please, call me Carole.'

'OK, Carole,' Leanne said. 'Where were you?'

'In the stalls, somewhere near the middle. I'm so glad our Rachel wasn't with me. Can you imagine? Chances are, I wouldn't be a grandmother right now,' Carole said. She had her phone in her hand and the deep lines on her brow eased when she found what she was looking for. 'Curtis Ethan Johnson. Seven pounds nine ounces. She waited such a long time for him. Forty-two she was.'

The phone was thrust towards Leanne and she obliged by scrolling through the photos while her mind placed Carole in the theatre that night. Carole was in the middle, Amelia to the left. She would have liked them to have been nearer. 'He's gorgeous,' she said, handing back the phone. 'Now, you were saying that you were in the stalls. Which exit did you use?'

'Well, I headed for the one at the back.'

'Why do you think most people ignored the side exits? Was the signage not good enough? Would you say the staff had been trained sufficiently?'

'Oh, I don't know. There was a lot of noise with the alarm, and no one stopped us from gathering up our belongings. I saw people carrying out tubs of popcorn. We thought we had all the time in the world.' Carole rubbed her forehead. 'There may have been calls to use the side exits, but I'm glad we were under the circle when the collapse happened. It shook the whole building. We were choking on the dust. Things got bad very quickly.'

'Can you describe it?' Leanne asked, wishing the knot in her stomach wouldn't tighten every time she asked someone this question.

'It was awful. Just awful. We were getting pushed this way and that, and I knew I had to find another way out or die trying. I'm not afraid to admit it, I thought I was done for. I remember telling myself, "That's it, Carole, you're never going to meet your grandchild."'

'But you managed to stay calm? Your daughter says you helped others,' Leanne prompted. Carole's modesty might be admirable, but it wasn't going to make a particularly good story.

Carole blushed. 'Like I said, we stuck together.' Her voice was a whisper when she added, 'It wasn't the time to be alone, and yes, I suppose I helped along the way. I grabbed hold of one young woman and made sure we got out of there. I don't know what came over me. It was grim determination, pure and simple. I had to live for Curtis, not that I knew he was a Curtis then, or a he for that matter. Our Rachel didn't want to know beforehand.'

'And who was the woman you helped?'

'No idea. She was in the seat next to me and I'd shared my wine gums with her, but I wouldn't know her name. She was in a terrible state, I can tell you that. Hysterical at one point, but she wasn't the only one. People had become separated in the confusion, many not knowing if their loved ones had made it out or not. I was glad I'd gone on my own. Outside, I heard a little boy crying out for Mrs Clarke, saying she was trapped, and it broke my heart – especially now we know what happened to poor Hilary.' She paused for a moment and rubbed her arm as if she had a sudden chill. 'I saw one man carrying a little girl in his arms. We all thought she was dead, but the para-medics started working on her straight away.'

'Could it have been Amelia Parker? Did you read about her in last week's paper?'

Carole pressed her chin to her chest, casting her eyes down to hide her tears. 'I saw the article. It could very well have been her. God bless whoever saved that child.'

'I don't suppose you saw Amelia earlier on?'

'Sorry.'

While Carole blew her nose, Leanne took a series of printouts from her rucksack. 'If you don't mind, I'd like you to look at some photos to see if you recognise anyone else.' She passed Carole an image of Angela Morris. 'Do you recall seeing this lady? She was someone who became separated from her friends.'

'Isn't she one of the victims?' Carole asked, taking the sheet of paper. It trembled briefly in her hand before she handed it back. 'No, I didn't see her, or if I did, I can't place her. The problem was we were all covered in dust and the emergency lighting wasn't that strong.'

'And how about this lady?' Leanne asked, offering a photo of Lena Kowalski. 'She's another one who didn't make it out.'

'I'm afraid not. Most of what happened is a blur. I could have come nose to nose with Elvis Presley in one of his white sequined suits for all I know.'

Leanne was ready to leave it there, but her conversation

with Beth a couple of days before was playing on her mind. 'Have you heard of Claudia Rothwell?'

'Who hasn't? Did you see her on *BBC Breakfast* this morning? I don't watch the other side, that Piers Morgan gets on my nerves.'

Leanne didn't know about the TV interview, but wasn't surprised. Claudia was grabbing as much media attention as she could, albeit for a good cause. 'Do you remember seeing Claudia inside the theatre?'

Carole shook her head. 'I'm afraid not.'

As Leanne began packing away her things, she tried not to dwell on why she had brought Claudia into this particular conversation. She didn't seriously think Claudia had anything to do with Amelia's rescue, even though she couldn't articulate exactly why. It was a gut feeling.

'Will my story be in this Saturday's paper?'

Leanne wasn't sure there was much of a story to tell, but the idea of a pensioner keeping the crowd calm had a certain appeal. She could make it work, and besides, didn't Mrs Brody deserve her fifteen minutes of fame along with everyone else? 'I expect we'll save it for the weekend after next, which will be our commemorative issue.'

'Don't you want to take my picture before you go?'

'I certainly do,' Leanne said, retrieving her Nikon DSLR from her rucksack. The *Courier* had one full-time photographer, and Mal reserved Henry's professional treatment for the likes of Claudia Rothwell, not Carole Brody. 'Do you mind if I open your blinds so there's enough light to show off the lovely colours in your hair?'

'I can give you the number of my hairdresser if you like,' Carole promised.

113

While Carole touched up her make-up, Leanne worked out the right angle to take the photo. Carole had already decided which was her best side and was happy to direct.

'I tell you who I did see,' Carole said as she flicked through the images Leanne had just taken.

'Who?'

'Well, maybe I didn't see him exactly, but I did hear his voice.' Carole handed back the camera, allowing the tension to build. 'I think the second one will do, don't you? Or perhaps number eleven?'

'Second one's perfect,' Leanne said, switching off the camera. 'You were saying, you saw someone?'

'The bloke who caused the fire.'

Leanne almost dropped the camera. 'Declan Gallagher?'

'That's the one. I didn't put two and two together at first, and for a long time, I couldn't think about the fire at all, or what I'd seen. But when I read about him being from Northern Ireland, I knew it had to be him. It was the accent.'

'But you said it was noisy in there. How can you be sure?'

'He was calling out to his sister. Her name's Karin.'

'Yes, I know,' Leanne said, not liking that this corroborated the general view that Declan had been looking for his sister. Carole was edging her towards the front door, she had her Zumba class to get to, but Leanne was reluctant to leave. 'But if you didn't see him, you might be mistaken.'

'We were crossing the auditorium to reach the side exit. Bits of ceiling were still falling here and there, and I kept looking up, expecting to be buried alive at any minute. Even through the gloom, I could see up to the circle. It looked half destroyed, but thankfully it was empty. Except for him.'

'Wait, are you saying Declan was upstairs?'

'I only saw a glimpse, but I'm guessing I was one of the last to see him alive,' she said, opening the front door. 'I feel awful saying it, but it's probably for the best that he didn't make it out. If it had been me who killed all of those people, I wouldn't have wanted to live.'

After saying goodbye to Carole, Leanne came to a stop on the pavement outside. Her thoughts were spinning. Although there were vague reports of someone who might have been Declan arriving at the theatre, Mrs Brody was the first witness to have seen him inside the Empress, placing him where no one expected to find him. What the hell was he doing up in the circle?

As she searched for an answer, Leanne looked up and down the road. The figure of a man caught her attention. He had been leaning against a wall, but straightened when he saw Leanne. He had his phone in his hand and shoved it into his pocket as he strode towards her. Joe had tracked her down.

Leanne's car was parked at the kerb, but she had to walk towards Joe to get to it. Thankfully, she was nearer, but she lost valuable seconds rooting around in her rucksack for her keys. Her fingers clasped the car fob and, without looking up, she unlocked the car and got behind the wheel. Joe appeared in her peripheral vision and, as she turned the ignition and hit the central locking mechanism, a man's hand slapped against the window.

'Leanne! I just want to talk!'

Keeping her gaze fixed straight ahead, Leanne pulled away from the kerb. She didn't look in her rear-view mirror. She wouldn't look back.

8

Leanne stood behind Mal with her arms folded as she glared at his computer screen. The latest edition of the *Courier* had been published that morning and they could now concentrate on the mock-up of next week's commemorative issue. It was going to be published just four days before the first anniversary of the fire.

Thanks to Frankie and Leanne's hard work, Mal had ten pages packed with articles that celebrated the lives of the victims and the good deeds of those who had tried to help, but the front page was proving contentious. Mal's current draft consisted of a three-by-four grid of photos; twelve faces to put to twelve names. Each one meant something to Leanne. She knew their story. She felt their family's loss. And she felt her own when she allowed her gaze to pass over Lois's smiling face. Her heart turned to stone when she looked at the bottom right-hand corner.

'You can't put Declan Gallagher's face on the front page,' she said. 'I'm telling you now, the people of Sedgefield won't accept it. It's an insult to the memory of the eleven people he killed.'

'What am I supposed to do, Leanne? I can't leave him out. We don't know exactly what went wrong yet.'

'I could hazard a guess.'

'I'm sure you could, but for now, you can keep your theories to yourself,' Mal warned.

Leanne kept her arms folded as she walked around Mal's desk and sat down on the sofa. 'What if I have evidence to support those theories?'

Mal released a huff. He didn't want to hear this, but he had no choice.

'I have a witness who saw Declan inside the theatre, and it turns everything we assumed about him on its head, or should I say, it turns what everyone else thought about him on its head.'

Mal mirrored Leanne's body language by folding his arms and resting them on his beer gut. He leant back in his chair. 'I'm listening.'

'The theory is that Declan saw the fire from his flat and ran into the burning building to save his sister, knowing that the second-rate restoration job he'd been overseeing had turned the theatre into a death trap.'

'Not exactly the accepted version, but go on.'

'Now, bearing in mind that Declan had given his sister tickets for the show, it's safe to assume that he would have known to look for her in the stalls.'

From his grim expression, Mal was not finding this slow reveal as exciting as Leanne. 'Agreed.'

'In which case, you would expect him to head straight to that part of the theatre.'

'I suppose.'

'So why didn't he?' Leanne said with a glint in her eye.

'According to my source, Declan was upstairs after the ceiling collapse, if not before.'

Mal's mouth twitched, but he said nothing.

'He was hardly going to save Karin from up in the circle, now was he?' Leanne continued.

'He could have gone upstairs for a better view.'

'But the circle overhangs the stalls. Even if he thought there would be enough light to see what was going on, most of the people trapped downstairs were taking cover beneath the circle, waiting to get out through the foyer.'

Mal raised an eyebrow. 'And how reliable is your witness?'

'It was after the first ceiling collapse, and she admits she couldn't see clearly, but she recognised Declan from his accent.'

'She spoke to him?'

'No, she was in the stalls when she heard him calling out.'

'Calling out to his sister by any chance?' Mal smiled when Leanne winced. 'So he *was* looking for her?'

Leanne gritted her teeth. She must not lose her temper. She most certainly shouldn't swear. She wasn't sure she could manage both. 'My point is, he was upstairs when he had no reason to be.'

The door behind them creaked open, and Frankie poked her head through. 'Sorry I'm late,' she said, before realising her two colleagues were in the midst of a staring contest. 'What have I missed?'

As she took a seat next to Leanne, Mal gave a brief summation. 'Despite orders to the contrary, Leanne has been pursuing a story on Declan. She claims to have a witness who saw him up in the circle after the first ceiling collapse. Is that about it?' he asked Leanne.

118

'I don't *claim* to have a witness, she very much exists. And I didn't go digging, Carole Brody offered the information without any prompting from me.'

Mal laughed. 'You're telling me your star witness is a decrepit old lady who could allegedly see through dust and smoke?'

'You wouldn't dare call her decrepit if you met her.' Realising from Mal's blank stare that she was getting nowhere, Leanne turned to Frankie, shifting her body until she had her back to her editor. 'I accept visibility wasn't great, but the dust would have been settling by then, and the smoke was thickest up near the roof. We have lots of accounts from people who saw more than they would like and, as I explained to Mal, Carole *heard* him calling out to Karin. I might be speculating here, but I don't suppose there were many men in the theatre that night who had a Northern Irish accent and were looking for someone called Karin.'

Frankie glanced at Mal and arched an eyebrow. 'She has a point.'

Emboldened, Leanne added, 'I don't dispute that at some point he was looking for his sister, but it's not unreasonable to ask why he would extend his search to the VIP area upstairs when he knew there was no way she would be up there. I've been thinking.'

Mal made a grumbling noise, but didn't interrupt.

'The accounts of him racing into the building are unverified. What if it wasn't him? What if Declan Gallagher was in the Empress from the start? He could have been working late and, funnily enough, the only parts of the building still under construction were the function rooms on the first floor. What if he wasn't simply responsible for the fire through

119

negligence? What if he'd been working late and actually caused it?'

'And what if that's an assumption too far?' Mal said, mimicking her. 'Even if we accept that he was in the building before the fire started, it doesn't necessarily follow that he set the place alight. We may not know what caused the electrical fault or how the fire spread, but it was an electrical fault, the fire service have said as much.'

'And, as we all know, Declan is an electrician,' countered Leanne.

'It could explain why there's confusion over his injuries in relation to where his body was found,' offered Frankie.

Mal shot her a look. He had instructed Frankie not to mention this little nugget of information in front of Leanne, but when he noticed Leanne failing to react, he shook his head. 'Do either of you ever listen to a word I say?'

'I'm not disputing that Declan cared for his sister,' said Leanne. 'In fact, Carole Brody's account confirms that he did, but if he had been at home, he would have gone straight to the stalls. To my mind, the only explanation for him being upstairs is that he was already there.'

Mal unfolded his arms. 'You're forgetting that the evidential hearings established that the fire started in the roof space.'

'And that's where the electricians fed all the wiring. They would need to work up there to access the trunking,' replied Leanne. She was leaning forward in her seat now. 'The project was behind schedule and I bet Phillipa was on Declan's back for not having it completed in time for her grand opening. I heard a rumour he was worried about the quality of the work.' She chose not to mention how Declan had been using his sister as a spy. Mal didn't need to know she had spoken to Beth. 'He could have been burning the candle at both ends. Pressure like that can lead to mistakes.'

'I'm not saying you haven't got something, but you're basing all this supposition on the recollections of someone who was, by her own admission, terrified of not getting out alive.'

'You can't use that to dismiss what Carole Brody saw and heard.'

'That may be so, but I stand by what I've said before. We wait for the public inquiry to draw its own conclusions.'

'And what if it's a whitewash?'

'Listen to yourself, Leanne,' Mal said, shaking his head. 'You've lost perspective along with the rest of the town. You want someone to blame, and I understand that, but you risk twisting the evidence to fit the crime. I'm not paying you to conduct a personal campaign against Declan Gallagher and Phillipa Montgomery.'

Mal didn't repeat his threat to move her to a less challenging role, not in front of Frankie, but Leanne could read between the lines. Was he right? Had she lost her perspective? She couldn't be sure, not enough to make it worth getting into a fight with her editor. She slumped back into the sofa cushions.

Ignoring Leanne's sullen silence, Mal showed Frankie the mock-up of the *Courier*'s front page. She didn't like it either.

'We could use the photos from Ashley Denton's cortège as an alternative,' Frankie suggested, referring to the fire's youngest victim. 'That's an impactful image.'

'It might work, but we've used it before.'

'What if we zoom in on the people who lined the streets to pay their respects? Make the image about the town's mourning and not one particular victim,' Frankie replied.

'Ideally, I'd like to run with something uplifting. What about it, Leanne?' Mal said, his voice loud enough to shake her from her mood. 'Is there any hope of identifying Amelia's rescuer? I take it we're all agreed that whoever this woman was, she must have perished in the fire? She would have come forward otherwise.'

'I've shown everyone I've interviewed the photos of Angela Morris and Lena Kowalski, including the man who carried Amelia outside,' Leanne explained without meeting Mal's eye. 'No one's been able to offer anything new.'

'So that's it then? You've given up?'

Leanne forced herself to sit up straight, not because Mal was challenging her, but because she was challenging herself. Had she done enough for Amelia, or had she allowed her personal feelings to get in the way? Leanne had never been that interested in finding heroes, not really, not when Lois hadn't been able to find hers.

'There is one lead I could pursue,' she said, 'but I don't think we should read too much into it. I doubt it has anything to do with Amelia anyway. In fact, I don't know why I'm mentioning it at all.'

'Because you think there's something to it,' Mal said. 'What is it, Leanne?'

'I was talking to someone who saw Claudia.'

'And?'

Leanne chewed her lip. 'As we know, she made it out through the fire doors at the side of the theatre, but was hanging back to make sure everyone else got out safely. We don't pick up her story again until Justin finds her wandering around Victoria Park. There's a period of time that Claudia hasn't accounted for.'

'So?' Mal asked.

'I have a new witness who saw her reach safety, then turn around and go back inside.'

There was a spark in Mal's eyes. 'Claudia went back? Into the auditorium?'

'It's possible, but I'd hate to make assumptions,' Leanne said, raising an eyebrow. She was stinging from Mal's earlier criticism, but she had other reservations too. 'My witness only recognised Claudia from the paper and, given how they were all covered in dust, it might be a case of mistaken identity.'

'But if it was her,' Mal said, 'it would explain how she was exposed to the levels of smoke that led to her miscarriage.'

'The question is, why would she go back?' added Frankie. 'She was on her own. She wouldn't be searching for someone in particular.'

'Unless she had seen Amelia waiting for her mum,' Mal said, finishing the thought for her. 'Does she meet the description we have, Leanne?'

'If by that you mean, is she an adult female between five foot seven and eight with a nice voice, then yes, she matches the description.'

'You know, the more interviews Claudia has given, the more you realise she's the type to put herself at risk for the sake of others,' Mal said.

Leanne pouted. 'She also comes across as the kind of person who would have come forward by now to keep herself in the limelight.'

'And you're coming across as someone who doesn't want Claudia's actions celebrated because of her association with

Phillipa,' Mal said just as quickly. 'I can't believe you were ready to dismiss this. I'm worried your judgement has become clouded. It's becoming a real concern, Leanne.'

He had a point. Leanne had convinced herself it was gut instinct that made her discount Claudia, but was it a matter of simply not wanting it to be her?

'Is it possible that Claudia had seen Amelia earlier on?' Frankie asked, breaking the stalemate. 'Where was she sitting?'

'All I know is that she was in the stalls.'

Frankie looked thoughtful. 'I'm surprised she wasn't upstairs in the VIP area.'

'She was a mystery shopper who was expected to mingle with the average punters.'

'Or else Phillipa didn't think she deserved to be in the posh seats because of her less than privileged background,' mused Frankie.

It was a possibility Leanne had chosen not to dwell upon. It was harder to keep that chip on her shoulder if she considered Claudia to be one of Phillipa's rejects. Leanne's judgement really was skewed.

'Either way, the evidence is stacking up, assuming your witness is to be believed,' Mal said. 'Who is it, Leanne?' His eyes narrowed into slits. 'Please don't say it's your Mrs Brody again.'

Leanne clenched everything. This was another reason she had kept quiet. 'No, it's Beth McCulloch.'

It took a fraction of a second for Mal to register the name. His face turned puce. 'And why the hell were you speaking to her?'

'She's Karin Gallagher's partner, and I thought she might

124

have a story too. The fire took its toll on them both, Mal. Beth feels guilty about leaving Karin for dead amongst the ruins.'

'Bollocks,' Mal said. 'Keep away from them.'

'They don't want to speak to me anyway.'

'Was it something you said?' Mal guessed. 'You do realise you've probably lost any chance we had of getting a quote from them once the findings of the public inquiry are known? You need to sort yourself out, Leanne. Maybe you should take a break, go home to your family and recharge your batteries.'

It was a tempting offer, but Leanne couldn't leave now, not before the anniversary, and not while there was unfinished business. 'What about Claudia?'

'I could speak to her,' Frankie said, but without enthusiasm. This was Leanne's story.

'If Claudia does have more to tell and is choosing not to come forward,' Leanne said, 'I'm the best chance we have of prising another confession out of her.'

All eyes were on Mal. He couldn't send Leanne away *and* have his headline for next week's issue. 'Fine,' he said at last. 'Leanne can do it. As long as she remains focused.'

'Not a problem,' Leanne said in a tone that didn't convince either of them.

The Empress Theatre
Sedgefield, Cheshire

As Leanne walked down the jetty, she could see a red glow in the sky, but she was more interested in the light coming from inside the boat. She wondered if Lois had decided against going to the theatre after all. They needed to have a serious talk, and the sooner the better, which was why Leanne had stopped off at the petrol station to pick up a box of Ferrero Rocher and a bottle of wine. She was ready to say sorry and admit she was in the wrong.

Closing the hatch, she noticed the paintings on the back of the doors. Lois had been working on her fish again, but when Leanne called out her friend's name, it echoed through the empty boat. Damp paintbrushes were resting on the drainer and, as Leanne picked one up, she felt a lump in her throat. She didn't often give in to the urge to cry, but tears pricked her eyes.

Ever hopeful, Leanne checked her phone in case Lois had sent a message since their argument. Nothing. She checked Instagram next to see if she had posted photos of the ballet. Leanne's timeline was filled with images of a roof engulfed in flames.

Racing back through the boat, Leanne flung open the hatch and tumbled onto the deck. She fought with the awning, and the boat rocked as she jumped on to the jetty and turned towards the glow on the horizon. She had assumed it was the sun going down, not registering that it was in the wrong place. It was really happening. The Empress was on fire.

Rex Russell refused to look at the falling embers as he and his wife stumbled between rows of seats to reach the other side of the auditorium. The fires at ground level were nothing compared to what he had glimpsed raging above their heads. He should have acted sooner.

Carrying his granddaughter, he called over to the writhing crowd that surrounded the main exit and begged people to stop pushing. Things were getting desperate and he could see a child being lifted over heads and passed along. Between ragged breaths, he urged those closest to him to follow, but they wouldn't listen, or didn't hear.

Rex paused before beginning their final journey. They would have to step out into the open to reach the last accessible exit. His heart felt like it was about to give in.

'Put me down, Granddad,' his granddaughter urged him. 'I can walk.'

Rex did as he was told, knowing they could move faster, and they did move fast. In no time at all, they were halfway across the auditorium, getting closer to safety. His family were going to make it, but before relief could lighten his step, guilt slowed Rex's pace. He cast his gaze across the damaged stalls. Was he thinking of that little girl again, or had movement caught his eye?

Through the swirls of smoke and dust, Rex watched a grey figure rise up from the carnage like a statue coming to life. When it struggled to move its limbs, he realised there were two figures, the smaller draped in the other's arms. He couldn't turn his back. Not this time.

'You go ahead,' he said to his wife, pressing their grand-daughter's hand into hers.

'Wait, what?' His wife was aghast, then realised what had caught his attention.

'I'll be right behind you. Please. Just go!'

Rex didn't wait for a response. If his wife had held his gaze a moment longer, he would lose what little courage he had. He cut across the rows of seats and climbed over debris, vaguely aware of water droplets falling onto his bald head. High above him, there was the hiss of water turning to steam. The fire brigade was tackling the blaze, but this was not the time for Rex to stand down.

'Help me!' the living statue called out.

Rex realised it was a woman imploring him. Darker roots peeked beneath hair layered with dust, but he could discern little else about her, not even her age. If he took in any detail at all, it was the torn nails hanging from her bloodied and blackened hands as she gripped the child.

The girl looked to be around the same age as his grand-daughter. Could she be the very one he had seen earlier? If that were the case, it would almost be better living with the torture of not knowing her fate. The child's lifeless body was covered in dirt and blood, her head was tilted backwards and her little mouth gaped open. She made no response when she was thrust into his arms, and he was grateful that her eyes were closed. He was too afraid to look death in the face.

9

Leanne had made a point of checking her socks for holes before setting off to meet Claudia, only to be faced with a new challenge while swapping her boots for guest slippers. Her laces had become tangled and she was bent over for so long that when she straightened up, she felt hot and flustered.

'Sorry about that.'

'I have the same problem with my riding boots,' Claudia said pleasantly, with no trace of the nerves that had plagued her during their first meeting. 'Come through, there's fresh coffee brewing.'

When Leanne had phoned to request the interview, Claudia couldn't have been more accommodating and agreed to meet Leanne first thing on Monday morning. She had ensured that the reporter drove through the security gates unheeded, and she had been waiting to welcome her guest when Leanne reached the top of the stairs.

There was a marked change in Claudia's appearance too. Her dark hair had been pulled back into a smooth, shiny ponytail, her make-up was immaculate, and she wore a perfectly pressed polo shirt. Her beige jodhpurs emphasised the sway of her hips while Leanne trundled behind.

'I didn't know you were into horse riding.'

Claudia gave a throaty laugh. 'Neither did I, but Bryony offered the use of one of her ponies. She's teaching me to ride,' she said in her best telephone voice. 'It's surprisingly good exercise.'

Instead of continuing to the kitchen, Claudia opened the door to a sumptuous sitting room and directed Leanne to one of the two sofas facing each other on opposite sides of a large, Afghan rug. There was a heavy oak coffee table taking up the space between, and a tray had been set with two china cups as big as bowls, as well as the French press.

Leanne was more concerned with the cream damask of the sofa cushions she was meant to sit on. One of the downsides of living at the marina was that she was always getting mud everywhere and, although the weather was dry, Leanne couldn't be sure she wasn't going to shed flakes of mud. She perched on the edge of the sofa while Claudia poured the coffee.

Leaving Leanne to add her own cream and sugar, Claudia picked up her cup and sank back into her seat. 'I should start by saying I owe you a debt of gratitude. I didn't want anyone to know about the baby, but I can see how much it's helped our cause. The response has been breathtaking, and humbling too. The memorial service has grown into something more than I could ever have imagined. I can't believe it's only a week on Wednesday. It's come around so fast.'

It was possible Leanne was being unfair, but Claudia sounded as excited as Phillipa had done when counting down to her grand opening. 'When can we expect the final programme?' she asked, taking out her phone and resting it on her lap. She didn't bother switching on the voice recorder, not yet.

'We're going to hold a press conference next Monday,' Claudia replied. Holding up her hand, she added, 'I realise that doesn't give the *Courier* time to include any late announcements, which is why I thought it only fair to speak to you today. I can't give you a confirmed line-up, but your readers can rest assured that the start time and venue won't change. I can share some good news though. We've managed to procure a proper sound stage, which means at least the performers will stay dry if it rains.'

'Great.'

Leanne's flat response gave Claudia a moment's pause. Her tone was more sombre when she said, 'Whatever happens, the show is going to be incredibly moving. The dance school invited me over for a sneak preview at their dress rehearsal and I must confess, they had me in tears. Hilary Clarke would be so proud of them.'

'Do you think the kids will cope on the night?'

Claudia glanced at the phone resting on Leanne's lap, then at her rucksack on the floor. A frown creased her brow. She was wondering why Leanne wasn't taking notes.

'We're doing all we can to minimise their anxiety,' she said. 'We had planned to bring them on immediately after the reading of the names, but on reflection, that would have been too much, so they're going to be one of the opening acts. We've booked an opera singer to cover their original spot. She's a friend of Bryony's.'

Claudia's eyes were bright. She was waiting expectantly

for Leanne to become enthused about the opera singer, but Leanne had stopped listening the moment Claudia mentioned a roll call of the victims. 'Is Declan Gallagher's name going to be read out?'

The sound of his name made Claudia flinch and Leanne was reassured that they still had some things in common. 'It's so awkward, isn't it? I don't see how we can leave him out. He has a sister in Sedgefield.'

'True, but Karin Gallagher hasn't tried to defend Declan, so why should we? It would help if she could explain what exactly he was up to in the theatre.'

'You think she knows more than she's letting on?'

'According to her partner, Karin has absolutely no recollections from the disaster, and I'm inclined to believe her. From what I've heard, I'd say Karin blames Declan as much as anyone.'

'That may be so, but in the absence of any request to exclude him from the reading, we have to go ahead as planned. At least the list is in alphabetical order, so he won't be the first name people hear, nor the last before we stop to reflect.'

'I suppose that's something.'

'It's about making the best of a very difficult situation.'

From an adjoining room, Leanne heard the glass doors of a bookcase sliding open. 'I take it your husband's working from home again.'

'Justin claims he's saving the planet by cutting down on his commute.'

'He could switch to a smaller car,' Leanne suggested. She couldn't help herself. The new Claudia served only to darken the clouds affecting Leanne's judgement. She wouldn't be too disappointed if she left without another confession.

'Actually, Justin's car is an Audi hybrid,' Claudia replied, her tone cooling to match Leanne's. 'It's my car that's the gas guzzler. It's the white Mercedes you're parked next to.' Point scored, she relaxed with a smile. 'Not that I use it much, but I can tell you it's a lot more comfortable than being thrown about in the back of my dad's old work van.'

'I'm sure a Merc comes in handy for all those trips to the stables,' Leanne noted. 'I had the impression from our last interview that you weren't particularly close to Bryony Sutherland.'

'I wasn't, but since your article, new alliances have been forged. When I set up the charity, my guess is everyone thought I was trying to take advantage of Phillipa's fall from grace. As if I could ever take her place.' She went to laugh, but Leanne's cold stare stopped her. 'Thanks to you, they're beginning to understand that I'm simply a survivor searching for a way to heal. It feels good to be accepted at long last. Is that so bad?'

'These new alliances you've made, do they include Phillipa?'

Claudia took a sip of coffee, creating a pause before she answered. 'No, not at all. From what Bryony's told me, Phillipa has shut herself off from everyone. She's still in the South of France, and I can't imagine her coming back.'

Leanne couldn't decide if she should feel angry or relieved. It was right that Phillipa kept away, but it made it far more difficult for Leanne to take aim. With every fibre of her being, she needed to hurt Phillipa for Lois's sake, and for all the others who had suffered at her hands. Did that make Claudia fair game in her absence? When had Leanne become so cruel? She was beginning to see herself through Mal's eyes.

As Claudia waited for the cross-examination to continue, she placed her cup on its saucer. The nervous rattle of china was the only sound to break the lengthening silence.

'I'm sorry,' Claudia said at last, 'but is there anything else you need from me, Leanne?'

'Actually, there is something. Do you mind if I record this?'

Claudia's eyes darted to the phone Leanne had picked up from her lap. 'Fine,' she said.

'Can you tell me where you were sitting in the stalls?'

Claudia pulled a face, unsettled by the unexpected line of questioning. 'I couldn't say exactly and I'm afraid I've thrown away my ticket stub. As you can imagine, it wasn't a memento I wanted to keep.'

'A general sense of where you were would do. Was it the middle section? To the left? The right? Near the front? At the back?'

'I was somewhere in the middle,' she said vaguely.

'I don't suppose you remember seeing a young girl, do you? Her mum got up in the middle of the performance to go to the Ladies. It would have been only minutes before the alarm went off.'

'Are you talking about Amelia Parker?' Claudia's fingers twitched and china rattled again. 'I read her story.'

'Did you see her?'

There was a quick shake of the head. 'Why are you asking?'

'We're extremely disappointed that the woman who rescued Amelia hasn't come forward. It would have been nice to hold a reunion to lift the town's spirits as we prepare to relive our darkest hour. Don't you think?'

'I can't imagine the town is short of heroes. What about

136

the firefighters?' asked Claudia. She was back to her previously modest self, eager to turn the spotlight elsewhere. 'As everyone was scrambling over each other to get out, they were going in. They knew part of the roof had collapsed and were experienced enough to know there could be another cave-in, and yet they put their lives on the line and brought out people who weren't able to walk out themselves.'

'But during those time-critical minutes before help arrived, other people had to step up,' Leanne countered. She was trying to find a version of Claudia she could, and should admire. 'I was just wondering what made you go back inside.'

Claudia's intake of breath caught in her throat. 'What?'

Leanne placed her phone face up on the coffee table. 'What was so important that, when you reached the exit, you turned around and went back inside?'

Still leaning forward, Leanne pulled her coffee cup towards her before adding a dash of cream and two spoons of sugar. Claudia didn't answer until Leanne looked up from stirring her coffee.

'I don't know what you're talking about,' she said, but she blinked one too many times. Beth had been right. She had gone back.

When Leanne tapped the teaspoon on the rim of the cup, Claudia's eyelids fluttered. The last time she had looked that nervous, Leanne recalled how Claudia had dropped a teaspoon on the kitchen floor as a distress signal. As it happened, her husband's arrival had been fortuitous. It wasn't Leanne who had teased the confession from Claudia, it was Justin. Would it work again?

'You were seen going against the flow of people trying to escape.'

Leanne had balanced her teaspoon on the saucer at a precarious angle, but was aware that the Afghan rug underfoot would muffle the sound if she dropped it. She held the cup over the tray as she wriggled back awkwardly in her seat. Her jerked movements caused the spoon to tremble, then fall, hitting the sugar bowl before landing on the tray with a clatter.

'Oops!' said Leanne, slopping coffee into her saucer for added authenticity. She looked at the dark liquid threatening to spill and placed the cup down on the tray, making yet more noise. 'I'm so sorry.'

'It's not a problem,' Claudia said, setting down her own drink and rising quickly. 'I'll get you another cup.'

Leanne stood with her. 'You don't have to. I need to cut down on my caffeine anyway.'

Unwilling to relinquish her chance of escape, Claudia continued towards the door, but it was already swinging open. Justin stepped into the room.

'We meet again,' he said to Leanne with a bright smile before turning his attention to his wife. There was concern in his eyes. 'Everything OK?'

'Leanne needs a fresh cup, that's all,' Claudia said, preparing to shoo Justin away.

'I was asking your wife to go over what happened on the night of the fire,' explained Leanne. 'I wanted to talk about the people she might have helped – the people she might have saved. It must have taken some courage to reach safety then turn around and go back inside to help those less fortunate.' To her surprise, the admiration in her voice wasn't forced.

Claudia kept her back to Leanne. It was impossible to see

her expression, but the look on Justin's face was easy to read.

'She didn't tell you?' asked Leanne. When neither responded, she sat down, leaving no doubt that she wasn't about to give up. She repeated her question, more softly this time. 'Why did you go back, Claudia?'

'I think I'd like to know the answer to that too,' Justin said.

Claudia backed away from her husband and sank down onto the sofa. She kept her head lowered and her hands clasped tightly in her lap as Justin joined her. He put a hand over hers. After what felt like minutes, they heard Claudia swallow hard.

'I'm sorry,' she whispered. 'I couldn't leave her there.'

'Leave who?' asked Justin. 'What are you talking about?'

'Amelia Parker,' Leanne said, when Claudia couldn't.

'The girl in the paper? The one who was pulled from the rubble by a . . . Are you saying that was you?'

'When the alarm sounded, it was obvious to anyone who saw Amelia, that she wasn't going to leave until her mum came back. And she was right where the ceiling collapsed,' Claudia said, avoiding a direct answer to Justin's question. She had to go through it, step by step. 'I suppose it was easier to believe that she had moved out of the way in time, or if she was beneath the rubble, that she hadn't suffered. But . . . some of the people coming out mentioned those who had been left behind, calling for help. I suppose I had to know for sure if there was more I could do.'

She pressed herself against her husband, but Justin had tensed and it must have felt like snuggling into a slab of granite. His knuckles were white where he held his wife's hands. Claudia inhaled deeply. 'I know I should have stayed outside, but I couldn't walk away. I don't know, maybe it was the hormones.'

Claudia's voice was growing bolder, and Leanne understood why. She had to justify her actions, not because she had saved someone and kept it a secret, but because she and Justin had paid a terrible price for her bravery.

A sob escaped when Claudia added, 'She was a child, and I thought I was going to be a mother. I couldn't just leave her.'

'It's OK,' Justin whispered. His shoulders slumped. 'I would have done the same thing.'

Claudia lifted his hand to her quivering lips. 'I wish I could go back,' she said. 'If I'd known I was making a choice, I might have chosen differently. We might be a family now.'

'We are a family.'

'What happened when you went to look for Amelia?' Leanne asked, aware that her voice had become scratchy.

'The dust had cleared, but the auditorium was filling up with smoke. I knew I didn't have long, but it took a while to work out where Amelia was buried. There was so much debris it was hard to make sense of it all, but eventually I found her,' Claudia said breathlessly, as if she were back there in the auditorium. 'I saw the top of her head, then her face. I thought she was . . .'

Claudia was staring into space as Justin put an arm around her. She pressed her cheek to his chest, leaving damp trails of tears on his cotton shirt.

'I thought I was too late and I did consider leaving her where I found her, but I couldn't un-see her body,' she continued. 'I moved a piece of timber to get closer and when

I touched her arm, I felt it twitch. I can't tell you how relieved I was, and scared too. I somehow managed to free her, but lifting her was almost impossible. She was a dead weight in my arms. And I did think she was . . .'

'You saved her,' Justin told her.

'I stumbled towards this man.'

'Rex Russell,' Leanne confirmed.

'He doesn't remember me?'

'I think he was too concerned with Amelia.'

'So was I, but I was thinking of our baby too,' Claudia said to Justin. 'I didn't want to strain myself any more than I already had, but I guess the damage was done.'

'Is that why you've never told anyone?' Leanne asked. 'Is it guilt that stopped you coming forward?'

'Guilt?' Justin demanded. 'She saved a child's life.'

'No, Leanne's right. I do feel guilty. The miscarriage wasn't simply one of those things that happened.' Claudia's lip trembled. 'I made it happen.'

Justin responded by hooking a finger under her chin and lifting her gaze. 'You have nothing to feel guilty about.'

Able to sit up, Claudia glanced at Leanne's phone on the table. Everything she had said had been recorded. 'Do you have to publish this?'

'You don't want to?' Leanne asked, but she was beginning to understand. Claudia didn't court publicity. Somehow it came to her unbidden.

'I'm scared of what people might say,' she said frankly.

'People are going to adore you, Claude,' Justin said. 'You're a hero.'

'I don't feel like a hero.'

Leanne could feel Mal breathing down her neck as if he

141

were in the room with them. 'Amelia thinks you are too,' she said. 'And because you haven't come forward, she's worried you died saving her. We can't let her go on believing that, can we?'

'You can do this,' Justin said to his wife.

Claudia bit her lip. She was on the verge of agreeing.

'Amelia would love to meet you,' Leanne said, giving her one last push. She could already imagine the scene. 'Her family will want to thank you.'

'No,' Claudia said firmly. 'That's too much to ask. I can't. Write what you like and I'll send her a note if that helps, but I can't face her.'

'We understand,' Justin assured her before Leanne could make a counter-argument. 'It's too soon to think about that, and I'm sure Amelia's family will respect your wishes.'

Leanne picked up her phone and closed the voice recorder. It was time to leave while she was ahead. 'Thanks for your time, Claudia, and I'll see you next week at the press conference. We'll be leading with your story this weekend, so you can expect a lot of interest.'

'I don't want this distracting from the memorial service,' Claudia said.

'Nor do I,' Leanne agreed, but she doubted either would get their way.

10

The Three Pheasants Hotel was a Georgian mansion house on the outskirts of Sedgefield surrounded by rolling hills and dense woodland. A popular venue for weddings, it had a decent-sized car park, but Leanne had to do two circuits through driving rain before she found a free parking space.

Swept into reception by a howling wind, she was hit by a cloud of warm, scented air wafting from the hotel's exclusive spa, but relaxation was furthest from Leanne's mind. She was directed to the largest conference suite where a podium had been erected in front of row upon row of chairs. The place was rammed with fellow journalists who wouldn't have given Leanne more than a passing glance a month ago. They eyed her with envy now. As predicted, Claudia's story had made the front page of the *Courier* on Saturday, and had gone on to make national headlines. Leanne wasn't afraid to look smug.

She found Frankie two rows from the front. She had reserved the seat next to her, and Leanne picked up the press pack before sitting down. 'You're a lifesaver.'

'I think you'll find Claudia Rothwell is the lifesaver,' Frankie replied. 'I can't wait to see the legend in person.'

Although Frankie's description was meant to be tongue-in-cheek, a casual glance around the room suggested there was growing anticipation of Claudia's arrival. 'Has there been any sign of her yet?'

'No, but I've spotted a few of her cohorts,' Frankie said, leaning in and surreptitiously pointing to the front row. 'The woman with the blonde bob is Bryony Sutherland, and next to her is Harriet Healey.'

Harriet was the treasurer to the Empress Memorial Fund and was sitting amongst several other notable names from Sedgefield's elite. These were the same people who had apparently been too busy to give their time to Claudia's cause before she hit the headlines. They were flocking to her now and when a ripple of applause travelled from the back of the room, they were the first to stand up and cheer her arrival.

Claudia wore a dark trouser suit and a white silk shirt that emphasised the red stain of embarrassment creeping across her neck and cheeks. She batted away the applause as she made her way to the podium, and took her time adjusting the microphone. She didn't dare lift her gaze as she shuffled her papers.

A woman with mousy brown hair and a floral dress who had been flanking Claudia, quickly poured a glass of water from a carafe and handed it to her.

'Thanks, Yvonne,' Claudia said, before facing front. 'Hello, everyone.'

She took a sip of water as she waited for the second round of applause to die down. 'This is all too much, and I know a lot of you are here today because you've read the piece in Saturday's *Courier*, but I'm sorry, I'm not going to answer any further questions in that regard.' She glanced towards Leanne and nodded. 'I've said all I want to say.'

If they had been alone, Leanne might have put a hand on Claudia's arm and apologised for the distraction caused by her article, but it had been necessary. The truth had to be told. Heroes had to be celebrated. It was time for Claudia to accept that, and Leanne too.

'I'm glad that Amelia Parker is happy and healthy,' Claudia continued, 'but we're two days away from marking the anniversary of the fire. It's going to be a painful milestone for Sedgefield, and I hope we can all play our part in making the memorial service a fitting tribute. It's taken a lot of hard work to get to this point, and our challenges aren't over yet. If you've seen the weather reports, you'll be aware that the storm we hoped was moving south, seems to have veered north, but come what may, we intend to go ahead with our plans. Now, if you could all turn to the press packs Yvonne has circulated.'

Despite initial nerves and a wobble in her voice, Claudia was commanding the room. Disgruntled journalists flicked through pages of information that detailed the line-up for Wednesday's event. The pack included biographies of those taking part, and quotes from others directly affected by the tragedy, explaining why the memorial was so important to them. Claudia was determined to divert attention away from herself and seemed to be getting her way.

There were one or two quiet groans when Claudia stepped down from the podium and invited the treasurer to go through the finances. On the face of it, Hilary was about to bore the room rigid, but the rise in donations was eye-watering. The fund had grown exponentially in line with Claudia's press exposure, and it was little wonder that the plans for the service had been supersized in recent weeks. They had more money than they could possibly need.

'I'm sure you're all wondering what will happen to the fund once we pass the anniversary,' Claudia said, after swapping places with Hilary. 'And it's a question that has been discussed ad nauseam with my fellow trustees and within the working party. We did consider commissioning a monument, and that might be something the people of Sedgefield want in the future, but personally, I don't feel now is the time for splashing out on a slab of stone or a tonne of twisted metal. We might be a year on, but there are those who continue to struggle. With that in mind, we've agreed that our next priority will be the establishment of a hardship fund to provide financial relief and mental health support to survivors and families of the bereaved.'

A hand went up. 'Isn't that a duplication of effort? I understand the victims have been offered counselling already,' said a TV reporter.

'You're right,' said Claudia. 'And there has been some financial support too, but from the messages I've received to date, it's not enough. It's never enough. If it took two years to restore the theatre, the least we can do is invest the same amount of time, if not more, repairing the damage the fire has caused to people's lives.'

Another hand shot up. 'Since you're taking questions,' said a journalist from one of the tabloids. 'I note from the programme that you're not intending to give a speech on the night. Why is that?'

'I will be onstage at various points, but I would prefer to leave the speeches to the likes of the mayor. Now back to—'

'And let him take the credit?' the journo asked.

'The running order is tight, and we've promised the council we'll be finished by ten thirty,' she tried. 'I'm sure Sedgefield can do without me droning on.'

'Rubbish,' Bryony called out from the front row. 'People will want to hear from you.'

Claudia pursed her lips. 'We'll have to see,' she promised.

'What are your plans for meeting up with Amelia Parker?' someone shouted, talking over another question that was being fired at Claudia. Her inexperience at dealing with the press was beginning to show.

'I'm sorry, I've said I wouldn't take ques—'

'Have you spoken to her yet?' another voice called out.

'No, I . . . I've written a letter to her. That's all I intend to say. Sorry, thank you,' Claudia said, before quickly stepping away from the microphone.

Yvonne took her place and offered to take any further questions, but the press were out of their seats and swarming around Claudia. In a week where the papers would be full of memoriam pieces, editors were looking for an upbeat story to add a touch of light. Mal had done the same.

'I'm going to get closer, see how she handles it,' Frankie said.

Leanne held back to take in the spectacle. Bryony had grabbed Claudia's arm and was trying to insert herself into the discussions, pausing now and again with a perfect pout whenever a camera was aimed in her direction. Yvonne had given up trying to draw attention back to the podium and was gathering up the papers Claudia had discarded, while

Harriet fielded questions from the reporters who couldn't get close to Claudia. The hero of the hour had been backed into a corner, but she was growing in confidence. With the wave of a hand and the occasional pointing of a finger, she worked the semicircle of journalists as a conductor might an orchestra. She didn't appear to notice when Bryony was forced out of the melee.

'Who knew Claudia would become so popular?' Leanne said. Her tone suggested she was talking to anyone who would listen, but the comment was directed at Claudia's ousted friend.

Aware that she was in a room full of journalists, Bryony eyed Leanne with suspicion. 'It's nice to see her getting the recognition she deserves after such a testing time.'

'Do you know her well?'

'Sorry, which paper are you from?'

'I'm with the *Courier*. Leanne Pitman.'

'Ah, so you're the one who finally persuaded her to tell all.'

'That's me. So you were saying you're a close friend,' Leanne prompted, knowing this wasn't entirely true, but she would like to hear Bryony's exaggerated version.

'Yes, I'm giving her riding lessons at the moment. She needs to find time to relax, get out into the fresh air. You can tell just by looking at her that she has a huge weight on her shoulders. How she kept everything to herself for so long, I don't know.'

'Perhaps she was dealing with the loss of her baby,' suggested Leanne.

Bryony placed a hand to her chest. 'It was such a shame, for her, and poor Justin too. He's desperate to be a father. Did she tell you they've been trying ever since the miscarriage?'

she asked, too eager to prove she was a trusted confidante to worry about breaking a confidence.

'No, she never mentioned it. Presumably because she wanted to keep some things private,' Leanne reminded her. Before Bryony could defend herself, Leanne attempted to catch her off guard. 'What do you think Phillipa would make of this?'

'Phillipa?' Bryony asked, eyes widening. 'She'd support our cause if she could. She cares a lot about this community.'

'Have you spoken to her about it?'

'No, not for a while.'

'Then how do you know? Has she made a donation?' Leanne felt heat pumping through her veins at the very thought. If Phillipa had dared to offer blood money . . .

'Not a penny,' Bryony said quickly, only to become flustered. She didn't know which of her comrades she was meant to defend. 'What I mean is, she did offer, of course she did, but Claudia couldn't accept it.'

'Good for her,' Leanne said, glancing over at Claudia. Things had quietened down, and only a handful of reporters were left to press her for soundbites. She was sharing a joke, and even Frankie was laughing. Claudia Rothwell never failed to surprise, and Leanne had stopped fighting against her instincts. She was ready to admit she was starting to like her. 'I don't imagine the rebuff went down well with Phillipa.'

'This whole ordeal has devastated her, but if I know Phillipa, she won't stay down for long.'

'She won't be welcomed back, not in Sedgefield,' Leanne warned, unable to repress the snarl.

Bryony tensed. 'I know this isn't what people want to hear, but . . .' She pressed her lips together. 'Never mind.'

'If you have something to say, I'm happy to keep it off the record,' Leanne promised, pulse rising.

Bryony tipped her head back just so she could look down her nose at Leanne. 'Phillipa's intentions were honourable throughout. She wanted only the best for this town, the whole town. Time will tell, but if you ask me, it's Declan Gallagher who should be hung out to dry, or at least his corpse should. He was a Jack the lad who took risks in every aspect of his life. This is his fault.'

'You knew him?'

'Not intimately,' Bryony said. She smiled. 'Not like some.'

'What does that mean?'

'Declan drew a lot of interest. There were rumours,' she said, arching an eyebrow. 'My theory is he was too busy offering his personal services elsewhere to pay attention to what was happening on site.'

'Do you know who he might have been seeing?' Leanne asked, but, before Bryony could answer, she felt a hand on her back. Frankie had grown bored of the circus around Claudia.

'I need to make a move,' she told Leanne.

Leanne had glanced away for only a second, but when she turned back, Bryony was in retreat. She smiled at the two journalists politely. 'I'll leave you to it.'

'Sorry, did I disturb something?' Frankie asked, as Bryony walked away.

'I'm not sure,' Leanne mused. 'But I think I'll hang around a little longer.'

People had started to drift off, but a handful of dogged journalists continued to demand Claudia's attention. Leanne was one of them, but she would have to wait her turn. Claudia was currently recording an interview for the local radio station.

Biding her time, she gravitated towards the refreshments table. All of the Thermos flasks for tea and coffee had been depleted, but amongst the empty cups she spied a rogue mini-pack of biscuits. She had skipped breakfast and went to reach for it just as someone else had the same idea.

'Sorry, you have it,' said the smartly dressed woman who looked to be in her mid-thirties. She pulled at the waistband of her trouser suit. 'You'd be doing me a favour.'

'How about we share?' Leanne suggested as she tore open the packet. 'Are you a journalist?'

'No, I'm supposed to be in the room next door for a very tedious management course. I thought I'd have a little nosey in here instead, see what all this fuss is about our Claudia.'

'You know her?'

The woman smiled. 'We were good friends once. We were at school together,' she said, eyeing Leanne carefully. 'I take it you are a journalist.'

'It was my article that caused this furore,' Leanne admitted. Before the old school friend had a chance to consider the wisdom of continuing their chat, she added, 'What was Claudia like?'

'Eager to impress. Eager to be liked. She wanted to be everyone's best friend,' she said, lifting her biscuit to her lips, then pausing. 'And I sort of get why she'd run into a burning building to save that little girl, but then again, she knew she was pregnant. Wouldn't you want to protect your unborn child over the life of a stranger?'

'I take it you weren't there at the theatre,' said Leanne,

feeling the need to push back on Claudia's behalf. This 'friend' appeared to be the type who enjoyed presiding over other people's misfortunes.

'No, thank God.' She nibbled on her biscuit. 'Not that it turned out too bad for Claudia in the end. Only she could put herself in the middle of a disaster and come out as the nation's sweetheart.'

'So tell me, why do you think your friendship drifted?' Leanne asked, although having spent less than five minutes with this woman, she could hazard a guess.

Claudia's friend wrinkled her nose. 'Oh, this and that,' she said vaguely. 'Once she had Justin, she didn't want to have people around who might tell tales about her misspent youth, or her childhood woes.'

'You mean like her mum dying?' Leanne said, shocked by the woman's callousness.

The old school friend didn't respond. She had caught Claudia's attention and waved at her with a smile that might have been a smirk. 'What you see with Claudia isn't what you get.'

There was no time to press for an explanation. Claudia had shrugged off the last journalist and was making a beeline for them.

'Kim, how lovely to see you! It's been too long,' said Claudia, hugging her friend.

'It certainly has,' Kim said with a cheesy grin. 'I bumped into your dad the other month in Chester, and I was telling him it had been a while. Didn't he mention he'd seen me?'

'No, well, you know . . .'

'Yes, he did say you don't speak much. You must be *so* busy.'

'Like you wouldn't believe. The charity has taken over my life,' Claudia said. 'Isn't this madness? I wish they'd all go away.'

Leanne cleared her throat.

Smiling, Claudia said, 'You're the exception, obviously, but the last few days have been crazy. I really wish everyone could put aside this business with Amelia. There are more important things this week.'

'I'm afraid there are also more important things today,' Kim said. 'You've caught me sagging. I'm meant to be in the training room next door, and I must go.'

'Let's not leave it so long next time,' Claudia said, and the two friends made plans to meet up without managing to firm up any details whatsoever.

'She seems nice,' Leanne said when Kim had left.

'Yeah, the best.' Claudia's tone matched Leanne's for politeness. 'Did you talk much?'

'Not really. She might have mentioned a misspent youth, but unfortunately she didn't share the details.'

Claudia attempted a laugh. 'If anyone had a misspent youth, it was Kim. Don't think for a second that this morning was her first experience of playing truant.' She took a deep breath and let the tension leave her with the exhale. 'I'm glad this is over, and I'm so, so sorry, but I need to head off. I promised Harriet I'd meet her back at the office for a de-brief.'

'I was surprised not to see Justin here today,' remarked Leanne, ignoring Claudia's prompt to leave.

'Unfortunately, he does have to show his face at work once in a while. It was a choice between coming along today, or being free on Wednesday, and this one I could handle on my own. The anniversary is going to be a challenge, especially if the storm doesn't pass in time. I know I said we'd press on either way, but it would be so much easier if it wasn't blowing a gale. But whatever happens, I promise to give the *Courier* one of the first post-event interviews. It's the least I can do after all you've done for me, and the charity of course,' she added.

Leanne had surreptitiously positioned herself in front of Claudia in case she had any ideas of scooting off. 'Do you mind if I ask you a quick question? It's something Bryony mentioned.'

'Oh, OK.' Claudia looked nervously around the room, where hotel staff were stacking chairs. Bryony was long gone. 'What did she say?'

'We were talking about Declan Gallagher. She seemed to think he was involved with someone, and since the rumours haven't hit the ears of the press, I'm guessing it's because your peers have closed ranks.' She left a pause to give Claudia time to close her gaping mouth. 'Which can only mean it must involve one of you, and now you're such good friends with Bryony, I imagine you know who she was talking about.'

Playing with the collar on her jacket, Claudia said, 'Yes, I'd heard the rumours, but it's not something I care to repeat. The truth is, I don't like to engage in that kind of gossip and I don't believe in kicking someone when they're down. Now, if you'll excuse me.'

Claudia was going to have to walk straight through Leanne if she wanted to escape, because Leanne wasn't budging, not now. 'What do you mean "kick someone when they're down"?' She stopped to consider her own question and the chuckle that tickled her throat was coated in wickedness.

'Are we talking about *Phillipa*? Declan Gallagher was having an affair with his boss?'

'Technically, she wasn't his boss,' Claudia hit back. 'I'm sorry, Leanne, I thought the *Courier* was better than this. Their private lives are no one else's business, and I won't say another word. I really do have to go.'

Leanne should get moving too but, unlike Claudia, who raced out of the hotel at lightning speed, Leanne slowed down when she reached reception. She had tried to ignore the smell of essential oils leaching out of the spa on her arrival, but she could no longer hold back the bitter-sweet memories they evoked. Lois had treated her brokenhearted friend to a blissful day of beauty treatments soon after her arrival in Sedgefield. Lois had loved everything about this hotel and had had dreams of marrying Joe here.

Plunging into the storm, the shock of rain washed away the warm memories, and Leanne was left bitterly cold. She glanced around the car park. Joe could have worked out where she would be, but there was no sign of him. Had he given up on her? She hoped so.

There was one familiar car she recognised as the headlights of a white Mercedes cut through the murk. Claudia was behind the wheel, but her car didn't slow, and Leanne was getting too wet to pay it much heed. She used her rucksack as an unwieldy umbrella and was crisscrossing the car park when another car passed in front of her. Leanne stopped in her tracks and stared at the receding taillights, oblivious to the puddle she had stepped in. Raindrops dripped down the inside of her jacket collar and a shudder ran down the length of her spine. Phillipa was supposed to be in France. She was supposed to stay away. The bitch was back.

The Empress Theatre

Sedgefield, Cheshire

As Rex watched the paramedics working on the broken body of the girl, he steeled himself for the moment they would turn to him and explain it was hopeless.

'They're doing all they can,' his wife reassured him. 'You've given her the best chance.'

'It wasn't me,' Rex said, refusing to take credit. If it weren't for his impatience, his wife might have persuaded the girl to leave when the alarm had sounded.

The alarm was no more than a bleat from inside the theatre now and, when Rex wasn't staring at the paramedics, his gaze was trained on the fire doors. There had been a slow trickle of survivors coming out, but he had yet to see the woman with bloodied hands. When he had taken the child from her, he had assumed she would follow, but he hadn't looked back to check. He tried to convince himself that she was already out. He could easily have missed her. He had spent the first few minutes seeking medical help for the girl, and a good amount of time after that had been occupied with hugging his wife and granddaughter.

157

Rex watched on with growing despair. He should have made sure she was safe too.

The alleyway had been crowded when Claudia had left the theatre. She had spotted the paramedics performing CPR on the little body pulled from the rubble, but she couldn't watch. She didn't want to think about life and death at all. She wanted to go home, but her car was in a side street, blocked in by emergency vehicles.

Reluctantly, Claudia had been ushered towards Victoria Park. Someone wrapped a foil blanket around her, but she didn't need it, and when she stumbled upon a man curled on the grass weeping, she placed the silver wrap over his shoulders.

'I watched her die,' the man sobbed. 'I didn't want to leave her, but she disappeared, and I kept getting pushed along. She's dead. Lois is dead.'

Claudia patted his shoulder. 'You did what you could.'

Wandering aimlessly through the park, Claudia checked her phone. There had been several missed calls from Justin and when she got through, his relief was palpable. He was already close by and, as she waited, she looked at the stains on her once cream coat. Added to the handprint on her sleeve were soot marks and a small tear. It couldn't be repaired. She would need a new coat.

Why on earth was she worried about a new coat? Stuff didn't matter. Things could be replaced. Lives couldn't. Anger forced her to take a sharp breath that caught in her inflamed throat. The smoke had been noxious.

Someone close by heard her coughing fit and she was handed a bottle of water. She savoured the coolness against her throat, but kept some of the liquid to wash the dirt from *her hands. Two of her acrylic nails were peeling away and she pulled them off. Her chest hurt, and the stitch in her side had returned, but compared to some of the others, she was fine. She was going to walk away from this unscathed. The worst was over, and she had done as much as she could.*

11

The sky had darkened to sapphire with enough light left in the day to pick out the skeletal forms of oaks and beeches stripped of their leaves by the storm. Victoria Park had taken a battering in the last few days, but on the day of the anniversary, the clouds had parted and the wind was no more than a despairing last breath.

Leanne was loitering by the bandstand, some distance away from the crowds concentrated around the sound stage that had been erected hurriedly on the playing field that morning. Claudia had been extremely fortunate not to have her plans blown away by seventy-mile-an-hour gales, and some might say she led a charmed life these days, but perhaps she deserved it. Claudia certainly looked as if she had the world at her feet as the lights came up and she stepped onto a stage that wouldn't look out of place on a field in Glastonbury.

Unlike any festival Leanne had ever been to, the crowd stilled; a solemn reminder that they weren't there to be entertained. They were there to remember and, as Leanne scanned the horizon, she searched for the glow in the sky that had been a forewarning she had initially ignored a year ago. She pushed her face into the scarf wrapped around her neck and breathed in the scent of damp wool to force the memory away. She was cold to the bone, but not numb. She could feel the collective pain of the crowd. There wasn't a single person in Sedgefield that hadn't been touched by the deathly fingers of the fire.

'I would like to start by saying that we shouldn't be here,' Claudia said, her voice remaining sharp and clear as it was amplified across the park. 'But it might be more appropriate to acknowledge the people who *should* be here with us. Our friends and neighbours, our parents, our brothers and sisters. Our children.' Overcome with emotion, she pressed her fingers to her mouth. An eerie silence pressed down on the crowd as they waited patiently.

Claudia's voice was stronger when she said, 'Our loved ones are gone and the memories we should be making with them are lost for ever. It's pain that fills the void. And for the survivors, there are physical and mental scars too. Our lives have changed. We have changed. We're here this evening to remember that awful night and to show the world that we will never forget.'

The first ripple of applause was almost lost to the soughing of the breeze, but after a tentative start, it became a wave that thundered through the crowd. Claudia wiped tears from her cheeks and, when she was ready, she raised a hand. At her will, the audience quietened.

As Claudia continued with the speech she had vowed not to give, Leanne turned away. She didn't want to be at one with the town and its collective grief. Claudia was right, they shouldn't be there.

162

Following the path that cut through the centre of the park, Leanne kept the main event at a safe distance as she checked her phone. Frankie and the *Courier*'s photographer, Henry, were milling around somewhere, collecting snaps and sound-bites. They weren't due to meet up until the end of the service, at which point they would regroup for a climax that wasn't on Claudia's itinerary.

Leanne's boots squelched on wet, decaying leaves as she veered off the path. She had hoped the refreshments marquee would be empty, but she wasn't the only one avoiding the throng. There were groups of families and friends huddled by the entrance with steaming cups of coffee and hot chocolate. Claudia's team had decided against serving alcohol. No one would be drowning their sorrows tonight, or at least not until the service was over.

Leanne acknowledged one or two familiar faces, but she refused to be drawn into a conversation. There was only one thing people wanted to talk about, and she had to step over guy ropes to avoid them. She wasn't quick enough, and felt a hand on her shoulder. Her body turned before she had the chance to prepare for who it might be. She could tell from the way Joe's grip tightened that he expected her to bolt.

'Leanne, please.'

'I don't want to hear it,' she hissed.

'But we need to talk.'

'And you choose now? Today of all days?'

'On this day especially,' Joe said, raising his voice to match hers. 'And I don't care how many times you walk away, I'll keep coming back.'

'No, Joe, you'll give up eventually. That's what you're good at!'

Joe's body jerked at the force of her words. 'You have every right to hate me, I hate myself, but I can't let you cut me out like this. At least give me a chance to explain.'

She tried to tug her arm free, but he wouldn't let go. 'So you can feel better? Well I have news for you, Joe. I don't want you to feel better. Now let go of me or I swear I'm going to punch you.' Her hand curled into a fist.

'I'm sorry,' he said, his voice breaking. 'I'm sorry for not being enough—'

Joe's words were cut off by the blow Leanne landed on the side of his face. Her knuckles cracked painfully, but the punch had the desired effect, and Joe released his grip. Leanne flexed her hand as she hurried away from the marquee and plunged into the swell of the crowd.

Claudia had been replaced onstage by the Lord Mayor of Sedgefield. It had been the right decision to have Claudia speak first. The mayor's words were drowned out by boos when he attempted to extol the bravery of the fire service. As a councillor, he had been party to the decision to close down the fire station.

Consumed by the crowd, Leanne slowed long enough to check behind her. Joe wasn't there, but there was a face that caught her attention, if only because the woman dipped her head the moment Leanne locked eyes with her. Despite her throbbing fingers, Leanne made another fist.

Phillipa Montgomery had dressed down for the occasion, wearing jeans and a padded jacket with a fur collar that matched her hat. In her late forties, she had kept her figure and timeless looks, although Leanne imagined that without the money and the polishing, she would be quite ordinary. It was what Phillipa was hoping to pass for now. She held her collar against her cheek as if the storm still raged, but it was a pathetic attempt to conceal her identity. She appeared to be alone. Her husband Robert was six foot five and would give his wife away too easily. Leanne eyed Phillipa as an animal might its prey and took a step forward.

Aware that her cover had been blown, Phillipa backed away and turned. The crowd filled the space between them and Leanne moved sideways rather than attempting to push ahead. She moved fast, too fast for those in her way, but she rode the wave of dissent and circled Phillipa, pouncing where the crowd had thinned.

'Leanne Pitman from the *Cheshire Courier*,' she announced as she blocked Phillipa's path.

'I know who you are.'

'Care to make a comment?'

'Only that I want to be left alone.'

'And yet here you are,' Leanne said tersely. 'I saw you outside the press conference too.'

'You can't blame me for wanting to see how people are coping. This is my town.'

Leanne mocked Phillipa with her laughter. 'Are you sure it isn't jealousy? Claudia Rothwell seems to have taken your crown.'

Phillipa pursed her lips, forming a tight seal. She had decided the interview was over, but Leanne wasn't done with her yet. 'Is that it, *Mrs Montgomery*?' she asked, her voice not quite loud enough for others to hear, but her inflection was a warning. Her name would be shouted through the treetops if necessary.

With her face deep in shadow, the reflected light from the stage gave Phillipa's features a ghoulish countenance. On closer inspection, her year in exile had not been kind to her. Her shoulders were hunched and she looked older than Leanne recalled from their last encounter a week before the Empress's grand opening. Phillipa had been perfectly preened back then, with shoulders pulled back and her chest puffed out like a bird of paradise. Claudia's comment onstage about them all changing was true, and Leanne was glad to see that Phillipa had withered out of the spotlight. If her frailty was meant to engender sympathy, it didn't. The reporter, like the town, was spent in that regard.

'What do you expect me to say?' Phillipa asked, with a note of resignation that Leanne hadn't anticipated.

Her face twisted into a snarl. 'You might want to start with an apology.'

'I have apologised, and I'll keep saying it until my dying day. I am sorry, so very sorry.'

'You should have been in that fire.'

'Do you think I don't wish that too?' Phillipa's chin wobbled. 'I'd give my life for any one of those victims if I could.'

'Any of them? Or is there one person in particular? Was there someone you were closer to than you should have been?'

Leanne's last conversation with Claudia had been a gift. Phillipa and Declan. It was all beginning to make sense now. According to Frankie, Declan's workmates had mentioned he had a habit of letting them down at the last minute whenever he had a better offer. Unfortunately, he had refused to breathe a word about the woman who could demand his attention at will and, without firm evidence, it was pointless running the story past Mal. He wouldn't print salacious gossip, but that didn't stop Leanne wielding the threat as a weapon.

Phillipa flinched at the accusation, but she wasn't completely disarmed. 'What are you talking about?'

'Do you know what Declan Gallagher was up to that night?'

'Should I?'

'He was your right-hand man,' Leanne said with a smirk that was deliberately engineered to unsettle.

'He was employed by the contractor, not me.'

'But he took orders from you, pandered to your every whim,' challenged Leanne. 'He died for the sake of your vanity project, and took eleven innocent souls with him. How does that make you feel, to know every person here tonight has suffered because of you?'

When Phillipa's body stiffened, it had the effect of straightening her posture. She wasn't as broken as she would have Leanne believe. 'I know what part I played, and if the investigation finds me wanting, I'll accept the consequences.' She tilted her head when she added, 'But where I can defend myself, I will. I have no idea what Declan was doing in the theatre.'

'He wasn't with you?'

'I was at a dinner party, as has been widely reported and can be corroborated by a dozen people.'

'But you did spend time with Declan. The two of you made quite a pair,' Leanne said, shifting to the left as Phillipa went to pass her.

'This is nonsense.'

As Phillipa attempted to shove Leanne out of the way, Leanne gripped her arm. 'I don't think so.'

'If you seriously think you can hurt me more than I'm hurting already, do your worst,' Phillipa whispered in her ear.

Tired of their little dance, Leanne let her go and Phillipa was about to stride away, but stopped. Something was happening onstage that made her glance back. Leanne turned too. There was a young girl beneath the spotlight, a sheet of paper in her hand. Her nose twitched like a bunny rabbit. It was little Evie, the last performer to grace the stage of the Empress Theatre.

'This is the poem I wrote for Mrs Clarke and everyone else who died in the fire,' Evie said, reading from her script.

The microphone picked up the sound as she cleared her throat. She took a breath. The crowd did the same.

'If I could go to heaven, I'd dance my way to you. I'd make each step a happy step, cos I'd be closer too. I'd smile my biggest smile and tell you what you've missed. I'd ask you if you were watching us and if you were im— impressed. And when it was time to go, I know I would not cry, because if I could go to heaven, I'd – I'd bring you down from the sky.'

Leanne felt a lump in her throat despite telling herself it was sentimental mush, and it was about to get harder. Claudia had reappeared. She took Evie's hand and announced the start of the two minutes' silence. It was 8.06 p.m.; the time the show had been brought to a stop by the sound of the alarm.

Squeezing her eyes shut, Leanne refused to follow Claudia's instructions to remember those they had lost. She chose instead to think about the people who had caused this misery, and what she would like to do to them. She listened to the

168

sobs echoing across Victoria Park and, when the first notes of 'Ave Maria' filled the air, she turned back to Phillipa. She wanted to witness her adversary's conscience breaking her completely, but she had already scuttled away. Leanne took her notebook from her rucksack and scribbled the quote as best she could recall. 'Phillipa Montgomery dared to show her face at the memorial service and said, "I know what part I played and I accept the consequences."'

As Leanne made her way backstage to the performers' tent, she caught a glimpse of Claudia prowling in the wings. She hadn't strayed far from the spotlight all night and was clapping along to a local band who had written a song especially for the occasion. It was one of the last acts, chosen specifically to lift the mood and ensure that the people of Sedgefield left the park with hope in their hearts. Leanne wasn't ready to be uplifted. She had a job to do.

'Are we all set?' Frankie asked when Leanne caught up with her in a quiet corner that would be perfect for their covert operation.

Leanne had her phone in her hand. 'I've just shared my location with Amelia's mum so she can track us down. They're on their way over, and all we need now is for our main attraction to fall into the trap.'

'It's not a trap,' Frankie reminded her. 'As far as we're concerned, it'll be a happy coincidence that Claudia and Amelia are reunited.'

'If you say so,' Leanne replied. This hadn't been her idea. Mal was getting jumpy, convinced another media outlet would beat them to this one-off opportunity.

Frankie caught Leanne staring off towards the stage and

Claudia. 'Don't look so worried. If you ask me, Claudia's loving being centre of attention, and she'll get loads of mileage out of this. She's nothing like I expected. I know you said she had a case of imposter syndrome, but I can't see it from where I'm standing. She's a hard one to figure out.'

'What you see isn't always what you get,' Leanne said, repeating the phrase Claudia's friend, Kim, had used to describe her. Claudia had many layers, and Leanne was still working out where the real Claudia started and the imposter began. 'She told me it was never her intention to fill Phillipa's shoes, but she's having a good go at trying them on for size. Speaking of Phillipa . . .' There was a mischievous glint in her eye.

'She's not about to close the show, is she?' Frankie said, laughing.

'No, but she was here.'

'No way! Did you speak to her?'

'Briefly, and I have a quote we can use. I'll tell you all about it later. First, we need to get this over and done with.'

Leanne had lost sight of Claudia, but she could hear her announcing the finale; a school choir who would give a rendition of 'Fields of Gold'. School kids dressed in black T-shirts had gathered in the wings, and Leanne recognised one of the volunteers organising them into line.

'Here, hold my phone and watch out for Amelia,' Leanne said, not wanting Amelia's mum to track her location to a spot where Claudia would see them. 'I won't be long.'

Justin was watching his wife welcome the choir onto the stage when Leanne approached.

'It's gone really well, hasn't it?' she shouted into his ear.

Justin spun around and beamed a smile. 'Isn't it amazing? I can't believe Claudia has pulled this off. She's even managed to conquer the weather gods.'

'You must be very proud of her.'

He nodded. 'I am. And thank you for your support. A lot of tonight's success can be credited to you and your articles.'

'In that case, I wonder if you could do me a small favour?' she asked, swallowing back her reservations about the reunion. 'I don't want to disturb Claudia now, but she promised us a post-event interview. Ideally, we'd like to catch her straight after the service.'

'Not a problem,' he said. 'There are other journalists who've asked for a quote, but I'll make sure she speaks to you first.'

Leanne pointed to where she would be waiting. 'See you later then.'

'Hold on a minute,' he said, catching hold of her arm. 'You might want to see this.'

A woman in a paramedic's uniform had appeared next to them. She was holding a stunning bouquet of flowers. 'Shall I go on now?' she asked.

Justin took her hand and squeezed it. 'The stage is yours.'

Claudia had been about to leave the stage and looked momentarily confused by the approaching paramedic. The choir had been prepped and their voices provided gentle background music as the woman handed over the bouquet and kissed Claudia's cheek. She held Claudia's hand to prevent her from rushing offstage.

'I've been asked to say a few words,' the paramedic began. 'I know this service is for each and every one of us, but it

171

would be wrong to end the night without reflecting on how much we appreciate Claudia Rothwell's extraordinary efforts in bringing us all together, and to acknowledge that Claudia has had to battle with her own heartbreak.'

'I was on duty a year ago, and spent hours in this park attending to the walking wounded. I must have treated tens, if not hundreds of people and some were more seriously injured than others. It's remarkable, therefore, that I remember Claudia at all, because she didn't have a mark on her. Maybe that was what made her so memorable, but I'd say it was her selflessness that struck me. She told me not to waste any time on her. She was convinced that she had survived without a scratch, and I wish that had been the case. I'd personally like to offer my condolences.'

'Honestly, you don't have to . . .' Claudia insisted.

She looked uncomfortable, and it was a feeling that Leanne shared. The picture painted by the paramedic was at odds with the image that had formed in Leanne's mind during her countless conversations with survivors in her quest to identify Amelia's rescuer.

As the paramedic continued, Leanne turned to Justin. 'Did she really not have a mark on her? I thought she lost finger-nails?'

Justin's eyes were glassy. 'A couple of false nails, a few stains on her coat, that was about it – if you discount how much she reeked of smoke,' he said. 'And it was the smoke that did the damage.'

'Of course. I'm so sorry,' Leanne said. She had great sympathy for Justin, but her feelings for his wife, however, were more difficult to define. A new layer to Claudia had been exposed. 'I have to go. I'll see you later.'

Leanne rushed back to Frankie and was relieved to find that Kathryn and Amelia Parker were yet to arrive.

'Where's my phone?' she demanded.

'Is everything OK?'

Leanne grabbed her phone and connected her earphones. 'I don't know.' Her heart was hammering as she searched through her interview recordings until she found the one she was after. She didn't have time to listen to the whole thing, and skipped the first couple of minutes of the telephone interview with Rex Russell before pressing play.

'Did you see Amelia before the ceiling collapse?' Leanne had asked him.

'Well, erm, I'm not sure. Erm, no, probably not. I don't remember.'

Leanne fast-forwarded again and with a little toing and froing, found the section she needed to hear.

'When you saw this figure coming towards you, what can you remember about her? How about the colour of her skin, or her hair?'

'She was a walking statue. Grey. Covered in dust.'

'Was she short? Tall?'

'She was tallish. I'm only five foot seven on a good day and she was at least my height, maybe an inch more. I'm sorry, I don't know what else to add. I was looking at Amelia,' Rex had replied. 'I was thinking how she was roughly the same age as my granddaughter, how it could have been her.'

'I know it's hard, but try visualising the woman coming closer. What do you see?'

'The girl,' he had insisted. His words were pained as he forced the memory. 'The woman was carrying her as if she were a dead weight and . . . I do remember her hands being

173

blackened and covered in blood. Presumably, that's all she had to dig Amelia out, and you could tell, they were covered in cuts.' He had left a pause, drawing forth the memory. 'And, God, yes, there were a couple of her fingernails hanging by a thread. I know it's not much, but—'

Leanne cut the recording. She had heard enough. The person Rex had described – Amelia's hero – was nothing like the one described by the paramedic. As much as she wanted to believe confusion might explain the contradictions, Leanne couldn't quite convince herself. She'd been fighting her gut instinct that told her not to trust Claudia, and now she knew why. Her stomach lurched. As unthinkable as it was, Claudia and Amelia's hero did not appear to be one and the same. Claudia was a fraud.

12

Standing in the wings as the school choir sang, Claudia looked out across a galaxy of flickering lights. It was as if a thousand stars had descended from the heavens to light up Victoria Park with people waving their phones. If anything, it was more like two thousand.

Was it only a year ago that she had raced towards the burning theatre, fearing the life she had made for herself was about to go up in flames too? She didn't dare imagine what might have happened if she hadn't realised in time. She would have been exposed, cast out of the social circle she had fought so hard to break into. On the other hand, she would have been a mother.

When Leanne Pitman had said Claudia had a case of imposter syndrome, she had been right. Her apparent delight when Phillipa had given her the tickets for the amateur ballet had been a performance worthy of an Oscar. Lying to Justin had been harder, but Claudia had needed them all to believe that she deserved their trust. Lies were often easier than the truth, but that particular one had gone on to divide and multiply like a virus, or an embryo.

If it was wrong, Claudia had endured the consequences. Her baby may have been little more than a collection of cells, but her pregnancy had offered the completeness she and Justin had longed for. How different would her life be now, if only she had stayed by the fire doors and not gone inside? As she listened to the lyrics of the song being sung by the choir, she conjured her own fields of gold, and she remembered.

Sensing his wife was on the verge of tears, Justin slipped his hand into hers, and she was reminded of what she had, not what she had lost. She couldn't love Justin more than she did at that very moment. What had she done to deserve him? And what had she done to deserve this? she asked herself as the final notes of the children's sweet voices faded and she stepped onto the stage to the thunderous applause that rose up from speckled darkness.

'How incredible was that?' she asked the crowd, turning to the choir and joining in the applause. When she stopped, so did everyone else. 'I don't know about you, but I was dreading today. I don't think I could have got through it on my own, and I'm so glad to be here with you all. Before we close, I'd like to thank each and every one of you for sharing this night as one community.'

Claudia went on to express her thanks to all those who had taken part in the service, before concentrating on the ones who had worked behind the scenes. She was grateful for the surprise speech by the lovely paramedic, but she wanted it to be known that this was not her achievement alone. She mentioned Bryony and some of the others who had been late to the party, but her expressions of gratitude were more heartfelt when she got to Yvonne, the primary school teacher whose only previous experience had been organising the school fete, and to Harriet, who ensured the charity met its fiscal and legal obligations.

'I'd also like to thank my husband, Justin, for being so supportive in the last year. I'm blessed to have him in my life,' she said and, as she reached out her hand, Justin joined her onstage. He was holding yet another bouquet of flowers. Their apartment was going to look like an explosion in a florist shop. 'I don't think any of us will take our loved ones for granted ever again, so if you're here because you can't hold the hand of someone you love, I hope tonight has helped ease your pain. You're not alone. We are not alone.'

When Claudia finally made it offstage, her ears were ringing. Even the people backstage paused to applaud her, and Yvonne came over to give her the biggest hug before relieving her of the bouquet to put with the other flowers.

'You did it, Claudia,' she gushed.

'*We* did it,' she replied, with a rush of exhilaration that made her eyes sparkle.

Justin pulled her to one side. 'There's a long list of journalists who want to interview you,' he warned, 'but if you've had enough, I can always send them packing. You must be exhausted.'

Claudia hadn't slept a wink the night before and, in the wee hours before dawn, she had feared it was her conscience keeping her awake. She had to remind herself that she didn't deserve to feel guilty about anything. She was a good person. That's what everyone else thought, and she needed to start believing it too.

'Who's first?'

Justin kissed her forehead. 'Leanne. I thought you might find it easier starting with her?'

'Sure,' Claudia replied. 'And the sooner we get it done, the sooner we can go home.'

As they weaved their way through the throng of performers who were busy packing up, there were more words of appreciation and congratulations. Claudia was so distracted by the pats on the back and arm squeezes that she didn't notice Leanne until they had reached the far corner of the tent. The reporter was with the *Courier*'s photographer, Henry, who had made Claudia feel so relaxed for what had been the first of many photoshoots. There was another reporter too, one that Claudia recognised from the press conference, but it was Leanne she greeted first.

'How lovely to see you,' Claudia said as she strode towards her with her arms open wide.

She could hear lots of camera clicks in quick succession, but she kept her gaze fixed on Leanne. She knew these photos would be splashed across the internet in a matter of hours, and her expression had to convey the right message. The tears she had been fighting back since leaving the stage rimmed her eyes as she committed to the hug. She could feel the reporter tensing and hoped she wasn't ruining the shot.

'How do you think it went?' Leanne asked, her voice monotone.

'It's a difficult one, isn't it?' Claudia pressed a palm to her chest and swallowed hard, overcompensating for Leanne's lack of emotion. 'We've been planning this for months and it's been stressful at times, especially in the last week with the storm, but I think we did OK.'

'You did more than OK,' said Justin, slipping an arm around her waist.

'Time will tell,' Claudia warned. Noticing the second reporter had her phone trained constantly on her, she realised they were being videoed too. 'And I hope it's not just about pulling together tonight. The first year might be over, but this is a lifetime's journey for the victims' families. I want them to know that we're still going to be here when they need us.'

Leanne appeared thoughtful. 'I'm sure tonight has resurrected some painful memories for a lot of people, but understanding exactly what happened is part of the healing process, wouldn't you agree?'

'Absolutely.'

'It's like one big puzzle,' Leanne continued, wrinkling her nose as if she were struggling with a tricky brainteaser. 'And it's time to bring two pieces back together to see how they fit.'

Claudia was confused when Leanne took two steps to the side. The second reporter moved away too, but kept her phone at eye level.

With a rush of adrenalin, Claudia realised the gap the two reporters had left wasn't a gap at all. Two figures had been concealed behind them, waiting to pounce at the very last moment.

'Hello,' said Amelia.

Claudia took a sharp intake of breath and was too shocked to release it. Her lungs burned and her eyes were so wide they stung. She wanted to turn and run, but this was being played out in front of the camera, not to mention a ten-year-old girl who was waiting for Claudia to respond. She couldn't speak. The blood pounded in her ears.

'Oh, wow,' Justin said, breaking the silence.

Claudia had to say something, but she was gripped with terror. She glanced sideways at Henry, who was clicking away with his bloody camera. What a mess. What an awful mess. She hadn't meant for it to go this far.

13

Despite her certainty that Claudia Rothwell had taken the credit for someone else's heroic deed, Leanne wanted to be proven wrong, but as she watched Claudia's complexion pale, her heart sank. The reaction was exactly as one might expect from someone who had been caught out on a big, fat lie.

Amelia's reaction was off too, and Leanne was waiting for her to look straight past Claudia and ask when the woman who rescued her was getting there. It was so surreal that Leanne had to stop herself from releasing a nervous laugh. She wasn't entirely sure she succeeded.

'Hello,' Claudia said at last.

'Hello,' said Amelia.

The awkwardness continued as the girl and her so-called hero waited to see who blinked first. Leanne shared a look with Frankie. Amelia had shown up before Leanne had been able to explain what was going on to her colleague, but Frankie must realise something was amiss.

When Leanne thought she couldn't stand the suspense a second longer, Claudia clasped both hands over her mouth to suppress a sob. She dropped to a crouch, her eyes welling up. 'Oh, Amelia. Sweetheart. You look so well. I don't think my heart can stand it.'

'I was covered in dirt last time,' Amelia conceded. She had pressed her body against her mother's side, a handmade card clutched in her hand. She made no move to approach. 'Is it really you?'

No, it bloody isn't! Leanne wanted to scream. She had considered calling the whole charade off, but she needed Amelia to confirm her suspicions. She wanted reassurance that she wasn't going mad.

'It's me,' Claudia said, as a single tear spilled down her cheek.

There were tears in Amelia's eyes too, and even Frankie gave a sniff. Working the crowd, Claudia spread her arms wide. Amelia let out a sob and raced into her embrace. There was a collective gasp, and a sigh of relief from Henry; he had his money shot. Only Leanne remained unmoved.

'We've spent the last year not knowing who we owed for saving our girl,' explained Kathryn. She had a crumpled tissue in her hand and blew her nose. 'It doesn't seem enough, but thank you, Claudia. Thank you.'

Claudia had cupped Amelia's face in her hands. 'It was Amelia's determination to get back to you as much as anything. I did what I could.'

'Do you remember the light?' asked Amelia.

'Oh, sweetheart,' Claudia said. 'All I remember is you. I was scared you weren't going to make it. You were such a fighter.'

'What light?' asked Leanne, unwilling to gloss over the finer details that would make or break Claudia's claims.

'The torch. She gave me a torch.'

'She's never mentioned it before,' Kathryn said, in response to Leanne's quizzical look. To her daughter she added, 'Are you remembering something new, love?'

Amelia's brow furrowed. 'I think so. Claudia gave it to me to hold while she dug me out. I was crying.'

'Could it have been a light from a phone?' suggested her mum.

'No, it was a proper one.'

'You didn't mention a torch,' Leanne said casually to Claudia.

Ignoring the question, Claudia stood up to check her husband's reaction to the unfolding scene. It was a reminder to them all that whilst Kathryn had her daughter, the Rothwell's remained childless. Claudia gave Justin's hand a squeeze.

'The torch?' Leanne asked again. Claudia's misdirection had bought her time, but she wasn't going to evade the question completely.

Claudia's sigh had a hint of exasperation. 'I'm a bit like Amelia. I remember snapshots, and it's hard to put everything in order.' She glanced at Frankie's phone, trained on their little group. 'All the ushers had torches.'

'No, it was a little one,' Amelia said. 'It was on a key ring.'

Claudia's expression was fixed. There was a smile of sorts. 'And do you remember what I said to you?' she asked. 'I told you to keep it safe. I told you it was going to lead us out.'

'Yes, you kept talking to me,' Amelia said eagerly. 'What else did you say?'

Claudia's smile broadened. 'I said you were very brave. I said you were going to see your mum again very soon.'

Amelia turned to her mum. 'She did. I kept closing my eyes, but she was still there when I opened them again.'

'I couldn't leave you,' Claudia replied, her words thick with emotion.

Leanne lowered her head. She didn't believe any of it, but without Amelia's corroboration, she wasn't sure she had enough to publicly accuse Claudia of being an imposter, not without putting her professional neck on the line.

'Here,' said Amelia, handing Claudia the card she had been holding. 'I made this for you.'

Amelia had written Claudia's name on the envelope with a red felt-tip pen. The *Courier*'s readers would find it sweet that she had misspelled her hero's name – and the reunion piece would undoubtedly be published, Leanne would never be able to convince Mal otherwise.

The card pulled from the envelope was just as saccharin, with a hand-drawn heart on the front enclosing two figures, one adult and one child-sized. There was a lengthy message inside and, as they waited for Claudia to finish reading it, Leanne made one last stab at uncovering the truth.

'What happened to the torch, Amelia?'

The girl shrugged. 'I gave it back.'

'Do you still have it, Claudia? Where did it come from?'

Claudia pressed herself against her husband, apparently needing his support to keep her upright. 'I carry all kinds of junk in my bag,' she admitted. 'You never know when it's going to come in handy, and I guess I was right. I've no idea where it went.'

'I could draw you a picture,' Amelia said.

Claudia stifled a yawn. 'Maybe another time,' she replied. 'I still have a few more interviews with the press before I can go home, but it was lovely meeting you again.'

'Can we have some photos of both families?' Henry suggested. When he noticed Leanne slinking away, he added, 'And you too. Mal wanted one with you in the group.'

'I don't think so.'

'Oh, come on, Leanne,' said Claudia. 'After everything you've done, it wouldn't be complete without you.'

Leanne was minded to repeat her refusal, but she was forced into the huddle. Slipping behind Justin, she hoped to be lost in the background, but he noticed and stepped to the side. When Henry was satisfied with the pose, Leanne was standing with a hand resting on Amelia's shoulder, and Claudia's arm was around her waist. It was too much. Leanne couldn't leave without saying something, so as the group disbanded, she pulled Claudia into a tight hug.

'I know it wasn't you,' Leanne hissed quietly into her ear.

Claudia wouldn't be shocked for a second time. She matched the force of Leanne's embrace. 'You know nothing about me.'

14

There were three tumblers on Mal's desk and a bottle of single malt in his hand. He seemed to be under the impression they had something to celebrate. The latest issue of the *Courier* was ready to go to print, and Claudia Rothwell was on the front page yet again. Leanne was only marginally relieved that the photo Mal had chosen was one of her welcoming Hilary Clarke's dance students onto the stage. The shots of Amelia being hugged tightly by her 'hero' were buried inside, but not deep enough in Leanne's opinion.

Mal poured a generous measure of whisky into each glass. 'You did a good job. Both of you.' He glanced only briefly at Frankie before concentrating back on Leanne, keenly aware of which member of staff needed the pep talk. 'We've given the town a happy ending of sorts.'

'It's not over.'

Mal sighed as he pressed a drink into her hand. He went to say something in response, but thought better of it. He sipped his whisky before trying again. 'In another month we'll know the root cause of the fire. We have to bide our time.'

The whisky burnt Leanne's throat and the notes of smoke

made her want to gag. 'I wasn't talking about the investigation,' she said. 'I'm talking about Claudia. There are some serious questions that need answering.'

Mal picked up a set of page proofs and found Leanne's feature set around endearing photos of Claudia and Amelia. 'There are no questions as far as I'm concerned. Amelia has her hero. Hell, the town has its hero. It's here in black and white.'

'I wrote what you told me to write.' There had been a lengthy telephone call the day before when Leanne had been struggling to submit her copy, and it was fortunate that she had been working from home. Slamming down the phone wasn't a sacking offence. Hitting your editor might have been. Her only push back had been to slip a line into her article about Claudia losing her mum, if only because Claudia had asked her not to, but it was a hollow victory. 'I follow orders,' she said.

'Good. Let's remember that, shall we?'

Frankie had grown tired of waiting to be passed her drink and grabbed the remaining glass from Mal's desk. 'Cheers,' she said wryly.

'What do you think, Frankie?' asked Leanne.

'It's not Frankie you have to convince,' interjected Mal. 'It's our readers, the ones who trusted you to find Amelia's hero and believed you when you said you had.'

'I was wrong,' Leanne said, struggling to free herself from the web of lies she had helped Claudia construct. 'If I'd heard the paramedic's description of what Claudia looked like after the fire, I would have known she couldn't be the same person Rex Russell described.'

'If you were so convinced Claudia was lying, why go

ahead with the reunion?' Mal challenged. 'I'll tell you why. There was a little voice inside your head telling you that you might be wrong. Victims of trauma make unreliable witnesses. One of yours had seen hundreds of people that night, and I doubt very much that she could recall the detail of Claudia's injuries as well as she claimed. And as for the other, Rex has said all along that he can remember very little. Did you try speaking to him again?'

'Yes.'

'And?'

Rex had apologised for feeding Leanne the wrong information, having been there at the service to hear the paramedic's speech. 'He doesn't want to go against the swell of public opinion. The blood could have been Amelia's. The torn fingernails could have been false.'

'Then why are we still having this debate?'

'Have you looked at Frankie's video yet?'

'Yes.'

'And?'

'Amelia suffered head injuries. Her recollection was never going to match Claudia's, and especially twelve months on.'

'Except it was Amelia who remembered the torch quite clearly,' said Leanne. 'And it wasn't a detail that had simply slipped Claudia's mind. She didn't have a clue what Amelia was talking about. You don't confuse an usher's full-size torch with one you can fit on a key ring, especially when it's something you supposedly own.'

'Claudia thought she was pulling a dying child out of the rubble and she went on to suffer a miscarriage. Memories can be repressed, and besides, the two of them seemed quite clear about what Claudia had said to her that night.'

'You've just said we can't rely on the memory of someone with a head injury. Amelia is open to suggestion, and Claudia quoted things that I'd expect anyone would say in that situation.'

'Sorry, Leanne, but I'm not convinced. You never wanted Claudia to be our hero. You've been against her from the start,' Mal said. He drained his glass. 'You've been blinded by your personal feelings and, to be blunt, I don't trust your judgement.'

'What about mine?' asked Frankie, finally able to get a word in between the warring factions. 'I've spent the last month or so speaking to genuine victims. You say the town found a hero, well read your own paper, Mal. There were plenty of heroes that night. People who were caught up in circumstances they hadn't been prepared for and who lost their lives while saving others. The seventy-one-year-old who pushed a child away from certain death, the man who lifted children over his head before the crush squeezed the last drop of life from him, not to mention the firefighters who went in and saved more lives. I'm sorry, but it doesn't feel right including Claudia in that list.'

'Why not?'

'For the same reason as Leanne. It's a gut feeling.'

'I'm not pulling the story based on a gut feeling,' Mal said. 'We launched the search for Amelia's rescuer and the only person to come forward was Claudia. Quite frankly, I don't care if she is or isn't the person who actually saved the girl. The only alternative is that the real hero is amongst the dead, and she's not exactly going to come back from the grave to dispute Claudia's claim now, is she?' His cheeks glowed with the effects of alcohol and frustration.

'So that's it? We let Claudia get away with this?'

Mal sank into his chair. 'You have to move on at some point, Leanne.'

'And I will,' she said, putting down her drink. 'But I'll be the one to decide when that should be.'

'No,' Mal said. 'You've worked hard on this, but I was wrong to let you become so involved. You need to take some time out.'

'I'm fine,' she hissed.

'No, you're not, and this isn't a request,' Mal said softly. 'You haven't taken any leave for months. I want you to go home to your family, and let someone look after you for a while. I don't want to see you back here until you're able to see things rationally.'

15

The inner sanctum of the spa was warm and humid, the lights dim, and the air filled with the sound of distant waterfall and birdsong. Claudia was being transported to another world, although it would be more accurate to say she had finally arrived, and in her home town no less. The journey had been arduous, but she couldn't have been happier as she settled against the undulating curves of the day lounger.

Her fluffy white robe slipped off her shoulder, revealing recently buffed skin that smelled of neroli and orange blossom. Or was it ylang-ylang and sweet geranium? Claudia didn't care. The therapist had tailored her treatment to promote her well-being based on her current needs. They had gone through a detailed assessment upon arrival, and Claudia wished she could have bottled the expression on the therapist's face when she realised Claudia was *the* Claudia Rothwell.

She was still smiling when she said, 'I could get used to this.'

'If anyone deserves it, you do,' Bryony told her.

Her friend was sprawled out on the lounger next to her,

but this wasn't such a novelty for Bryony. As a regular, she was on first-name terms with the staff at the Three Pheasants spa, but she was enjoying Claudia's reaction.

'Stop, or you'll make me cry,' Claudia said, wafting a hand in front of her face as tears pricked her eyes.

In the last few days, she had been overwhelmed by the love directed towards her, and it had gone some way to make up for what Leanne had done to her. After reading the reporter's profile on LinkedIn, Claudia had gone to great lengths to win Leanne over, and there was no disputing that their partnership had worked to both their advantages. She felt extremely let down.

What annoyed Claudia most was that Leanne was there to witness the incredible results of their combined efforts on Wednesday night in Victoria Park, and her response had been an attempt to ruin it. Setting up the surprise reunion had been bad enough, but Leanne's parting shot had been downright cruel. What had she expected Claudia to say? 'Fine, I admit it. I lied about Amelia, but only because I knew it was what you wanted to hear!'

It had been a test of nerves waiting to read the reporter's write-up of the night, but rationally, Claudia knew she had nothing to fear. If Leanne were so convinced that Claudia was lying, why whisper it in her ear? Why go ahead with the farce of a reunion in the first place? Because she had no proof, a fact borne out by Saturday's article. The *Courier* wasn't going to kill the golden goose that kept the run-down rag in print. Claudia had the power. Leanne didn't.

It would be interesting to know what had made Leanne turn against her, but it didn't keep Claudia awake at night, nor did her conscience. For the best part of a year, she had worked hard to give the town what it needed, and that had included a hero for little Amelia. Where was the harm in that? She refused to allow Leanne to take the shine off her glory.

Picking up a tall glass from the side table, Claudia took a sip of the green slime that was apparently going to be a treat for her digestive system. It didn't seem that long ago that a McDonald's strawberry milkshake had done the same. How things had changed.

'You'll have nothing to do with yourself now,' said Bryony.

'I have a feeling the work has only just begun,' she said, aware that her greatest weapon against the naysayers would be to continue her good deeds. 'We have the administration of the hardship fund to figure out next. The money has been flooding in, and we have to find a way of getting it into the hands of the people who need it, and quickly.'

Bryony yawned. 'My dear Claudia, you have to realise that the world is divided into two kinds of people. There are the thinkers, and there are the doers. You've *done* enough, and besides, it's Sunday afternoon. We're here to relax, remember?'

'It may take more than one session.'

'Then we'll make it a regular treat. I used to come here with Phillipa all the time.'

This wasn't news to Claudia. She had heard Phillipa mention her twice-monthly rejuvenating sessions, and had made a point of asking questions, fishing for an invite that never came. It was one of the many pitiful attempts she had made to gain Phillipa's favour. To think she had been Claudia's role model once, but not any more. It wouldn't be long before they were saying, 'Phillipa who?'

'Have you spoken to her? Did you know she was coming home?'

'I had no idea,' Bryony said, her words clipped. 'I had to read it in the paper like everyone else.'

The *Courier* had broken the news of Phillipa's return and, although it was no more than a couple of lines about her surprise attendance at the memorial service, it hadn't been complimentary.

'I can't believe she sneaked into the crowd,' Claudia said. 'She was asking for trouble.'

'Oh, one shouldn't underestimate Phillipa. She might look like a shadow of her former self, but she's made of sterner stuff.'

Claudia turned her head so fast her neck hurt. There had been no recent photos to accompany Phillipa's mention in the paper. 'You've seen her?'

'She paid me a visit yesterday,' Bryony said. She sounded as if she were gloating to have received the honour. Despite everything, she still wanted to be one of Phillipa's chosen ones. 'She apologised to me for not being in touch.'

'How is she?' asked Claudia, concern etched into her features with the precision of a sculptor's chisel.

'Restless, I think.'

'So she's not planning on staying?' Claudia asked hopefully.

'She and Robert would normally wait until the boys are home from school before setting off on their winter break,' Bryony said, as if it were normal practice for a school run to span a whole term. 'But she wants to leave as soon as possible.'

Phillipa's return to exile couldn't come too soon in Claudia's opinion. She didn't relish the prospect of their paths crossing. If anyone could make Claudia feel like a fake, it was her. 'Justin thinks they'll eventually sell up and move for good.'

'He might be right. There's nothing left for her here. She likes a cause to champion, but she can't do that now that you've cornered the market.'

'You make it sound like I've ousted her. That was never my intention.'

'I'm not sure Phillipa sees it that way,' Bryony replied. She laughed. 'Don't look so worried, I'm only playing with you. If anything, Phillipa was impressed with the show you put on.'

Claudia pressed a hand to her throat. She could feel the sudden rush of blood heating up her skin. 'You talked about me?'

'Only in passing. She was more interested in that reporter, Leanne Pitman.'

'What about her?'

'She was the one who got the quote, taken out of context naturally, after Leanne pounced on her. Whatever passed between them has left Phillipa livid. She wouldn't share the details, but it was something personal, and she's determined to find out where the cow got her information. Has Leanne ever asked you for gossip to disparage Phillipa?'

'She's tried, but what can I tell her?' Claudia replied, not looking Bryony in the eye.

The spa had become unpleasantly hot. Claudia wasn't scared of Leanne, but the same couldn't be said of Phillipa. If she had known she was back in town, she would never have dropped the not-so-subtle hint about an affair when the reporter had asked about Declan Gallagher's private life.

She had thought she was being clever. It wasn't as if the rumours didn't exist, but she shouldn't have said anything. She didn't need to be Phillipa's friend any more, but neither did she want her as an enemy.

'What about you?' Claudia asked, deflecting the question. 'I saw you talking to Leanne at the press conference. Could it have been something you said?'

'Gosh, no, I don't like talking to the press at the best of times. As I recall, we were remarking on what a great job you were doing.'

When it became clear that neither of them was inclined to continue the conversation, Claudia relaxed back on her lounger. Taking mindful breaths, she told herself that Phillipa didn't know where the information had come from, and there was no reason to believe she would ever find out. Whatever Leanne's current feelings towards Claudia, it was eclipsed by her hatred of Phillipa, and the two would not be sharing notes.

'I'm sorry about your mum by the way,' Bryony said, just as Claudia felt herself dozing off. 'I hadn't realised you were only five when she died.'

'It's not something I like to talk about,' Claudia replied. She had been furious to see it mentioned in yesterday's *Courier*, having expressly told Leanne not to refer to it, but if that was the worst Leanne could do, so be it.

'I bet your father's proud of you. Do you see him much?'

'Oh, you know how it is,' Claudia said, quite certain that Bryony wouldn't have a clue.

The assumption might be that the absence of a mother meant her relationship with her dad had been stronger as a result, but for most of Claudia's childhood, she had known poverty and neglect that was beyond Bryony's comprehension. Her dad was a painter and decorator by trade, but you would never have guessed it from the state of their tiny, two-bed terrace. Money had been tight, clothes threadbare, and little Claudia had often relied on the goodwill of neighbours to feed her while her dad was at work. It wasn't a happy childhood, and when her dad had sold the family home and moved to Chester not long after Claudia had married, he hadn't given his daughter a forwarding address and she hadn't asked for one.

'I know exactly what you mean,' proclaimed Bryony. 'My parents decided to swan off and travel the world after plonking the management of the company onto me and my brother.'

Before Bryony could continue with the comparison of their family woes, Claudia's phone began to vibrate on the table next to her.

'Is that Justin checking up on you?'

Claudia could see the caller's name from where she was and waited until the phone stopped before picking it up. 'No, he'll be in front of the TV watching the Grand Prix, or else packing for his flight to New York.'

'I thought he was cutting back on his business trips?'

'He did for a while, but he can't stay at home playing nursemaid for ever.'

'And it's not as if you need it.'

'Exactly,' Claudia replied, trying not to sound deflated. It was true that she felt stronger than she had a year ago, and she didn't want to be reliant on Justin, but that wasn't the point. Every time he went away, she felt abandoned.

'Are you still trying for a baby?' Bryony asked gently. 'Is that the problem?'

Claudia pulled the thick, towelling dressing gown around her tightly. 'I'm scared that we had our one chance and I blew it.'

'Now that you have more time to relax, it might happen. These things have a way of taking you by surprise,' Bryony said. 'But it must be hard for both of you. It can't help that Sasha's pregnant.'

Sasha was Justin's first wife, and Claudia had always felt she was being measured against her, if not in Justin's eyes then in the eyes of his friends and family. When Claudia had become pregnant, something Sasha had failed to do, she had thought she had the match all sewn up. She should have known. Life for Claudia was a constant battle.

Bryony looked expectantly at the phone clasped in Claudia's hand. 'So, was the call important?'

'Absolutely not,' Claudia said. She considered making something up, but there was an important point to be made, and one that might eventually reach Phillipa's ears. 'It's Leanne Pitman. She doesn't know when to give up.'

'Is she becoming a nuisance?'

'They all are, I'm afraid,' Claudia said. 'I didn't mind getting caught up in the media circus ahead of the anniversary, but each time they've written something about me, or wheeled me onto some magazine show or other, I've felt like another piece of me has been taken. I had an invitation to go on *This Morning* and do the whole re-run of the reunion with Amelia, but I can't. I just can't.'

'You shouldn't feel guilty. You've given more than enough to the cause. This is your time, Claudia.'

'Thanks, Bryony. You're a good friend.'

Bryony's expression became clouded. 'I try to be,' she said.

'You're still worrying about Phillipa, aren't you?'

'It's hard not to. Now that the anniversary is out of the way, we're counting down to the public inquiry report. I can't imagine how difficult it must be for poor Phillipa, and I feel guilty about being here without her.'

'Me too,' Claudia said softly. 'It's a terrible world we live in, where someone can be condemned simply by association.' She left her vague observation open for interpretation. Was she talking about Phillipa and the Empress fire, or was this a warning to Bryony about old loyalties?

Bryony took a deep, cleansing breath, but her voice remained strained with anxiety when she said, 'Maybe it would be better if she sold up and moved away. It would give us all a chance to start afresh.'

Claudia slipped her phone into her pocket and felt a shudder of anticipation. A fresh start with new friends was exactly what she needed. 'I don't know about you, but my stomach's growling. How about we get dressed and have some lunch?'

'As long as we can forego the green slime,' Bryony said with a glance at their barely touched drinks. 'I could really do with a glass of bubbly.'

'I think we deserve it, don't you?'

Claudia was looking forward to an afternoon of over-indulgence, but when they returned to the changing rooms, she found an envelope taped to her locker.

'Is there a problem?' asked Bryony, hovering behind Claudia.

'Not at all,' Claudia replied, stuffing the message back in the envelope before Bryony could read it. 'There's a query over the bill for last week's press conference. I need to sort it out before I leave.'

'Good grief, can't they leave you alone?'

Claudia wiped a clammy hand against the towelling of her dressing gown. 'Apparently not.'

Claudia air-kissed her friend at the hotel reception and waited for Bryony to leave before taking the lift to the second floor. The note had requested that she go to room 215, and when she arrived, there was a housekeeping trolley parked outside and a bag of laundry propping open the door. A chambermaid was sitting on the edge of a freshly made bed clutching a dust cloth.

'Karin?' Claudia asked.

'You know who I am?'

'I've seen your photo in the paper enough times,' Claudia said, although she had already guessed the identity of the note writer by the initials used in place of a signature. She was more interested in knowing why their meeting should be so urgent or so secretive.

'Then you know who my brother was?' Karin asked, her accent not dissimilar to Declan's. She had his eyes too.

'Yes.'

Karin stood up and backed away, giving Claudia the confidence to step deeper into the room. She kicked the laundry bag out of the way and let the door close. 'What do you want, Karin?'

'To say I'm sorry,' she began. 'For everything he did. For everything he put us all through.'

Claudia's hands had been tightened into fists, but she forced them to relax. This broken woman meant no harm, unlike her brother, who had caused untold damage. 'You shouldn't blame yourself.'

'Easy for you to say. You're not the one being punished for his sins.'

Karin's lip trembled. She wanted more from Claudia than to offer an apology. 'Why have you brought me here?'

With her chin pressed to her chest, Karin said, 'I know I don't deserve it, but I need help. I was in Victoria Park the other night, and I heard what you said about how our suffering goes on. I used to be a bar manager, but I couldn't go back to work after the fire. Sure, keeping any job is a struggle.'

Claudia watched as Karin twisted the dust cloth in her hands. 'From what I've read, you were injured quite badly. You must have been traumatised by what you went through.'

'I was on life support for a while, and needed physio when I came out of the coma, but I'm good now. It's not the physical stuff that keeps me from work, it's people. Once they realise who I am, they look like they might spit in my face. Actually, someone did.'

'That's so unfair.'

'No, what's unfair is seeing my partner, Beth, suffer. Unlike me, she didn't lose her memory. It was hours before she found out I'd been pulled out alive, and weeks before she knew I was going to make it. If anyone should have the nightmares, it should be her.'

'But it's you?'

Karin stared off into space. 'When I wake up, my heart is thumping in my chest, but I don't know why. Well, obviously, I do. I'm reliving what happened or, more likely, I'm making it up. The doctors say my memory has gone for good, and the snatches of dreams I do remember don't make sense.'

201

Claudia remained silent, letting Karin speak. She had spoken to enough survivors to know that listening was the best way to encourage them to open up.

'I'm looking for Declan in my dreams, but I swear, I didn't know he was there. I know from my phone log that he tried calling, but Beth had my phone in her bag. I guess he saw the fire from his flat and came running.'

'He died trying to save you.'

'But people say such awful things about him.' Karin wiped her nose with the twisted cloth. 'I'm scared they're right. I don't know how I'll cope if it's proven he was responsible.'

'No one's suggesting it was deliberate.'

'Am I supposed to feel better knowing it was his incompetence that killed eleven people?' Her hand dropped, she looked aghast. 'And your baby too. Beth said it was in the papers.'

'It's OK.'

'I wish everyone was as nice as you.'

'You're a victim too, Karin. You can't lose sight of that. What support have you had so far?'

'A bit of counselling. They only gave me twelve sessions, but then my counsellor left for another job halfway through. I didn't want to start again with someone else, but I'm fine, I don't need it.'

Karin was looking at the floor. She needed something and she thought she could get it from Claudia. That was why she had left the note.

'What can I do to help?'

'Beth applied for an emergency grant a while back, but it wasn't enough. I couldn't claim benefits because I was declared fit for work long before I could face looking for a new job. Beth's done her best, this isn't her fault, but we've ended up with huge debts, and that's not including the money we've borrowed from family. I swear, we're trying to get ourselves straight.'

'How much do you need?'

'Over a thousand if we're to stop the landlord evicting us, but anything would help,' she said. Her head remained lowered, shame weighing her down. 'If it was just me, I'd accept whatever happens, but you know, I have to think of Beth. I hate what this is doing to her. She was ambushed by a reporter the other week and she was ready to sell her story. I could do the same, I've had all kinds of silly offers, but I refuse to make money that way. It's hard enough asking you.'

Claudia took a business card from her bag and handed it to Karin. The hardship fund wouldn't be in a position to accept applications for weeks, but Claudia wasn't going to let bureaucracy get in the way. She would use her own money if necessary. 'Send me an email with your account details and I'll arrange an urgent payment. It might not be everything you need, but it'll be a start.'

Karin took the card in her shaking hand. 'I don't know what to say.'

'My advice would be to say nothing,' Claudia said. 'Especially to the press.'

'I won't. And thank you.'

'It's my pleasure,' Claudia said. She was tempted to offer a hug, but she thought Karin might break.

It was cruel how the press were hounding her, and they would bleed her dry if they could. Wasn't that what Leanne had done to Claudia? She hadn't gone to the press looking to share her personal experience. Leanne had coerced her into making a confession she hadn't wanted to make. The press didn't play by the book, so why should they?

Claudia was about to leave, but her steps faltered. Her recent conversation with Bryony had unnerved her. She didn't want to take the blame for spreading the rumours about Phillipa. She needed someone to muddy the waters, and who better than Declan's sister?

'Can I ask you something?' she began. 'What do you know about your brother's private life?'

'That it was private,' Karin said. She pushed Claudia's business card into the pocket of her tabard. 'Why?'

'I don't mean to pry, it's just that, I don't know if you've heard, but there's a rumour being circulated about an affair.'

'With who?' Karin demanded.

Claudia paused to give Karin warning that she wasn't going to like this. 'The press are saying he was involved with Phillipa Montgomery.'

'That's rubbish!'

'Is it? Did he ever mention her?'

'Of course he did. He talked about her all the time. I guess he liked her, but she's married.'

Claudia tilted her head, waiting for Karin to consider the possibility.

'Maybe they were involved, I don't know,' Karin said, refusing to meet Claudia's gaze. 'But Christ, haven't the press got better things to do? What does it matter? He's dead.' The reminder caused her to gasp. Whatever anger Karin felt towards her brother hadn't stopped her from loving him, and it was painful to watch.

'It matters to Phillipa,' said Claudia.

'Phillipa? Why should I care about protecting her? She didn't protect Declan, did she?'

Claudia didn't have an answer to that, nor did she need one. All she had to do was hold her nerve. In a few short weeks, the findings would be published and, whatever the outcome, Phillipa wasn't going to come back from this. Claudia would be free to start her new life with a clean slate, which was all she had ever wanted.

16

Sitting cross-legged on the futon with her laptop resting on a cushion, Leanne closed her eyes and listened to the gentle lap of water hitting the sides of the boat. She was entering her third week of enforced leave and was getting nowhere fast. She hadn't been ashore for days, and spent most of her time surfing the internet. Today's session had drawn another blank, and there wasn't a YouTube video, witness account, or committee report left that she hadn't dissected and devoured.

When she slammed her laptop shut, a chorus of quacks rose up nearby. The resident family of ducks had wrongly assumed that the noise heralded an appearance on deck, but the container of oats and seeds that Lois had kept to feed her feathered friends was empty, and had been for some time.

Rearranging her work environment without getting up, Leanne shoved her laptop between a cereal bowl plastered with the dried-up remnants of breakfast, and a buttery plate from last night's supper. From beneath some clean, or possibly dirty laundry, she retrieved a file that had grown at the same rate as her frustration. It contained a typed transcript of the exchange between Claudia and Amelia on the night of the anniversary, and the notes that Leanne had put together from all her other interviews, including the most recent ones.

Leanne had managed to track down the paramedic, but she had nothing new to add. Apparently, her speech had been vetted by Justin, and everything else would remain confidential. Reading between the lines, there was nothing more anyway.

Rex Russell, meanwhile, was happy to talk to Leanne, but it had reached the point where, if someone wanted to suggest that Amelia's rescuer had been walking around in a Donald Duck outfit, he would happily agree. As leads went, it was a dead end.

Leafing through her accumulated evidence, she picked up a child's drawing of a torch. It was the sketch Amelia had promised her, but it lacked any real detail, even for a ten-year-old. The schoolgirl could remember the light, but distinctly less about the item that had produced it, and her depiction was based almost entirely on its shape and touch as she clenched it in her fist. It wasn't much, but it was all Leanne had.

Two things struck her about the torch. Firstly, there was no doubt that it was small enough for Amelia to hold in her palm, so it couldn't be the kind used by ushers, and Leanne had already spoken to an ex member of staff to confirm this. The second thing was that there were at least two keys also attached to the key ring, according to Amelia's drawing. If they were house keys, it would explain why the woman who rescued Amelia had made sure to get the key ring back, and it would also indicate that it was an item in daily use. It wasn't something half-forgotten at the bottom of a designer handbag. It didn't sound like it should be forgotten at all.

After staring at Amelia's drawing until her eyes stung, Leanne closed the file. One notable omission from her investigation was a follow-up response from Claudia. She was ignoring Leanne's calls and, although Leanne had considered camping outside the Rothwells' security gates, she was unsure what would be gained from it. The opportunity to catch Claudia out had been missed. Leanne should have delayed the reunion until she had set her trap properly, but deep down she hadn't wanted to believe that Claudia had fooled her. She had fallen for the reluctant hero act, along with everyone else.

At least Claudia knew now that not everything she said was being believed, but was it too late to prove she was a fraud?

With a groan, Leanne let the file slide off her lap and onto the mound of scrunched-up clothes. Averting her eyes from the mess, the clutter, and the unfinished painting on the back of the cabin doors, she uncurled her legs and stood up. The circulation was returning to her tingling toes when she heard a tap on the window behind her. She turned to see a pair of legs standing on the jetty. The man wore brown brogues and green corduroy trousers, which immediately excluded Joe. She wondered if it might be a fellow boater, but there was only one person in her life who dressed like a seventies schoolteacher.

'Shit,' she muttered. 'Oh, shit.'

Leanne scooped up the discarded clothes and shoved them under the futon, which was already crammed with stacks of paperwork and other rubbish she kept out of sight. She heard the awning being unzipped and, a moment later, the boat rocked as it adjusted to the weight of a heavyset man. Mal was on board, waiting by the hatch to gain entry. Or at least she hoped he was waiting. The cabin doors weren't locked.

'I won't be a minute!' she shouted as she picked up her bowl, two plates, and a selection of mugs that had been growing mould. She stacked them on the draining board on top of other dirty dishes before covering the mountain of shame with a tea towel.

Leanne cast a glance around the boat. Hopefully her editor wouldn't ask to use the bathroom, which was full of rubbish bags she had been planning to take to the marina's disposal point at some point today, possibly. It was mostly empty pizza boxes and wine bottles. She grabbed a can of air freshener and sprayed generously before attending to her guest. It was only as she was opening the doors that she realised she was still in her pyjamas, and stained ones at that. She raked her fingers through her unwashed hair.

'How did you get into the marina?'

'Morning to you too,' Mal said as he climbed down the short set of steps into the boat. Balanced in one hand were two coffee cups with the Raven Brook logo stamped on the front. 'These are courtesy of Dianne.'

Leanne took a proffered cup, but kept her scowl. 'I'm surprised she let you through.'

Mal patted the pocket of his waterproof jacket. 'Press pass. I told her you were expecting me.'

'I wasn't. You never come here,' she said. She remained standing. 'Why *are* you here, Mal?'

Her editor unzipped his jacket. 'Phew, it's warm in here. That log burner kicks out some heat.'

Mal looked at the aforementioned log burner as if it were the most fascinating piece of archaic technology he had ever seen. It gave Leanne the chance to catch up with her thoughts. Mal never made house calls, which meant it had to be bad news and, even though that was something the *Courier* thrived upon, this was going to be personal. She briefly considered if he was about to turn her sabbatical into a permanent arrangement, but Leanne's anniversary articles had paid dividends for the paper. That couldn't be it. She shuddered despite the heat that enthralled Mal. The fire.

'It's the public inquiry, isn't it? You've seen the findings.'

The lines around Mal's eyes deepened, then softened. 'Why don't we sit down?'

'Tell me,' she said, but in that moment, she knew. Not trusting herself to hold hot liquid, she placed her coffee cup on a shelf. 'Phillipa's got away with it, hasn't she? I told you they'd cover it up! I knew it! I fucking knew it!'

Mal set down his cup too. He went to put an arm on Leanne's shoulder, but she shrugged him off. Her cheeks burned, her eyes blazed, and any tears that threatened were eviscerated by her anger. She would not cry.

'The report is embargoed until tomorrow, but yes, I've seen it,' Mal said. 'Leanne, it's not a whitewash. There is the possibility of legal action against some, but—'

'But not Phillipa.'

'There will be lessons learnt.'

'Lessons?' she mocked. 'How does that help any of the families who lost the people they love?'

'There's no evidence that the restoration work was below standard. All the building regulations were met, the correct materials were used, in fact there's some praise for the levels of fire retardancy that delayed the spread of the fire on the lower levels. It was an electrical fault in a control panel. The initial fire burnt out quickly, but sparks had travelled into the roof space where it was contained long enough to spread without being detected. By the time the alarm sounded, it was already out of control.'

Leanne had turned away with her hands over her ears, but Mal carried on.

'It was a freak combination of failures that, on their own, would have caused minimal damage, but combined together, it was . . . Well, we know what it was.'

'It was the end of the world,' she said, her voice failing her.

'The control panel was made in Lithuania, and the manufacturers have issued a recall. There may be a case for corporate manslaughter if it can be proven that they knew the fault existed before the fire, and that's something that will be actively pursued. Justice might not look like we imagined, but it will come.'

'And what happens to Phillipa?' Leanne asked, twisting around to face him. 'Does she get a slap on the wrist?'

'Not even that.'

'But she opened the theatre before the restoration was complete.'

'The completion works in the function rooms were purely cosmetic and were only being carried out when the theatre wasn't in use. All the health and safety measures were in place, every box was ticked.'

'We can all tick boxes, Mal. It doesn't mean a job's been carried out competently,' she said. 'And what about the bad wiring? It must have contributed to the fire.'

'There was no bad wiring. The building contractor has been exonerated. Declan Gallagher has been exonerated.'

'But the alarms didn't go off—'

'The smoke was in the roof, above the sensors. Again, that's something the investigators have picked up in their recommendations. And there's some criticism too of the response from the fire brigade.'

'Of course there is,' Leanne sneered. 'Let's blame the men and women who risked their lives that day. Let's point the finger at them so we're not looking at the politicians who cut the budgets and decided that what Sedgefield needed was some swanky bistro with a fireman's pole rather than an actual fire station.' She stopped to suck air into her lungs in one gulp. 'And let's not upset the people who cared more about the aesthetics of the town than the well-being of its citizens.'

'Leanne,' Mal said, far too gently.

'Stop!' she replied, backing away. 'Don't be nice to me.'

'Let's sit down.'

Tremors rocked Leanne's body. 'People died,' she reminded him. 'Innocent people who would have been terrified at the end. They knew they were trapped. They couldn't breathe, and they knew they were going to die. What must that have felt like, Mal?' The answer came not with words, but with the tightening of her chest and a constriction in her throat. 'Do you think maybe, just maybe, they thought about us in their last moments? Did they wonder how we'd carry on? At the very least, they would have expected us to make the bastards pay for what they did!'

'They would have thought about their loved ones,' Mal agreed. He took a step closer. 'Lois would have thought about her best friend, and how she was going to cope without her.'

'Don't,' Leanne begged, her words coming out as a gasp.

'She would want you to search for the truth, whatever that looked like,' Mal said. 'I don't think she'd want revenge for its own sake, but then again, I never knew her. You did. What would she want, Leanne?'

Leanne's eyes darted around the home she had once shared with her best friend. She had bought the boat, but it was Lois who had made it their home. And even though Lois was planning to move in with Joe, she had considered Leanne in her plans. She had promised faithfully that she wouldn't leave until everything was shipshape. She wasn't going to suddenly disappear.

Leanne's heart clenched. She was dead. Lois was dead, and if it wasn't Phillipa's fault, who could she blame? Joe? Herself? Unable to go there, Leanne let out a cry that became muffled as Mal pulled her into a bear hug.

'What would Lois want?' he repeated.

Leanne's legs wobbled from the sheer energy it took not to let the tears flow. Now was not the time. She dropped onto the futon and Mal sat down next to her. She took a breath and puffed out her cheeks as she released the air slowly, bringing her heart rate down so it wasn't thumping so hard against her ribcage. 'She'd want me to stop torturing myself. She'd expect me to find a happy ending,' she said, glancing at the unfinished painting of the slippery, golden fish that her friend would never complete.

'Happy endings are for fairy tales.'

'That was Lois,' Leanne said, attempting a smile.

Mal stretched the muscles in his neck. She could imagine he'd been dreading this conversation, but Leanne appreciated his efforts to come and tell her personally.

'I'm going to send you the report,' he said. 'Read it with an open mind. You won't be the only one who's going to find it difficult, and our job is to guide our readers towards acceptance.'

'You want me to write it up?'

The only article Leanne wanted to publish had been written months ago. It hadn't been what Mal had wanted then, and he certainly wouldn't accept it now, but that didn't matter to Leanne. Despite the new narrative, Phillipa Montgomery was culpable of something, even if it was only conceit and snobbery. She had run away to her little chateau in the Dordogne or wherever it was, and her behaviour reeked of guilt. Leanne had seen it in her eyes on the night of the anniversary. It was like looking in a mirror.

'I've asked Frankie to put something together,' Mal said, interrupting her thoughts. 'I know you're still on leave, but this might be the time to write that final article on the Empress fire. You can connect with our readers in a way that no one else at the *Courier* can. This is your town, Leanne. Lois was your friend. You're looking for resolution just like everyone else in Sedgefield.'

'I won't do it. No, definitely not.'

'Grief has a way of eating you from the inside if you let it,' Mal warned. 'One day, you wake up and you see someone you don't recognise.' His gaze had a glassy quality as if he were looking directly into the past. 'I don't want that to happen to you.'

Leanne hadn't known Mal when he lost his wife, Jill, six years ago, but she had seen photos of him before his beer gut and frayed edges. According to Frankie, the couple had been saving up for a retirement cottage in the Lake District.

214

He had never talked about retirement in all the time that Leanne had been at the *Courier*.

'I accept what you're saying,' she replied, 'but I'm not there yet, and I won't be the only one in Sedgefield who feels like that. Some wounds won't heal while there are questions to be answered.'

'It could be years before families get their day in court, and the defendants aren't going to be the ones you'd imagined taking the stand. It's time to stop this witch-hunt.'

Shuffling back against the futon to create distance from the advice her editor was giving, Leanne's hand touched the file she had been working on earlier. She explored it with her fingers as if feeling for the pulse of a dead animal. What would Claudia make of the findings? Would she act as the town's spokesperson, while Leanne was left choking on her words?

'Even if I could accept the findings, I can't close my eyes to every injustice. If anything, it makes me more determined to seek them out,' she said, searching for a new course for her anger to surge towards. 'You said the other week that you didn't care if Claudia had saved Amelia or not, but are you sure you can live with that? Because I can't.'

'I spoke out of turn. I do care, of course I do, but my main concern at this moment in time is you.'

'Then let me do this. I need to know for sure that the person we've been applauding is a hero and not some glory-seeker. These people can't hide behind their good causes and expect us not to notice when they're taking us for idiots. Claudia didn't save Amelia, and I'm going to prove it, with or without your blessing.'

'I don't know. This can't be good for you.'

'No, Mal. Stuck here with nothing to do but stew is no good for me.'

'You were supposed to go home to your family and recharge your batteries.'

'Oh, they're recharged,' warned Leanne with a glint in her eye. 'And if you're not interested in this story then you'd better hope that I don't find my proof, because it could be a national paper grabbing the headline, not the *Courier*.'

Mal closed his eyes and tipped back his head.

'I'm doing this for Lois,' she said. 'Heroes might exist, but they're few and far between. We can't all be saved, and we shouldn't be worshipping false gods.'

Straightening up, Mal reached for his coffee. 'I think I need something stronger,' he said after taking a sip. He sighed. His body deflated. 'If I say yes, it doesn't mean it's going to be top priority, and you have to promise that when it comes to nothing, you'll draw a line under it and move on.'

'Agreed,' she said without hesitation. It wouldn't come to nothing. The truth was waiting to be uncovered.

The Empress Theatre
Sedgefield, Cheshire

When Declan Gallagher hurried out of his flat and towards the theatre, he thought it would be a simple matter of resetting the alarm. They would need clearance from the fire officer, but it was only eight o'clock. There was plenty of time to get the audience back in and restart the show. He didn't need to be there, but he would be interested to know what had triggered the sensors so he could add it to the snagging list. The theatre had to be perfect when the project was signed off. Phillipa Montgomery was one of the few people who still believed in him, and he wanted this for her.

It was as Declan drew closer that the smell of smoke stopped him in his tracks. A moment later, the ground shook. 'Sweet Jesus,' he said.

In less than a minute, he had reached the theatre and couldn't believe what he saw. Flames licked at exposed rafters in the roof, but Declan was more interested in what was happening at ground level. There were people flooding out, many of them families with children, but nowhere near enough for what equated to a sell-out show. There were people still inside.

A terrible thought struck him. What if this was his fault? Had he taken his eye off the ball? Had he been distracted by love? He couldn't think about that now. He had to make sure everyone was safe, including his sister. He knew what Karin was like. She would take her time no matter what the emergency. He was always telling her she would be late to her own funeral.

Declan made the mistake of attempting to get in through the front entrance and lost precious time caught up in the confusion inside the foyer. There was no sign of Karin, and no way he could get into the auditorium; people were climbing over each other to get through the exits, and the sweeping stairwell to the VIP area had been blocked off by a collapse. There were so many in need of help and only so much Declan could do. He scooped up one of two children a mother was trying to protect, and helped them outside.

After he had re-emerged onto the street, Declan tried a different tack and slipped down the alleyway. It was calmer here, which made it impossible to ignore the sobs of a little boy coming out through the fire doors. He was covered in dust and his wails chilled Declan to the bone.

'Someone has to help Mrs Clarke! She's trapped upstairs!'

Declan's worst fears were being realised. Whatever the cause of the fire, not everyone was going to make it to safety. Whether it was a member of his family or someone else's, he would never forgive himself if a single person died.

And while Declan was forcing his way inside, Karin Gallagher was very much concentrating on staying alive. It was a small miracle that she had escaped the crowd clogging up the main exit, and when Beth had yelled, 'We have to go! Now!' Karin hadn't hesitated.

They had almost made it too, but she hadn't been expecting to hear someone call her name.

'Karin!' Declan screamed. 'Karin, are you there?'

She stopped in her tracks and looked up. Thick smoke churned in the roof space; dust and more smoke swirled on the ground; but in the space between, she could see clearly enough. A front section of the circle had been destroyed, but where the balcony remained intact, there was Declan. She waved to him, but he was already turning away.

Karin opened her mouth to call to him, but someone thumped into her back. She was blocking the aisle and was forced into one of the rows to let people past. 'Declan!' she called out, but it was too late. Her brother was gone.

When she looked back towards the side exit, Beth had disappeared too. She had made it out to safety and Karin ought to follow, but how could she leave now that she knew Declan was looking for her?

17

Claudia wasn't sure how she was meant to react to this latest turn of events. Should she pretend to be relieved that no one close to home was going to be held to account for the fire?

'Do you think Phillipa and Robert will want to spend more time in Sedgefield now?'

Justin didn't look up from the newspaper spread out on the breakfast table. He had been reading out snippets of the *Courier*'s take on the public inquiry to Claudia, pausing now and again to agree with its sentiment. The investigation appeared to be fair in his view, even if the findings weren't necessarily what had been expected.

'Judging by her statement, I can't imagine they've changed their minds.'

'Phillipa's issued a statement? What does it say?' Claudia wanted to grab the paper off him. She didn't need someone serving up the news in bite-size chunks. She was perfectly capable of reading it herself.

'Basically, it says that although her name had been cleared, her conscience hasn't. "I feel personally responsible for the twelve victims and will do so until my dying day. I welcome

221

the report and hope that it will help families find closure, but it brings me no comfort." Quite an admission.'

'That won't do anything to mend her reputation.'

Something in her tone made Justin look up. A touch of glee?

'It's a real shame,' Claudia added, for clarity.

And it was a shame in some respects. When Justin had first introduced Claudia to Phillipa, she had been awe-struck. Phillipa had a presence. People looked up to her and followed her lead. If she considered you someone to be noticed, you were noticed by everyone, or else you were ignored. Claudia's phone number had never been high up on anyone's list, but that was then. Her phone hadn't stopped ringing in the last couple of months. Was it so wrong of Claudia not to want to be pushed back into obscurity?

'No response yet from Declan Gallagher's family,' Justin continued, 'but I imagine they'll be relieved. It must have been truly awful having to deal with the speculation and not have him there to defend himself. We need to make sure they know our charity is there to support them too.'

My charity, Claudia wanted to remind him, and she was already looking after Declan's family thank you very much. The hardship fund would be launched very soon, but Karin had given Claudia the impression she couldn't wait. Claudia had transferred money from her personal account. Not all of her secrets were bad.

'We'll do all we can,' she agreed.

Appearing satisfied, Justin resumed reading the newspaper, leaving his wife to fret. She had just reached the point where she had stopped waiting for Leanne to make her move, and now she had to worry about Phillipa's potential resurgence.

Claudia tried not to huff as she picked up her mobile and slipped into the sitting room to make a call. If Justin couldn't give her the reassurance she needed, she would try someone else.

Bryony must have heard the news by now, but when Claudia tried to call her, she didn't answer. Was she too busy stalking Phillipa? There would inevitably be a long line of Sedgefield's finest offering to build bridges and, knowing Bryony, she would push her way to the front of the queue. How long would it take for her to entice Phillipa back to the spa, just like the old times? Would she offer insider knowledge on Claudia as a bargaining chip? Would they laugh at her attempts to dethrone the queen of good causes?

Claudia told herself she was being paranoid. Whatever Phillipa and her minion were up to, it didn't change the fact that Claudia remained in a position of power. The outcome of the public inquiry hadn't changed that. Or had it?

18

Leanne was sitting on a leather chesterfield sofa in a quiet corner of the Bridgewater Inn, which wasn't going to be quiet for long. It was Saturday evening and the place would be rammed in a couple of hours. She checked her watch. There was plenty of time to numb the pain, and she looked forward to self-medicating on several gin and tonics.

When Frankie returned from the bar, Leanne took one of the fish-bowl glasses. The chesterfield cushions creaked and ice cubes clinked as Frankie sat down next to her. Her friend tucked her legs beneath her and rested an arm on the back of the sofa so the two reporters were mirroring each other. Leanne would be returning to work on Monday, and this was her gentle reintroduction to the workplace.

'Is this where you used to come with Lois?' Frankie asked.

Hearing her friend's name spoken out loud in the place where it had once been yelled across the room, whispered conspiratorially, and even sung on occasions, made Leanne's heart bleed, and yet she smiled. 'We came here more times than I care to remember, or should I say, more times than I can actually remember,' she said. 'Oh, Frankie, I miss her so much. She should be here.'

Frankie sipped her drink, leaving her friend to fill the silence. Leanne should know better than to fall for the trick she often used herself.

'Someone should have looked after her. Joe was right there and he did nothing. How come he got out and she didn't?'

'Joe was pinned in too,' Frankie said. 'They were packed so tight that his arms were trapped at his sides. He watched her die, Leanne, and he thought he was going to die too. When I interviewed him, he told me he wished he had. He loved her.'

'He didn't know her. They'd been going out for less than a year.'

'He loved her, and so did you,' Frankie said softly, choosing not to remind her that Lois and Joe had been about to move in together. It was a mere detail. 'You should speak to him.'

'I'm not sure there's anything we could say that would make either of us feel better.' Leanne checked her watch again. If she stayed long enough, there was every possibility she would find out one way or the other. This had been Joe's favourite watering hole too.

'I'm worried about you,' Frankie said. 'Joe wasn't to blame for Lois's death. And neither was Phillipa.'

Ice cubes knocked against Leanne's teeth as she gulped her gin. She had gone over the report line by line, and she had read Frankie's article. She couldn't fault a word of it. One by one, the people she had held accountable for her friend's death had been vindicated. There was only one person she could never forgive. And it wasn't Joe.

'If I had been there . . .' Leanne started. She felt her cheeks

225

burn with anger. She should have been there. That was the problem. Claudia wasn't the only one capable of lying.

'If you had been inside the Empress, you would have been one of the victims, or one of the survivors,' Frankie said.

'Neither a hero, nor a villain,' Leanne mused, wishing it were true. She had a villainous streak.

'I wish you'd consider talking to someone, like a counsellor.' Frankie played with the stem of her glass. 'Mal said he'll pay if you need to go private.'

'Did he now?' Leanne replied, not liking the idea that the state of her mental health had been a topic of discussion between her colleagues.

'If not a counsellor, talk to someone else. Lois's parents have said they miss you.'

'No,' Leanne said before Frankie had even finished. 'I'm sick of talking about the fire. Let's talk about something else. What about Declan Gallagher?'

Frankie gave her a wry look. 'Yeah, that's a change of subject.'

Leanne pursed her lips and waited for Frankie to continue.

'Fine,' Frankie conceded, 'but I'd say Declan is becoming less of a mystery, wouldn't you? He definitely wasn't working inside the theatre before the fire started.'

'I know,' Leanne said. When the findings had been published, CCTV footage was released showing Declan running down the high street towards the theatre soon after the alarm had sounded. 'But Mrs Brody was right. He had been upstairs.'

'At least now we know why the coroner waited for the investigation to be completed. He was the only victim to have sustained injuries from a fall.'

Leanne shuddered. It was the word Frankie had used to

describe Declan. A victim. She wasn't sure she could get used to it.

'He must have been trapped,' Frankie continued. 'The stairwell leading to the foyer had been sealed off by the first ceiling collapse and later on the remaining exit became blocked by a second. He would have seen the balcony as his only means of escape.'

'Hardly an escape. He fell to his death,' Leanne said, forced to reimagine Declan's last moments. 'Chances are Karin saw him, and that's why she was found so close to his body.'

'It would explain why she's blanked out the memory.'

'The stuff of nightmares,' Leanne said, recalling something Karin's partner had said. 'I'm glad Beth stopped me from confronting her. I can be such a horrible person at times.'

'You're bloody-minded, I'll give you that, but that's what it takes to be a good journalist. I'm too soft.'

'You're better than I am.'

Frankie looked at Leanne over the rim of her gin glass. 'You need to give yourself more credit. And you also need to think about what you want to do with the rest of your life. You can't stay at the *Courier* for ever. It's only a matter of time before it closes down for good, despite the late rally in circulation figures.'

'It's not finished yet.'

'Mal said you think there's one more story to write. Are you sure it's a good idea to go after Claudia?'

'Answer me truthfully, do you think my judgement is compromised? Am I so angry with the world that I'm seeing villains where I should see heroes? Do you think she's lying about Amelia?'

'I agree wholeheartedly that Claudia isn't all she appears to be, but unless you can find incontrovertible evidence, you'll have a hard job disproving her claims.'

'I'll get the evidence.'

'If you have to pursue this, please make sure you're doing it for the right reasons.'

'I am. I'm doing it for the twelve victims,' Leanne said, for the first time counting Declan amongst the innocent lives lost. 'And I'm doing it for the person who *did* save Amelia. I still think Angela Morris and Lena Kowalski are possible candidates.'

'Not one person we've spoken to has been able to connect either of them to Amelia, or given us a reason to discount Claudia.'

'But we haven't interviewed *everyone*. If I can find out who was sitting where, I can target witnesses. I'm not expecting one person to have the whole picture, otherwise they would have come forward by now, but even the tiniest fragment might lead to something bigger. I'm not giving up.'

'And how do you propose to identify who was sitting where?'

'The investigator's report had a seating plan.'

'An incomplete one. They were only interested in the movements of the victims. How are you going to fill in the gaps?'

Leanne drained her glass. 'Ready for another one?'

Frankie scowled. 'What?'

'If the investigators were able to obtain the information, maybe I could use the same source.'

'The theatre company?' asked Frankie. She didn't like the way Leanne kept her poker face. 'Please don't say you're going to approach Phillipa Montgomery.'

'Now that's an idea,' replied Leanne, as if the thought had never struck her before. 'I'm sure she'll be more than happy to help now that she knows we're not gunning for her.'

'Need I remind you that last time you spoke to her, you accused her of having an affair with Declan? She won't talk to anyone from the *Courier*. I've already tried. I was surprised we managed to get any kind of statement from her at all.'

Leanne had been surprised too. Phillipa's official response to the findings had been surprisingly meek. It was as if she were intent on self-flagellation now that the press and the prosecutors had no appetite to punish her.

'She might talk to me,' Leanne said.

'Because?'

'Because I'm bloody-minded,' Leanne said, playfully. 'Now do you want another drink? I don't know about you, but I'm here for the duration.'

By the time Frankie left to catch the last train, the low table in front of the chesterfield had acquired an impressive collection of empty glasses and crisp packets, the latter bought to soak up the alcohol because Leanne had been trained well. Lois always made sure they didn't drink on empty stomachs.

Lois Granger had been the kind of person who insisted her fellow students couldn't party until their essays had been handed in. She was the one who kept a ten-pound note in her shoe for a taxi at the end of the night, and she was the one who made sure Leanne drank a glass of water before she went to bed. Even Leanne's ex, whom she had lived with for three years, hadn't looked after her the way Lois had.

Her dead friend continued to influence Leanne's life decisions and, in the last few days, she had wondered what Lois would want her to do next. It kept coming back to Joe. It was why she had ordered another gin instead of leaving with Frankie. She had been expecting to see his face in the crowd all evening, but the pub was as busy as it was going to get. She had no idea what he did these days, or who with. She checked her watch. She should go home. At least she had tried. Except Lois would have expected her to try harder.

When Leanne took out her phone, it took a second to focus on the icons. She was more drunk than she realised, which helped with the next decision. She sent Joe a message to let him know where she was and that she would be there for the next fifteen minutes. She didn't bother unblocking his number, so if he replied, she wouldn't know.

It wasn't long before Leanne's glass was empty. She dug out the slice of cucumber, a valuable source of Vitamin C according to Lois, and, as she nibbled on it, she detected movement in her peripheral vision. She didn't turn towards the figure in dark jeans and a loud shirt, but felt the cushions dip next to her.

'Hello there you,' he whispered in her ear. 'I don't like seeing you looking so sad. Where's that smile?'

Leanne swayed ever so slightly as she turned to fix her gaze on the wide grin assaulting her. Anger bubbled up from the pit of her stomach. 'I don't know who you are, but you can fuck off right now,' she hissed.

'I was only trying to be friendly,' the stranger said. He looked shocked, despite being the kind of bloke who must surely be used to this type of rebuff. 'You know that saying about girls looking gorgeous when they're angry. That isn't you.'

Another figure appeared in Leanne's wobbling vision. 'Everything all right here?'

Joe was standing next to the table and had left enough room for Leanne's uninvited guest to make a withdrawal, but it was Leanne who had had enough. 'I'm leaving,' she said, standing up and kicking the legs of the stranger out of the way so she could join Joe.

Without saying a word to each other, they weaved through the crowd, Leanne leading the way with fierce determination. The damp air outside provided a cold shock, and she thought she might be sick, but after a couple of deep breaths, she convinced herself she had sobered up enough to face Joe. She turned to find him half bent over, with his hands on his knees.

'Are you OK?' she asked.

Joe panted. 'Just give me a minute.'

When he straightened up, there was a sheen of sweat on his brow. He wiped it away with a shaking hand.

Sudden concern for Joe took Leanne by surprise. 'Are you ill?'

'No, it's nothing. I don't do crowds very well these days, that's all,' he said. His breathing had slowed and, as he looked at Leanne, the world around them stilled. He smiled. 'I wouldn't have gone in there for anyone else. And I wouldn't have needed to if you'd answered your bloody phone.' When Leanne didn't reply, uncertainty got the better of him. 'I presume the fact you invited me over is because you want to talk.'

'I don't know what I want,' she said. Now that he was there, she wasn't sure what to say. 'This was a bad idea. I should go home.'

'Do you want a lift?'

They didn't speak again until they were in his car and on

their way to the marina. Even then, the silence was easier than the words that must come.

'I've been so angry,' Leanne said at last.

Joe rubbed his chin. 'I noticed.'

'Sorry about that. I'm sure my knuckles hurt more than your face.'

'I wouldn't bet on it.' Joe took a couple of breaths, then added, 'I just want you to understand what happened . . . Why I let her down. Will you let me try?'

Leanne stared at the road ahead. It wasn't only Joe who needed to explain, but if he was willing to go first, she wouldn't stop him. 'Go on.'

'I was supposed to save her.'

Leanne had told him as much at Lois's funeral, or to be precise, she had screamed it at him. Since then, she had heard enough accounts from survivors to know that Joe had been powerless to help, but she couldn't stop wishing that he had been able to make a difference. 'So what did happen?'

'I had my arm around Lois as we were queuing to get out, and then all hell broke loose,' he replied. 'We were in the worst possible place, right in the centre of the corridor. The people pushing from behind went left or right, while we were trapped in the middle. At one point I was aware that my arms were digging into Lois's back and I pulled away to free up space. It didn't help, and the next thing I knew, she was on one side of our logjam, and I was on the other. I tripped over something, I think it was a body.'

The pause Joe left was wide enough for Leanne to plunge headfirst into the image he was conjuring of her best friend's last moments.

'When my eyes adjusted to the light, I spotted Lois at the same time she saw me. I couldn't breathe and I could see that she was struggling too.' Joe's breathing had become laboured as he relived the horror. 'I wanted to reach her, but I couldn't. We just held each other's gaze, and I could see her lips turning blue. There was no air, and it felt like I was falling into a black hole.' His voice faded. 'I didn't want to leave her.'

'You know exactly how Lois felt.' It wasn't an accusation.

'I can imagine, yes,' Joe replied as he turned the car into the marina. 'I often do.'

'Me too.'

'I tried, Leanne, I really did. I passed out at some point and only stayed upright because we were packed in so tight. When I came round, she'd disappeared.'

Leanne wiped a hand across her dry cheek. She hadn't allowed herself to cry since Lois's funeral. She couldn't until she faced what she had done. 'It might have been different if I'd been there.'

'You can't—'

'No, let me finish.' If Leanne didn't do this now, she never would. Her chest heaved and she could feel her fingers tingling. 'The last time I spoke to Lois, I lied to her,' she said quickly. Joe had pulled up in front of the security gates and Leanne took hold of the door handle, ready to leap out. 'I didn't want to go to some ballet put on by a bunch of school kids, so I made sure I had to work late.'

'She knew,' Joe said, 'and she understood.'

Leanne couldn't agree. Lois had been angry.

'I don't believe this, Lea! We're supposed to be leaving in an hour,' she had shouted down the phone. 'I knew you were going to bail on me. It's all right for you, you've had the grand tour of the theatre, I haven't.'

'I've only just found out,' Leanne had insisted.

'I thought you hated liars,' Lois had replied. 'Never thought you'd be one.'

'You can still go with Joe,' Leanne had said, dodging the accusation. 'He'll have to get used to your bad taste in culture at some point, it might as well be now.'

'Yeah, I can still go with Joe, but I wanted to go with you. I wanted you to know that even though I'm moving out, it won't stop us doing things together.'

Leanne could remember rolling her eyes. 'It's one crappy ballet production I'm missing. It's not the end of the world.'

Shoving open the car door, Leanne staggered towards the marina gates, only to realise she had left her handbag in the car with her keys in it. She grabbed hold of the rusted bars and shook them with a rage that had been building for over a year. A sob tore from her throat and when she felt Joe's hands peeling away her fingers, she let him turn her around. She pressed her face into his jacket and she howled. It *had* been the end of the world, the end of Lois, the end of their friendship, the end, the end, the end.

'It's my fault,' she sobbed. 'And I didn't just hurt her, did I? I hurt you too. You shouldn't have been there.'

All this time, Leanne had told herself she didn't want to see Joe because she blamed him, but it was another lie. She didn't want to see the pain she had inflicted, but if she was waiting for Joe to tell her she was wrong to blame herself, he couldn't do it. He was sobbing too. As much as she was clinging to him, he was clinging to her. They stayed like that for the longest time.

Eventually, Leanne found her keys and, when the gates were unlocked, she insisted Joe come to the boat. Leanne was feeling the first inklings of a hangover and they were both dehydrated from all the crying. It was only when they were nursing two cups of coffee that they were ready to resume.

'It could so easily have been me watching her die,' Leanne said in a whisper. She was sitting next to Joe on the futon, both staring ahead. 'Or else I might have persuaded her to use the side exit.'

'I could have been faster getting up after the alarm went off,' Joe replied. 'Or slower. Or Lois could have bought tickets for a different show, or just a different night. She could have picked up that stinking cold of hers a week later than she did, in which case she would have been home drinking Lemsip when it happened. We took a thousand small and insignificant steps to reach that point and if you change any one of them, it could have saved her life, or caused the death of someone else. But we are where we are and there are a million other decisions ahead that are going to lead us down one path as opposed to another. If you think about that too much, it can drive you mad.'

'I'm sorry, Joe.'

He turned to look at her. 'I'm sorry too.'

Leanne rubbed an eye, leaving her fingers tacky with smudged mascara and eyeshadow. When she attempted a smile, she knew she must look like Joaquin Phoenix's Joker, but she tried anyway.

'Please say you're not so drunk that you won't remember any of this,' Joe said. 'I don't think I could go through it twice.'

'I'm not that drunk,' she said, sipping her coffee and ignoring the throbbing at her temples.

Joe didn't look convinced. 'I'll leave you in peace for now,' he said, 'but I hope we can catch up again.'

'We'll have to.' Leanne stood up and took a spare set of keys off the hook in the galley. 'You'll need to borrow these to get back through the gates.'

It was like old times when Joe had visited, but not quite.

'Don't forget to leave some water and paracetamol by your bed,' he instructed.

It was something Lois would have said if she had been there, and Leanne could feel pressure behind her nose as tears threatened again. 'I won't.'

Joe poured away the rest of his coffee in the kitchen sink and was about to turn away when he noticed the drawing of a torch stuck on the fridge door. Amelia had written her name on the bottom. 'I read about what Claudia Rothwell did.'

'Yeah, well, there might be more to that story if I can figure it all out. I'll explain it to you some time.' Leanne was feeling woozy and tired. She was eager for her bed, but there was something about the way Joe kept looking at the drawing. 'I don't suppose you remember seeing Claudia or Amelia, do you?'

'No, but I recognise that torch. I had one.'

Leanne straightened up. '*You* did?'

Joe was bemused by her reaction. 'I suspect half the town had one at some point. Ronson Construction were giving them away like sweets during the open day for the restoration project.'

'I think I was in Ibiza at the time, with Lois,' Leanne said distractedly. It was years ago, before Lois had met Joe. 'Do you still have it?'

'I found it in a drawer after the fire and when I saw the logo and realised what it was, I chucked it in the bin. To be honest I don't think it ever worked. It was cheap tat.'

The comment stayed with Leanne long after Joe had left. If it was cheap tat, why on earth would Claudia carry one around? The answer was obvious. She wouldn't. If ever Leanne's judgement had been clouded, it wasn't now.

19

Leanne had planned a remorseless campaign to secure an interview with Phillipa, but it had taken precisely one call. Leanne didn't explain why she wanted a meeting, and Phillipa hadn't asked. The hardest part had been agreeing a time in the day that didn't provoke suspicion in Mal. She had only been back at work two days, and would rather her editor didn't know exactly how hard she was prepared to push her investigations. Leanne's next challenge was to remain civil long enough to persuade Phillipa to hand over a seating plan.

It was Phillipa's husband, Robert, who greeted her at the door before leaving Leanne to wait in the library. It was all very grand, with wall-to-wall bookshelves that required a ladder to reach the uppermost tomes; a room befitting a mansion house set in grounds so vast it warranted a sweeping drive. Taking a seat in a Georgian armchair, Leanne tapped her fingers against the polished mahogany armrest. From the other side of the door, she heard the rattle of teacups. Her hand stilled.

Phillipa glided into the room wearing a satin wrap dress

and open-toed shoes that revealed a perfect pedicure. Her auburn hair shone, and her make-up was immaculate, if not on the heavy side. Whatever Phillipa had gone through in the last year, her standards had not slipped. She nodded briefly at Leanne, before returning her attention to the silver tray, which she placed on a reading table next to a stack of newspapers.

Leanne had checked through the papers when she arrived, expecting to find copies of *Horse and Hound* amongst a collection of broadsheets, but the newspapers were all back issues of the *Cheshire Courier*. Somewhere in amongst those pages were photographs of Lois, and Leanne hated the idea that Phillipa had them in her archives. Since meeting Joe last weekend, she had been coming to terms with the possibility that a group of faceless company directors were ultimately responsible for the tragedy, but old habits were hard to break. She gripped the armrests hard enough to turn her knuckles white.

Phillipa perched herself on an armchair matching Leanne's. She crossed her feet and tucked them under her chair before turning her body to face Leanne. She ignored the tray with the fine china tea service. Unlike Claudia, Phillipa hadn't asked her guest if she preferred tea or coffee, how she took it, or even if she wanted a drink at all. She had taken it upon herself to dictate Leanne's needs with an air of effortless sophistication and entitlement that Claudia could only emulate.

'I think we're ready to start,' Phillipa said, with perfect poise and control.

Fumbling, Leanne grabbed her phone to open the voice recorder.

Phillipa looked down her nose at the contraption being pointed at her. 'I'd prefer it if you didn't record this.'

Leanne's arm remained extended. Her breaths sharp and painful.

There was a lilt of amusement in Phillipa's voice when she said, 'Of course, if you insist, this is going to be a very short interview.'

Leanne waited a second or two, but it was a weak attempt at bravado. 'Fine, I'll keep it switched off, for now,' she added as a warning. She tapped the screen and dropped her phone into her lap, all without rolling her eyes.

'Well done. Now, I expect you're wondering why I agreed to meet you,' Phillipa began. 'As you have no doubt realised, I have accepted everything the press and the public has thrown at me. Some have called the Empress Theatre my vanity project, and I wouldn't disagree. It was, in many ways, a reflection of my personal aspirations.'

'And now it's a burnt-out ruin.'

Unflinching, Phillipa lifted her chin and stretched her neck. Her pose was meant to be superior, but the light coming from the sash windows emphasised dark shadows beneath her eyes that layers of make-up hadn't dispelled completely.

'I was willing to accept my punishment, whatever the findings produced, but two things have given me pause for thought. One of them is you. I take great exception to the ugly rumours you've been spreading about me.'

Leanne attempted to look puzzled for a moment. 'Oh, sorry, do you mean what I said about your affair with Declan Gallagher?' Her heart was hammering in her chest. She couldn't tell yet if her previous attack had pierced Phillipa's Achilles heel, or stabbed a hornets' nest.

There was a spark of anger in Phillipa's eyes that relit her features. 'In the last twelve months, there is only one person who has stood by my side, one person who never doubted me, who made me believe that we could endure this, and that man is my husband. We've been married for almost twenty years and I would *never* cheat on him.' She pointed towards the door that Robert had disappeared through earlier. 'I adore that man and, while I can accept the attacks on my character, I won't stand idly by and let you debase my marriage.'

'You can't blame me for—'

'People like you think it's a game. You tell one person and they pass it on to the next, then the next, until one day Karin Gallagher is screaming in my face. That was the second thing that happened. The final straw. I will not let this go unchallenged.'

If the sharpness of Phillipa's tone was meant to penetrate Leanne's cold heart, it didn't work. 'If Karin has a problem with you, it has nothing to do with me.' Leanne's lips curled into a snarl. 'Quite frankly, I couldn't care less about the state of your marriage. Maybe you did have an affair with Declan, maybe you didn't. So what? Others might be interested to hear the ins and outs of your private life, but I'm not. That being said, if you'd like to save the *Courier* the cost of some ink by not circulating the gossip, I'm sure we can come to some arrangement. You might be able to help with other matters I'm investigating.'

Phillipa shook her head. 'You don't know me very well, do you, Leanne? I'm not the type to be manipulated. I asked you here because I thought it was simplest to cut out the poison at the source.'

241

'You think I'm the one who started—'

'Please, let's not get into a debate,' Phillipa interjected. She cleared her throat, adjusted her tone. 'It seems that you've formed quite a bond with a friend of mine. Claudia Rothwell?'

Leanne kept her expression neutral. Even a cursory glance at the articles written in the last couple of months would make her look like Claudia's personal champion. 'I can appreciate how it would seem like that.'

'And I suppose you talked about me in your cosy little chats, and Declan too,' said Phillipa. 'I'm disappointed that Claudia has gone on to repeat your vile claims to his sister, but that's another matter. You must be very proud of yourself.'

'Oh, please,' Leanne said, rising to her feet. She couldn't bear one more second of Phillipa's company. She would find another way to obtain the information she needed. 'If anyone has spread poison and misery in this town, it's you. We're all getting told to move on, well, move on, Mrs Montgomery. Go back to the South of France or whatever hole you choose to hide in. Sedgefield doesn't want you. You're a blemish in its history that needs to be expunged.' Her voice trembled and she blinked hard. She wouldn't let Phillipa see her tears.

Phillipa stood to face her. 'Don't make an enemy of me, Leanne,' she warned. 'I still have influence.'

'Save your threats for someone who cares. If I had my way, I'd have nothing more to do with you and your nest of vipers. And that includes Claudia. You think I told her about your affair? It was the other way around. You're malignant, the whole lot of you.'

Leanne slung her rucksack over her shoulder.

'Wait. Please,' Phillipa said. Her expression remained fixed, but the iron rod up her backside appeared to have buckled. 'I know what you think of me, and I understand why. I'd feel exactly the same if I'd lost someone dear to me.'

Leanne stepped back, her calves knocking against the chair. 'I don't know what you mean.'

'I made it my job to find out everything I could about those who died,' Phillipa said, far too softly. 'If I hadn't taken it upon myself to renovate the theatre, it would still be hiding behind a row of dilapidated retail units, and Lois Granger would be living her best life, with her best friend.'

'No, don't you dare mention her name.'

'I'm sorry for your loss, I truly am,' Phillipa continued. She too had tears rimming her eyes. 'I can't change what happened, however much I'd like to try. Hate me if you must, but please, sit back down and let's start again. I believe I've misjudged you.'

Leanne was torn between her desire to escape and her need to understand what was behind the sudden switch in her disposition. When Phillipa sat down, Leanne followed suit, but she kept her rucksack on her lap.

'If it helps, I hate myself too,' Phillipa began. 'When the fire station was closed down, I was as worried as the rest of the town, but I could appreciate that efficiency savings had to be made. So one of the first things I did was to bring in an expert to check over the house and improve our fire safety.'

'While the rest of us could burn.'

'I put my family first, yes,' Phillipa said, looking away briefly. For someone who objected to being shamed about an affair, she was content to pour shame on herself. 'But I

243

did make fire precaution a priority at the theatre too. Not that it was enough, but there you have it.'

'Why are you telling me this?'

'I simply wanted to apologise. My heart breaks for each and every one of the victims and, since I know you're going to ask, that does include Declan. I worked with him for over two years, and I'd go as far as to say I liked him. He was attractive,' she said, arching an eyebrow. 'He was also very charming, but a bit too much of a charmer in my view. I could certainly understand why his wife divorced him. He wasn't my type, Leanne, not by any stretch of the imagination.'

'As I've already stated, I'm not interested.'

'I realise that now, and I'm not above admitting I've made an error. When Declan's sister came to see me, I managed to glean from her that her misinformation had come from Claudia. I connected the dots in a straight line back from Karin, to Claudia, to you. I see now that it was more a web with numerous strands, all connecting to our mutual friend. It would seem I underestimated Claudia Rothwell.'

'I know how that feels,' Leanne admitted.

'I had thought you were her biggest fan.'

Leanne followed Phillipa's gaze to the stack of newspapers. 'I had her down as the reluctant hero. Not any more.'

'She is quite a character, isn't she? She tried so very hard to fit in after marrying Justin. Whenever we met, it was obvious she had done her homework, dressing in a way to compliment my style, exploring interests she knew I was passionate about, turning up in places she knew I frequented. I don't mean to sound like a snob, and my reticence about Claudia has nothing to do with her background. It was simply that everything she did felt contrived.'

Leanne thought back to their first interview. Claudia had gone out of her way to appear relatable, right down to the instant coffee and Custard Creams.

'I never felt as if I got to know the real Claudia,' Phillipa continued, 'but I'd say she's starting to reveal her true colours now. She's enjoying her elevated status, and I've reached the conclusion that she thinks she can keep it by undermining me.'

'And that would be why Claudia made up this story about you and Declan?'

'I'm pleased to hear you calling it a story,' Phillipa said. She tipped her head towards the silver tray. 'Now, how do you like your tea?'

Leanne dropped her rucksack on the floor. Her lips were parched, so she allowed Phillipa to play hostess. They had reached a truce of sorts if only because they shared a common adversary.

'Would it be possible for you to do me a favour, Mrs Montgomery?' Leanne asked, balancing her teacup on the saucer.

'I'd certainly consider it.'

'There's a story in the *Courier* that I believe has been misreported. As you can imagine, not every witness I've spoken to has been as reliable as I would like,' she said. She wouldn't share specifics, but she hoped Phillipa would read between the lines. 'It would help enormously if I had a better understanding of who was sitting where in the theatre. I noticed from the public inquiry that you were able to provide the investigators with seat locations for the victims. Would you have the whole picture?'

'I'm afraid it would have been the theatre company who

provided that information, but I'm still in contact with some of the staff. From what I gather, they looked at payment transactions, so the information won't be complete. Customers would have bought groups of tickets, and there were cash sales too.'

'And complimentary tickets.'

'Absolutely,' replied Phillipa with a curious smile.

'Could you obtain a seating plan for me?'

'It would be a breach of data protection,' she replied, appearing to dismiss the request out of hand. 'So if you do happen to receive one, it couldn't have come from me.'

'I'll bear that in mind.'

Leanne drained her cup and, as she placed it on the silver tray, she noticed the papers again. 'Have you read Amelia Parker's story?'

'It's very hard to avoid it.'

'Someone mentioned that Ronson Construction had merchandise that was very similar to the key ring torch Amelia describes.'

'They gave away anything one could stamp with a logo,' Phillipa said with a shrug, but then her expression changed. 'Actually, yes, I do remember those.'

'You don't happen to have one, do you?'

'Do you honestly think I'd collect that kind of rubbish?'

'No, I don't imagine someone like you would,' Leanne said. It was the last hint she would drop. She had shared as much as she could. 'I think that's it then. Thank you for your time.'

Leanne hadn't been obliged to take off her footwear on entering the house, so when Phillipa showed her to the door, there was no awkward wait for her to lace up her boots.

'Will you be at home for a while?' she asked, her parting question.

'It won't be my home for much longer. The house is about to go on the market and we have our eye on something just outside Wilmslow. My intention is to remain until we have everything packed up and ready to go.'

'You're leaving Sedgefield for good?' Leanne said, surprised that the prospect didn't provide the level of glee she would have expected.

'I'd say it's for the best, wouldn't you?' Phillipa asked. 'And I'm sure there will be someone to fill the breach.'

20

Leanne cast a long shadow across the small patch of lawn in front of the Parkers' house, aware that another day was ending without any real progress. She hadn't expected to receive Phillipa's seating plan after only twenty-four hours, nor was she surprised that Claudia continued to ignore her calls, but she had to do something. She was pinning her hopes on one little girl's broken memory.

The temperature had dropped low enough to turn Leanne's breath to vapour as she waited for the door to be answered. Each time she inhaled, she was painfully aware of how effortless it was to draw the cold air into her lungs. On average, a person takes twenty-five thousand breaths per day – reflexively, without effort, or thought. You took it for granted. Until you didn't.

With the next exhale, a cloud curled around Leanne's face. It could easily be mistaken for smoke. Fighting the urge to hammer on the door and beg to be let in, she saw a light flicker inside the house. A figure appeared in silhouette and the door opened.

'Come in, you look frozen,' Kathryn Parker said, offering a smile.

Grateful to use the cold weather as an excuse, Leanne made no attempt to disguise her dithering.

'They're saying we could be in for record lows this winter,' said Kathryn, taking the coat Leanne was reluctant to peel off.

'And it's going to snow at Christmas,' said Amelia confidently. She had appeared in the hallway with a clutch of Sharpies in one hand and a piece of paper in the other.

'Have you been drawing again?' asked Leanne.

When the girl turned the sheet of paper around, Leanne scanned it hungrily for what might be another of Amelia's clues. There was a Christmas tree in the centre of the page and a smattering of figures sporting elf hats. It was a happy family scene; no flames, no fire, no dead bodies littering the ground. Leanne forced a smile. 'That's lovely.'

'Let's go through to the living room,' suggested Kathryn. 'I can make you a hot drink if you like?'

'I'm fine, thanks.'

'So how can we help?' Kathryn asked. 'I wasn't sure if the *Courier* would be doing any more interviews. We've stopped getting calls from all the other reporters and researchers. It's a real shame, Amelia would have liked to have met Holly Willoughby.'

'You were going to be on *This Morning*?'

'Only if Claudia came with us,' Amelia said, her lip protruding. 'But she said no.'

'Have you seen her since the anniversary?'

'Not a word,' Kathryn said, lowering her voice. Amelia had sprawled out on the rug in front of them and was absorbed in a new drawing. 'It's been disappointing for Amelia, but I completely understand. I'll never forget what Claudia sacrificed for us.'

'And how is Amelia doing?' Leanne asked, matching Kathryn's whisper.

'She's much better, thanks.'

'Has she had any more flashbacks?'

Kathryn's brow creased. 'It's hard to say. Her counsellor has been encouraging her to draw as a way of visualising her fears.' She closed her eyes. 'Some of them are quite disturbing.'

'Would you like to see them?' Amelia asked. She had been listening after all, and abandoned her work in progress; the outline of a woman.

While they waited for Amelia to return from her bedroom, Kathryn watched the reporter expectantly. Leanne had yet to explain why she was there.

'I wanted to speak to some of the survivors, to gauge a reaction to the findings of the inquiry. How do you feel about it?'

'I'd say my emotions are mixed,' Kathryn said. 'On the one hand, it's a relief to know how the fire was caused, but it's frustrating that no one can say for sure if there'll be any prosecutions. At least we can stop pointing the finger at our neighbours. I feel guilty that we were so quick to blame Phillipa Montgomery.'

'There are worse people in the world,' Leanne agreed.

'Got them,' Amelia said, rushing into the room and dropping a stack of paper into Leanne's lap.

As she leafed through the artwork, Leanne was aware that Kathryn had turned her body to the side so she didn't have to look at them too.

'Are you sure you don't want a cuppa?' she asked.

'No, but don't let me stop you if you need one,' Leanne replied without looking up.

There were twenty or more drawings to go through while Amelia's mum was in the kitchen. Some were simple pencil sketches, while others were busy scenes with gaudy colours and grotesque shapes. Some of the less disturbing included a picture of Alice and the white rabbit standing by a cavernous rabbit hole, but the one that made Leanne's hand shake was a sea of faces with mouths open in silent screams and tears sliding down cheeks.

'Do you remember this?' asked Leanne, horrified by the glimpse into the child's mind.

'No, I just remember the screams and not being able to move,' Amelia said. She was standing at Leanne's side and leant over to point out something Leanne hadn't noticed. It was a broken body beneath a sea of chaos. 'That's me.'

'You must have been awake just after the roof collapsed.'

'I suppose so.'

Leanne moved on to the next drawing. There was no mistaking Amelia in this scene. It looked like a bonfire, with the same figure buried beneath the rubble, and a speech bubble with the word, 'Help,' written inside. 'Do you know how long you were there?' she asked.

'Until after the screaming stopped.'

'And what could you see?'

'There was dust over everything. The torch wasn't that good,' Amelia said. She took charge of the drawings and found one similar to the picture stuck on Leanne's fridge.

Since speaking to Joe, Leanne had looked up merchandise companies online and found similar items that could be stamped with any company logo. She strongly suspected the one Amelia had been given had come from Ronson Construction, but it would be useful to have it confirmed.

She took out her phone and found an image she hoped Amelia would recognise.

'Does this look familiar?'

The graphic was a blue circle with the letters R and C layered on top of each other in white. Ronson Construction.

Amelia was close enough for Leanne to feel a shudder run through the young girl's body. 'I've seen it before.'

'Was it on the key ring?'

Amelia wrinkled her nose. 'It might have been.'

It wasn't the eureka moment Leanne had been hoping for and when Kathryn reappeared, she was ready to call it a day.

'I'll leave you to it,' she said.

'Wait!' said Amelia, returning to her drawing on the floor. 'I want you to give Claudia a picture from me. I won't be a minute.'

'You don't need to rush. I'm sure you can give it to her yourself, or post it.'

'We wouldn't know where to send it,' explained Kathryn, 'and there's no answer from the phone number Claudia gave us.'

'I could give you her address.'

'It doesn't matter,' Kathryn said with a shake of the head. 'It would feel like we were imposing. If she doesn't want us to have her contact details, we should respect that.'

'But I want to give her this,' pleaded Amelia, glancing up from her work. To Leanne she added, 'Please, wait.'

There was an awkward attempt at small talk with Kathryn as Leanne willed Amelia to hurry up and finish her drawing. The composition was of a woman holding a child and, after adding Claudia's dark hair and red lipstick, Amelia wrote, 'Thank you,' across the top of the page.

She was writing something at the bottom when she let out a loud huff and said, 'Oh, no,' admonishing herself.

'It's OK,' Kathryn said, leaning over to see what had caused her daughter's frustration. 'If you cover up the mistake with a heart, you can write her name again.' She glanced at Leanne and said, 'She struggles with Claudia's name.'

'It's not an easy one to spell,' Leanne said, hoping the encouragement would be enough for Amelia to continue with her drawing and not scrunch it up and start over.

'Here, I've finished,' Amelia said at last.

Despite herself, Leanne searched the drawing for some hidden message buried inside Amelia's psyche. Amongst a smattering of hearts, there was Claudia's name. It didn't deserve to be next to Amelia's.

'It's lovely,' Leanne said. 'And I'll make sure Claudia gets it.'

Amelia smiled, but her expression became clouded as she glanced at Leanne's necklace. Leanne touched the silver pendant self-consciously. It was in the shape of a loop that crossed in the middle, like a figure of eight on its side. Lois had given her the eternity symbol shortly after announcing she was moving off the boat. It was meant to represent their friendship.

'Do you like my necklace?'

When Amelia looked straight through her, Leanne sensed the child being drawn towards an elusive memory. Instinctively, she checked the drawing again. 'Is that a chain around Claudia's throat too?'

'Yes.'

'Claudia was wearing a necklace when she found you?' When Amelia nodded, Leanne asked, 'And can you remember what it looked like?'

Amelia shrugged. 'It was a bit like that,' she said, pointing back to Leanne's pendant.

'This shape?'

Amelia stared intently at the eternity symbol. 'I don't think so, but it was silver.'

Leanne picked up a handful of Amelia's other drawings. In every sketch, the woman with dark hair had the same semicircle around her neck, and in every one, the detail was lacking. The pendant was nothing more than a dot in the centre of a thin, grey line.

'What are you looking for?' asked Kathryn.

Leanne straightened up. 'To be honest, I don't know, but I think I just got closer.'

The Empress Theatre
Sedgefield, Cheshire

Angela Morris was sitting with her four friends two rows from the front. They worked together at Bridgewater Primary School and when one of their students appeared onstage as the white rabbit, a squeal carried through the group. A few minutes later, Angela casually fixed her hair, not entirely necessary with her shortly cropped afro, but since her hand was up in the air anyway, she gave Evie a furtive wave.

They were just getting settled when the alarm sounded, and the group of friends shuffled out of their row. Angela had reached the aisle when Evie's mum, Sarah, appeared in front of her. She was on her way backstage to collect her daughter, but stopped to say hello to the teacher who had been in the job long enough to have taught her too.

'You must be so proud of Evie, I know I am,' Angela said. One of her friends tugged at her arm, but she waved them on. 'I'll be right behind you.'

'Wasn't she amazing?' gushed Sarah. 'I hope they don't send everyone home. Evie couldn't sleep last night with nerves, and this will only make it worse. At least there'll be another show tomorrow.'

'Not for me,' Angela said, her dark brown eyes dimming with disappointment. 'I'm keeping my fingers firmly crossed that tonight isn't over yet. Now you get on and find your superstar.'

While Angela was praying that the show would restart, Lena Kowalski was hoping it would be cancelled so they could get a refund. Lena and her boyfriend, Peter, were at the back of the stalls, not far from where Rex would find temporary refuge only a few minutes later. She was fuming. Peter had bought tickets for what must be the worst seats in the house. They were underneath the circle and as far away from the stage as you could possibly get.

Their position should have meant they were one of the first out when the evacuation started, but Peter had chosen that moment to drop his bottle of Coke. It disappeared under the seat in front of them.

'Leave it,' she said.

'But what if a kid picks it up and drinks it?'

'And?' She shook her head slowly. Peter the penny-pincher had smuggled two bottles into the theatre and had been very particular about which one he gave to his girlfriend. 'Did you put vodka in yours?'

He was on his knees searching. Too busy apparently to answer. 'There, got it.'

'I thought you were driving home?' she demanded. 'It's your turn.'

'But you're not bothered about drinking.'

'I am now. You're such a knobhead, Peter,' she said, using one of the English insults he had come to regret teaching her when they had first met. She turned to check the exit. 'Look at that, there's a long queue to get out now.'

'We can push in,' he said with a shrug.

'Or we could use one of the side exits.'

'But everyone's going through the foyer,' he said, pointing with the bottle in his hand.

'Then you go that way,' she replied through gritted teeth.

'I will.'

'Fine. See you out there,' Lena said, turning her back on her boyfriend and pushing against the flow.

Anyone hearing their exchange might think that Lena didn't like Peter, but that couldn't be further from the truth. She loved him with all her heart, but that wouldn't stop her staying mad at him. They would have a blazing row later and she would exaggerate the hurt. Peter would beg forgiveness and they would make up. And so it would always be.

And as Lena made her way to the side exit that was destined to become blocked by falling rubble, Angela was delayed for a second time.

'Amelia Parker, what are you doing all by yourself?' She had spotted the girl sitting in an otherwise empty row.

'I'm waiting for my mum, miss. She went to the Ladies, but she'll be back soon.'

'I think you should come with me.'

'No,' the child said, panic in her eyes. 'I need to wait.'

Angela looked along the aisle to the main exit. Mrs Parker wasn't going to get through that. 'I tell you what, I'll go and see if I can find her.'

21

The meeting wasn't entirely necessary, but Claudia could do with a boost from her working party disciples. Justin was away on business and she had too much time on her hands. She worried about the shifting sands she had built her new life upon, and her anxiety levels increased every time the phone rang. She should block Leanne's number and have done with it, but in truth, she was just as uncomfortable when her phone remained stubbornly silent.

Claudia needed to know how Phillipa's closest friends had reacted to the verdict of the public inquiry, but so far they were keeping their thoughts to themselves. Bryony had eventually responded to one of Claudia's many messages, but only to offer her apologies for the meeting. The clock was ticking down on Claudia's fifteen minutes of fame.

'That was a quick meeting,' Yvonne said as she practically skipped out of Harriet's offices into bright, wintry sunshine.

'I was disappointed with the turnout,' replied Claudia sourly. 'Setting up the hardship fund may not be as glamorous as planning the memorial service, but it's just as important, if not more so.'

The schoolteacher glanced at the papers in her hand. 'They probably saw the agenda and didn't think they were needed. It was quite a dry meeting, but sometimes that's for the best. It's good that we can get on and do things instead of wasting hours simply talking about it.'

Claudia was reminded of what Bryony had said about the thinkers and the doers. Watching Yvonne shove her papers into her fake Burberry satchel, she knew which group she preferred. 'I won't keep you in that case. I'm sure you have lots to be getting on with.'

'Oh.' Yvonne looked crestfallen. 'I was going to suggest we go for a bite to eat. But if you're in a hurry?'

'Ah, that's a shame. Maybe another time.'

Claudia made a show of returning to her car, but the idea of going home to an empty apartment held no attraction. She checked her phone as she waited for Yvonne to disappear out of sight and cleared another missed call from Leanne before dialling Bryony's number. To her surprise, she answered.

'Hi, Claudia. How are you?'

'I've just come out of my meeting. I needed to make sure the hardship fund was being progressed properly, you know how it is,' she said, one businesswoman to another. 'I was wondering if you wanted to meet up.'

'Oh, was it the charity meeting today? Sorry I couldn't make it, but I'm sure you didn't need me there,' Bryony chirped.

Claudia left a beat, waiting for Bryony to respond to her offer to catch up. Obviously, if Bryony had been too busy to make the meeting then she wouldn't be available right now, but she could at least suggest a convenient date for their diaries. It wasn't that Claudia was desperate for Bryony's company, but still. 'So do you fancy a get-together some time?'

'A get-together?' Bryony repeated.

'Or a trip to the stables if you'd prefer some fresh air.' It hadn't gone unnoticed that Bryony's offers of riding lessons had dried up lately.

'Yes, darling, a horse ride would be lovely, but can I get back to you?'

Claudia pressed the phone to her ear and listened intently. She didn't like the way Bryony kept repeating what Claudia had said. She wasn't alone.

'Make sure you do,' Claudia said with mock sternness that wasn't all pretence.

Short on offers for alternative forms of amusement, Claudia slipped her mobile into the side pocket of her briefcase and strolled towards the high street. There were a number of exclusive boutiques nearby where she could fritter away Justin's money for a few hours. He might baulk at the credit card bill at the end of the month, but what did he expect for leaving her on her own? And she was very much alone.

Noticing a gaggle of young mums that were bearing down on her, Claudia crossed the street, but not before she glimpsed chubby cheeks and tiny hands poking above the pram covers. The pang of loss made her heart clench. Justin kept reminding her that if they could get pregnant once, it would happen again, but Claudia didn't share his confidence. The fire had taken so much from her, and she was still being punished. It wasn't fair.

As she passed an estate agent's window, her pace slowed. Only select properties deserved a window placement, and

Phillipa's stately pile took up half the display. Despite being on the market for only a matter of days, Claudia was surprised that it hadn't been snapped up yet. If things didn't happen soon, she would have to put in an offer herself – anything to ensure Phillipa's speedy departure. Justin had said they couldn't afford it, but they had talked about buying a house when they had a family and, if he was so sure that would happen, he should put his money where his mouth was. She could see herself living in a place like Phillipa's. She would be harder to ignore.

As she stared at the window, Claudia caught her reflection in the glass and for a second, she glimpsed the girl she used to be, the one Justin had fallen in love with. Where had she gone?

In her formative years, Claudia was always known as the little girl without the mum, but at least it had secured the invites to the birthday parties, and she could always count on kindly neighbours to gift her money and clothes that obscured the neglect. She made sure she was one of the popular girls and, as her confidence grew, she had stopped relying on pity and strived for respect. Why had she been forced to go to extraordinary lengths simply to gain the approval of people she didn't respect or care for? But, why did it always have to be a battle? Her reflection blurred. She could hear hurried footsteps drawing closer and a face appeared next to hers in the window. Reluctantly, she turned.

'Hello, Karin. How are you?'

Karin was panting. 'Can we talk?'

They walked in silence, past the artisan bakery and Declan's flat above, past the theatre with its boarded-up doors and soot-stained façade and into Victoria Park. They followed the path as it sloped towards the lake, and found a bench.

'Are you still working?' asked Claudia, fully expecting Karin to say no. She had made no effort to cover up the acne breakouts and dark shadows beneath her eyes. Her hair was pushed into a woollen hat and the matching scarf was wrapped tightly around her neck as if it alone kept up her head.

'I can't manage long shifts but, you know, we're getting by,' she replied. 'Thanks so much for the grant money. You never did send me the forms, but I'm happy to fill them out whenever you like.'

'It's not necessary,' Claudia said. She had gladly handed over the cash. She was a good person at heart. 'Was it enough?'

'Enough to take the pressure off, and right when we needed it,' Karin said. She took a shaky breath. 'I thought the anniversary was going to be bad enough, but when I read the findings . . . I lost it completely.'

'How so?'

'Everyone had been blaming Declan, saying it was his incompetence or his arrogance that had caused the fire, and I believed them. And sure, Dec did have this way about him. Too confident for his own good.' She managed a weak smile as she stared out across the lake. The smile vanished. 'I should have defended him, but I looked at the photographs of the other victims, I read their stories, and I hated my brother. I *really* hated him. And now I hate myself.'

'You believed what you were being told. It's understandable.'

'Not to me, it isn't. He was my big brother and I looked

up to him. He was the one who encouraged me to leave Donegal and see the world, you know. Take chances and live my best life. I backpacked across Asia, climbed volcanoes in New Zealand, and got very seasick once on a fishing boat in Papua New Guinea.' Karin hunched her shoulders, pushing her chin into the folds of her scarf. She was aware that she bore no resemblance to the young adventurer she described. 'I would never have taken those first steps if it hadn't been for Declan. He believed in me, and I should have believed in him.'

'I'm no counsellor, but it can't be good for your mental health to torture yourself like this.'

'What else am I to do? There are huge chunks of Declan's life that are a blank, and I don't mean just on the night of the fire. I keep thinking back to what you said about him being involved with someone. I had to go and see her.'

Claudia's heart skipped a beat and she pressed a hand to her chest. 'You went to see Phillipa Montgomery?'

'I thought she would know what made Declan go up to the circle. He can't have been looking for me. It had to be her. And wasn't the VIP area up there? Did you know he fell?'

Claudia swallowed hard. She didn't care about Declan. 'What happened with Phillipa?'

'I told her she was the reason he got trapped, that she killed him. I was so angry,' Karin said, her last words tangled with a sob. 'She says she wasn't there that night, and she laughed at the idea of an affair. I screamed at her, told her she was a liar, said that even her friends knew about it.'

'What exactly did you say to her, Karin?' When Karin didn't reply immediately, Claudia's stomach somersaulted. 'Did you mention me?'

'I, well, yes, I suppose I did.' She glanced up. 'Sorry.'

Claudia struggled for breath. 'No, it's fine,' she managed. 'When was this?'

'Last week, the day after the report came out.'

Squeezing her eyes shut, Claudia found she could see more clearly. Phillipa knew what she had been saying about her. She was the reason Claudia was back to being *persona non grata*. That was why Bryony was so difficult to pin down. And if they had been together when Claudia had phoned earlier, it would have caused no end of amusement. Claudia told herself that Bryony didn't deserve her friendship, but the rejection hurt more than she would like.

'I won't stop until I find out what happened,' Karin was saying. 'I was thinking I'd speak to the press, see if they can find out more. I've started reading the papers again. The *Courier* is listing Declan as one of the victims at long last, so maybe they do have a conscience.'

When Claudia looked at Karin, she wanted to drag her by the scarf to the lake so she could dunk the stupid bitch in the water. She exhaled slowly, and the next breath was easier. She was firefighting, and not for the first time.

'You can't trust the press, Karin. They're not looking to help the likes of us, I can promise you that much. I know it sounds churlish given how the *Courier* has written such nice things about me, but when Leanne Pitman told the world about my miscarriage, I felt violated afterwards. And as for that reunion with Amelia, I'll be honest, I faked it.'

'How do you mean?'

'I didn't want to see Amelia again. I didn't want to hold another mother's child when I couldn't hold mine.' The ache in Claudia's voice was very real, but when Karin took her

265

hand to comfort her, Claudia squeezed it briefly before pushing it away. She wasn't looking for sympathy. 'I'm telling you this only so you can learn from my experience.'

'I just wish I could set the record straight. I would have been nearby when Declan died, but there's so much I don't know, or can't remember.'

'My advice to you is, if you find yourself overthinking things, stop. Distract yourself. Move on.'

'Easier said than done. It was bad enough that I could hear Declan calling out to me in my dreams, but now I see him. I think I saw him fall.'

'You couldn't have done,' Claudia said, keeping her voice soft. 'The theatre was full of dust and smoke. No one could see anything.'

'Beth said the dust was settling . . .'

'Believe me, once the smoke took over, you wouldn't have been able to see what was happening in the circle.'

'I suppose,' she said. She pursed her lips. 'So you were there after most people had left. Do you remember seeing me, or hearing Declan?'

'All I can tell you is that it was chaos in there. I'm pretty sure whatever you're remembering is simply your mind playing tricks.'

'Do you really think so?'

Karin was seeking permission to forget about her brother. 'You've become fixated on Declan because you think solving some mystery you've concocted over his death will solve all your other problems. It won't. And making an enemy of Phillipa will only end in more grief. You can't confront her again, Karin. Those reporters you think will help you are more interested in protecting their own. Phillipa is good friends with the *Courier*'s owners. They'll close ranks and, if you're not careful, they'll destroy you, and Beth too,' Claudia said. A shudder ran down her spine. She should listen to her own advice.

'Would they do that?'

'You never know what someone is capable of until they're pushed into a corner,' warned Claudia. 'Do you trust me, Karin?'

'Of course I do. You were the only one willing to help when everyone else treated us like lepers.'

'And I want to help you now. You need to keep away from Phillipa and the papers. Will you do that for me?'

Karin frowned, but Claudia held her gaze until her features relaxed. 'Sure,' she said. 'You don't have to worry about me.'

22

Within days of their encounter, Phillipa made good on her promise and sent Leanne the seating plan, or at least she forwarded the information someone else had produced. Leanne had opened the spreadsheet in the office, expecting to find a nice graphic of the theatre's layout. What she had actually been given was a table of information presented in rows and columns – a simple list of names and seat references. That was it.

It would take time to create a clear picture of who was sitting where, and Leanne couldn't do that in Mal's line of sight. He tolerated her continuing investigation, but only just, and the less he knew the better. She accepted all the assignments he could throw at her, which meant she didn't have a chance to look at Phillipa's information until her day off on Sunday.

Needing space, she relocated to the café and commandeered a large table. She used two cruet sets to pin down a blown-up graphic of the theatre's layout, and set about transposing names from the printed spreadsheet.

'Where do you want me to put this?' Dianne asked when she appeared with a mug of coffee and a plate of toast.

'Over there's fine,' Leanne said, pointing to the upper left corner of the plan. It didn't matter if the plate covered seats in the circle, she was only interested in the stalls.

Breathing in the heady scent of dark, roasted coffee, Leanne returned to her spreadsheet, and it took a moment to realise Dianne hadn't left. Leanne followed her gaze. Joe was heading towards them, edging nervously through the busy café.

'Do you want me to hang around?' Dianne asked.

'It's OK, I invited him.'

Dianne had never come out and told Leanne she thought it was wrong to keep Joe at arm's length, but the relief was written all over her rosy cheeks. 'He's a good lad.'

'I know.'

Joe couldn't get past Dianne without being enveloped in a hug, and the blush was still spreading up his neck and face as he pulled out a chair and sat down opposite Leanne.

'You look in better shape than you did last week,' he said, handing over the spare keys he had borrowed.

Leanne eyed him carefully. She was no longer sure if Joe's flush was embarrassment after all. 'Is this a bad idea? I forgot about you not liking crowds.'

'This I can manage.'

Leanne remained unconvinced. Joe wasn't the man she remembered from a year ago. His broad shoulders had narrowed and he had acquired a frailty that hadn't registered when she had been too drunk, or too angry to notice. 'You should eat more. Here, have some toast.'

'I can't say I'm hungry,' he replied, ignoring the plate she had pushed towards him.

'Are you sure you're OK?'

'I'm feeling better than I did last week too,' he admitted. 'I needed to take positive action, and speaking to you has been top of my list for a long while. It feels good to have ticked it off.'

'I'm sorry it took so long,' she said, bowing her head and making a silent apology to her absent friend for not doing better.

When she looked up, Joe was scrutinising the diagram on the table. So far she had written down the names of all the victims, including Angela Morris and Lena Kowalski. Joe slid a hand across the paper until his fingertip touched another name scrawled in red across two seats. Lois. 'Is this your way of coping?'

'I suppose it is,' Leanne replied. 'But it's not about Lois.'

'Then who?'

'What did I tell you about Claudia Rothwell the other night?' asked Leanne. She hadn't been so drunk that she didn't remember their last conversation, but it was hazy around the edges.

'Not much more than I've read in the paper. And the fact she has a penchant for corporate merchandise,' he said with a smile.

'I saw Amelia the other day, and I think she recognised the Ronson Construction logo. It should all fit. Claudia was involved with the project, so she might have had one, but I can't see why she would hang on to a crappy key ring when she's become accustomed to the finer things.'

'She wasn't born with a silver spoon in her mouth though, was she?' Joe remarked. 'She went to Sedgefield High like the rest of us.'

Leanne's jaw dropped. 'Did you know her?'

'Not really, she was a year above me. It was one of my mates who recognised her. I don't think I would have made the connection otherwise.'

Leanne recalled the brief conversation she had had with another of Claudia's school friends. At the time, she had thought Kim was the one with the issues, but maybe it was the other way around. 'Can you do me a favour? Ask around and see if there's a story to tell.'

'Like?'

'I don't know. Let's just say I have some misgivings about what I've written.' She picked up her phone. She would let Joe decide for himself. 'Here, take a look at this and tell me what you see.'

While Joe watched Frankie's video, Dianne appeared with a second coffee for the new arrival. Her eyes were glassy as she gave Leanne a wink before leaving.

'Well?' Leanne asked after Joe returned her phone.

He picked up his drink and held it an inch from his mouth. Steam billowed in front of his face. 'She didn't know about the torch, did she?'

'It could have been the trauma. Selective memory,' suggested Leanne, playing devil's advocate.

'But you would expect her to know if she'd ever owned a key ring like that.' He put down his mug and saw things more clearly. 'You think she's lying?'

'When I interviewed Rex – he's the bloke who carried Amelia out of the theatre – he described someone with bloodied hands and torn fingernails. He was quite graphic about it, and yet the paramedic who treated Claudia says she didn't have a scratch on her. Even her husband says she lost a couple of false nails, but that was it.'

271

'Which means someone else saved Amelia, and Claudia just came along and took the credit. Jesus,' he said, with a mixture of disbelief and disgust.

'It would explain why she was so adamant about not meeting Amelia. We had to set up the reunion as a surprise, and now I wish we hadn't.'

Joe sat back in his seat and looked around the busy café. 'It's sickening how much we've been hailing her as a hero. I take it you're writing a piece to expose her?'

'Oh, I'd love to, but if I'm going to take down Claudia, I need irrefutable proof. Unfortunately, Rex isn't a reliable witness, and I'm going to have to find someone else who is.'

'Will this help?' Joe asked, returning his gaze to the seating plan.

'Maybe. That's why I asked you over. I need a second pair of eyes.'

While Leanne explained what she needed, Joe repositioned himself next to her so they could work together transferring the information to the seating plan. By the time Leanne had crossed off the final entry on the spreadsheet, their coffee cups were empty and the plate of toast no more than a puddle of melted butter and a sprinkling of crumbs.

'Are you two ready for a refill?' Dianne asked as she cleared the table.

Leanne was surprised to see that they were the only customers left. She turned to Joe. 'Are you staying?'

'I'll have another cup if you're having one.'

'Two more coffees, please, Di,' said Leanne.

When they returned their concentration to the seating plan, Joe asked, 'What next?'

'Good question.'

They had been working methodically, and Leanne had avoided getting sidetracked by the emerging picture until the job was done. 'I need to see who was sitting close to Amelia Parker,' she said, searching the names that Joe had written down while she called out the seat references. 'Where is she?'

Joe pointed to the left-hand side of the plan. 'Row F, seats 9 and 10.'

Leanne examined the other names in that row and was surprised to find Rex Russell's. It was interesting, but added nothing to her current lines of inquiry. 'Where's Claudia?'

'Row I, seats 8 and 9,' Joe replied, moving his finger three rows back. She had been sitting almost directly behind Amelia.

'Shit, it looks like this proves Claudia could have seen—' Leanne stopped. She had been distracted by another of Joe's annotations scribbled across the solitary aisle seat next to Claudia's. 'What does that say?'

'C Brody,' he said, squinting at his own handwriting.

'Oh, my God, it's Carole Brody,' Leanne said. 'I've interviewed her. She went alone because her daughter was heavily pregnant. But, she told me she was in the middle of the auditorium, not on the left.'

Joe shrugged. 'I suppose she was in one of the middle rows.'

'She talked about helping a woman who had become hysterical,' Leanne said. Her eyes widened. 'It was someone she had been sitting next to.'

'You think the woman was Claudia?'

Oh, please, God, let it be Claudia, Leanne thought, but her nose wrinkled. 'Carole said she hadn't seen Claudia. I suppose it's possible she was too traumatised to connect the woman she helped to the slick photos of Claudia in the press.' She rubbed her temples with the tips of her fingers. 'Damn, even if it was her, I have another witness who saw Claudia go back inside anyway. It doesn't prove she didn't save Amelia. This is the problem. There was so much confusion that it's given Claudia the opportunity to make up what she likes. I practically gifted her the story that set her up as the town's hero.'

'There was chaos everywhere,' Joe agreed. 'It wasn't as bad around the side of the theatre, but there was a crowd milling around the fire doors.'

'You were there? Could you have seen Claudia, or Carole maybe?' asked Leanne. She grabbed her phone and found an image of Carole on the *Courier*'s website.

Joe shook his head. 'It was like sensory overload. My mind registered only what I needed to see to reach my goal, and that was getting back to Lois.' He closed his eyes as if that would help. 'I ran around to the side hoping I could get back in. It was possible. Declan Gallagher obviously managed it, but a policeman stopped me. I did try, Leanne, but I couldn't get to her. I often wonder if it would have made a difference . . .'

For a brief time, they had been able to concentrate on something other than the loss they shared, but it would always come back to Lois. Losing her had almost broken them, but they were holding on. Leanne could forgive Joe because he had done nothing wrong. One day she hoped to forgive herself too, but that didn't mean she was ready to stop fighting. Not every injustice had to be accepted.

23

When Leanne awoke, her head throbbed, and there was an irritating buzz in the bunk room that made her ears hurt. She and Joe had spent most of the previous day in the pub after leaving the café. It wasn't quite like old times – they had spent the entire afternoon huddled next to an outdoor heater in the beer garden – but it was close. They had laughed and they had cried, they had drunk in Lois's honour, and they had drunk to drown their sorrows, but most of all they had acknowledged the empty chair at the table. Leanne wasn't sure what time she had staggered home, but it couldn't have been particularly late because she had apparently had a productive evening. The bedlinen smelled fresh, and she had a vague recollection of putting on a pair of Marigolds.

Peeling open an eye, Leanne admired the delicate ice patterns on the inside of the windows. The central heating hadn't kicked in yet, and she considered rolling over and going back to sleep for another hour or two. She had a court case to cover in Chester, but it wouldn't matter if she missed the preamble. She needed more sleep, but first she had to find the source of the buzzing. Slapping a hand blindly across the small bedside shelf, she found her phone. Whoever was calling was persistent.

'I hope I didn't wake you,' said Carole Brody.

Preferring to snuggle down rather than sit up, Leanne pulled the duvet over her head. 'No, it's fine,' she said as brightly as she could muster.

'I'm sorry I couldn't take your call last night. I was babysitting Curtis and I didn't want him waking up. He's a little bugger. Barely a year old and he has us wrapped around his little finger.'

'Thanks for getting back to me,' Leanne said, even though she didn't recall phoning her in the first place. 'I have some news. I might have tracked down the woman you helped out of the theatre.'

'Oh. I see.'

It wasn't the excited response Leanne was hoping for. 'You did say she had been sitting next to you? You shared some wine gums.' It was a detail that Leanne was surprised to recall, but it would have been included in her notes and there was every possibility she had gone through them last night. 'I know you said you didn't see Claudia Rothwell last time we spoke, but is it possible you were mistaken? I think it might have been her next to you.'

'*The* Claudia Rothwell?' Carole asked, the shock only hitting her now. She laughed. 'Oh, no, it wasn't her.'

'You're sure?'

'Without a shadow of a doubt.'

The throbbing in Leanne's head intensified and she wanted to throw up. How did Claudia manage to dodge every attempt to corner her, and all without trying? No one was that good.

Leanne pulled the bedclothes away and braved the cold, hoping the shock would get her brain firing on all cylinders.

'What about the second seat along?' she asked. Two complimentary tickets had been issued, even though Claudia had used only one. 'Could she have been sitting there?'

'Hmm, I don't think so,' Carole said, quashing Leanne's remaining hope. 'There was another lady, but no, I'm absolutely certain it wasn't Claudia.'

'Are you sure? Would it help if you took another look at her picture?'

'No. I'm one hundred per cent certain it wasn't her. And I'm sorry, but I do have to go. More babysitting duties.'

'That's OK.'

'Bye then,' Carole said. The line went dead.

Leanne grabbed her dressing gown, pushed her feet into her slipper boots, and hobbled through to the galley where works surfaces had been cleaned, and dishes washed and cleared away. She was too cold to admire her handiwork, and moved towards the back of the boat and the equally tidy saloon. The log burner had been cleaned and stacked with fresh kindling and logs. She thanked her former drunken self as she struck a match to the firelighter and watched the flames take hold.

As she crouched down to absorb the heat, she noticed the rolled-up seating plan resting next to the steps by the door. She should be relieved that she hadn't left it in the pub, but at that precise moment, she was more inclined to feed it into the fire. As her cheeks began to tingle with warmth, she sat back and crossed her legs, resting her back against the corner of the futon.

Claudia wasn't Carole's hysterical woman, nor was she

277

in the second seat, which made sense, because surely Claudia would have mentioned giving away the spare ticket, or taking a companion – not that Claudia had ever given information freely, but still. Breathing in through her nose, Leanne let go of her disappointment with a long exhalation. Her mind stilled.

'Oh. My. God,' she said out loud.

Cogs whirred inside her head and she ignored the fresh wave of nausea. Neither of the two women had been Claudia. So where the hell had she been sitting?

24

Leanne became fascinated by the droplets of condensation that shimmered like pearls on the inside of her windscreen. Once they reached critical mass, they etched a seemingly random path down the film of moisture clinging to the glass. Or were they random paths? Like her thoughts, the droplets zigzagged this way and that, absorbing whatever they touched, growing in weight, moving faster, and then plop. Game over.

In terms of her investigation, Leanne was very much at the zigzagging stage and no closer to knowing what the final outcome would be. When she had spoken to Carole Brody earlier in the week, she had been expecting some form of answer, only to be given another question. And a subsequent call from Joe had thrown something new into the mix. He had done some digging of his own and had uncovered another anomaly; a discrepancy between a younger Claudia and her public persona.

Using the sleeve of her jacket to wipe the window, Leanne could see Claudia's Mercedes through the security gates. She had been staking out the apartment for two hours, and had positioned herself in the passenger seat of her Fiesta so she could get some work done on her laptop. It would be pointless ringing the intercom, just as it had been pointless waiting for her calls to be answered. Claudia no longer trusted Leanne, and with good reason. Whatever the outcome and whatever the protests from Mal, Leanne would not be writing any more positive pieces about Mrs Rothwell. She didn't deserve it.

As time crawled, Leanne's laptop went into sleep mode; her sleeve became sodden from wiping the window, and her hopes of a confrontation dwindled. She had lost sleep rehearsing how this would go, and it could all be for nothing.

Leanne checked her watch for what she decided would be the last time, when she heard the clatter of metal as the gates hummed into life. She could see only the bonnet of Claudia's Mercedes, but the car was moving. She snapped shut her laptop and slid it into the footwell before grabbing an envelope.

As Leanne took up position in front of the partly opened gates, vapour issued forth from her nostrils as if she were a fire-breathing dragon. She was ready for this, unlike Claudia, who had been driving slowly towards the gates when she spotted Leanne. The car juddered to a halt and Claudia's mouth fell open, only to snap shut again as the reporter approached.

Leanne stepped into the path of the Mercedes. If Claudia chose to stay behind the wheel, Leanne's questions would be shouted at her, or she could preserve some dignity and get out of the car. Wisely, she chose the latter.

'What do you want?' Claudia demanded. Her dark hair had been tied back into a tight ponytail that sharpened her features. She was in her gym gear and pulled her hoodie tight across her chest.

'A little chat, that's all.'

'I'm rather busy. Can we do this another time?'

Leanne considered the request. 'Erm, no.'

Claudia took a deep breath and attempted a smile that cut a sharp line across her face. 'So how can I help you, Leanne?'

'I've been continuing my investigations.'

'If you're after something newsworthy, you could always write about the hardship fund,' Claudia suggested. 'We've been inundated with applications and should be making our first payments soon. I'll send you the press release when it's ready, but until then, I have nothing to add.'

The dismissal had no effect. Leanne held her position. If Claudia wanted to pretend that Leanne hadn't called her out about being Amelia's hero, she could play that game too. 'Amelia's quite upset that you haven't returned her calls.'

With her arms remaining across her body, Claudia squeezed her shoulders together. She was shivering, which would have made her appear vulnerable in someone else's eyes. 'I haven't received any calls from Amelia, or her mum.'

'Could there be a fault on your line?' asked Leanne mischievously. 'You haven't answered my calls either.'

'I'm sorry, that was deliberate,' Claudia said. 'The last few months have been overwhelming and I've needed to take a step back.'

'That's all right. I thought it might have been something I said.'

'Look, Leanne. I can assure you I haven't been avoiding calls from Amelia. I can only presume her mother wrote

281

down the wrong number. We were all a bit emotional at the time.'

'I can double-check with Kathryn.' It wasn't meant to sound like a threat. Or maybe it was.

'Please, I never intended to upset anyone,' Claudia tried. Met with only a blank stare, she crept closer and lowered her voice. 'Off the record, I've had some health issues since losing the baby. I'm trying to get back on my feet again, but it isn't easy.'

The confession made Leanne feel awkward, but she had no sympathy for the woman who was standing next to her Mercedes in top of the range gym gear, begging Leanne to see her as a victim. Her loss didn't cancel out the lies she had told, or the glory she had stolen from someone less fortunate. Did that make Leanne a heartless bully? Or was that simply how Claudia wanted her to feel?

Leanne opened the envelope she had taken from the car and took out a sheet of paper. 'Amelia asked me to give you this.'

'That's so sweet, thank you,' said Claudia, reaching to take the drawing. Leanne held on to it.

'I think she's remembered a few more details. She keeps drawing you with a necklace.'

Claudia's smile was fixed as she looked more closely at the sketch. 'So I see.'

'What was the pendant like?'

With a firm tug, Claudia took the sheet of paper. 'It was over a year ago. I'm sorry, I don't have a clue. What did Amelia say?'

'She was almost as vague as you.'

Leanne wanted to take Claudia's evasion as further

confirmation that she was no hero, but could anyone be expected to recall what jewellery they had been wearing on the night of the fire? Actually, Leanne could. It was the eternity symbol she wore now. Lois's gift.

'Well, thank you for delivering this.' Claudia stepped away.

'Did Phillipa tell you I interviewed her?'

Claudia spun around. 'An interview? When?'

'Last week. I must say I was surprised when she agreed to see me.' Leanne laughed as if the next thought tickled her. 'She seemed to think you and I were best friends.'

'Why on earth would she think that?' Claudia asked. Realising she had made the suggestion sound like an insult, she quickly backtracked. 'Not that I'm saying we haven't developed a bond of sorts. You were the one who persuaded me to admit I saved Amelia, after all. I would never have come forward if it weren't for you.'

Leanne didn't flinch. 'Oh, I don't think I should be taking any credit for that particular story.'

Claudia waited for Leanne to explain why she had spoken to Phillipa, and when she didn't, she was forced to ask, 'What did you and Phillipa discuss?'

'She mentioned you may have been talking to another survivor – Karin Gallagher. Have you?'

'None of your business,' said Claudia. Her hand reached for the car door. 'What I mean is, I speak to many survivors who have contacted the charity, but it's in the strictest of confidence. I can't confirm or deny who we've been supporting.'

'Did you know Karin tracked Phillipa down after the findings were published? She accused her of having an affair with her brother and implied the information had come from you. Phillipa presumed I was the original source.'

'And what did you tell her?'

'The truth,' Leanne answered, wondering if Claudia recognised the word. 'That you told me.'

'This is ridiculous. I don't know why I'm getting the blame,' Claudia said, a little too petulantly. She had visibly paled. 'I might have indulged in a bit of gossip, but can you blame me? You made me realise how Phillipa deserves to take some responsibility for the fire. Why should I care about protecting her reputation? She killed my baby.'

'So you made up a story to get back at her?'

'I didn't make it up. Who's to say it's not true? Everyone knew how secretive Declan could be, and he did have quite a track record. He slept with his wife's own sister for goodness' sake.'

Leanne wasn't listening. 'But as we know, you are good at making up stories.'

Claudia wiped the sheen of sweat from her upper lip.

'How did your mum die, Claudia? Because your old school friends don't remember it quite like you do.' Thanks to Joe, one of Claudia's lies had been discovered and verified. It wasn't the dramatic reveal Leanne longed for, but it was a start.

'Have you been harassing them too? If you're not careful, Leanne, someone is going to put in a complaint about you.'

Rather than respond to the threat, Leanne waited it out.

'Why are you doing this?' Claudia demanded. Her grip on the door handle tightened. 'You really want to know what happened with my mum? Fine! She didn't die, she left us. I was five years old. Dad promised she'd come back, but she never did. He was stringing me along, doing everything he could to avoid accepting sole responsibility for his daughter. He's the liar!'

284

'Is that why you don't see him any more? Or is it because you're afraid Justin will find out you've been lying to him? Wouldn't it have been less painful to simply tell the truth?'

'Is it a crime to want people to think better of you?'

'I expect that depends on the lie.'

Claudia shook her head in despair. 'I thought you were better than this, Leanne. This isn't news. Why are we even having this conversation?'

'I don't know, Claudia. Why do you think we're having this conversation?'

Claudia didn't answer. There was no smile now, forced or otherwise.

'Don't you want to know what else I'm working on?'

With one hand on the car, the other resting on her hip, Claudia had miraculously become impervious to the cold that had been making her shiver. She held Leanne's gaze and refused to be baited.

'I've acquired a seating plan of who was sitting where in the theatre.' Leanne didn't say how she had acquired the information because Phillipa had asked her not to, but Claudia's eyes widened. She knew. 'For instance, I have it on very good authority that your tickets were in Row I, which was three rows behind Amelia. You would have been in either seat 8 or 9. Do you remember which?'

'No.'

Leanne's nostrils flared. 'Funny thing is, I know the lady who was sitting in seat 10, which was the aisle seat.' She didn't offer any more information on Mrs Brody either, given their pithy telephone conversation.

'Is there a point to this?'

'The lady in question is adamant that you weren't one of

285

the two women sitting next to her. Two tickets. Two seats. And you were in neither. So I suppose my point is, where were you?'

Claudia raised her gaze to the skies. Thinking time presumably. 'If you must know, there was a mix-up at the box office and someone was already in my seat when I got there. I didn't want to cause a fuss so I sat somewhere else.'

'Where? Was it in the same row?' Leanne knew it couldn't be. Every other seat in that row had been occupied, she had checked.

'I don't recall. It was in that general location,' Claudia said, her voice clipped.

'Could you be a little more specific?'

Claudia's eyes shone. 'Are you suggesting I wasn't there?' she asked, her words scratching against a constricting throat. 'Because if that's the case, maybe you should go back and speak to the witnesses who were ever so keen to tell you that they'd seen me. I don't know what your problem is with me all of a sudden, but this is getting silly. Whatever your game is, please stop.'

'You're right, let's stop playing games, Claudia. I don't dispute that you were at the theatre at some stage, but I don't believe that you went into a burning building to save Amelia. So tell me, what were you doing?'

Claudia's eyes were no longer shining, they were shimmering with tears. 'I'm getting back in my car and I'm driving through the gates, whether you're standing in front of them or not.'

'That's OK. I think we're done,' said Leanne. 'Thank you for your time.'

Walking back to her car, Leanne didn't look over her shoulder to watch Claudia drive away. The car's loud revs told her all she needed to know. She had rattled Claudia, and that felt good. She was still mulling over their conversation when she heard her phone ring.

'Where the hell is your update on the McVey case?' Mal demanded. 'You were supposed to have it over to me first thing this morning.'

'I'm working on it,' Leanne lied as she slipped behind the wheel. She closed the door gently so her editor wouldn't work out that she was in her car.

'Finish it,' he hissed. 'And then get into the office. We need to talk.'

25

Leanne skulked past Mal's office in the hope that he wouldn't notice her arrival. She had submitted her copy, or to be more precise, she had cobbled together the required wordage.

'What's wrong with Mal?'

Frankie looked up from her screen. 'Nothing that I know of.'

'Ah, so it's just me he's got it in for,' Leanne said, hoping it was only her missed deadline that had riled him.

Her friend grimaced. 'I'd say we're about to find out.'

'When did you get back?' Mal asked before Leanne had a chance to turn around fully.

'Just now.' She made a point of sliding off her jacket. 'I was going to make a hot drink. Can I get you one?'

'That can wait.'

Mal lumbered back to his office, taking it for granted that Leanne would follow. She did, and when he came to an unexpected halt, she almost walked into him. 'Actually, Frankie, I might need you too.'

By the time Frankie had closed the door, Mal was back in his chair with his hands behind his head. His bloodshot eyes bored into Leanne. 'I can only presume your exposé on Claudia Rothwell has gathered pace considering you've let the ball drop on all your other assignments.'

Leanne sat down on the battered sofa. 'I suppose it has taken some interesting turns,' she said, and was about to give Mal the edited highlights containing all of the highs and none of the lows, but he was ahead of her.

'Why don't you start by explaining why you felt it necessary to pay Phillipa Montgomery a visit?'

Leanne made sure not to glance at Frankie, who had joined her on the sofa. Her colleague wouldn't have been the one to tell Mal, and Leanne didn't want Mal to know she had been aware of the plan.

'Has she been in touch?' she asked.

'Not directly, no, but I had an interesting chat with Evelyn,' he said, referring to one of the *Courier*'s owners, who was a particularly close friend of Phillipa's. 'She wondered if we could do a feature on Phillipa, something that might seed a change in attitude, revert perceptions back to the pre-disaster era so she can leave Sedgefield with her head held high.'

Mal didn't need to explain that when Evelyn made a suggestion, it was a direct order.

'Evelyn seems to think you would be the best person to write it,' Mal continued. 'She's under the impression that Phillipa trusts you.'

'Technically, it shouldn't matter if Phillipa trusts Leanne or not,' Frankie chipped in. 'Assuming you want her to write an honest observation and not a piece of propaganda.'

Frankie had tensed. She was squaring up for a fight to protect Leanne from doing something that her conscience wouldn't allow.

289

Mal rubbed a hand over his face as he straightened up. 'Anyone else want a drink?' he asked, opening a drawer. He picked up a half-empty bottle of whisky and added a splash to his stained coffee cup.

'It's not a problem,' said Leanne, surprising them both. 'I'll write a piece about her.'

Mal knocked back his whisky and topped up his cup before putting away the bottle. 'Evelyn would especially like you to focus on the strength of the Montgomerys' marriage. Something about how they have been a constant in each other's lives, blah, blah, blah.' He was testing her. 'Apparently there was a rumour about an affair with Declan Gallagher. Heard anything?'

'Bits,' Leanne said vaguely. 'But there was nothing to it.'

'Are you sure you want to do this?' asked Frankie.

'Look, I know I've spent a year using Phillipa as target practice, but it turns out she's not all bad. I'd go as far as to say the events of the past year have left her ever so slightly humbled.'

Frankie tutted. 'Not enough to stop her pulling strings and grabbing some self-promotion.'

'She likes power,' Leanne said. 'Would we be so critical if she were a man?'

'Yes,' Frankie said quickly.

'I don't think she's doing this simply for her own benefit. She's accepted that her position in Sedgefield is untenable,' explained Leanne, as shocked as her colleagues that she should be defending Phillipa.

'So why bother?' asked Frankie.

'She wants to put one particular person in her place, and I don't see why that can't work to our advantage too.'

'Have we come full circle back to Claudia?' Mal guessed. 'Do you want to fill us in?'

'I've been putting together a detailed plan of who was sitting where at the theatre, all in my own time,' she said, for her editor's benefit. 'And guess what? Two, as yet unidentified, women were in the seats allocated to Claudia.'

'Then where was she?' asked Mal.

'That is a very good question, and one I put to her this morning,' Leanne said, enjoying the change in atmosphere she was creating. The tension had left the room, replaced by growing anticipation. 'She claims there was a mix-up with the tickets.'

'And was there?'

'Not that she's ever mentioned before. Her latest story is that she managed to find an empty seat nearby, but she was very evasive about where, and I'm not surprised. The stalls were packed that night.'

Mal had his cup halfway to his mouth. 'Are we saying Claudia was never at the theatre?'

'I don't think anyone can argue that she wasn't there. She suffered the effects of smoke inhalation, and Beth McCulloch saw her turn around at the exit, which implies she was there to begin with,' Leanne said, but she didn't feel as comfortable with this assertion as once she had.

Frankie sensed it too. 'Did she actually see Claudia turn around? That suggests one quick movement, but if you look at the comments online since the anniversary, quite a few people mention seeing Claudia standing for a while by the fire doors.'

'Let me check.'

Leanne's cheeks burnt with a mixture of humiliation and

fury as she realised her mistake. She had seen the comments too, but had dismissed them because they appeared to support the argument that Claudia had been helping people. She searched her phone for the recording of Beth's interview.

'Here it is,' she said, after a few false starts to find the right place. She pressed play.

Above the rush of wind against the microphone, they listened to Beth explain: 'She was encouraging everyone to get out, reassuring us that the fire crews were on their way, and then she pushed her way back inside.'

'I can't believe I missed it,' Leanne said.

'You missed nothing,' Frankie told her. 'None of us ever considered the possibility that Claudia, or anyone for that matter, would have the gall to lie the way she has.'

'We've all been taken in by her,' Mal said. 'Unless . . . If we're not disputing that she did go inside at some point, couldn't she still be Amelia's hero?'

'No!' Leanne and Frankie said in unison.

'Look,' Leanne continued. 'We have to forget every assumption we've ever made about Claudia. She's a compulsive liar who creates new versions of herself to combat her insecurities. She had a tough upbringing, and it was probably a defence mechanism she learnt early on. When she married Justin, she cut herself off from her old life, smoothed over her accent, and did her best to assimilate, but she would have felt every slight. She wanted to break into Phillipa's inner circle, and it must have stung when she was given complimentary tickets to an amateur performance, knowing it was probably because no one else wanted them. Of course she didn't go.'

'Then where was she before the fire?' asked Mal.

'Not at home,' Leanne said. 'I'm sure Justin isn't in on her lies. He wouldn't have known she was skipping the show, which means she would have gone someplace where she wouldn't be spotted.'

'It would need to have been close if she heard the alarm and got to the theatre before the emergency services cordoned off the area,' Frankie added.

Leanne smiled. Her investigation had gathered momentum, much like the drops of condensation running down the windscreen earlier. 'Or she was with someone who had a text alert.'

Mal leant forward. 'Where are you going with this, Leanne?'

'Claudia became defensive earlier when I tackled her about the rumours of Phillipa and Declan's affair, and I'm not sure, but I think she slipped up. She talked about Declan having a track record with women.'

Frankie shrugged. 'I'd say that's common knowledge.'

With her overdue article and the drive to Chester, Leanne hadn't had time to figure it all out, but having now established that Claudia was missing when the fire started, the pieces fitted together with surprising ease. 'But how many people know that when he cheated on his wife, it was with her sister?'

'Is that true?' Mal asked Frankie. She had been the one to interview Declan's ex-wife.

'If it is, I'm pretty sure his ex doesn't know about it. So how the hell did Claudia find out?'

Both Mal and Frankie were looking to Leanne to say what they were all thinking. 'Bryony Sutherland was the first to mention the rumours of an affair to me, and I'm convinced

Claudia threw Phillipa's name into the mix as a decoy. It was Claudia who was involved with Declan,' Leanne said, shocked to hear the revelation spoken aloud. She had thought Claudia and Justin were the perfect couple, but it was all smoke and mirrors, much like the rest of Claudia's life.

'But if Claudia was with Declan, why wasn't she in the CCTV footage of him running to the theatre?' asked Mal. 'He was caught on two cameras on the high street, and he was definitely alone.'

'I don't know the answer to that,' Leanne admitted, 'but I do know Claudia is devious enough to have made the extra effort to avoid detection if she were having an affair. And let's face it, there's a hell of a lot of other questions left to be answered, like why she went inside at all, risking the life of her unborn child.'

'She might have gone in after the baby's father?' asked Frankie.

Mal didn't blink. 'Unbelievable.'

'Are you still questioning my judgement?'

'No, Leanne. I'd say you're doing a fine job despite your interfering editor.'

Mal sat back in his chair and, the longer he looked at her, the more colour returned to his cheeks. He was fighting a smile. They all were.

26

Justin rested a hand on Claudia's back. 'Feeling better?'

She smiled in answer, not trusting herself to speak. No, she didn't feel better, she felt sick to the stomach and the sensation had intensified the moment she had stepped across Phillipa's threshold. Justin had been telling her that they should make the most of Phillipa's company while she was still in town, but what did sweet, naive Justin know? She didn't deserve him, but she suspected she did deserve whatever Phillipa planned to serve up that evening.

'Not feeling well, dear?' Robert asked. 'You do look a little peaky.'

'It's nothing,' Claudia said, slipping her hands beneath the dining table to hide her tremors.

'What's this I hear? Are you coming down with something, Claudia?' Phillipa asked, arriving in the smaller of their two dining rooms. She carried a platter of salmon terrine on a bed of endives, supplied no doubt by professional caterers.

The smell of fish made Claudia's stomach heave. If she had known it was going to be an intimate dinner party for four, she would have cried off. She had been left drained and exhausted by Leanne's impromptu visit earlier in the week. Her worst fears were being realised. The truth was being revealed, one lie at a time.

'Honestly, it's nothing,' Claudia said, smiling sweetly.

Robert lifted a bottle of Sancerre from a wine cooler on a silver stand. With the air of a sommelier, he removed the cork cleanly and began filling glasses, careful to have the label on show for the benefit of his guests. In her youth, Claudia would have been more interested in the label on the back. The higher percentage proof, the better.

Robert stood with one hand behind his back as he leant forward, but he didn't immediately fill Claudia's glass. 'I could get you a soft drink if you prefer?'

From the corner of her eye, Claudia noticed Phillipa stiffen. Good grief, they thought she was pregnant. 'Wine is absolutely fine. I'm hoping it will settle my stomach,' she insisted.

'We are trying to cut back,' Justin said above the glug of wine being poured. 'Claudia wants us to do Dry January.'

'I didn't know people still did that,' replied Phillipa. Her idea of a detox was more likely to be a week at a premium wellness retreat, complete with colonic irrigation.

'The truth is, we're trying again for a baby,' Claudia said, to clear up any doubt about her current condition. 'And the fitter we are, the better our chances.'

'It's a shame about what happened,' Robert said, repeating what had become a worn-out platitude.

Phillipa sliced into the terrine. 'It must be so difficult when there's constant news of other couples having babies,' she said. To press home the notion, she added, 'I suppose you heard that Sasha had a little girl?'

Justin twisted the stem of his wine glass. 'Yes, we heard.'

Their host gave Justin a look of apology, while keeping his wife in her peripheral vision. 'Sorry, I shouldn't have brought it up. I know how much you and she longed for a family, but if it can happen for Sasha, it can happen for you two.'

'We sent a small gift,' Claudia said brightly.

And it had been very small; a token gesture that said they were happy for the new parents, and that it wasn't awkward at all.

'That's so sweet of you,' Phillipa said in a tone that was usually accompanied by a pat on the head. Instead she offered Claudia a slab of salmon mousse.

Robert topped up Claudia's glass before the first course was over – the wine had made the food more palatable. She forked tiny slivers of terrine into her mouth, using her teeth to scrape it off the tines so her lips didn't have to touch the food. There were times like this that she longed for some salt and pepper ribs from her favourite Chinese takeaway. Salmon terrine was the price of her success. She hoped it was the only price.

The conversation moved on and Claudia chose not to engage in talk about the housing market, until Justin dropped her in it. He really thought they were amongst friends.

'Claudia wanted me to put in an offer for this place.'

'Here?' Phillipa said, her cool demeanour slipping a touch.

'Too late, I'm afraid,' Robert said. 'There was a bit of a bidding war, but we accepted an offer this afternoon, so it's all systems go.'

'Does that mean you'll be moving soon?'

Phillipa laughed. 'My, my, Claudia, you make it sound like you can't wait to see the back of us.'

'Now that couldn't be further from the truth,' Justin replied with a chuckle that was shared with Robert. Their husbands were oblivious to the underlying tension between their wives. 'You've been the perfect role model for Claudia. She wouldn't be where she is today without you.'

'Oh, I don't think I can take any credit for what Claudia's been doing lately.'

'I haven't done anything that—' Claudia's half-hearted attempt to say something that was conciliatory but not cowed was drowned out by Justin.

'Nonsense,' he said. 'And I'm sure Claudia could benefit from your guidance going forward. Wilmslow isn't that far. We should do this more often. It's been a while.'

If Justin was thinking back to a previous dinner party when it had been a cosy foursome at the Montgomerys', he was travelling back further than Claudia's time as his wife. She imagined Justin and Sasha had been invited over for dinner regularly until his first wife had called an end to their five-year marriage.

When Justin had bumped into Claudia all those years ago at the tennis club, his heart and pride had been wounded. He would tell her later that his friends thought he was on the rebound when he announced he had fallen head-over-heels in love again. And of those who chimed in with advice, Claudia suspected that Phillipa's voice would have been amongst the loudest.

'We want to offer you support too, Phillipa,' Claudia said, deciding it was her turn to point score. 'You must have felt very isolated when the whole town turned against you.'

'It was a dark time,' Robert said solemnly. 'And we didn't quite appreciate how dark until we came home. Some of the vile stories that have been circulating are outrageous.'

298

Robert Montgomery was too polite to say what particular products of the rumour mill were causing his cheeks to glow crimson. He was normally a stoic man, submitting quietly to a self-imposed exile and accepting there was no way back despite Phillipa's exoneration. This was different. His present angst had nothing to do with the Empress fire, and everything to do with his wife's reputation.

Phillipa placed a hand over his. 'It's not worth getting upset over, darling. I said the truth will out, and the piece in the *Courier* today was certainly a slap in the face to some.'

'It was a lovely article,' Justin said. 'And long overdue.'

The feature Justin had read out to Claudia that morning had been vomit-inducing. It had set out a convincing argument to hail Phillipa for her past achievements, envy her for her happy marriage, sympathise with her for the guilt she would always carry and, most controversially, to forgive her.

Claudia had checked the online version later in the day, hoping to find a torrent of abuse in the comments section, but the piece had been well received, not least because it had been written by Leanne Pitman, trusted champion of Sedgefield. It would seem that the reporter and Phillipa had joined forces, and it didn't take much of an imagination to work out who they were gunning for. Claudia's attempt at misdirection had backfired spectacularly.

'It was good to read something positive for once,' Phillipa said, 'but we shouldn't forget how fickle the press can be. They raise you up as a hero one minute, and rip you to shreds the next.' Turning to Claudia, she added, 'You need to be very careful, my dear. You could be next.'

'Now if that happened, I'd lose all faith in the world,' said Robert, clearly not privy to the subtext of the discussion.

'Thank you, Robert, but I agree with Phillipa. I for one would rather keep the press at arm's length. If they can exploit a situation, they will. And they do like to play us off against each other.'

'It's a sad truth,' replied Phillipa. 'All it takes is one reporter holding a grudge to make our lives a misery, and Leanne Pitman falls into that category, I'm afraid. She lost her best friend in the fire and, while I'd say she's finished with me, her crusade is far from over.' Despite the dire warning, Phillipa's eyes sparkled with delight. 'It won't matter that you saved a little girl's life, the likes of Leanne will want to know how you dared to make a profit from it.'

'I've never taken a penny,' Claudia said, aware that she and Phillipa had entered a weird game of cat and mouse, where both wanted to be the cat. 'Even the payments I received for my interviews went straight to the memorial fund.'

'I wasn't talking about financial benefits, but surely you've profited in other ways,' suggested Phillipa. Sensing the restlessness around the table, she quickly added, 'Not that I, or any of your friends see it that way, but in my experience, you have to be especially careful when it comes to public perception, or else you'll be accused of having inappropriate affiliations.' She wrinkled her nose to ensure the idea sounded particularly seedy. 'I always made sure never to be caught with a pen or a notepad that had a business logo on it.'

'Thanks, I appreciate the advice,' Claudia said, draining her glass. Before she could look to Robert for a top-up, Justin reached for a carafe of water and filled a tall glass. A not-so-subtle hint that she was drinking too fast.

'And if you can bear some more,' Phillipa said, eager to

dispense the next nugget of wisdom. 'You might want to deny that torch you used during your rescue mission had anything to do with Ronson Construction.'

'Sorry, I don't understand,' said Justin.

He was looking at his wife, but Phillipa was quicker with a response. 'Ah, you weren't at the open day, were you, Justin? Ronsons had lots of merchandise on offer, including these funny little torches on key rings. It was a great way to sneak their name into the public consciousness, but they were *very* cheaply made. I'm surprised Claudia's was still working, what, two years later? Or did you go back for more?' She could answer this question too. 'I know our contractors liked to look after our visitors.'

The salmon terrine churning in Claudia's stomach threatened to reappear. 'I didn't get the torch from Ronsons.'

'That's the ticket!' Phillipa said, laughing. 'You keep to that story.'

Except it wasn't a story. Phillipa was fishing in the right place, but she had chosen the wrong bait. Claudia had never owned a single one of those ugly key rings, but she could remember the day they were being handed out. It was the first time she had met Declan Gallagher, and Phillipa was right in one regard. The contractors did like to look after their visitors.

'Can I tempt you with a freebie?' Declan had asked, twirling a pen in his hand.

They were in the town hall, and Claudia had been admiring the architect's model of the revamped theatre when Declan Gallagher had interrupted her thoughts. He was dressed in hi-vis and a hard hat, somewhat unnecessary, but as she would soon discover, Declan liked to draw attention.

Claudia moved away with a polite refusal.

'How about a torch? Look, this one actually works,' he persisted.

Claudia caught the flash of a light being aimed at her, but didn't raise her gaze. 'No, thank you.'

'Come on, there must be something I can give you to raise a smile?'

Claudia wasn't sure if it was his Northern Irish accent or his cheesy banter, but she looked up and made the mistake that would become her downfall. She smiled at him.

'Now doesn't that feel better?' he said, smiling too.

Declan was a little younger than Justin, his dark hair curlier, and his hazel eyes were brighter and kinder too. Not that Justin wasn't kind. They had been married for just over a year at that point, and she didn't doubt that he loved her. It was just that there had been a noticeable change of late.

In the early days of their courtship, Justin had enjoyed introducing Claudia to a lifestyle vastly different from her own, but the novelty had worn off and her new husband was away on business more and more often. He knew Claudia was capable of establishing a new life without further handholding, but what was the point if he wasn't around to cheer her on? Claudia had felt lost and abandoned, and there was Declan, shining a light towards her with one of those stupid key rings. A thousand butterflies had taken flight in her stomach.

Saliva filled Claudia's mouth at the memory, and she thought she might be sick.

'I can't say I ever saw this torch of Claudia's,' Justin was saying, 'but I'm glad she had it.'

'I dread to think what else they carry around in their handbags,' Robert said with a wink.

Phillipa gave a throaty chuckle. 'There are some things you're better off not knowing.'

Claudia was tiring of their battle of wits. If Phillipa had invited her over to watch her squirm, then she had succeeded. Hopefully, it was enough to settle the score. It would have to be, because right now Claudia needed to choose her battles, and this wasn't one of them. 'I'll drink to that,' she said, reaching for her wine to signal a truce. Her glass was empty. It felt like a bad omen.

27

When Leanne finally persuaded Carole Brody to agree to another interview, she wasn't on the hunt for more information on Claudia, but she did want to know more about the two women who had occupied her seats. They were the proof that Claudia wasn't where she had claimed to be, and if Leanne could prove one lie, the rest would fall like dominoes. Or that was what she hoped as Carole opened the door.

'Thanks for agreeing to see me.'

Carole's face was creased with wrinkles. 'Come in.'

There was no offer of refreshments and, although the house was warm, Leanne didn't take off her coat.

'I want to put this all behind me,' Carole said, wringing her hands.

'I know, and I'm sorry for making you go over it again, but if I've learnt one thing in the last year, it's that you can have six hundred people experience the same thing and every one will tell a different story. I wasn't there, but even I came up with my own version of events, and it's one I'm currently rewriting. I can't imagine what it must be like for you.'

Carole pressed the tips her fingers to her lips.

'I don't mean to upset you, Carole.'

'Ignore me, I'm being silly,' she said, but her voice wobbled. 'I never could hold back my emotions. Too sensitive for my own good.'

'You care too much about others. It's like your super-power.'

The joke was met with a howl as Carole put her hands over her face and slumped down onto the sofa. Leanne grabbed a box of tissues from a shelf.

'I'm sorry,' Carole said, grabbing a handful and blowing her nose. 'I knew I'd be found out. It was only a matter of time.'

Leanne sat down on the armchair. Her mouth opened, then shut again.

'You think you know what you'd do in an emergency, but the reality is very different,' Carole continued between sobs. 'I was terrified I wasn't going to see our Rachel again, but I was just as scared for her as I was for myself, and that's the truth. I imagined the police knocking on her door and her collapsing with shock. She could have lost the baby.'

'What are you trying to tell me, Carole?'

'I wasn't a hero, not in the slightest,' she admitted. 'It was me who needed help getting out. I grabbed hold of this woman and refused to let go of her. Have you found her? Does she remember me?'

'Carole—'

She wiped her nose. 'It's OK. I knew this day would come.' The confession had lifted the weight from her shoulders and she managed to raise her head to meet Leanne's puzzled gaze.

'I'm not investigating you, if that's what you've been worried about. I'm looking into something else entirely.'

'But when you asked about Claudia Rothwell, you said you were tracking down the woman who was with me.'

'And I would very much like to find her, but right now I don't have any other leads. I was hoping you could help.'

Carole was quiet for a moment. 'I was deliberately vague with you before. I was worried that if you spoke to her, you'd realise I'd been lying. I didn't want my daughter to be ashamed of me and, worse still, for Curtis to grow up knowing that his nanna was a coward.'

'You're not a coward.'

'Oh, but I was selfish,' Carole replied. 'That poor woman was so busy looking after me that she didn't realise she'd lost her friend. I was clinging to her for dear life. I hope they're both OK. What do you need to know? I don't remember much.'

'Can you tell me what they looked like?'

'The lady we lost had dark hair, but that's about all I can say. Her friend was the one who sat next to me. Now, I think I'd recognise her again. She had shorter hair. Golden, like a halo.'

'OK, good. Now, can you cast your mind back to the start of the evening? The reason I asked you about Claudia was because her tickets were for the seats next to yours. I've been told there might have been a mix-up at the box office.'

'A mix-up?' Carole asked. She dabbed her eyes with a crumpled tissue. 'Not as far as I could tell. I was already in my seat when the two ladies arrived. I was knitting a baby blanket for Rachel, so there was a bit of a kerfuffle letting them past.'

'And you didn't notice anyone challenge them?'

'No. If anything, I was impressed with the whole organisation considering the staff were so new. What an induction they had that night.' She shook her head.

'I know this is going to be difficult, but I want to show you something that might prod your memory,' Leanne said, taking out her phone.

Joe had suggested Leanne take another look at the videos of the disaster that had been uploaded by members of the public onto YouTube. She had felt voyeuristic, but it was necessary and it had been fruitful.

'I've come across a recording that was taken further back in the stalls. The stage is bright so it only shows the audience in silhouette, but I think I've spotted you,' Leanne said. 'Would you be OK to look at it?'

'No,' Carole said, but she was smiling as she took the phone.

As Carole watched the clip, Leanne asked, 'You can just make out the two figures sitting next to you. Does it trigger anything new?'

Carole shook her head. 'I'm afraid not. Are there any others?'

'Nothing that gives more detail.'

'You know, I took some videos. Obviously I was filming what was happening onstage, but you never know,' Carole said. 'You're lucky, I was going to delete them.'

After checking her mobile, Carole handed it over to Leanne. There were three recordings, each no more than thirty seconds long. The first was a close-up of the performers onstage, and the second looked like it was going to be more of the same.

'When you talked to the women, did they sound local?' Leanne asked as she continued to watch the screen.

Carole seemed to consider her answer. 'The blonde was definitely local, but I can't be sure about the other girl. They were mostly chatting to each other before the performance, whispering and giggling. A lovely couple.'

Leanne had reached the end of the second clip at the point where Carole had tilted the phone ever so slightly as the recording stopped. The image was frozen on an image of a woman's lap. She had her hands folded gently on top of each other.

Realising what Carole had just said, Leanne looked up. 'They were a couple?'

'They were holding hands at one point. I thought it was nice.'

Returning her attention to Carole's recordings, Leanne was about to play the final clip, but the frozen image of the hands gave her pause. At first she had thought the woman was wearing a mustard-coloured skirt, but it was a beret resting on her lap. Leanne could almost hear the sizzle of synapses making connections inside her brain.

'I've seen that hat before,' she said, and after a quick internet search, she found the Facebook image she had looked up months ago. 'Is this who you were sitting next to?'

Carole gasped. 'You've found her. Who is she?'

'Her name is Beth McCulloch.'

Beth had been wearing the same beret when Leanne had pounced on her in the car park. It made perfect sense, of course it did. Claudia had passed her unwanted tickets to her lover, who had passed them on to his sister and her partner. If nothing else, this proved the connection between Claudia and Declan.

Carole's eyes filled with tears as she looked at the second woman in the photograph. 'What happened to her girlfriend?'

'She survived,' Leanne assured her. 'Remember what you told me about Declan Gallagher calling out to his sister? Well, that's her.'

Carole bit her lip. 'Is that why she didn't follow us out? She heard him calling out to her?'

'I think so,' agreed Leanne. It felt good to have some of the unknowns revealed at last.

'Oh, the poor thing. She nearly died, didn't she? And then she had that awful business with the press vilifying her brother.' Carole paused, a look of apology on her face. 'Present company excepted.'

'No, you're right. We did demonise him, and it wasn't deserved. I have to say I'm seeing everyone in a different light.'

'Including me.'

Leanne wanted to reassure Carole that she was still a hero, but she let the comment slide. It was time to stop twisting the truth to suit the narrative. 'I'm wondering now if Declan was shouting because he was trying to find Karin, or because he was trapped. Can you remember hearing a second crash, it would have blocked the remaining stairwell?'

'With all the wailing I was doing, it was a wonder I heard Declan's shouts.'

'What about at the exit? Did you see Claudia Rothwell there? Beth told me she did, so you would have passed her too.'

'I'm sorry. I was looking at the door, not the people around me. I just remember savouring that first gulp of fresh air, even if it did taste of smoke.'

Leanne put her hands on the arms of the chair, ready to stand up. 'Well, I think that's about all,' she said. 'Thank you so much, Carole. You've been a great help.'

'That's it?'

'Unless there's anything else you want to add?'

Carole played nervously with her hands. 'Are you going to publish what I've told you?'

Sensing a reticence to share whatever else was bothering her, Leanne said, 'If I do write another article, I don't see why I'd need to revisit what I've already written about you.'

'What about Amelia?'

Leanne's pulse quickened. 'Why do you ask? Did you see her?'

Carole nodded. 'It was when the alarm went off. She was waiting for her mum and it crossed my mind that I should make sure she was OK, but it looked like everyone filing past was doing the same. Later on, as I was leaving the auditorium, I looked across to where I'd last seen her. There were bits of masonry all over the place, and I remember thinking . . .' She pursed her lips. Took a breath. 'I remember having this terrible fear that she must be underneath it, but it was too much to bear. I was already wailing like a banshee by then and convinced myself she had to have got out. I wasn't brave enough to go back for her, but I'm glad someone did. She had a guardian angel that night.'

'Yes, she did,' said Leanne, grateful that Carole hadn't mentioned the angel by name. Leanne had been instrumental in placing Claudia on that particular pedestal and, when the time was right, she would take great pleasure in knocking her off it. She was already taking aim.

The Empress Theatre
Sedgefield, Cheshire

Lena was lying flat on her stomach and couldn't remember how she had got there. Her cheek was pressed against a carpet of grit and it took long seconds for her to realise she was in the theatre. Rising unsteadily to her feet, she was surprised to find she was unhurt except for the painful throb in her knees, which had taken the brunt of her fall. The air was thick with dust that tasted strongly of smoke and she knew she had to get out, but couldn't work out which way was which. Her eyes stung, making her limited vision blurry, but she was aware of a glow the colour of amber that grew in intensity as she lifted her gaze.

Horror struck her as she realised the fire was above her head and she cried out. 'Peter! Where are you?'

Using the position of seats that hadn't been ripped from their fixings, she found her bearings. The main exit was somewhere behind her. That was where the screams were coming from.

Angela had been closer to the middle of the auditorium when the collapse happened, and had landed against the back of a seat with enough force to wind her. The air was polluted with dust that irritated her airways and what little she could suck into her lungs was difficult to expel. Normally when her asthma was bad, she would tell herself to stay calm, but these were exceptional circumstances. From the screams and calls for help, everyone was panicking. She gripped the back of the seat and worked through a plan of action before daring to waste precious oxygen attempting to move. Her inhaler was in her handbag. She needed to find it.

'You'll be OK,' she said between wheezes as she explored the ground with her foot.

When she connected with something solid, she crouched down only to discover it was a crumbling piece of plaster. She stayed on the floor, unsure if she had the strength to stand up again, and felt around some more. She couldn't find her bag. Her hands moved faster, more desperately. It wasn't there.

She forced her thoughts to slow. If she couldn't find her inhaler, she could and she would reach crisp, clean air. As she imagined the coolness of the night filling her lungs, she reached the aisle and that was when she remembered Amelia. She wanted to cry.

Lena rubbed her eyes. She was beginning to make out shapes in the gloom. The dust was settling and she found an illuminated sign pointing to a fire exit, the one she had been heading towards, but the doors themselves had vanished behind an avalanche of burning timber and masonry. She would have to return to the back of the stalls. It was getting quieter back there so it must be clearing. Peter had made the right choice. She should have stayed with him. They shouldn't have argued. She should have said she loved him. A tear slipped down her cheek.

Ignoring the fire raging in the eaves, Lena climbed over the chunks of plaster and skirted around the small fires that were struggling to catch alight. She would feel less scared once she reached the others. There was safety in numbers, and she felt calmer as she approached the point where the circle overhung the stalls.

On the far side of the theatre, away from the collapse, Carole Brody had stopped crying long enough for her vision to clear. She was hurrying towards the undamaged side exit, but she couldn't stop herself from looking at the destruction all around her. She could see where the ceiling had been devoured by an inferno and where the upper tier had been damaged. That was when she noticed a lone figure in the circle, and she almost tripped over.

Holding onto Beth McCulloch's sleeve, Carole had to look again. Her eyes hadn't deceived her. There was a man shouting for someone called Karin. He turned away and, a moment later, a large piece of masonry crashed onto the balcony close to where he had just been standing.

The near miss was a reminder of how exposed she was and Carole snapped her head to the front again, searching out her escape route. She didn't see the falling missile continue on its trajectory, or witness it take another victim of the Empress fire; a young woman who would never get to kiss and make up with her boyfriend. Carole kept moving, and made it through the side exit and into a corridor. As she drew nearer to the fire doors, she passed someone moving in the opposite direction, but the idea that anyone would want to go inside was so alien to her that her brain cancelled out all memory of Claudia Rothwell.

Angela, meanwhile, wanted to curl into a ball, but she

knew she shouldn't give up. Her legs trembled as she stood up and surveyed the emerging scene. She found the spot where she had last seen Amelia and gagged on the air she squeezed from her lungs with a tight wheeze. The poor child. Where once there had been red velvet seats, there were smouldering fires amongst the rubble. Angela felt an ache in her heart for Mrs Parker and the pain that lay ahead for her. Angela had lost one of her babies before he could take his first breath. That had been over twenty years ago, and it still it hurt. Before grief could overtake her, she heard a child's cry.

'Please! Help me! Please! I want my mummy!'

28

The windscreen was clear of condensation, but if the temperature continued to fall, Leanne would be scraping ice off the windows soon. She had brought her laptop in case the boredom became too much, but there were no pressing deadlines. Mal had approved her latest stakeout and had gone as far as to say she could claim expenses for coffee and doughnuts.

Licking vanilla sugar from her lips, Leanne stared through the gates to the car park beyond. There were two people under surveillance this time, which doubled her chances, and she was prepared to stay as long as was necessary. There was no alternative. Karin continued to ignore her calls, and the email she had sent to Beth had bounced back.

Sipping a gingerbread latte, Leanne kept an eye on the blue Peugeot, hoping that Karin and Beth weren't so short of money that the petrol tank was empty. It bothered her that she couldn't see the entrance to their apartment, and she considered reclaiming her previous spot by the canal, but it was the beginning of December, and she wasn't prepared to freeze to death. Or was she?

Zipping up her coat, Leanne was getting ready to patrol the block, when two figures appeared from the direction of the apartments. One wore a woollen scarf that seemed too heavy for her hunched frame, and the other a padded jacket and mustard beret.

Leanne locked the car and slipped through the narrow pedestrian entrance next to the main gates. She didn't run in case she drew attention to herself, but she walked fast enough to reach the Peugeot at the same time that its indicators flashed and the doors unlocked.

'Please, can we talk?' Leanne said before either woman had a chance to react to her arrival.

Beth stepped in front of Karin. 'Leave us alone,' she hissed.

Leanne stepped away from the car, signalling to Beth that she didn't want to be considered a threat. Her new position also gave her a better view of Declan's sister. She hadn't met Karin before, and her first impression was that she looked nothing like the pre-disaster photos the *Courier* had acquired. Her dark hair hung limply around her face and disappeared beneath the folds of her multi-coloured scarf. Her eyes were also multi-coloured; bloodshot with purple shadows beneath.

'Who are you?' Karin asked, holding on to her girlfriend's arm.

'She's no one,' Beth said.

'I'm a reporter with—'

'I've been advised not to talk to you,' Karin said before Leanne could finish.

'I work for the *Courier*. My name is Leanne Pitman and—'

Beth was opening the passenger door. 'It's OK, I'll handle this.'

Red blotches had bled into Karin's cheeks, but it was

316

impossible to tell if it was from the cold or growing anxiety. 'You wrote about the wee girl.'

'Amelia?' asked Leanne. 'Yes, do you remember her? You would have been sitting a few rows behind.'

'Stop!' Beth said. 'The last thing she needs is someone forcing her to relive stuff she's better off forgetting.'

'I'm sorry,' Leanne said as she watched Karin get into the car.

Beth was about to close the car door when Karin popped her head back out. 'She's OK, isn't she? I thought she was dead.'

'She's fine.'

The door closed and Beth rested her hands on the car roof, her head bowed as if she didn't have the strength to turn to face Leanne again. After a couple of breaths, she twisted around.

'Whatever you want from us, we've got nothing left to give.'

'I've found the woman you were sitting next to at the theatre.'

'So fucking what?'

'I thought you might want to know. Her name is Carole Brody.'

'I know who she is, I read your article,' Beth said with a bitter laugh. 'I recognised her from the photo, although I have to say, that story of hers was a real work of fiction. It took me a while to realise the distraught woman she practically carried out of the theatre was supposed to be me.'

'I'm sorry about that. I have spoken to her again and she told me it was you who helped her.'

'No, I didn't!' Beth said, her eyes blazing. 'I thought I was

317

helping Karin. I thought she was the one holding my arm.' She wrapped a hand around her upper arm to illustrate. 'When I realised my mistake, it was too late. I'd lost Karin, and that stupid woman wouldn't let go of me.'

'I'm sorry,' Leanne said, knowing she was inflicting pain, but continuing anyway. 'Mrs Brody said she heard Declan calling out for Karin. If she was next to you, you must have heard him too. He was up in the circle. Did you see him? Did you see anyone with him?'

'I don't know!' Beth looked as if she didn't want to say more, but this new piece of information forced her to reconsider. 'A year ago I would have said absolutely not, but Karin goes over it again and again and I've forgotten what's real and what isn't. She obsesses over the tiniest detail of every account of the disaster like she's expecting to find pieces to her own puzzle.'

'I want to help.'

'No, you don't,' Beth said, spitting her accusation back at Leanne. She took a step towards the front of the car, heading for the driver's side, only to realise she would be leaving Karin unprotected. She pressed a button on her key fob and locked the car.

Leanne stared at the collection of keys in Beth's hand. There was a torch dangling from a chain.

'That key ring,' she stammered. 'Did you get it from Declan?'

Beth hesitated, confused by Leanne's reaction. 'We had a whole drawer full once,' she said. 'They come in handy when we're walking along the canal in the pitch dark. Not that they last long. Not that we go out for walks in the dark any more.'

'It's the same key ring Amelia Parker remembers holding,' Leanne said, trying not to read anything into it. Lots of people would have had them.

'So what?'

'I'm revisiting some of the stories I reported on the Empress fire. Carole Brody isn't the only one who stretched the truth.'

Beth shuffled her feet, growing restless. If Leanne was going to keep her attention, she needed to shock her. There was nothing else for it. 'I don't think Claudia Rothwell saved Amelia,' she said.

'My God, you were the one who broke the news. Are you saying you made it up?' Beth replied with a laugh that was meant to mock. It worked.

'Claudia lied. In fact she's lied about a lot of things. When you saw her by the exit, she wasn't going back inside, she hadn't been in there to begin with. She had tickets, but she gave them away.' Leanne left a beat before adding, 'Did you know she was having an affair with Declan?'

Beth's jaw dropped and then she laughed again. 'More stories? You're getting good at this. I read that rubbish you printed about the wonderful Phillipa Montgomery. Is that what this is about? Are you trying to frame Claudia so we'll forget it was Phillipa who was involved with Declan?'

'And where did the rumour about Phillipa come from? Was it Claudia?' When Beth didn't answer, Leanne added, 'When I said Claudia gave away her tickets, who do you think used them?'

Beth gave nothing away. 'Should I care?'

'You and Karin were in her seats,' Leanne said slowly. 'According to Claudia there was a mix-up at the box office. Surely you remember the confusion over tickets?'

'It sounds like you're the one who's muddled. We had the right tickets. We were meant to be mystery shoppers.'

'No, Beth, that was Claudia's job. I have a list of all the complimentary tickets that were issued and none went to Declan. He acquired Claudia's tickets – a man she claims not to have known.'

'This is ridiculous. Declan's dead. Can't you let him rest in peace?'

'I know I'm as guilty as anyone for believing he was the villain, and I understand why you don't want Karin talking to me, but I promise you, that's not what this is about. I want justice for the people who died in the fire, as well as those who continue to suffer,' she added softly, wanting Beth to know that she saw her suffering too. 'I think Claudia is using Amelia as a cover story. I don't know what made her go inside the theatre, but it wasn't to pull a girl from the rubble.'

'And you know that because?'

'Because she's a liar. Claudia walked away without a scratch on her. Does that sound like the same person who dug Amelia out with her bare hands? Claudia saw an opportunity, and she took it. No one else had come forward, and not one person could describe the rescuer, not even Amelia.'

From inside the car, Karin was peeling away her scarf with gloved fingers. Amelia wasn't the only one to have suffered memory loss.

'The person who saved Amelia had a key ring just like yours, but Claudia knew nothing about it when Amelia brought it up. It almost caught her out, but she talked her way out of it because that's what she's good at.' Leanne looked towards Karin, forcing Beth to follow her gaze. It was a tenuous connection, but worth a try. 'Did Karin carry one of those key rings?'

'This is ridiculous,' Beth said. If she harboured the same thoughts, she dismissed them with a shake of her head. 'Claudia has been good to us. We're not going to be used as weapons against her.'

'Don't you want to know the truth?'

'Will it pay the bills?' Beth snapped back. Her jaw was clenched when she added, 'I can't and I won't help you. Karin's lost another job, and we need Claudia's support.'

'You've applied to the hardship fund?'

'We'd have lost the apartment by now if she hadn't bailed us out.'

'You've had payments?' Leanne asked. 'I didn't think the fund had issued any money yet.'

'Claudia found a way.'

'And now you're beholden to her,' Leanne said, her heart sinking. 'All I want is to find Amelia's true hero. Maybe I'm clutching at straws, but what if it was Karin, or someone else who can't come forward? How does it feel to know Claudia is buying your silence?'

'Don't you dare! You have no idea what it's like!' Beth cried out, but her anger was quickly spent. 'I can't cope with any more of this. Please, just leave us alone.'

Leanne held up her hands and said no more as Beth raced around to the driver's side. When she was safely inside the car, Karin tried to console her. She didn't look as fragile as she had earlier, but Beth was right, neither of them had anything left to give.

Once Beth had sniffed back the tears, she started the engine and reversed the car out of the parking space, passing within inches of Leanne. As the car came level, Leanne got a closer look at Karin. Her scarf hung loosely from her neck, and a silver chain glinted in the winter sun. The car sped away.

When Karin and Beth were forced to wait for the gates to open, Leanne didn't want to appear to be pursuing them. She left her car and strolled towards the canal while her mind attempted to force Karin into the mould she had once pressed Claudia into. She was the right height, but did she look like someone who would fight a natural instinct to escape? What if she had gone searching for Declan when she heard him calling out to her? Would she have been distracted by the plight of a little girl? From the broken woman Leanne had seen today, it was almost easier to believe Claudia had saved Amelia.

As Leanne reached the towpath, she continued the internal debate. Karin had asked about Amelia and said how she thought she was dead. Had she seen where the roof had caved in and made the same assumption as Carole Brody? Or had she thought it was a dead child she was placing into Rex Russell's arms? Beth hadn't denied that Karin had a torch that night, even if she hadn't confirmed it either.

Leanne blinked against the sun that was reflecting off the canal's still waters and immediately recalled the flash of silver around Karin's neck. How many women in the theatre had been wearing silver pendants that night? How many possessed Ronson Construction torches that had been given away like sweets? How many couldn't come forward and retell their feats of bravery because either they, or their memory, hadn't survived the tragedy?

Opening her rucksack, Leanne searched for her sunglasses,

but pulled out her phone instead. She had taken a photograph of the drawing she had been asked to pass on to Claudia. Amelia's guardian angel had dark hair, as did Karin, but what about the pendant? Leanne zoomed in on the line around the woman's neck, but the little dot in the centre remained just that.

Frustrated, Leanne tapped her phone harder than was entirely necessary to zoom out to the full image. She hated seeing Claudia's name appended to Amelia's, but she couldn't with any certainty change it to Karin's, or anyone else's for that matter. She was almost at the point of admitting defeat when she saw it – the clue hidden in the sketch that Amelia had covered up with a pink heart.

29

With no better place to be, Claudia rested her back against the flock of duck-down pillows she had spent the last ten minutes rearranging. She shuffled up the bed, then down again, dug her left shoulder into her nest, then did the same with the right, but to no avail. Unable to cure her restlessness, she distracted herself by smoothing out the creases on the white Egyptian cotton sheet that protected her from the heavy damask of the duvet cover. The strap of her silk chemise slipped down her arm. She pulled it up, almost snapping it.

Claudia didn't understand why everyone was ganging up on her. She had made a few errors of judgement, but she had made up for it since. Why couldn't she be left in peace? Other people made mistakes. Why did hers have to happen in the midst of a disaster that had to be brought up over and over again?

Justin was bemused by her moods and seemed to think the best way to deal with Claudia was to give her some distance. She couldn't remember the last time he had worked from home. He was back to his old ways, leaving early and coming home late. He was living for his work instead of living for his wife.

Shoving an elbow into her pillow, Claudia realised she had never felt comfortable in this bed. She closed her eyes and willed herself someplace else, and Declan's scruffy little flat above the bakery came to mind too easily. She had always felt at peace there. It was somewhere where she never had to pretend to be something other than what she was.

'What if it could be like this for ever?' Declan had once asked her, kissing her bare shoulder as she lay tangled in sheets that were thin and scratchy.

'You have to go back to Ireland, for your kids,' she reminded him. It had been part of the initial attraction. Declan would return home when the theatre project was signed off, and no one need ever be the wiser.

'I'll be home soon enough, but what if you came with me?'

'My life is here.'

'Is that so? Then tell me, who's your best friend? Who knows your darkest secrets? It's not the likes of Phillipa, that's for sure. And it's not Justin either.'

'Don't,' she said. Her husband was the one subject that was barred from their pillow talk.

'Can your relationship be so great if you can't even be open with him about your past? There's a reason we fit together so well,' he whispered, sliding a hand beneath the covers.

Claudia had only told Declan about her mum because he had been droning on about how difficult his childhood had been. She had wanted to trump his absent father with an absent mother, and it had been liberating to talk about it.

Declan had understood why she had felt the need to re-imagine her past. He shared the sense of rejection and the shame too. He knew what it was like to feel not good enough.

Justin had no similar point of reference. His childhood had been blissfully uneventful and he would have been appalled by her tale of desertion and neglect. A dead mother and a father debilitated by grief had been far more palatable, for both of them.

Declan on the other hand, had embraced the imperfections in his life. He wasn't afraid to mess up and had messed up spectacularly on occasion, but he carried on regardless. Claudia didn't doubt that he would celebrate her mistakes too and, as his hand explored the subtle rise of her belly, she knew he had worked out that her latest was one they had made together.

'Oh, my sweet Claudia,' he said. 'I promise you here and now, I'll never leave you.'

Her life had felt uncomfortably crowded back then, so how had she ended up so alone? Where was Declan when she needed him? She consoled herself with the knowledge that their secret had died with him, although when Karin had first confronted her, there had been a moment when she thought she had been found out. She had worried for nothing. Declan's loyalties had been with Claudia right to the end. It was unfortunate that not all her mistakes were dead and buried.

Stretching a hand across the damask, she picked up Amelia's drawing. From Leanne's swagger when she had handed it over, Claudia had expected it to reveal more than she would like, but it was a poorly executed sketch, with no detail.

Lifting the sheet of paper to examine the figure holding the child, Claudia allowed herself a brief twinge of guilt for taking credit where it wasn't due. She had seen Amelia's limp body and was surprised the paramedics gave her any chance at all. If it had been Claudia who had stumbled upon the girl, she would have left her where she found her. But it wasn't Claudia making those decisions. It was the woman with the silver pendant and that damned key ring torch.

They should rename Leanne Pitman, Leanne Pitbull. Claudia hadn't realised the reporter's friend had died in the fire until Phillipa mentioned it. It made sense now why she had become so obsessed, but she had to give up eventually. Didn't she?

Claudia felt tears prick her eyes as she stared at the drawing. Against the light from the window, she could see each pen stroke. She brought the paper closer. Not all the hearts surrounding her name were completely pink. One heart had lines inside that were the same shade of purple as the pen used to write Claudia's name. Amelia had made a mistake and tried to cover it up. Claudia could make out three dark lines that formed a letter.

Glancing again at the pendant drawn in grey, Claudia made the link she hoped no one else would, not even Amelia. There was a reason the child had been misspelling Claudia with a K. It was the block initial hanging from the silver chain around the neck of her rescuer. Karin Gallagher still wore it. That might be a problem.

30

'Thanks for coming over so quickly,' Karin said after offering Claudia a seat. 'I know you must be busy.'

'It's no trouble,' Claudia replied, even though she had been the one to suggest a visit. She had phoned that morning with Amelia's drawing still clasped in her hand. 'You sounded upset and I didn't want to let you down.'

'You've been so kind. There's only a few people left I can trust,' Karin said, perching on the edge of a battered leather sofa. Her open-plan apartment was small, and it looked as though the dated furniture was included in the rent and had suffered one too many occupants.

'I'm shocked you and Beth have been ambushed again. Are the press looking for another angle on Declan?'

'I wouldn't be surprised. It was Leanne Pitman, the one who wrote about you and Amelia.'

Claudia knew it would be. It was one of the reasons she had come over so quickly. 'What did she say exactly?' By which she meant, what had passed between them, word for word.

'Beth spoke to her while I was in the car. All she's told

me is that Leanne has tracked down the woman who was sitting next to us at the theatre.'

Claudia wiped a clammy hand against her trousers. Not only had the reporter worked out that she wasn't in her allocated seat, she knew who had taken her place. Shit.

Swallowing down a wave of panic, Claudia reminded herself that all of the evidence against her was circumstantial. Leanne couldn't prove that Claudia hadn't gone to the theatre, she *had* been there, and any link to Declan remained tenuous. And as for saving Amelia, there was nothing to disprove her claim except a mishmash of unreliable memories and the pendant hanging around Karin's throat. Claudia wanted nothing more than to yank it from her neck and run, but she forced a smile and nodded at Declan's sister as if only mildly interested.

'Does Beth know why Leanne's still working on the story?'

'I don't think so,' Karin said. She glanced at the wall clock. It was half past three. 'But she might be able to tell you more. She'll be home in about half an hour, depending on the traffic.'

Karin had mentioned that Beth was at work and Claudia had wrongly assumed she would be home much later. 'I'm afraid I can't stay long,' she replied, thankful that she hadn't taken up the offer of a drink. She would have to keep the visit short. 'I only came to give you this.'

Claudia took from her bag a smoky brown bottle with a pretty label. 'My aromatherapist, Maggie, made this up for me to reduce my anxiety. It's a massage oil, and I thought it might help you too.'

'Oh, I couldn't take it.'

'I have lots more at home. Please, I insist,' Claudia said.

'You could try it now, if you like?' Just rub a few drops on your neck and chest. The smell is incredibly calming.'

Karin looked uncomfortable, but if she thought it was an odd request, she was too polite to refuse. She went to undo the cap.

'You might want to take your necklace off first. Apparently it can tarnish silver.'

'Oh, OK,' Karin said, reaching behind her neck to undo the clasp. 'It was a present from Declan. I'd hate for it to get damaged.'

'Here, let me take it. I'll put it somewhere safe.'

'Sure, thanks,' replied Karin as the chain was snatched from her hand. 'Would you mind putting it over there on the shelf by the kitchen? There's a little bowl.'

No longer interested in Karin and her massage oil, Claudia wandered over to the shelf. With the necklace cupped in her hand, she grasped one end of the chain between her thumb and forefinger and lifted it up. The silver pendant slipped off and remained secreted in her palm. 'Sorry, where do you want me to put it?' she called out. She wanted Karin to witness her setting down the necklace.

Karin rubbed scented oil across her throat as she joined Claudia. 'There,' she said, pointing to a bowl shaped like a lemon.

As Claudia dropped the chain amongst other bits of jewellery, she spotted a set of keys on the shelf next to it. Karin noticed her gaze falter.

'Do you recognise the key ring?'

Claudia shoved her hand into her trouser pocket, depositing the stolen pendant. 'Should I?'

'I had a torch like the one you gave to that little girl.

Except I lost mine after the fire. All that was left was the screw cap on the end, so I squashed it into a disc.'

The smell of lavender and chamomile from the massage oils did nothing to relax Claudia. 'Do you remember using it that night?'

Karin went to the sink to wash her hands. The leathery patches of healed burns on her palms had become invisible to her, as were the sharper scar lines, but Claudia noticed.

'I can remember switching it on,' Karin said, 'but that doesn't mean anything. I have this infuriating need to fill in my memory gaps and sometimes, when I read someone else's account, it's as if I lived it too.' She chewed her lip. 'Even what happened to Amelia. I dream that it was me with her.'

With her head bowed in shame, Karin rinsed the soap suds from her hands. She thought she was stealing Claudia's memories instead of recapturing her own. That was good.

'Beth still has her torch though,' she continued. 'That reporter was looking at it.'

'She was?'

Picking up a tea towel, Karin took time to dry her hands. She hadn't looked up yet and for the first time, Claudia suspected she wasn't being as open as she could be.

'Did they talk for long?'

'Quite a while.'

'And what else do you think they chatted about? Beth must have said something to you.'

'Bits,' she admitted. 'There must have been some talk about our theatre tickets because Beth asked if Declan had told me who he got them off. I presumed it was Phillipa, but Beth asked if it might have been you.'

'You know that's not possible. I've told you before, I don't think I ever met him.'

'I know,' Karin answered quickly. 'I'm not suggesting there was something going on.'

Claudia felt a rush of blood to her cheeks. She didn't like the way Karin's mind had made the leap to a suggestion of impropriety, or how her brow remained furrowed. 'Good,' she said.

'But, are you sure you didn't see him inside the Empress?' Karin asked. 'Isn't it possible you bumped into him? I have this image of him looking down at me. And I see you too.'

As Karin spoke, she held out her hands in front of her. It looked as if she were reaching for the ghost of her brother only to grasp thin air, but Claudia knew differently. She was mirroring something she had seen.

Noticing the look of horror on Claudia's face, Karin said, 'Sorry, I told you my memories are jumbled. Of course you weren't up there.'

Claudia rested a hand on the kitchen counter. 'No, I wasn't, and if it's not too much to ask, I'd rather you didn't say things like that again, not to anyone, not even to Beth. The press would love to link me to your brother just for the fun of it.'

'I can't believe they've let Phillipa off the hook.'

'Maybe that's for the best. The press started the rumours because they didn't expect Phillipa to be around to challenge them, and I think we all fell for it. I wouldn't be surprised if he wasn't seeing anyone at all. You didn't think he was, and I'd trust you above any reporter.'

'Actually . . . I wasn't completely honest with you when we first met,' Karin confessed. 'The thing is, I'm pretty sure

332

Declan was seeing someone. He never talked about her, but there was this one time when I called at his flat and there was a cup on the side with red lipstick on it. He wouldn't say who it belonged to, and I remember thinking it was because he wasn't serious about whoever it was, but maybe he had to be secretive because she was married. If it wasn't Phillipa, then who was it?'

Claudia held her nerve and Karin's gaze. 'Whoever it was, Declan must have cared a lot about her to keep that secret from his family. And the best way you can respect his memory is to say nothing and keep away from the press.'

Putting her head in her hands, Karin said, 'I don't care if I never talk about any of this again. It's already driving a wedge between me and Beth. I ask questions that she can't answer and we both end up feeling frustrated. It's so hard, and things have been getting worse.'

'That's why I'm here,' Claudia said gently. 'Each time we meet, it's like the fire is still eating away at you and I can only imagine how it's affecting Beth too. Whenever there's any kind of disaster, the victims are counted by the lives lost, but the survivors pay another price. The pain goes on and for some it becomes unbearable.'

'Beth refuses to go for counselling.'

'She's too busy worrying about you.'

'I wish she wouldn't. I'm not worth it,' Karin said, pressing her fingers against her eyes to staunch her tears. 'I hate that Declan died trying to reach me, and that three kids have lost their dad. It was nice to blame Phillipa for a while, but I despise myself. He'd be alive now if it wasn't for me.'

Claudia had to turn away. She was tired of being Karin's emotional crutch, and wanted to tell her to grow a backbone.

If only she knew that Declan hadn't died because of her. He had died because of Claudia.

'It's natural to feel guilty,' she said, not sure if she was talking about Karin or herself. 'But the best way to honour his memory is to go on and lead a happy life.'

'But I'm not happy, am I?' Karin whined. 'Nor is Beth. If she isn't babysitting me, she's out working. I don't know how long we can go on like this.'

Claudia checked the time. 'I'm sorry, but I have to go. Please stop blaming yourself for other people's decisions, Karin. If Beth chooses to work herself into the ground, it's only because she loves you.' She stopped short of saying how sorry she felt for the poor cow who had been landed with Karin as a girlfriend.

Karin was sobbing as Claudia left. She hoped she hadn't pushed her over the edge, but on the other hand . . . it would solve all their problems if Karin found she couldn't go on.

The Empress Theatre
Sedgefield, Cheshire

After Declan had disappeared from view, Karin used the backs of seats to navigate her way across the auditorium while she continued to scan the balcony. The closer she moved to the open wound in the ceiling, the hotter she became, and she hoped it was only the effort of breathing that made her sweat.

'Declan! Where are you?'

When no answer came, Karin wanted to believe it was because her brother was already on his way out, but how could she leave without knowing? What if he was still looking for her? She glanced over her shoulder to make sure Beth hadn't done something stupid like turn back for her. She didn't need two people to worry about. Where was Declan?

As she moved along the row, glowing embers rained down and she patted her scalp now and again to make sure her hair wasn't on fire. She was getting further away from the only viable exit.

'Declan!' she cried out again, unsure how much longer she could fight the urge to flee.

'Help.'

The voice was as much a wheeze as it was a whisper. Karin looked around, unsure if she had imagined the sound above the crackle of fire and the diminishing wail of the alarm. Shadows stretched and contracted above her head, the orange glow inside the smoke cloud twitching like a beating heart. Karin stepped into an aisle strewn with rubble and was horrified to see one of the shadows reaching out to her.

'Please.'

Karin rushed towards the woman crouched on the floor. Her short cropped hair and her face were layered with dust, and her lips were a violent shade of blue.

'It's OK, I'm here,' said Karin. 'I'll get you out.'

'Not me. The girl. She needs help. Under there.' She pointed. 'Go.'

Karin looked to where the woman was pointing and immediately recalled seeing a girl who had refused to move from her seat. If she was under the rubble, she couldn't have survived. Karin was about to refuse to even look, when the woman gripped her arm with more force than she could spare.

'She's alive. Go.'

'I can't.'

'You must.'

Reluctantly, Karin left the stranger and began her search. She felt in her pocket for her phone to use as a torch, only to realise it was in Beth's bag, but at least she had her keys. The key ring torch was the last of a job lot Declan had given her. They weren't particularly reliable and when she switched it on, she was relieved to find it worked.

As she climbed the mounds of rubble, Karin was terrified

she might be stepping on the girl, but there wasn't time to clear a path. The rest of the ceiling could come down at any moment, exits could become blocked, the fire could spread. There were no end of reasons why Karin should abandon her quest, but she was too scared to think beyond finding the girl.

It was when she moved a scorched piece of timber that she saw a small hand, but it was too soon to know if this was a cause for celebration or sorrow. Tentatively, she cleared away more debris until she spied the top of a head. She pointed the torch and miraculously, the head tilted up towards her. The girl was alive. Karin wanted to laugh, but it caught in her throat as the head slumped forward again. She heard the thump as the girl's forehead hit masonry.

'Please wake up. Oh God, please wake up,' Karin urged. The child couldn't die now.

The head moved again. 'Mum?'

'It's OK, I'll have you out in no time.'

As the girl flitted in and out of consciousness, Karin clawed away at the debris. She didn't feel the cuts and scratches, or the burning as she pulled away glowing pieces of timber, but she couldn't keep hold of the torch for long and gave it to the girl to hold. She felt reassured each time the light flickered across her face.

The child was hanging on, but only just, and when Karin pulled her from her tomb, the shock and pain must have been too much for her broken body, and she passed out. Karin retrieved the torch and, as she prepared to lift her casualty, she refused to accept that she didn't have the strength. Rising unsteadily to her feet, she began the trek back towards the exit. She could see a scattering of survivors

337

rushing towards the same destination and one of them, a short, bald man, stopped to look at her.

'Help me!'

Once she had handed the girl over, Karin was tempted to follow them out, but there was someone she couldn't leave behind, and this time, it wasn't Declan. Telling herself that her brother was sensible enough to have left the theatre by now, she gave the upper tier only a cursory glance as she called out his name one last time. Detecting no movement, she was unaware that she was being observed from above.

Karin retraced her steps back to the woman with blue lips, who was exactly where she had left her. She crouched down to touch her arm, but it was too late. This stranger's last act had been to send Karin off to save someone else, and she had died alone.

'I got her out for you,' Karin whispered as she kissed the top of the woman's head.

Mourning the loss of a hero she couldn't name, Karin clamped a hand over her mouth and released a wail, which quickly transformed into a cry of pain. Her hands were burnt and bleeding and some of her fingernails were hanging by a thread.

To match the tears running down her cheeks, Karin could feel drips falling onto her scalp as if the Empress was crying with her. She heard the same hiss of water evaporating as Rex had done, but as she looked up, her gaze came to rest on the balcony. Her brother hadn't left after all.

'Declan!' she cried out with a rush of relief. They were both still in danger, but they had found each other. It was going to be OK.

31

Feeling conspicuous with her solitary glass of gin, Leanne weaved through the crowded pub and took up a holding position next to her favourite chesterfield. A small gathering of friends were sprawled across it, waiting for their table to be called and, after only five minutes, Leanne's patience paid off. The group left her to reclaim her seat with only echoes of their boisterous chatter.

Settling in for what might be a lengthy duration, Leanne tried to picture Karin working in such a demanding environment. The Sunday lunch crowd was good-natured enough, but the pub could get boisterous on a Saturday night and it would take a manager with nerve to keep drunken patrons under control. Would Karin be able to use her past skills to stand up to Claudia? Did she have the mettle to stake her claim as the rightful hero?

Leanne didn't think so, and as the Christmas decorations twinkled above the occasional ripple of laughter, she wasn't sure anyone would care. If this scene were a barometer of the town's mood, then Sedgefield was looking forward, not back, and Leanne had chosen a battle she wasn't sure she could win. She couldn't change the ending to the town's worst tragedy. The dead would remain dead.

When her phone vibrated, Leanne wasn't surprised when she saw it was from a withheld number. She connected the call, knowing what would happen next.

'Hello?'

The line went dead. It was the fifth such call in three days.

Leanne had a block on cold calls and she had dismissed the possibility of a nuisance caller, who would surely choose an indecent hour to unnerve her. She couldn't be absolutely sure it wasn't Claudia getting her own back, but the put-downs had started soon after she had spoken to Beth, and it didn't feel like a coincidence. Leanne had left her with some serious doubts to wrestle with, and if Beth was coming to the same conclusions as Leanne, today would hopefully provide the incontrovertible proof that had evaded the reporter so far.

Sipping her gin, Leanne scanned the crowded pub, concentrating on the female guests in particular. She didn't see Joe until he dropped a catalogue onto the low table in front of her.

'Jesus,' she said. Gin had slopped onto her hand and she sucked it up before it dribbled onto her grey hoodie.

'I thought you might want some company,' he said, unapologetically.

Although Joe had become a useful sounding board, she hadn't invited him on her latest quest for good reason. She scrutinised his face, feeling his panic rise up inside her too. 'Are you sure you want to be here?'

Joe kept his eyes on Leanne and only Leanne. 'As long as you don't freak me out by drawing attention to the fact that this should freak me out, I'll be fine.'

340

'OK,' she said warily. 'So what's this?' She pulled the shopping catalogue towards her, giving Joe something to concentrate on other than the crowd ebbing and flowing around them.

'Inspiration,' Joe said. 'Why don't you have a flick through while I get a pint? Do you want anything?'

'Do you want me to go?'

'Nope,' he said, his gaze fixed.

'Then I'd love another gin.'

By the time Joe returned with their drinks, Leanne had the catalogue open at the jewellery section.

'Anything take your fancy?' he asked, as if she were choosing a present.

The two pages on view offered a range of pendants in differing styles, but all on the same theme. They were initials. Some in gold, some silver, and some had embellishments. Leanne tapped a finger on the image of a silver chain with the letter V hanging from a loop. 'This one's closest,' she said. 'The font was definitely sans serif.'

'And in English?' asked the gas engineer.

'The lettering was a bold block type. No squiggly lines.'

Joe peered at the description beneath the photo. 'Wouldn't it be better if we put this off until we can buy one with the right letter? I'm sure we could get a refund once we've finished with it.'

'No, I can't wait. And besides, I'd rather Amelia made that leap on her own,' Leanne said, looking up to scan faces again.

When she had first interviewed Amelia and her mum, she had mentioned how they came to the Bridgewater Inn for Sunday lunch. Leanne could have arranged another interview, but she thought this way would be less stressful, and Amelia's memory might be more prone to a nudge if she wasn't expecting a trigger. It wasn't exactly ethical, but she hoped the family would forgive her if it led to the right results.

'And what happens if she doesn't recognise it?'

Leanne folded the corner of the page and closed the catalogue. 'Then I'll have to find another way of trapping Claudia.'

'And you will.'

This was why Leanne liked talking things through with Joe. If she were with Frankie or Mal, they would be cross-examining her, pushing her to build her case and state her options. Joe only asked questions once Leanne had decided which angle to take. She poured the dregs of her drink into the fresh gin glass, pulled out the sliver of cucumber and crunched on it.

'If I can't prove that Karin saved Amelia, I'm just going to have to go to Plan B and prove that it couldn't have been Claudia. If only she'd been picked up by CCTV cameras coming from Declan's flat. I don't know how she did it.'

'She could have used the back alleyways, there's one that runs parallel with the high street.'

Leanne didn't know the street layouts as well as Joe, but if there was a way to get to the theatre unseen, Claudia would have taken it. 'It wouldn't be enough anyway. Proving she was in Declan's flat when the fire started, doesn't prove she didn't rush into a burning building to save Amelia.'

'If she was chasing after Declan, she must have loved him.'

'Do you think?' Leanne asked, not so easily convinced by any sentence that had Claudia and the word love in it. 'The first time I saw her with Justin, I bought into *their* love story, but now the only thing I can say with any certainty is that Claudia enjoys the trappings of their marriage. She wouldn't have given that up for Declan, a man who had an affair with his sister-in-law and walked out on his wife and kids. She took a huge risk getting involved in the first place.'

'And those stakes would have been higher still when she became pregnant.'

'It's funny how Claudia didn't have any trouble conceiving around the time she was seeing Declan, and yet Justin's fertility problems go all the way back to his first marriage.' Leanne had heard this from Phillipa. They had had a second conversation, ostensibly to prepare for the feature on Phillipa's marriage, but the conversation had touched on Claudia's too. Reading between the lines, Phillipa was harbouring the same suspicions as Leanne.

'I don't mean to sound *seedy*,' said Joe with a smirk, 'but what if Declan's real attraction was his sperm?'

Not amused, Leanne abandoned her cucumber for a large swig of gin. 'In that case she would have had what she wanted from him. So why follow him inside the theatre? And why did Declan end up trapped upstairs, but not Claudia?'

'She could have been looking for him somewhere else.'

'Yeah, like in the stalls,' Leanne said. 'Which again doesn't help me prove that she didn't save Amelia. What are we missing?' She was staring off into space, when movement caught her eye. Someone was waving frantically at her from across the pub. Amelia kneeling up on a dining chair and when she knew she had Leanne's attention, she said something to her mum.

'For now, it might be safest to stick to Plan A,' Leanne said as Amelia approached.

'Did you give Claudia my drawing?' asked Amelia.

'I certainly did, and she loved it.'

'I might make her a Christmas card next.'

Leanne could feel her lips stretching taut across her teeth as she attempted a smile. 'Are you excited for Christmas?'

'It's my absolute favourite time of year.'

'I hope you've been a good girl for Santa,' said Joe, jumping into the conversation and killing it stone dead. He didn't need Leanne's scowl to tell him he sounded creepy.

Amelia looked at him with mild curiosity. 'You do know he's not real, don't you?'

'It's probably just as well,' said Leanne, 'Joe would be getting a sack of coal.'

Cupping a hand over her mouth, Amelia whispered, 'Is he your boyfriend?'

'Actually, he's my best friend's boyfriend, which sort of makes him a substitute best friend,' Leanne admitted. It was the first time she had had to describe their relationship since Lois's death, and she had said the first thing that sprang to mind.

'I couldn't have described us better,' Joe said.

Leanne cleared her throat. 'We were just deciding what to buy for Christmas.' She put down her drink and placed a hand on the catalogue as if it were a holy scripture. She said a silent prayer.

'I've made my list,' Amelia told her. 'I want a Samsung Galaxy. A second-hand one will do.'

'Aren't you a bit young for a mobile?' challenged Joe.

Amelia gave him a look. 'I'm ten.'

Joe went to say something else, but Leanne rolled her eyes at him. He didn't have nieces or nephews, so had no clue how to speak to kids. Leanne had four, although it was sometimes easy to forget there was life beyond Sedgefield town limits. She would go back home for Christmas this year. She couldn't face another on her own, or the stress of making up a story of spending the day with friends to stop her mum fretting.

'My mum likes to know where I am *all* of the time,' Amelia said to Leanne.

'In that case, you should make sure it's a brand-new one. Better reliability,' Leanne said, arching an eyebrow.

'Good idea!'

'Now we've sorted you out, I need to work on my list,' Leanne said casually as she looked down at the catalogue.

'Do they have phones in there?' Amelia said, squeezing next to Leanne on the opposite side to Joe so the three were lined up in front of the low table.

'I think I'd prefer jewellery.'

As she spoke, Leanne slid her phone towards Joe as if she were moving it out of the way. At the same time, she gave him a nudge with her elbow and he picked it up. Leanne checked he was opening the voice recorder app before carefully opening the catalogue a couple of pages before the one she had earmarked.

'That's nice,' Amelia said, pointing out a gold bracelet encrusted with cubic zirconia.

Leanne turned the page. 'A necklace would be better. I'd wear it more often.'

'How about that one?' Joe said. He had leant forward with Leanne's phone in his hand and pointed at a Hello Kitty pendant.

Amelia pulled a face. 'Whatever your girlfriend sees in you, it can't be your taste.'

Leanne heard the sharp intake of breath and felt the same stabbing pain she knew had cut into Joe's heart. She swallowed and said, 'Joe was and always will be, the love of her life.'

Amelia made a retching sound, but it was the way Joe pressed his shoulder against Leanne's that made Leanne smile. 'Right, where were we?'

Watching Amelia out of the corner of her eye, Leanne turned to the page with the folded-down corner. She waited a moment, but there was no gasp, no recoiling in shock. Amelia continued to smile and her eyes remained bright. There was nothing in her expression to suggest that even the tiniest memory had been triggered.

Leanne felt her heart sinking and all hope with it. She wanted Amelia to know how important this was. If Leanne failed to expose Claudia as a fraud, she would never find closure. She wouldn't go home for Christmas, nor would she celebrate the start of a new year where the world continued to celebrate the villains simply because the heroes didn't fit the right mould. It had all rested on Amelia, and she was still smiling. Not a muscle in her face had moved. Her expression was frozen.

'What is it?' Leanne asked.

Amelia blinked. Twice. She took a breath. It was a short gasp, followed by another. As she raised her hand, she extended one finger towards the open page. 'I remember,' she whispered, but not in the playful way she had adopted earlier when asking if Joe was Leanne's boyfriend. She had lost her voice, or else she had rediscovered the one left behind amongst smouldering rafters and broken masonry.

Leanne put an arm around the girl. 'Tell me what you see.'

'She was wearing a necklace like that.'

Amelia was pointing at the same image Leanne had picked out.

'Exactly like that?' Leanne asked. They weren't there yet, but they were getting closer.

There was a pause, another prayer.

'No, it wasn't a V. It was a . . .'

Leanne couldn't tell if Amelia was struggling because she couldn't remember, or because she could and it didn't make sense. Everyone kept telling her she had misspelled Claudia's name.

'It's OK, Amelia. Say what you remember. Don't try to make it fit with what's happened since. What letter was around her neck?'

'It was a K,' Amelia said. She looked at Leanne, her face twisted with confusion that only intensified when she realised the reporter was grinning at her. 'Is that right?'

'It's the rightest thing I've heard in a very long time.'

Amelia returned her gaze to the image, and for a moment it was as if she were entranced. 'This might hurt a wee bit.'

'Sorry?'

'That was what she said to me. She was pulling things off and I was looking at her necklace.'

Leanne's broad smile was making her cheeks ache, but she didn't care. Amelia hadn't only repeated something Karin had said, she had added the faintest lilt of a Northern Irish accent.

'I should tell Mum,' Amelia said.

'I'll need to speak to her as well.'

They both looked over to where her family was sitting. Kathryn waved at her daughter. Their food had arrived and she was being called back.

'Do you want to come over now?'

'I'm afraid I have work to do, but tell your mum I'll be in touch in the next few days. You've helped me so much, Amelia. I'm seeing things so much clearer, and soon you will too,' Leanne promised.

32

When Leanne was roused abruptly from sleep, she realised she may have spoken too soon about not getting calls at an indecent hour. Grabbing her phone before it danced off the shelf, she retreated beneath the warm covers and blinked until her eyes adjusted to the glow of the screen. It was half past two, but she was ready for this. When she had left the Bridgewater Inn the previous afternoon, she had spent the rest of the day formulating a plan, and she suspected her mystery caller had a part to play.

'Please don't hang up,' she said as soon as she accepted the call. 'If you are who I think you are, then I have some news. The last time we spoke, I threw a lot of what-ifs at you, mainly because I was trying to make sense of it myself, but now I think I have. She did have one of those key rings on her, didn't she?'

When no answer came, Leanne held her breath. She couldn't be sure it was Beth on the other end of the line and if by some chance it was Claudia, she didn't want her to know how far her lies had unravelled. That conversation would come soon enough.

'Are you still there?'

The line was cut.

Leanne pushed her head into her pillow with a groan, but she didn't let go of her phone and she didn't fall back to sleep. Ten minutes later, the screen lit up again. She connected the call, but this time she waited for the caller to speak.

'You have to stop this.'

The stranger's voice gave Leanne a jolt. It wasn't Beth, nor was it Claudia, but the accent was familiar. 'Is that you, Karin?'

'You've made everything worse,' she replied. Her words were slurred and wet with tears. 'Why couldn't you leave us alone?'

'Are you OK? What's happened?'

'I don't have to tell you anything!'

There was the clink of a glass being lifted or put down, but no other background noise. Karin was presumably at home, but she wasn't being quiet or secretive. She was alone. 'Where's Beth?'

'Gone,' Karin said. 'She's better off without me, everyone is. You know, I wish I'd been left to burn in the fire along with Declan. I wish I'd never woken up.'

Leanne had a horrible vision of a bottle of pills next to Karin's glass. She had no desire to take on the responsibility of someone else's life, but she couldn't ignore the desperation in Karin's voice. 'Do you need me to come over? I realise you don't know me, but it might help to talk to someone.'

'A reporter?'

'I didn't mean like that,' Leanne said. She was surprised that tears had sprung to her eyes. 'You're not the only one who wished they'd died in the fire. I lost someone too, my

350

best friend, Lois. She was everything I wanted to be. She was the nicest person I ever knew. She could walk into a room full of strangers and leave having made friends for life. I felt so special because she called me her best friend, and when she died, I was a nobody again.'

The outpouring came from nowhere and took Leanne by surprise. She was huddled beneath the covers in an otherwise empty boat, in the middle of the night, in the middle of nowhere, and she understood exactly how alone Karin felt. There had been times when she had thought she wouldn't make it, but she had, and she wanted to believe it had been for a purpose. Karin might be part of that purpose, and Leanne wasn't going to lose her now.

'I want to make things better, for me and for you,' she said, sharpening her words to pierce the silence on the other end of the phone. She strained her ears and picked up the faintest of breaths. 'Please, Karin. Talk to me.'

'I'm sorry your friend died.'

'I didn't tell you so you'd feel sorry for me. I just wanted you to know that you're not the only one who wonders if it should have been them who died. If you need me to come over and sit with you, I promise, I'll leave my notepad at home.'

'It's OK. I'm drunk, but I'm not about to do anything stupid. I just want all the noise in my head to stop.'

'Is that why you've been phoning me? Do you think I can help?'

'You're the only one who's still looking for answers.'

'I am, and I'm getting closer to the truth,' Leanne promised. Karin's call had reminded her that this wasn't simply a story to be written and shared. The characters were real, and what had happened to them would affect the rest of their lives. She wasn't going to give up on them, not ever. 'I'm here to listen whenever you're ready.'

'I don't think I'll ever be ready. My mind's broken, and what memories I have can't be trusted.'

'I wouldn't be too sure about that. We can work with whatever fragments you have left of that night.' Wanting to give Karin hope, she added, 'A while ago Beth said you had dreams about seeing Declan.'

'Sure, I still get them, but they're mixed up with other things.'

'I've spoken to a woman who heard him calling out to you,' Leanne said. 'Her name is Carole and she was with you and Beth as you fought to get out. She saw him up in the circle and my guess is you saw him too.'

'I didn't just *see* him, I saw him fall,' Karin said in a hushed whisper as if she were sharing her worst secret. 'I mean, I picture him falling. The doctors say my memory won't come back.'

'Maybe those doctors don't know everything. What else do you remember?'

For a while, the only thing Leanne could hear was the sound of water lapping against the side of the boat.

'Can I really trust you?'

'Look, I know Beth told you not to talk to the press, but—'

'It wasn't Beth.'

It was Leanne's turn to leave a pause. 'Claudia?'

'She came over the day after we saw you. That's what started the argument with Beth,' Karin said. 'She doesn't think Claudia . . . Actually, I don't know what she thinks.'

'Beth doesn't trust her,' Leanne surmised. She would have punched the air, but she was too nesh to raise an arm outside the duvet.

'You told her Declan was having an affair with Claudia, but Claudia said it was Phillipa. Now she says forget all about it, let Dec keep his secrets, but I can't. I need to know what happened that night.'

'The difference between me and Claudia is that she will tell lies and make you believe them. I can only give you my best guess. I can't prove that Claudia was having an affair with your brother, but she knew things about him that no one else did, like the fact that he'd slept with his sister-in-law.'

'What— What did you say?' Karin stammered. 'How did you . . . No one was supposed to know about that.'

'Is it true?'

Karin groaned as if her thoughts hurt. 'He was so ashamed. He made me promise not to breathe a word of it to anyone. And I didn't, not even to Beth.'

'And his ex-wife still doesn't know, so I doubt her sister's been talking. Declan only told the people he thought he could trust.'

'And he trusted Claudia? But she said she didn't know him. How could she lie to my face like that? And not only that. You think she gave us our tickets?'

'Yes, and that's not a guess. It's a fact.'

'Claudia knows you're on to her, doesn't she? That's why she took my pendant.'

Leanne bit down hard on her lip to stop herself swearing. 'Claudia took your necklace? The one with the initial?'

'She gave me some massage oil to try, so I took it off. I did think it was weird but, you know, I thought she was a

353

friend. It was just a trick, wasn't it? I watched her put the chain down, but when I looked later, the pendant was missing. I searched everywhere. I was on my hands and knees on the kitchen floor looking under the cupboards. I even emptied the bin,' Karin babbled. 'Beth wouldn't help. She says Claudia stole it, but she doesn't know why. Do you? Is it because Declan gave it to me? Why would Claudia be that cruel? It means nothing to anyone else.'

And it shouldn't mean anything to Claudia, thought Leanne. Unless she knew it was Karin who saved Amelia.

'I thought she was a good person,' Karin continued. Her words remained slurred, but there was an edge to her voice. Confusion had been replaced by anger.

'So did I once,' Leanne said.

There was a gulp as Karin downed more of her drink. 'It's wrong, it's all so wrong.'

Leanne wasn't sure how much more information Karin was capable of absorbing, but she couldn't be allowed to talk herself out of her fury. Leanne had to keep up the momentum. 'Did Beth mention what else we discussed?'

'Is this about the torch thingy? You know I had one,' she said. 'But why does it matter?'

'Why do you think it matters?'

'I don't know,' Karin said too quickly. 'I lost mine. Guess I used it in the theatre. I didn't have my phone with me, but I remember light being flashed in my eyes. It could have been a paramedic, I suppose, or someone at the hospital.' Her voice was growing louder. 'I don't know. I can't remember!' She released a howl of frustration.

'It's OK, Karin, I will help you get there,' Leanne promised. 'If you'll let me, I'd like to introduce you to someone who remembers you. She's recognised the pendant Declan gave you.'

'Who?' Karin said. 'Is it the little girl?'

'You remember her?'

Karin refused to answer.

'She's real, Karin. That memory you're pushing away is real.'

Again, Leanne was met with silence. Karin needed time to sober up. 'Can we talk again tomorrow?'

'I need to speak to Beth first.'

'Would it help if I spoke to her? Could you give me her number? I bet she's as confused as you, but together we can work out what is the most likely truth. It's the best I can offer.'

'You want Beth's number?' Karin repeated numbly.

'Please.'

When Karin reeled off the eleven digits, Leanne had no choice but to jump out of bed to grab her notepad. She was dithering as she scrawled down Beth's number with only the light from her phone to illuminate the page. She squinted as she repeated it back to Karin. There was no answer. The line was dead.

The painful frost stole Leanne's breath and sharpened her wits. When Karin sobered up, she would phone one of two people, and if Beth wasn't speaking to her, the next person she would try was Claudia. Leanne would have to act fast, she wanted that pleasure for herself.

33

When Justin walked into the kitchen, he caught Claudia slumped over the breakfast table with her head in her hands. He squeezed her shoulder and she moved to press herself against him.

'Why don't you go back to bed?' he asked.

Claudia straightened and stretched her neck. 'I'm fine. You're the one who needs a lie-in.'

Justin had arrived home in the middle of the night, dumped his flight bag on the bedroom floor, and was snoring two minutes after telling his wife how much he'd missed her.

'Sit down, I'll make you some coffee,' she insisted. She picked up her empty cup to refill at the same time. 'Do you want something to eat?'

'I'm still on Washington time. Maybe later.'

As she waited for the fresh coffee to brew in the French press, Claudia rested her back against the kitchen counter. Aware that Justin was watching, she crossed one leg over the other, shifting her body so that her silk dressing gown fell open to reveal a smooth thigh and the lace of her chemise. She wanted him to want her.

He groaned as he rolled his shoulders. 'Maybe I should go back to bed, but that coffee smells too good to resist.' As Justin moved his head to the side, he tried not to make a show of checking the normally full wine rack. He was working out how much his wife had got through while he was away.

Claudia poured their coffee and returned to the table. 'I'm glad you're home,' she said. She had wanted to sound seductive, but her voice hitched. She felt stupidly emotional.

'What's wrong?' he asked. 'And don't say nothing. You've been acting odd for weeks.'

In that moment, Claudia considered telling Justin everything; how she had allowed a man to seduce her when she had been at her most vulnerable, and how everything that followed on from that single error of judgement had made her realise how much she loved her husband. For all the lies she may have told, this was the absolute truth. She needed him to know that, but words failed her.

Justin leant forward and parted the veil of tresses hiding Claudia's face. 'I don't know what to do with you, Claudia,' he said. 'What am I doing wrong?'

'Nothing.'

He kissed her gently and his lips remained close to hers when he said, 'I love you.'

'I love you too.'

Claudia wanted time to stop so they could stay like that for ever, but inevitably, Justin sat back in his chair. She picked up her coffee and swallowed back a swell of sadness.

'I'm going to tell the office not to book me on any more trips for a while,' Justin said, after mulling over the conundrum that was his wife. 'It's been an exhausting year for both of us, and we need to recharge our batteries. And not just because we want to get pregnant. Let's do it for us. We don't have to wait for Dry January to start cutting back our alcohol consumption. It would be nice to wake up for once without a hangover.'

He made it sound as if he were talking about himself. He wasn't.

'How about we go away for Christmas?' he continued. 'Bali might be nice, or the Seychelles?'

It was a tempting offer, but Claudia didn't think it was safe to leave Karin to her own devices yet. 'That does sound appealing.'

'But?'

'There's so much to do with the hardship fund. How would it look if I went off jet-setting while there are so many in need?'

'Phillipa always managed to find a balance. It can be done.'

'Isn't it time we all stop idolising Phillipa?' asked Claudia, her temper rising. She could cope with her so-called friends being sycophants, but not her husband too. 'She might have her successes, but her failures have been spectacular.'

'She's been a good friend.'

'No, Justin, she hasn't. Her actions led to the fire and we lost our baby because of it. How can you not be just the tiniest bit angry about that?'

Justin raked his fingers through his hair. 'We can't look at it that way.'

'Why not?' she asked, but she already knew. Justin liked perfect order to his world. The problems he couldn't fix, he airbrushed out.

'It doesn't matter now,' he replied. 'Robert tells me they're heading off to Geneva next week. They can coordinate the house move from there so they won't be returning to Sedgefield. Whatever people might think, the town has lost a great asset.'

The news of Phillipa's imminent departure added some much-needed balm to Claudia's mood. She gave a theatrical sigh to give Justin the impression that her misplaced anger was spent.

'Sorry, I didn't mean to snap. Of course they'll be missed, especially at this time of year.' She was reminded how Phillipa used the social calendar to establish her pecking order. Claudia may have overreached herself, thinking she could replace Phillipa at the top, but at the very least, she deserved a higher ranking. 'I was toying with the idea of a Christmas fundraiser.'

'I don't want you pushing yourself too hard.'

'I won't have to if you're here to look after me,' she said. 'And you will look after me, won't you?'

Justin smiled. 'Can I have a shower first?'

'I might join you.'

With her hair still damp and her skin glowing, Claudia left her husband snoring in bed and returned to the kitchen to clear away their abandoned coffee cups. Her head felt clearer than it had in months. Despite what Justin might have assumed, she hadn't been suffering from a hangover this morning. Preferring to keep her wits about her, Claudia had refrained from drinking since Phillipa's dinner party, but it did no harm for him to think she had a problem.

To Justin, Claudia was a broken toy that he enjoyed fixing,

only to forget to play with it later. She was the temp who overstated her experience and messed up an entire month's bookings at the tennis club; she was the daughter whose father let her down, requiring one of Justin's friends to give her away at their wedding; and she was the mother-to-be who suddenly wasn't. Each and every time, Justin had thought she needed fixing, and those were the times when his attention had been exactly where it needed to be. Claudia had him all figured out.

Pouring the cold coffees down the sink as she had done with all that expensive wine, Claudia told herself to relax. She still worried about Karin, but realistically, how much harm could she do? Her silver pendant was residing at the bottom of the canal, and Karin was left with no more than conflated memories and mild hysteria. Amelia's recollections could be dismissed just as easily. Claudia was in control, and with Justin home again and home for good, her confidence was returning.

Claudia's smile had a hint of smugness and it didn't falter when her phone rang and she saw Leanne's name appear. She told herself she had this.

'Good morning, Leanne,' she said brightly.

'I'd like to ask you some questions, Mrs Rothwell, if it's convenient.'

Claudia closed the kitchen door. 'Shoot away, Miss Pitman.'

'I'm writing an article on the events that took place on 21st October last year and I thought I'd give you the opportunity to respond.'

'That sounds very officious,' Claudia observed. She kept her tone casual, but her legs wobbled. She sat down and kept her phone pressed to her ear despite the unsettling sensation that it was about to explode in her hand.

'The last time we spoke, I had some questions about your seats at the theatre. I've since discovered that the two women who used your tickets were Karin Gallagher and Beth McCulloch.'

'I've told you before, no one else used my tickets,' Claudia corrected. 'There was a mix-up at the box office. I presume a duplicate set had been issued.'

'You don't think it's a coincidence that Karin and Beth should be in your seats?'

'I don't see how.'

'But you were in their home last week.'

Claudia's hand jerked, but she kept tight hold of the phone. 'As you seem to have worked out, they're receiving support through my charity, as are many other victims,' she said. 'I hope you haven't been hounding them.'

'Not at all. It was Karin who contacted me.'

'Well, that's something I suppose,' Claudia said with a note of relief she wished she could feel.

'I've been following certain lines of inquiry,' Leanne continued, 'one of which is to identify who actually pulled Amelia from the rubble.'

Claudia rested her elbows on the breakfast table. 'You're still going on about that? I honestly don't know why you've become so obsessed, Leanne. Why does it matter to you so much? Is it because no one swooped in to save your friend?'

'I don't like liars, that's all,' Leanne snapped back. Claudia was getting to her.

'Are you including yourself in that category? Because that's how your readers will see it once you start contradicting the story you were so eager to share with them.'

'I'd rather be damned for telling the truth than be lauded

for supporting a lie,' Leanne replied. 'Only we're not talking about one lie, are we?'

Claudia forced herself upright. 'If you want me to respond to your claims, it would save us both a lot of time if you simply stated your case.'

'I suppose it would. Time is of the essence and my editor wants this story ready for our Saturday edition,' Leanne replied, letting Claudia know that her ticking bomb had a timer. 'I aim to prove that the reunion we arranged between you and Amelia was the first time you ever met. You weren't the woman with injured hands that Rex Russell described carrying Amelia. The person who treated you on the scene has stated for the record that you didn't have a scratch on you. Then there's the small matter of the key ring torch. Your reaction when it was mentioned by Amelia was caught on camera, and we'll be sharing the video with our readers. They can make up their own minds as to whether your faux pas was genuine confusion, or if it shows how you've been making things up as you went along.'

'You would need parental consent to use that video.'

'I'm sure the Parkers will be more than happy to cooperate. In fact I was talking to Amelia only this weekend. We had a very productive chat.'

'And?' Claudia asked. She dug her fingernails into her unblemished palm, using the pain to remain focused.

'There was a reason she thought your name was spelled with a K.'

'I presume it was because her mum spells Kathryn with a K.'

'Now we both know that isn't the real reason. I could

explain, but my guess is you already know. That would be why you went to see Karin and stole her pendant.'

'This is ridiculous.'

'You've actually helped me out enormously. I'd say your actions have proven what was only a theory. And not just in my mind. You'll find you can't buy Karin's silence as easily as you thought you could.'

'The poor woman is unstable.'

'Which is exactly why you were able to manipulate her. She's been confused by memories she doesn't think belong to her, but that's about to change. It was Karin Gallagher who turned back for Amelia after the ceiling collapsed. She had the key ring torch, and she was wearing the same pendant around her neck that she wore up until last week. Amelia has confirmed that the necklace worn by her rescuer had a silver K hanging from it. It was Karin, not you, who pulled Amelia out of the rubble and handed her over before going back to look for her brother.'

'Well, good luck trying to convince your readers with that piece of fiction.'

'What did make you go into a burning building?'

'You're the reporter, you tell me,' Claudia said, almost laughing. It was a relief to have confirmation that Leanne didn't know everything.

Claudia savoured the silence on the other end of the line, and she was searching for another acerbic comment when the reporter found her voice again.

'I think you were following Declan.'

The smile on Claudia's face vanished. 'What?'

'You had been with him that evening, hadn't you?' Leanne asked. 'How fortunate for you that he learnt about the fire in time for you to get back to the theatre before you were caught out. I take it your husband still doesn't know about the affair?'

'You've gone too far,' Claudia hissed. 'And if you dare publish anything that links my name to Declan Gallagher's, I'll take your paper for every penny it has. It won't survive. Tell your editor that.'

'How strange,' Leanne said. It was her turn to sound amused. 'I've just told you we're going to expose your lies about Amelia, and you don't react. I mention Declan on the other hand . . .'

'You want a statement? Well here it is,' Claudia began. As she unclenched her fist, a trickle of blood ran from the half-moon wounds in her palm. 'I stand by what I've said previously. I was inside the theatre when the alarm sounded and, when I reached the exit, I realised there were people left inside who needed help. The emergency services were struggling. Not enough appliances had arrived because the local fire station had been closed down. I didn't realise at the time that they were concentrating their efforts at the front of the theatre. Time was running out for some of those trapped, and that was why I turned back. After various conversations with Leanne Pitman, she convinced me that I was the one who pulled Amelia from the wreckage. It's possible that I was mistaken and it was in fact another child. If that is the case, I implore whoever I did help to come forward so we can put this traumatic event behind us.'

'Is that it?'

Claudia loosened her shoulders. Her damp hair felt sticky, but her pulse was slowing. 'Unless you have any more questions.'

'No.' Leanne didn't sound so sure of herself now. She didn't have the scoop she thought she had.

'Would you like me to repeat any of what I've just said?' Claudia asked helpfully.

'I have it all on tape.'

'Of course you do.'

Claudia cut the call. There was no goodbye, no pleasantries, and no opportunity for Leanne to work out how deeply she had plunged the knife into Claudia's back.

It had been a mistake to give Amelia's mum the wrong mobile number. If Claudia had engaged with the girl more, she might have teased memories from her earlier. She could have moulded the recollection of the pendant into something that would support Claudia's claim instead of disproving it, but recriminations were futile. Past mistakes couldn't be undone, and if the worst that came out of this sorry mess was that Claudia had to acknowledge that she might not have been Amelia's hero, so be it. But it had to stop there.

The reporter couldn't be allowed to mine all that information Claudia knew was buried inside Karin's head. Despite everything she had done for her, it looked like Karin was turning against her. Was there no such thing as loyalty any more?

After a quick call, the arrangements were made and Claudia slipped back into the bedroom, where Justin continued to sleep through the tremors that rocked their happy marriage. She was pulling on a Lycra top when he began to stir.

'Are you off to the gym?'

'I thought I'd go for a run.'

He looked towards the window to gauge the weather beyond the closed blinds. 'It'll be bloody freezing.'

365

'I'll warm up,' she said, grabbing a hoodie and trainers. 'You go back to sleep, I won't be long.'

Justin yawned. 'I should get up. I need to check my emails.'

'Don't work too hard.'

'Same goes for you,' he said with a smirk.

Claudia would need to push herself. It was going to be quite a trek into town, but she didn't want to take the car. She had to get better at covering her tracks if she were to survive this.

34

Having not slept since her wake-up call from Karin, Leanne had started the day making calls of her own. The first had been to her editor and, despite claiming to be an early riser, Mal had still been in bed at six thirty, which was as long as Leanne could wait. She needed to know if she had a story. Actually, she knew she had one, but she wanted to hear it from Mal and, to her relief, there had been no mutterings of caution, no anxieties about legal action or upsetting the powers that be. He wanted a draft on his desk within days.

Leanne had spent more time preparing for her next call and had hoped to catch Claudia off guard, but Mrs Rothwell had remained unnervingly cool. Her explanation for the 'confusion', was almost plausible, but her veil of innocence had slipped. Leanne may not have worked out what Claudia and Declan were up to that night, but Claudia's reaction at the mere mention of his name proved the hypothesis that they were indeed having an affair.

Karin was the link that tied the whole thing together, but when Leanne called her back as promised, it went straight to voicemail. She had to settle for leaving a message.

'Hi, Karin, sorry for disturbing you,' she said, forcing a smile to lift her voice and disguise her anxiety. 'I hope you're feeling OK after last night. I'm not sure how much you remember, but I'm here if you need to talk. There's no pressure.' She winced at the lie. Her smile forgotten. 'I know it's tough, but like I said to you last night, *please*, don't let anyone tell you what you should remember. Accept your memories as your truth. Trust them. Trust me.'

She cut the call before she could scream down the phone, 'And whatever you do, do not trust Claudia Rothwell!' She hoped that was obvious, and if it wasn't to Karin, then it would be to Beth, but when Leanne tried her number, it went through to voicemail too. This message was shorter and to the point. She told Beth that Karin had phoned and left it to her to decide what that might mean.

Aware that she had a deadline to meet, Leanne made herself comfortable on the futon and opened up a blank page on her laptop.

They say you can't rewrite history, but I'm about to try. Claudia Rothwell is not who we thought she was. The image she projects is the product of not one lie, but many, and I apologise for being amongst those who helped create a false icon. Our search for justice is a search for the truth. Here is the truth as I know it.

Leanne stared at her words. It was going to be tough convincing the *Courier*'s readers that despite being wrong before, she was right this time. Would they believe her? At that moment, it would be enough if she could convince only Karin and Beth. When her phone rang, she crossed her fingers.

'What did you say to Karin?' Beth demanded.

'I told her that she might not be as confused as we all

thought. The memories she has of Amelia are real. I showed Amelia a pendant similar to the one Karin wore and she recognised it straight away. There's no doubt in my mind that after you and Karin became separated in the fire, she ended up with Amelia. She saved her, Beth. It wasn't Claudia.'

'The pendant's gone.'

'And you and Karin had an argument about it. You don't trust Claudia either, do you?'

'What you said hurt. She didn't pay us for our silence. We needed help, we still do, but that doesn't mean we can be bought.'

'I'm sorry if I offended you,' Leanne said. 'I was frustrated because I was beginning to see what no one else could. Heroes can be victims too.'

'Karin really saved Amelia?'

'Yes.'

There was a muffled sob as Beth clamped a hand over her mouth. 'I was scared she was losing her mind. She'd wake up in a cold sweat after dreaming about digging someone out. Karin still has the scars from the damage to her hands. We always assumed it was Declan she was trying to reach, and I've been telling her that her fixation on Amelia is unhealthy. I've let her down so badly.'

'You'll only be letting her down if you walk away from this.'

'It wouldn't be the first time,' Beth suggested. She swallowed hard. 'I could have gone back for her. I know I said it was Mrs Brody who stopped me, but the truth is, she didn't have to try very hard. I convinced myself that Karin must have found another way out, but it was only so I could give myself permission to do nothing instead of doing something. Karin chose differently. She might not know it, but she's stronger than I could ever be. She risked her life for a complete stranger.'

'I promise I'm going to make this right, Beth. If we can put Karin and Amelia in the same room, they'll see things more clearly. Claudia might present us with a problem, however,' Leanne warned. 'There are still questions about her that need to be answered. Will you help me?'

'I'm in work at the moment, in Chester,' Beth explained. 'I can't talk for long, but I could meet you later today. Karin's not answering her phone, but I'll keep trying and hopefully convince her to come along.'

The previous night's fears for Karin's safety resurfaced. 'Have you heard from her at all? It was two thirty when she phoned me. She was pretty drunk, and very upset.'

'And now she's hungover,' Beth said, not sharing Leanne's concern. 'She texted me before to let me know that she was still alive, and that she was going out for a walk along the canal to clear her head. She's not ready to talk yet, or at least not to me.'

'You have to keep trying,' Leanne said. 'I've spoken to Claudia, and she knows I'm writing a new piece on Amelia, so if you do speak to Karin, please warn her to keep away from her.'

'I've already said as much. Karin's in a dark place at the moment, she keeps saying I'd be better off without her and I think it was Claudia who put the idea in her head. What kind of monster is she?'

'The kind who knows she's trapped and is trying to claw her way out.'

'She only has herself to blame. It must have taken some

gall to spend a year pretending you were involved in a disaster when you were little more than a bystander. And if that wasn't bad enough, she goes and puts herself centre stage and tells even bigger lies? I don't understand her. Why would she do it?'

'I don't think I helped. I was asking questions she couldn't answer truthfully, like why she apparently reached the exit only to turn back.'

'I've been thinking about that. I didn't know who she was at the time. I wouldn't have connected her with Declan, but she stood out for a reason. Maybe it was because I was looking for Karin and they both have dark hair, but I think there was another reason. We were all covered in grime and she was there with her perfect make-up and her cream coat. Could that be why she went inside? Did she want to get as messy as the rest of us, or at least absorb the smell of smoke?'

'Some of those who got out first didn't have a mark on them, so it wasn't entirely necessary, but you might be right,' Leanne said. She closed her eyes and attempted to put herself in Claudia's position that night. It made her skin crawl.

The Empress Theatre
Sedgefield, Cheshire

As the white rabbit made her entrance onstage, Claudia was lying in Declan's bed. She was as focused as the little dancer, but there was no guiding voice inside her head, no choreographed next steps. The decisions she had to make were hers and hers alone.

'You need to tell him,' Declan said as he cupped Claudia's face and wiped away a single tear with his thumb. He thought she was crying for sweet Justin.

Claudia turned away, and when she dragged herself out of the bed, she knew it would be for the last time. 'I have told him,' she said as she began to dress.

Declan raised himself onto an elbow, his eyes alight. 'Why didn't you say sooner?'

'I mean, I've told him about the baby. He's thrilled. We both are.'

Unable to say what needed to be said while looking at the tangled sheets she could never return to, Claudia left Declan to grab his clothes and went into the kitchen to make some coffee. She hated that he only had instant.

Claudia hadn't intended to break up with Declan that

night, but he had become far too invested in her pregnancy. Unfortunately, because she was using the ballet as her cover story, the earliest she could arrive home without causing suspicion was ten thirty. It wasn't even eight o'clock. It was going to be a very long night.

With his shirt hanging open, Declan was buckling his belt as he joined her. 'You're staying with him?'

'Look, Declan, I'm not saying I don't love you, it's just that I love Justin too, and my life belongs with him,' she said, and her heart actually swelled. She had become visible again in her husband's eyes and, now that they were about to become parents, their life together was assured.

Justin had warned Claudia before they married that he and his first wife had seen a fertility specialist and that 'his little swimmers' weren't Olympic material. But he had never given up hope of fathering a child of his own, and Claudia's news had been exactly what he had been waiting for. She had succeeded where Sasha had failed.

'But you can't live a lie,' Declan insisted.

Claudia stirred two mugs of coffee and pushed one towards Declan. 'And what lie would that be?'

She hoped he wasn't going to accuse her of deliberately seeking him out as a glorified sperm donor because that wasn't true, not completely. She had allowed herself to fall for Declan's charms because she had been starved of Justin's attention. It was simply a happy coincidence that she had become pregnant.

Declan was shaking his head in disbelief.

'What?' she asked, prepared to make her argument.

Before he could respond, his phone bleeped. It was in his back pocket and he glanced at it briefly, intending to *continue their conversation, but his head snapped back to the screen.*

Claudia sipped her coffee. 'Is it important?'

In answer, Declan went to the kitchen window and opened it a crack. She could hear the wail of an alarm.

'Is that coming from the theatre?'

'I've had an automated message. I need to check it out before Phillipa finds out,' he said, but he stayed where he was. 'I don't know, maybe I should stay. This is more important.'

Claudia wasn't listening as she pushed past Declan and hurried to the tiny living room. When she had arrived earlier, she had hung her bag on the back of a chair, kicked off her shoes by the door, and hung her cream cashmere coat on a hook. She hadn't been expecting Justin to phone while she was at the ballet, so she had left her mobile in her bag, along with the programme for the ballet that Declan had given her to shore up her alibi. She gathered up her things.

'What are you doing?' asked Declan.

'I'm supposed to be inside the Empress. Phillipa will expect a blow-by-blow account of what happened. I have to be there.'

In truth, Claudia was perfectly capable of lying her way out of it, but she had delivered the bad news to Declan, and this was the perfect opportunity to leave. She would spend the next couple of hours sitting in the car if she had to.

Claudia left the flat by her usual route out the back. She knew the position of each and every CCTV camera littering the high street, having done everything she could to ensure her affair wouldn't be discovered. Now was not the time for mistakes.

'I'm not giving up without a fight,' Declan warned as he caught up with her. 'I want to be a part of this baby's life.'

'It's not yours.'

'You can't know that.'

Claudia would believe what she wanted to believe. It wasn't as if Justin was ever going to insist on a DNA test. He trusted her implicitly, and besides, it was possible that he was the father, if just a little unlikely when factoring in who she was with and when. Not that Declan needed to know that. 'The dates match when Justin was home, not when I was with you. It's his baby.'

'Either way, I love you, Claude. And I'll love the baby too.'

'You're not listening,' she hissed. 'I'm not going to leave Justin for you.'

They were zipping along the back alley that ran parallel with the high street. Unlike the pristine shopfronts, the back of the buildings were crumbling and she could smell rotting waste and cat pee. She wasn't giving up what she had for this.

'You'll love Donegal,' he said as if reading her mind. 'It's beautiful.'

'You expect me to follow you back to your ex-wife and her sister?'

'If you don't fancy Ireland, how about Scotland, or Wales? Or the South of France?' he asked. He was laughing as if the whole thing were a joke. 'We can go anywhere.'

'Not with a baby. And what do I do when you abandon us like you did your last family?'

He grabbed her. 'I phone my kids when I can, and I've promised they can come and stay with me once I'm settled somewhere permanent,' he said, ever the fantasist. 'I'm not my father.'

376

Oh, but you are, thought Claudia.

'I'll do right by all of you,' he insisted. 'Look, if you're too scared to tell Justin, I can do it for you.'

'You will not!'

Claudia pulled away, but Declan followed. 'I can't let you go. Just think about—' He stopped in his tracks and sniffed the air.

Claudia could smell it too. Smoke. She was about to remind him that Bonfire Night was only a few weeks away and it would be kids up to no good, but the ground shook and an eerie glow lit up the rooftops.

'Sweet Jesus,' Declan said under his breath, not needing to see the theatre to know it was alight. 'I have to get to Karin. She's in the stalls, right?'

'You can't go in there if it's on fire.'

'I have to, you stay here!'

'No, I need to be there too or I'll be found out,' she said as Declan shot off towards a side alley that would take him onto the high street.

'To hell with that!' Declan called back to her. 'You don't have to lie any more, not for me.'

Claudia wasn't doing it for him, and she ran as if her life depended on it, keeping to the back alleys until she reached the crowd of theatregoers spilling out onto the road in front of the Empress. The roof was ablaze.

Out of breath and with a stitch in her side, Claudia couldn't decide what to do next until she saw Declan coming out of the front entrance carrying a child. Not content with saving one person, he headed down the side alley. Claudia followed with her head down and her coat collar up.

It was surreal. The smell of smoke had intensified and the

377

people emerging through the fire doors were covered in dust. There was a little boy wailing loudly.

'Someone has to help Mrs Clarke! She's trapped upstairs!'

Declan stopped and glanced back. His eyes were wide with shock as he took one last look, and then he was gone. Claudia was slower to react, and it was only when a woman grabbed her arm to leave a bloodied handprint that she was spurred into action.

35

Claudia jogged at a steady pace as she crossed a footbridge that spanned the canal junction at Raven Brook Marina. She was unaware that Leanne lived nearby, but the reporter was on her mind. The *Courier* could print whatever it liked. Claudia had given her statement and she would stand by it.

She would explain how Leanne had placed her under unnecessary duress with leading questions, and how Claudia's answers had been twisted until she believed what was being suggested. It wasn't her fault. She was a victim like anyone else. Why couldn't Leanne simply accept that? It wasn't as if she hadn't suffered an enduring loss as a result of the fire, and not just the baby.

Overwhelmed with fear and sadness, Claudia longed for Declan's touch, but it was her hand that wiped the single tear sliding down her cheek. She had needed their affair to end, but not in the way that it had. For a long time, she had consoled herself that his death provided a neat ending, but as she jogged along the towpath, it didn't feel so neat any more. Karin was one loose end that needed snipping.

Navigating the occasional angler whose fishing rods criss-crossed her path, Claudia didn't miss a step. Her pace slowed only when the path narrowed into the approach of a forty-foot tunnel. The dull thud of running shoes on well-trodden earth was replaced by the thump of rubber on sandstone. It had taken a bit longer than she had expected to get there, but Karin had waited obediently.

'Sorry I'm late,' she said as the sound of her laboured breaths echoed off the walls.

Consumed in shadow, Karin's complexion appeared sallow. Her scarf was wrapped around her neck, and there was an unpleasant yellow stain on it. As Claudia drew closer, she could smell the bitterness of bile.

'You'll have to forgive me for not hugging,' she added. 'I'm quite sweaty.'

'Why would I want to hug you? We're not friends.' Karin's words were as sour as her breath.

'Oh, I thought we were. I hoped we were,' Claudia replied, unfazed by the welcome that was as cold as the frost clinging to the smooth edges of the canal. She released a sigh as she lifted her gaze to the arched roof and admired the graffiti inflicted by marker pens and penknives. 'I used to hang out here with my friends when I was younger. We had this challenge to see who could write their name up highest. I remember balancing on a boy's shoulders while his heels hung over the water. I don't know how we didn't fall in.'

She squinted at the old bricks. Was her name still up there? Justin would be horrified if he knew what she had got up to.

'Did you sneak down here with my brother?'

'Ah, you've been speaking to Leanne again.'

'So you're not denying it?'

380

'This is getting tedious. Karin. I never met your brother,' she said through gritted teeth.

'Then how did you know what happened in Donegal? Declan was ashamed of what he did. Even his ex doesn't know about her sister.'

'Gosh, he had an affair with his sister-in-law?' Claudia said, feigning shock. 'Little wonder he had to do a runner.'

'You already knew. Leanne—'

'Leanne told you,' Claudia said, her patience snapping. 'Can't you see she's playing with you? How many reporters did you have hanging around when Declan was suspected of causing the fire? How many do you think turned up on his ex-wife's doorstep, or her sister's for that matter? I don't know where Leanne got her information, but it didn't come from me.'

Karin placed the palm of her gloved hand on her forehead. Her bloodshot eyes closed briefly. 'You're the one who's trying to play me. The only reason I had tickets for that night was to do your job while you were with my brother. You were pulling the strings then, and you think you're doing it now.'

'That's simply not true. I won't deny that Leanne has made a compelling case, but she has her own agenda.'

'She lost a friend, I know. I lost a brother.'

'And I lost a baby,' Claudia reminded her.

'And whose baby was it? Did Declan know you were pregnant?' Karin demanded, her raised voice echoing through the tunnel.

Claudia shifted uncomfortably. The last angler she had seen was too far away to hear, but she couldn't account for dog walkers. 'I'm not your enemy,' she said softly, forcing the conversation to lower levels. 'You came to me, remember?'

Karin laughed. 'Do I remember?' she asked, mocking Claudia. 'Do you know what? I think I'm starting to.'

Claudia glared back at her. 'Fine, let's get this out there. Leanne phoned me this morning with some crazy story about you being the one who saved Amelia. Can you believe that?' When Karin didn't respond, she added, 'And I bet Leanne's gone out of her way to plant the idea in that poor girl's head, just like she's planted it in yours. She wants a new headline, that's all. She's ruthless.'

'I remember digging Amelia out.'

'You said yourself you've absorbed false memories from the news reports. You're reliving my experience, not yours.'

Karin pulled off her gloves and invited Claudia to look at the scars on her hands. 'I didn't get these from trying to reach Declan. He wasn't the one who was buried.'

'This is silly,' Claudia said, rubbing her arms. The sweat on her skin had turned to ice and she shuddered as she glanced at the still surface of the canal. The water was black and bottomless. 'You're not well, Karin.'

'I'm not as sick as you.'

Claudia's lip curled. 'I've had enough of this. I came here in good faith because I was worried about you, but if you're determined to do battle, so be it.' She made a show of looking Karin up and down. 'Who's going to believe you of all people? Seriously, you look half-crazed and that's being polite. Are you ready for the abuse coming your way when the public hears your ramblings? They won't believe you, Karin. You're a nobody.'

'I'm not interested in being in the headlines. I'm not like you.'

'No? Then why are you here?' demanded Claudia.

'Because I remember seeing you inside the theatre.' Karin let her gloves drop to the ground as she extended her arms. She was repeating the same movements she had made in her kitchen, reaching out for an invisible figure. 'I saw you, Claudia.'

36

After talking to Beth, Leanne returned to her laptop intending to make another stab at her article. The world needed to know that the woman who had stood onstage in Victoria Park demanding the world's sympathy had been no hero, but the words wouldn't come. Whilst Leanne was quite clear about what lies Claudia had told, she wasn't entirely sure she could explain her motives.

Beth thought Claudia might have raced into the burning building to add some authenticity to the story she would later tell her husband, but Claudia had been pregnant. Had she really been so desperate to conceal her affair that she would risk her life and that of her baby's simply to embellish her cover story? And why claim to have gone back for Amelia? Wasn't that a lie too far? Or was there something much bigger that Claudia was hiding?

Telling herself she needed space, Leanne slipped on her leather jacket and a pair of boots with a growing sense of urgency. It was only when she was on dry land that she acknowledged her mission. Beth had said Karin was taking a walk along the canal. Perhaps they could clear their heads together.

The sun shone in a clear blue sky, but it had yet to defeat the hoar frost covering the landscape. To keep warm, Leanne kept to a brisk pace as she circled the marina and joined the towpath. Chances were that Karin had returned home from her walk by now, or she had chosen a different route, but if their paths did cross, Leanne hoped Karin could help with some of the remaining questions, if not about Claudia, then about her brother.

What had Declan been doing up in the circle? He would have seen that the fire was in the roof as he approached the theatre. He would have known it was sheer madness to head upstairs, and yet he had done just that. Had Claudia been following him inside? Did one or both of them have a death wish?

The Empress Theatre
Sedgefield, Cheshire

It was seeing the handprint on her coat that had made Claudia realise she couldn't walk away. The fire wasn't going to be contained. Mrs Clarke wasn't going to be rescued. People were going to die. The only question left was had she done enough to protect herself from the fallout? No, not nearly enough.

As Claudia shouldered people out of the way, she locked eyes fleetingly with a woman coming from the other direction. Declan had shown her photos of Beth with Karin, but this woman was a replica of every other person streaming past, dazed and covered in a grey film of dust. There was no inkling that this brief encounter would change the course of Claudia's life. The stitch in her side was easing and she believed she was indestructible.

She needed to find Declan. If the fire was as big a catastrophe as she feared, this was her last opportunity to speak to him before he was placed under the media spotlight. She wouldn't be able to get near him afterwards, not without risking the discovery of their affair, but the biggest risk was Declan himself. He might be good at keeping secrets, but he was under the misapprehension that their secret was ready to be brought into the light. Over her dead body.

Ahead of Claudia, a group of stragglers came out from the stalls and she expected to see Declan amongst them. He ought to be coming out by now, but as she passed a deserted stairway, she realised why he hadn't. Before disappearing into the theatre, Declan had turned to look back. He had heard the boy crying for his dance teacher. The idiot had gone upstairs to find Hilary.

Declan Gallagher's overriding need as he raced towards the theatre had been to make sure Karin was safe, but as he drew closer, the true scale of the horror had dawned on him. He wanted to make sure everyone was safe and he couldn't ignore the little boy's pleas. Hilary Clarke was a legend and if she was trapped, he wouldn't abandon her.

As he reached the top of the stairs and entered the circle, he had his first glimpse of the dense cloud of smoke above his head. It flared briefly and his heart filled with dread. It seemed like only seconds ago that he had been lying in bed imagining a future for him and Claudia. He had wanted her to realise he wasn't afraid of commitment and responsibility. What would she think of him now? What did he think of himself?

Choking on the acrid air, Declan circled the site of the collapse. Despite the gloom, he could see where the front of the circle had been partly destroyed. He clambered over debris to get nearer the edge. He needed to look over onto the stalls even though he was terrified of what he might see.

Finding a section to the right of the collapse that looked relatively secure, he gripped the brass handrail and leant forward. Where once there had been neat rows of red velvet seats, there was devastation and chaos. Worst of all, there were people still down there.

'Karin!' he screamed. 'Karin, are you there?'

He saw movement almost directly below him. It was a woman, but she hadn't looked up. Whoever she was, she wasn't Karin and didn't appear to need help, so Declan turned his attention back to the circle. Luck must have been on his side because as he moved away, a large piece of masonry fell from the ceiling and glanced off the balcony roughly where he had been standing. He was about to look back down into the stalls, but something caught his eye, and he was spared the sight of Lena Kowalski's body. She had died instantaneously. Across the rows of the circle, on the outer edge of the collapse site, he spotted an arm protruding from the rubble.

Hilary Clarke's slight figure was hidden beneath a mound of debris with only one shoulder and arm protruding. Her white hair was covered in the same thick layer of dust that covered her face. Her eyes flickered open when Declan took her hand.

'Hilary? I'm going to get you out.'

She smiled. 'I suspect it's too late, but not to worry. I don't feel any pain – and I can't tell you how many years it's been since I could say that.'

Declan fought the urge to ignore Hilary and start digging her out, but she was so calm. He couldn't do anything to save her. She knew it and so did he. 'I'm so sorry.'

'Don't be sorry, be better.'

'I am trying,' he said, before searching for something to say that might prove as much. 'I found out recently I'm going to be a dad again.'

'Then you have something to live for.'

Declan gripped her hand tighter still. 'Tell me what I can do to help?'

'Stay with me. I don't want to be alone.'

'I'm not going anywhere,' he promised, just as a hand clamped on his shoulder. He turned with a jolt. 'Christ, Claudia! You shouldn't be here!'

'Neither should you.'

Claudia was out of breath again after climbing the stairs, and her lungs were desperate for clean air. Her coat collar was pulled across her mouth, and wasn't much of a face mask, but at least it hid her scowl. Surely Declan could see that the dance teacher was beyond help.

'I have to stay,' Declan said, drawing his gaze back to the dying woman. 'This is Hilary. Hilary, this is the mother of my child.'

Claudia's jaw clenched. Declan really didn't care who he told. He had become a liability.

'Did my students make it out?' Hilary asked.

'They're safe,' Claudia said, before demanding Declan's attention again. 'Shouldn't you be looking for Karin?'

'I'm sure she'll be heading out the front with all the others. She has to be,' he said. 'This is where I'm needed. Christ, where's the emergency services?'

'They'll need time to make everything safe.'

Declan was shaking his head. 'It'll be too late.'

He had kept his voice low, but Hilary had heard him. 'There really is nothing to be done for me,' she said, her voice drifting. 'It was quite some show, don't you think?'

Forced to wait, Claudia edged closer to the crumbling balcony. There were a handful of people heading for a side exit, but the rest of the stalls looked to be deserted, until she saw a figure the colour of dust pulling what looked like a child's body from the rubble. Claudia was mesmerised by the sight of what she presumed to be a corpse being handed over to someone else. If they were the child's parents, she was confused when the mother didn't follow the man out.

As the figure turned, she looked up, and Claudia dipped behind the shattered balcony. The theatre was full of noise, but she heard a name being carried above the useless cry of the alarm. Someone was calling for Declan and there was only one person it could be.

Remaining low, Claudia clambered back to Declan. 'We should go.'

Declan wasn't listening. 'It's OK, I'm still here,' he said to Hilary. He had her hand clasped tightly in his, but the dance teacher's long, white fingers had uncurled and were extended in a grim ballet pose.

'She's dead, Declan.'

'I know.'

'And so will we be if you don't let her go,' Claudia said impatiently. She should mention Karin, but it would be another distraction. 'Please, you have to listen to me.'

Declan placed Hilary's hand down gently. 'How many other people have died tonight?' he asked. 'If it turns out it's my fault, I'm not sure I could live with myself.'

'You can go back to Ireland, start again.'

Standing up, Declan moved towards her. 'I couldn't go without you,' he said, taking her hand. 'I need you, Claude. We have to stay together.'

Claudia forgot about the fire raging above her head. The real danger lay directly in front of her and, when Declan went to lead her away, Claudia pulled her hand free and shook her head. She stepped back. No.

'It'll be OK,' he promised.

'No, it won't!' Claudia yelled at him. She backed away until she was dangerously close to the exposed edge of the balcony and the void beyond.

'Jesus, watch what you're doing!' Declan cried out.

Claudia held his gaze as she took another step in the wrong direction.

As Declan lunged towards her, time slowed enough for Claudia to consider every possible outcome. She could simply fall back and bring this torture to an end; she could let Declan save her and commit herself to a life of purgatory; or she could step to the side.

Declan wasn't expecting Claudia to twist her body as he made a grab to save her. He misjudged his step and lost balance. As he began to flail, Claudia reached out a hand. It was pure instinct.

37

'You were standing with Declan. I can see you reaching for him,' Karin said, her face twisted with anguish. 'Why didn't you save him?'

Recoiling in horror at Karin's outstretched arms, Claudia stepped back. She could feel the flagstones sloping towards the water's edge. One wrong move could be her undoing. Wasn't it always the way?

The fire at the Empress had been one near miss after the other. If Declan's flat hadn't been so close; if he hadn't been notified of the alarm; if the emergency services had arrived sooner to cordon off the theatre; or if luck hadn't been on her side for a myriad other reasons, then Claudia's marriage would be over by now and she would be trapped with Declan in some crappy, rented house, hidden and forgotten. It was everything she had tried to escape, as her mother had before her.

Claudia wanted to explain to Karin that she had loved Declan. He was a good man, even if he had acted on impulse occasionally without considering the consequences. It was something they had in common.

Karin's eyes widened. 'Did you push him?'

Claudia continued to stare at Karin's outstretched arms as if they held the answer. She had reached for Declan as he began to fall and her fingers had snagged on his sleeve. 'I tried to save him,' she stammered.

'No,' Karin said, her confidence growing. 'I don't believe you.'

Claudia didn't believe herself either. In her defence, Declan had pushed her first, if only metaphorically speaking. She had never given him the slightest indication that she would ever consider leaving Justin. If Declan had paid more attention, he wouldn't have looked so surprised when Claudia reached out to urge him over the balcony and out of her life for good.

Karin blinked hard, determined to resurrect the memory. 'I saw what you did,' she said. 'My God, you killed him!'

There was only so much Claudia could take. Karin was almost as annoying as her brother for persistence. 'So what if I did?' she yelled.

'You bitch!'

Claudia was ready for her, and grabbed Karin's coat sleeve as she lunged toward her. She twisted her around so that it was the turn of Declan's sister to teeter towards oblivion. The heels of Karin's boots hung over the edge of the canal. All that Claudia had to do was let go.

394

38

Stepping over fishing rods and almost tangling herself in the lines, Leanne trudged on. Beads of sweat had turned to ice at the nape of her neck, and her leather jacket was too thin to offer much protection from the freezing temperature. If Karin had wanted to cure her hangover with a shock of cold, there was no need to stay out long. She could be home already and in no mood to answer the door if Leanne turned up.

Deciding she was ill-prepared for another stakeout, Leanne turned about-face, but she didn't immediately head back. The angler she had passed moments earlier was giving her a hard stare. He would need to move his rods again if she retraced her steps. She turned a second time and followed the curve of the canal.

Only vaguely aware of the tunnel ahead, Leanne reconstructed the events leading up to the fire. Claudia had just found out that she was pregnant and, whatever her feelings for Declan, the baby changed everything. Having Justin's child provided the kind of security Claudia had yearned for, and it wouldn't have mattered who the father was. It was only Declan who knew the paternity was questionable, and how fortunate for Claudia that the fire had neutralised that risk? Or was it luck?

Leanne's boots thudded against the dirt path as her brisk pace became a jog. It was as if her subconscious had registered the two figures inside the tunnel before her conscious mind recognised Claudia in the same gym gear she had been wearing on their last encounter. It took only a fraction of a second to realise the second figure was Karin.

'My God, you killed him!' she heard Karin yell.

'So what if I did?' Claudia shouted back, her voice reverberating off the tunnel walls.

'You bitch!'

Leanne broke into a sprint as she entered the tunnel. She could see the two women grappling with each other and time stood still as Karin's back arched over the water's edge. The canal was only one boat-width wide and if Claudia let go of her, Karin could swim easily to the other side, but that didn't factor in the temperature of the water. Cold-water shock could be fatal, especially at this time of year.

'You stupid bitch!' Claudia cried. 'Why did you have to remember?'

Leanne felt a fresh surge of adrenalin as she raced towards them. 'Stop!' she cried out, pushing Claudia away with one hand while making a desperate grab for Karin.

The only part of Karin that Leanne managed to grab hold of was her scarf. Karin's arms windmilled over the water's edge and her scarf began to unravel. Leanne yanked it hard, by which point Karin had built up enough momentum to propel herself forward. Their combined efforts meant Karin was thrust head first against the tunnel wall.

Karin's cry was lost to the sound of a scream. Claudia

had let go of Karin when Leanne ploughed into them and the shove had unbalanced her. Claudia could have fallen one of two ways, and fate decided that this was one disaster she wasn't going to sidestep. There was a human-sized splash.

Leanne knelt down and made a grab for Claudia's outstretched hand, but Claudia had done the one thing she shouldn't. When she hit the cold water, she had gasped for air and, as her head submerged, she breathed in a lungful of water. Her arms flailed in panic and when she did rise briefly to the surface, she was coughing and spluttering. Her eyes were wide with fear and she was looking directly at Leanne.

Karin had risen to her feet and pressed a hand to her bloodied forehead as she watched on silently.

'We have to do something,' Leanne said, glancing left and right.

Beyond the tunnel there were no boats moored along the canal bank, no lifebuoys or poles to hook out Claudia, not even a fence post or broken branch that Leanne could recover in time to save her. She reached out her arm again, fingers stretching towards Claudia, who was busy swallowing more water than she was coughing up. Her movements slowed and she couldn't keep her head above water. She seemed to know this and stopped struggling.

Leanne had trained for a situation like this and if it had been Lois slipping beneath the surface, she would have jumped in by now. It was probably for the best that she hadn't. It gave her time to take off her boots and jacket.

'What are you doing?'

'I can't watch her die.'

'She would have let *me* die. I saw her push Declan off the balcony, Leanne. She killed my brother!' Karin's voice was loud enough to block out the sound of air bubbles breaking the surface of the water. 'She's . . . She's not like us.'

'No. And we're not like her,' Leanne said with grim determination. 'You need to phone for an ambulance. Now!'

Without waiting for an answer, Leanne took a breath and held it as she jumped into the canal, her arms spread wide to reduce how far her head dipped beneath the surface. The pain was like nothing she had ever felt before. She knew she wouldn't have long before she succumbed to the cold, but she didn't act immediately. She floated on her back and waited for the shock to dissipate. When she allowed herself to move, she kicked her feet, exploring the dark waters with her legs until she connected with a solid form that she couldn't see. She took another deep breath.

Leanne plunged beneath the surface and moved her arms blindly as she searched for Claudia. Her hand glanced against what might be an arm, but there wasn't time to find purchase. Leanne's ability to hold her breath was dramatically reduced by the cold, and with her lungs burning, she rose briefly to the surface before trying again. At first she felt nothing. Her fingers were numb, but as her hand dredged the water one last time, she felt resistance and grabbed something that was soft and flesh-like. She kept hold as she broke the surface, gasped for air, and opened her eyes, only to discover darkness threatening to overtake her.

She wasn't going to make it. She was going to die and, although she didn't believe in an afterlife, she clung to the hope that Lois was waiting for her. She didn't need to conjure a tunnel, she was in one. She could see a hand reaching out to her.

EPILOGUE

Leanne was at the stern with her hand resting on the tiller bar as she steered the boat out of the marina. She could hear the bleat of lambs in a nearby field, and the trees lining the canal bore succulent green buds. The waterways were full of life too and her chosen course was temporarily impeded by a convoy of rented narrowboats. The holidaymakers waved and Leanne offered them a smile that almost broke her. She was leaving Sedgefield.

Dianne had organised a small farewell party at the Raven Brook Café where Leanne had said her goodbyes to friends and colleagues. Today she was on her own and, although it was a wrench to leave so much behind, she was grateful at least that she wasn't being parted from the *Soleil Anne*. She and Lois had christened their boat with an anagram of their names. Two lives entwined for ever.

What a life they had planned together in Sedgefield, and what a life they had lost. Ahead of Leanne was a whole future waiting to be rewritten and, even though it looked on the face of it as if she were running away, she was in fact moving towards something new. She hoped Lois would approve.

As the canal narrowed, Leanne had an unobstructed view running the length of the tunnel. The way was clear, but to be safe, she tooted the horn in case another boat was approaching from the other side. She hadn't been back here since her dramatic dive into the waters, despite being offered ridiculous amounts of money to be interviewed on location. She had agreed to some press, but the most compelling account had been reported in the *Courier*, written by Leanne from her hospital bed. It was some story.

Hypothermia had been setting in when Karin had dragged her out of the canal. Leanne's body had been shutting down, and the blood supply to her extremities had been diverted to vital organs. She didn't know how they had hauled Claudia's lifeless body out of the water, but they had done it together.

'She's not breathing,' Leanne had said, her body shaking violently.

Karin pulled off her coat and offered it to Leanne. 'An ambulance is on the way.'

'We can't wait. Do you know CPR?'

'Yes, but you can't ask me to do that,' Karin replied. 'Not after everything she's done.'

'You have to.'

Despite her protests, Karin had already positioned herself to the side of Claudia's prone body. Whatever she might say, she was the same person who had dug Amelia out of the rubble with her bare hands. Karin wouldn't stand by and watch Claudia die, but she might have cursed under her breath as she slipped a hand beneath Claudia's neck to tilt her head upwards. She scraped back dark tendrils of hair from Claudia's porcelain skin and parted her blue lips. Two rescue breaths. Fifteen compressions. Leanne counted them out until the paramedics arrived.

In Leanne's view, it was Karin who had shown the greatest courage that day. Claudia had thought she could manipulate and destroy Declan's sister as she had done to him. In return, Karin had saved her life. What an incredible human being.

Claudia, on the other hand, was the antithesis of a hero and, as Leanne steered the boat through the tunnel, she hoped that the cell Claudia currently occupied was equally dark and dank. She had initially refuted all of the accusations that had been levelled against her. In particular, she claimed that she had been acting in self-defence when she had grappled with Karin in the tunnel. In a perverse kind of way, her attack had been a means of self-preservation, if you accept that a fantasy life was worth killing for.

In relation to the more serious charge of murder, Claudia claimed she had followed Declan up to the circle with the single intention of helping Hilary Clarke, having heard one of Hilary's students mention she was trapped. Leanne didn't believe it, but she hoped the part about Claudia holding Hilary's hand as she died was true. It would undoubtedly form part of her defence and establish that Declan's murder hadn't been premeditated. Rumour had it that she was going to admit to a lesser charge based on diminished responsibility. Any admission of guilt would be a first for Claudia and suggested there was hope for her after all. Her husband must think so. Justin had been visiting her in prison.

Stretching her spine, Leanne glanced up at the roof of the tunnel. The light reflecting from the boat's headlights picked up faded graffiti on the brickwork. Was that Claudia's name? Leanne blinked and it was gone, but she had a feeling that woman would haunt her for a very long time. The Claudia Rothwell story had given Leanne the scoop she had been longing for, and there had been a flurry of job offers. The one that had taken her fancy was in television, and that was why she was relocating to Salford where she had already secured a new mooring. It wasn't as close to home as her mum would like, but Leanne had gone back to Leeds for Christmas and had promised to make regular return visits.

Leanne would return to Sedgefield too, although she might avoid the high street. The Empress had been boarded up for over eighteen months and remained an open sore. Some would like to see it torn down, but there was talk of a second restoration. Bryony Sutherland was putting together a proposal, and Leanne tried not to have a view on the subject. Her crusade was over. She was leaving behind small-town politics.

With two weeks to kill until she was due to start her new job, Leanne had one last assignment to complete for the *Courier*. Mal had accepted her resignation on the condition that she deliver that personal piece he had been urging her to write. It wasn't enough for him that she had reported on events that had involved her personally, he wanted her to express her innermost feelings, and so, with the echo of the boat's engine thudding against the arched walls, she began to compose her final article, albeit in her head.

Bravery doesn't come with a cape, but it does have a mask of sorts. It hides undetected until we are placed in extraordinary circumstances and find ourselves doing extraordinary things, and I'm not talking about racing into a burning building, or jumping into icy waters. It's having the courage to face what comes next. It's the parent who buries their

402

child, the spouse who takes over the role of two parents, the teacher who encourages her students to dance on, and the friends who gather around a table with one empty seat. It's these small acts of bravery that are often the hardest – the carrying on when you are very much aware of what you have left behind.

Leanne's eyes stung as she emerged into the light and at first she didn't recognise the figures on the bank, not least because she was temporarily distracted by the collection of helium balloons with good luck messages on them. She began to laugh, just in case any other emotions dared to make an appearance.

As she steered the boat towards them, Joe jumped on to the *Soleil Anne* and shuffled towards her along the gunwale running the length of the boat. He tied the balloons to the handrail before jumping onto the deck to plant a kiss on her cheek.

'I said no fuss.'

'This isn't a fuss!' Beth shouted over to her.

'We just wanted to see you off,' Karin added.

Leanne wasn't surprised that Joe, Beth, and Karin had been in cahoots. They had enjoyed some serious debriefing sessions in the Bridgewater Inn after Leanne's dip in the canal, and had been joined occasionally by Amelia and her mum. Karin refused vehemently to take credit for saving Amelia. It was as if there was a mental block, or perhaps a memory that refused to resurface. The Empress hadn't given up all her secrets and never would, but it had allowed a small group of friends to make bonds that would never be broken. This simple fact should have made it easier for Leanne to leave.

'Don't you dare make me cry,' Leanne warned.

She cut back the engine and allowed the boat to drift slowly along the canal without coming to a complete stop. She wasn't going to moor up. She didn't want to face leaving all over again.

As Karin and Beth linked arms and began walking along the towpath at a pace that matched the boat, Joe put his arm around Leanne. He pressed his head against hers. 'You're making me cry,' he whispered. 'I'm going to miss you.'

'And I'll miss you,' she replied as the boat thumped against the side of the bank.

Leanne moved the tiller bar to steer it back on course and pushed Joe away in the process. He needed a new start too and Leanne was holding him back. She didn't want to be around when he found a new love that wasn't Lois, and she suspected that was going to happen sooner rather than later. She hoped sooner. She really did.

'I get the message,' he said, giving her one last hug.

To rejoin Karin and Beth, Joe had to jump a couple feet to get ashore. He landed on an uneven patch of grass and for one heart-stopping moment it looked like he was going to fall backwards. Instinctively, Leanne revved the engine and steered the boat away from him to avoid hitting Joe or squashing him against the canal bank if he did fall in. Beth and Karin reacted too, and it was Karin who grabbed the hem of Joe's T-shirt and held on until he righted himself.

'Jesus, Joe!' Leanne called. 'Don't frighten me like that.'

'Don't worry, he's safe with us!' Karin shouted, her smile a beam of light and joy.

Leanne hadn't slowed the boat after Joe's near-miss and

the distance lengthened between them. 'Look after each other,' she called back, 'or I'll be back to sort you out.'

'You had better come back anyway!' Joe called.

Leanne tried not to look back for the longest time and when she did, she found only Joe had persisted in following in her wake. He waved furiously and when Leanne squinted her eyes, she tried so hard to place Lois next to him.

'Goodbye, my friend,' Leanne whispered, before turning to face the future.

Acknowledgements

It's fair to say that this book has given me many challenges, and the first was creating a world where I had to inflict a major disaster on a small community. I couldn't bring myself to wish harm on a real place, and that's why I decided to return to the fictional town of Sedgefield, somewhere in Cheshire, which has been used in some of my other books.

The disaster I describe isn't based on a real-life event, but my writing has been influenced by such tragedies. The victims of the Grenfell Tower fire were never far from my thoughts, as were the victims of Hillsborough. My thoughts and prayers are with those who lost their lives, and the loved ones left behind to fight for justice and mourn their loss.

When I started writing this story, I could never have imagined that I would be editing it in the middle of a pandemic, at a time when a trip to the theatre would be impossible and mass gatherings illegal. And while I never intended to put a date stamp on the events in my novel, I think we can all agree that it couldn't have happened in 2020. I can only hope that, you, the reader, are enjoying better times and we are once again savouring the joy of doing the things we once took for granted.

What could have been another challenge for me was having my editor go on maternity leave during the editing process, and I was immensely relieved to have the benefit of Martha Ashby's wise words and guidance on the first draft, literally days before she became a mum. A huge thank you to Kate Bradley, who had the unenviable task of taking me under her wing and has been the best surrogate editor I could wish for. Thank you also to Luigi Bonomi and Hannah Schofield from LBA Books for being the greatest champions of my work. I hope I've done enough to make you all proud.

Thank you as always to my family and friends for your love and support, especially to my daughter, Jess who couldn't escape from my plot ramblings despite being halfway across the world – you are the kindest, most thoughtful and bravest person I know. A special mention also to the Low Brow Book Club, who invited me to give a talk on one of my books a few years ago, and haven't been able to get rid of me since. Thank you to Catherine Ravens, Emma Prior and Helenor Watson for keeping our little group in check.

A very big thank you to my readers. It's a privilege to have my books published and I couldn't do it without you. I'd love to hear what you think of my latest novel, so please come find me on social media.

One final note. Soon after finishing this novel, a dear friend of mine died. I had known John Webster for twenty-five years, but it was only at his funeral that I discovered that when he was seventeen, he saved two children from a house fire. He never talked about it, but I should have guessed. He was a true gent, a best mate, and one of life's unsung heroes.